I'm Not the Hero

Book 2 • Secrets and Strife

SourpatchHero

Podium

For my wife and boys. The three of you inspire me daily. I wouldn't be able to write anything without all your support and snuggles. I love you.

Cover design by Jason Nathaniel Artuz

ISBN: 978-1-0394-5429-3

Published in 2024 by Podium Publishing
www.podiumentertainment.com
Podium

SECRETS AND STRIFE

Chapter 1

"Orrin, don't pout. Wave to them." Madi elbowed him and waved to the crowds.

Only two weeks had passed since one of the members of the ruling class of Dey had tried to kidnap Daniel, Orrin's best friend and the [Hero] of the magical fantasy world they'd been summoned to. Now, Orrin and Madeleine Catanzano, the only members of their party who remained, were stuck on an open-backed carriage, being paraded around as members of the [Hero]'s entourage. Daniel, in front, waved at everyone, smiling.

Orrin slunk down farther into his cape, trying to avoid the cheering.

Madi's father, Silas Catanzano, one of the lords of Dey, had been preparing this celebration since right after Lord Wendeln's fall from grace. His argument had been that the people needed something positive to focus on. The fact that a [Hero] was in Dey had become common knowledge overnight.

At first, the people revolted when they found out that a lord of Dey had been killed. It had taken a few days for the other lords to put down the looting and restore order. The news of what really happened had been circulated: Wendeln had tried to attack the city, and the [Hero] had saved them all. Nobody talked about the attempted kidnapping or the monster the younger Wendeln had set loose on the city. Nobody talked about the dozens dead or maimed. Yet the entire city whispered for days before the parade, and almost everyone turned out to witness the event.

Orrin had tried to get out of this. He wanted to remain incognito. Silas had ignored him. Madi had ignored him. Even Daniel hadn't fought too hard against the rising popularity.

"Stop trying to hide," Madi hissed.

Orrin groaned and leaned against the side of the carriage. They'd already been up and down four streets. The city guards were marching behind and in front, mostly wearing the Catanzano colors. The common folk cheered for the [Hero] and his party. Flowers were thrown. Orrin could have sworn he saw underwear tossed toward Daniel, too. Madi had quickly shoved those under the bench.

An hour passed, and when the driver waved, Orrin leaned forward to hear his conversation with Daniel.

"—to go around again. The people are pushing and climbing over each other to see you. Is that okay?"

Orrin punched Daniel in the side at the lopsided grin on his face. "Don't you dare say yes."

Daniel smirked. "Tell Lord Catanzano that we would love to make another pass for the people."

Orrin fell back and pulled his cape over his head again. This day was never going to end.

Three hours later, Orrin pulled himself out of the bath. They'd traveled the streets of Dey to let the people catch a glimpse of their savior, the [Hero]. What nobody had told him was how much dirt would get kicked up by the carriage. When they rolled back into the Catanzano estate, Orrin was covered in grime. Luckily, the staff had hot baths ready for them.

Orrin dried himself off and pulled on his backup outfit. He still had the basic clothes that Daniel had bought months ago when they'd first been summoned here.

If you call being run over by a truck being summoned, Orrin thought grimly.

After waking up naked in a forest, the two friends had managed to learn a lot about the system that granted different stats, like strength and intelligence, as well as magical abilities. Daniel had been given the class [Hero], along with Quests for him to perform. Instead of being given a class, Orrin had encountered multiple loading errors. He'd been granted the ability to create a class, [Utility Warder], and had unlocked something called Administrator Access.

He was still learning about that.

Despite their best efforts, Daniel's status as a [Hero] was quickly discovered. Their relationship with the Catanzanos had started off rocky, with a test to discover Daniel's powers turning deadly. Then Silas had tried to keep Orrin and Daniel apart. He still thought Orrin was a native of this world. As did everyone except the mind mage Tony.

Orrin had thwarted one kidnapping attempt targeting Daniel, and the two had decided to go on a mission to rescue the family members of a teammate. Orrin had unwittingly helped release a monster on the city. The culprit behind the scenes had been unmasked and the lords (and lady) of Dey had an epic battle in the streets. Daniel's status as a [Hero] became common knowledge, and already, emissaries from Veskar and Odrana had arrived to give gifts and assurances that the [Hero] was welcome and expected to make appearances before all the ruling members of the two countries.

Orrin looked at his status. In his efforts to rescue Daniel, he had used a new ability. By sacrificing a point of his own constitution, he had stolen ten points from an opponent they'd had no chance of beating. He'd had to use that skill twice.

Orrin
Utility Warder
Level 13 (380/4,000)
AP: 14
HP: 70/70
MP: 380/380
Strength: 9
Constitution: 7

Dexterity: 9
Will: 28
Intelligence: 11

He had yet to figure out a way to gain constitution with his Administrator Access skills. Of course, he hadn't had too much time to himself to experiment until recently.

The only good thing about being thrust into the limelight was the leveling. Each of the lords of Dey had sent Orrin, Daniel, and Madi out with a full retinue of guards to take down monsters. Orrin had been carried an entire level in only three days. The downside was that it was getting harder to go out. Everyone from the local baker to the stable boy wanted to witness the great [Hero] Daniel take down a monster. They hadn't been able to go out for days now.

Orrin started working through his list of daily chores. He used [Analyze] on himself while cycling the smallest amount of mana he could muster. Just as Tony had promised, he was starting to see some results, including a new counter of how much daily mana he'd used.

Mana Use: 320/???

It was both exciting and disheartening to see the progress. He could expand his status screen to see a full rundown of useless information about himself. His age, height, and even his weight. However, he knew how far he still had to go.

At least I'm making some progress with my project, he thought with a smirk.

The mana ticker had only appeared two days ago and still gave no indications that it would eventually tell him anything more useful, but Orrin had a good feeling that he was on the right path. Maybe he could even control how much mana he could cycle. Tony had theorized that he could work out his daily mana capacity like a muscle, pointing to mages from rich families who gained the ability to drink an extra potion a day. They usually had to drink their weight in mana potions to be able to do so.

But they don't have my blood cycling.

One of Orrin's skills, [Blood Mana], allowed him to exchange his health points, or HP, for mana points, or MP, on a one-to-one ratio. He also could heal himself for less than the difference, giving him a seemingly infinite mana glitch. Except using that much mana in one day would kill someone.

Enter Orrin's second skill, [Mind Bastion]. The system-given skill was a blessing and a curse. The ability made him more in control of his mind and thoughts, allowing him to analyze and process situations and outcomes without emotion. It also delayed the backlash of using too much mana . . . something he'd had to suffer through multiple times already. If he hadn't found Tony when he had . . .

Overall, the two skills let him use spells without care of the cost. He'd already spammed his current spells to the maximum multiple times, something that took regular people years to do. Looking over the abilities, Orrin started his internal debate again, the one that had kept him up at night more than the impending parade.

"I can't level anything," Orrin muttered as he pushed his screen around. "Should I get something new or just keep focused on what I'm doing?"

Using his math skills, Orrin had figured out that he could stretch his 380-MP pool into a little over a thousand total points a day without any side effects. He'd pushed himself daily, using his own [Increase Intelligence] skill to make spells cost less and his experience for each spell go further.

In the end, Orrin had been able to add over seventeen thousand points of experience across a few spells.

[Heal Small Wounds] Level 3 (5,740/10,000)
[Increase Intelligence] Level 3 (3,370/10,000)
[Increase Will] Level 3 (5,950/10,000)
[Increase Strength] Level 3 (1,945/10,000)

[Increase Dexterity] Level 3 (1,620/10,000)
[Camouflage] Level 2 (2,210/10,000)
[Remetabolize] (150/1,000)

He had made good progress, but Orrin knew it would be another few weeks before he was able to max out his spells—something most mages would take years to do—but still, he was pissed at his prodigious rate of growth.

Orrin heard talking from downstairs. Someone had worked Madi up.

With a sigh, Orrin looked around the room to make sure he had everything packed away in his [Dimension Hole]. The ability to store everything he needed in a magical subspace was probably still the coolest thing to him. He'd annoyed Daniel more than once by just making things appear from his pockets.

Orrin opened the door and started down the hall. Madi and Daniel were standing in the entryway with a young boy, a messenger, most likely, judging by the clothes he wore.

"What does this mean? Why does the Guildmaster think she has the right to demand Daniel's presence?" Madi all but screamed at the poor teenager who had delivered the message. He stumbled back from the fury of the daughter of the lord of Dey.

"I—I just deliver the messages, ma'am," the boy said, clutching his satchel and backing toward the door. "I don't know what's in them."

"What's going on?" Orrin asked as he came down the steps. The boy squeezed through the open door as soon as Madi turned her back.

"Damn," Madi spat. "He ran."

Daniel chuckled. "I'd have run, too."

Madi put her hand on her hip and tilted her head at Daniel. "You do realize that we have been lying low at your request? You're the one who asked for a break from all the politicking."

Daniel's smile faded.

"Can I see the letter?" Orrin reached out a hand. Madi practically threw it at him.

The outside envelope was addressed to Daniel, in the care of Lord Catanzano. The letter inside was written in a steady-flowing script.

> **To the [Hero] Daniel:**
> **Too long have we gone without meeting. I am looking forward to our dinner tonight at eight o'clock. You may bring your party, as after pleasantries, a request will be offered.**
>
> **Jennifer Pritus, Guildmaster of Dey**

"It doesn't really sound that bad," Orrin said, folding the paper back up. "Does this Jennifer chick have enough clout that it would be a problem if we just don't show?"

"Guildmaster Pritus. She's a relatively good politician, according to my father. She's got almost as much say in the running of the city as the lords do. She's probably on the list of people who have been denied an audience with Daniel."

Daniel stood with his back against a banister, looking off into space—the hallmark of someone reading their own status. Completely oblivious.

"Are you even listening?" Orrin kicked his friend in the shin.

"Hmm?" Daniel didn't react to the kick. "Oh, sorry. So, we have to have dinner with the leader of the Guild, right? Can they give us a quest to do? I want to get out of the city for a bit."

Orrin slapped his forehead. "You think everything will just work out that easy?"

Daniel pushed his status screen away and smirked, a mischievous glint in his eyes. "Doesn't it always?"

Chapter 2

Orrin groaned at his friend and looked around for something to throw at him. Madi noticed his gaze and stepped closer, calming him with a hand on his arm.

"I'll speak to my father and try to find a way out of it for you." Madi smiled. She smiled at Daniel and Orrin more these days, but Orrin noticed the sadness and anxiety on her face, too.

He sighed. "No. If Daniel is going to make an ass of himself, we should be there to rein him in a bit, I guess."

Madi patted his arm and turned to leave.

"Is Sir Bennett back?" Orrin let the words slip out. It had been two weeks since Brandt had left on sabbatical. Madi had sulked in her room for an entire day before her father demanded she join them on the outings to level sponsored by the houses of Dey and other powerful families. Her savagery against the monsters they'd encountered had given even Daniel pause.

". . . not yet," Madi whispered. Her eyes looked around the room furtively before she nodded to both of them and excused herself.

"Come on, O," Daniel admonished as soon as she was out of sight. "You know how much she's hurting. Why rub salt in her wounds?"

Orrin frowned. "Brandt left to clear his head. If Madi needs to do the same—"

Daniel took two quick steps and bopped Orrin on the side of the head. "Madi grieved for Jude, just like we all did. She's hurt because Brandt hasn't come back. They have some weird not-quite boyfriend-girlfriend thing going on. Or did you not notice that?"

Orrin's mouth dropped to the floor. Of course, that made so much sense. Madi had even called him "my Brandt" a few times. *How thick do I have to be?*

"You really didn't know, did you?" Daniel crouched a bit to stare into Orrin's eyes. "You're hopeless, man."

"Hey, at least I didn't hit on her like you."

Daniel's eyebrow went up. "When did I hit on her?"

Orrin raised his fingers one by one. "You always compliment her on what she's wearing. You pull back and let her win against you in our practice duels. You—"

"You saved her life in the dungeon. Does that mean you're interested in her?" Daniel interrupted him. "I can compliment anyone I like. It doesn't mean I'm flirting with them. And I let everybody win on occasion. How would you feel if I beat you every single time?"

Orrin's mouth opened and shut again. "You don't let me win."

Daniel laughed and pushed Orrin's shoulder. "Sure, buddy. Okay." He turned and started back up the stairs. "I'm going to get a nap in before dinner. All that smiling and waving hurt my face and shoulder."

"Your face is killing me, too." Orrin threw one last jab at his friend. Daniel just raised his middle finger as he climbed the stairs and rounded the corner.

Orrin glanced around. With everybody else gone, the front entrance hall to the Catanzano keep was quiet. Despite it being nearly time for dinner, no staff was present. Normally, maids or guards would be roaming this central point. After the last few weeks, Orrin realized Silas had his house operating on a skeleton crew.

He sighed and made his way up the stairs. Tony had sent him a few more books on [Vampires] and blood magic. They weren't fun to read, but Tony thought the more he knew about [Blood Mana] and the other skills used by [Vampires], the quicker he would be able to get [Analyze] to give more details on his otherwise dangerous skills.

The problem was the books were boring, with a capital *B*. Most of the tomes that had been delivered weren't even directly about

[Vampires], but other monster races in general. It was a hunt through what boiled down to encyclopedias.

"I miss the internet," Orrin muttered.

Three hours later, a guard knocked on the door of the library to tell Orrin the others were waiting. Orrin hadn't changed and didn't really need to after his earlier shower, but when he saw Daniel and Madi dressed in their nicer clothes, he began to feel self-conscious.

"Should I go change?" Orrin asked. Madi shook her head.

"You should fix your hair, though," Daniel answered. "It looks like you were trying to pull it out."

In fact, Orrin almost had. He'd run his hands through his hair in frustration as he'd realized each book was useless. Each contained only small snippets of information on [Vampires] and no actual useful knowledge on [Blood Mana]. He'd worn out his eyes and felt a small headache forming, but a quick healing spell took care of that.

Madi stepped forward and tousled his hair. "I think it suits him. The messed-up look makes him look a little wild."

Daniel quirked an eyebrow. "Wild?"

Madi put her hand on her hip as she appraised Orrin. "Unpredictable. Pritus knows me through my father. She'll know everything she can learn about you, Daniel. But Orrin will be able to rock the boat. Everybody in town has seen you, but nobody knows much about you. The few rumors about you that I've been able to get the guards to repeat are that you have mysterious magic and an endless mana supply. That's it. *I'm* not even sure exactly where your village was, but it must have been really remote." She brushed some wrinkles out of his clothes and continued. "Pritus knows my father. She'll think you're in his pocket or the [Hero] chose you specifically. So, you're either an obstacle to getting closer to Daniel or her best chance at getting an ally in the [Hero]'s party."

"Great," Orrin muttered. "Now I really don't want to go. Should I do anything in particular?"

Madi's smile reached her eyes as she took his arm in hers. "Be yourself. That'll confuse her more than anything else."

Daniel laughed as they walked out the door to the waiting carriage. Orrin could only grumble as they made their way to the Guild. The short trip was filled with Madi's suggestions to Daniel on etiquette and the best way to not get swept up in Guild drama.

"The Guildmaster is a bit of an enigma," Madi explained. "She is obviously a high-level adventurer, but she's been able to hold her own in the political arena as well."

"So, just keep your mouth shut and let Madi do the talking," Orrin summarized for his friend. "She's the smarter one when it comes to this political shit."

Daniel stuck out his tongue. Madi sighed.

"That might not be possible. From everything I've heard, she's clever. Everything she does or says will be a test. She loves to learn and has a knack for drawing out information from others. My father warned me that we should get in and out as quickly as possible."

"What about dinner?" Daniel asked. "I didn't have anything because I thought we were eating with her."

Madi shook her head and ignored him.

Stepping out of the carriage, Orrin realized how long it had been since they'd been to the Guild. Everything was always taken care of for the [Hero] and his party. The dungeon run had taken care of their need for the monthly quest requirement, and Silas had been creating quest requests for them based on whatever backdoor deals he made. Orrin had the suspicion that all the free monster kills they had received were benefiting the lord of Dey more than they knew.

Nobody waited outside the Guild for them. Madi shrugged and walked in first. Orrin followed close behind.

The receptionist glanced up and ignored the two of them but did a double take when Daniel followed a moment later. With a sputter, he fell back off his stool and rushed around the side of the small alcove desk to greet the [Hero], ignoring Madi and Orrin completely.

"It's an honor to meet you, sir." The lackey pumped Daniel's hand and spoke so fast his words almost slurred together. "My name is Jasper. It's an honor to meet you. Guildmaster Pritus is waiting for you. I'll be more than happy to show you the way to her receiving room. Please follow me."

Daniel tried to speak, but every time he opened his mouth, Jasper snuck another sentence in.

Orrin could only smirk as Daniel was essentially dragged down the hall. He followed with Madi, who also had a hand over her mouth.

Jasper led them through hallways Orrin and Daniel had never been to. The entire Guildhall had small plaques on most corners directing people where to go, and they'd never needed to go to administration before. Jasper stopped before a nondescript door in the middle of a hallway of doors and knocked twice. He opened the door and ushered Daniel inside. Orrin and Madi slipped in behind them.

"Guildmaster, the [Hero] Daniel has arrived," he announced.

Guildmaster Jennifer Pritus was not what Orrin had expected. The room spread out in the space-altering way rooms in the Guild's hall did, looking much bigger than it did from the outside. A table set for four was sitting in the middle of the room, just a few steps away from Daniel, with Pritus already sitting. A desk sat tucked away in the corner, but the rest of the room was filled with other tables or stands holding an assortment of beakers, floating dead things in jars, and books. Books piled up underneath the cushioned armchairs by the small fireplace, books covered her desk, and a book was in her hand that she put down with a finger holding her spot as she took in the group.

Jennifer Pritus was young. Not as young as Daniel and Orrin, but not too much older. Maybe her mid- to late twenties. She was also beautiful. Dark hair and eyebrows framed her face. She looked over and judged each member of the [Hero]'s party. Orrin could easily imagine her on the cover of a magazine or in a TV show back home. His heart beat faster as he stood straight, trying to make himself appear a little taller.

"Welcome, honored guests. Thank you for accepting my invitation." Pritus stood and placed a bookmark down before closing the book she was reading and placing it to the side. "It is promising to our future relationship that you would make the time for me. I appreciate it more than you know."

The Guildmaster bowed her head toward Daniel.

"And the [Hero] thanks you for the courtesy," Madi said and stepped forward. Pritus's brown eyes followed her like a cat's. "Daniel and his party are looking forward to a dinner with the great Guildmaster of Dey. The [Hero] has been keeping so busy lately, a quiet and filling meal is just what he needed."

Orrin immediately felt out of his depth. As the two ladies exchanged pleasantries, he realized more was being said than the surface words alone.

"Of course, we are all in his debt for unveiling such a heinous traitor in our midst. How is your father taking the loss of a fellow lord? A shame he could not be here." Pritus smiled. Orrin could watch her smile for days.

"My father is working hard to undo all the harm done by Wendeln's betrayal and rooting out all those who conspired with him . . . or knew of his plans. Of course, he is not a part of the [Hero]'s party, like I am. I will always be in the [Hero]'s debt and am so glad that Daniel has decided to entrust that position to me. We really do make a good team." Madi's response was quick.

"Yes, the [Hero]'s party. Young Catanzano and Orville, is it? What of the other? A knight of your father's? Is he not here? I heard he ran away after the entire fiasco. You're sure he wasn't in on it?" Pritus's smile took on a wicked edge.

Orrin opened his mouth to correct his name, but as the Guildmaster continued, he saw a look of pain and anger spasm across Madi's face.

So instead, what came out of his mouth was "Sir Bennett is taking time off after losing a close friend to that traitor and his goons. Brandt fought Lord Wendeln and his retainers. Funny, though, I don't remember seeing any other Guild members helping. Did Lord Catanzano tell you what was going on and you decided not to help, or did he not trust you enough to involve you in the entire fiasco, as you called it?"

Orrin's anger cooled as he finished his rant. He watched Pritus wince before her face cleared. He'd struck a point for his side.

"Oh, but Orville, are you not a member of the Guild? So, in a way, I think the Guild can take some credit for ending the life of a corrupt leader." She bowed her head and smiled at him with her eyes. "For that matter, I believe even the [Hero] is on our rolls. I'm told you joined together. What a joyous occasion for us all."

Orrin couldn't be sure, but he could swear Madi was grinding her teeth.

"Since we are all brothers and sisters of the Guild, why don't we sit down and eat? I have a proposition for you. One that I'm sure you will accept."

Chapter 3

Daniel started to speak, but Madi quickly stepped on his foot.

"We would of course listen to a request from the head of the Guild," Madi said slyly. "But whether the [Hero] deems it worth his time is another thing. While we are members of the Guild, precedent dictates the [Hero] and his party are free from the restraints of politics and required memberships."

Pritus nodded and gestured for them to sit. She glided around the table and sat in the same seat she'd been in when they arrived. "Of course, the [Hero] is not to be tethered by any power. He is to be free to receive any and all invitations and requests, is he not?"

Orrin squirmed in his seat. He knew Silas had been gatekeeping all the fan mail sent to Daniel. Now he wondered how many real requests for help had been sent. It wasn't like Daniel could actually do anything about them all, but it still galled Orrin to think of Silas being in charge of that.

Daniel slumped in his seat. "Okay. This back-and-forth you two have going on is getting annoying. Can you just tell me what it is you want?"

Madi closed her eyes in frustration while Pritus smiled.

"Over dinner," the Guildmaster said with a glint in her eye and picked up a bell. With a flick of her wrist and a tinkle in the air, two servers—or, more likely, Guild members—entered the room and poured wine.

Another woman entered and stood at the side of the table. She began to recite a list of possible options to eat.

"Can I just see a menu?" Daniel asked.

The woman stopped speaking and raised an eyebrow. "Would you like me to write it all down for you?"

Orrin leaned forward. "That won't be necessary. He'll have the chicken and roast potatoes. I'll have the same. Madi?"

Madi hid her mouth behind her hand as she turned. Orrin didn't see what was so funny until Pritus spoke.

"Does your party dictate all your decisions?"

Daniel leaned his chair back and assumed his normal air of being too cool for the room. "Orrin usually knows what I like to eat. I trust his judgment."

Madi and Pritus gave their orders, too, and the servers left. Daniel picked up his wine and swirled it around the glass. He sniffed it and promptly choked.

"Are you okay?" Madi quickly clapped him on the back, while Orrin took a small sniff of his own wine. The dark-red liquid had a pungent smell of wood and smoke. It burned his nose.

"That's not wine, is it?" Daniel got out between gasps. "It smells like my dad's whiskey."

"It's a dwarven drofka. They drink it like wine, but it does have more resemblance to a whiskey." Pritus picked up her glass and took a sip. "I apologize if it is too much for you."

Orrin groaned internally, hoping Daniel wouldn't take the bait.

He did. While they chatted about inconsequential things, like how Pritus had gotten this particular vintage from a trader for next to nothing or the rebuilding of the parts of the city destroyed by the monster that Wendeln had let loose, the food was delivered.

Orrin had to spend the next thirty minutes quietly casting [Remetabolize] on Daniel after he finished glass after glass of the dwarven "wine." His friend drank three glasses before Madi pointedly pushed the glass away from him.

Orrin tried a sip but didn't like the taste. The chicken was delicious, though.

Daniel put his fork down. "This has been nice, but why not just ask your question in a letter?"

Pritus shook her head, amused. "Is he always so . . ."

"Blunt?" Orrin volunteered.

"Focused," Madi said at the same time.

The Guildmaster looked between the three of them carefully. "Daniel, if I paid gold, could I place a member in your party?"

"How much gold are we talking about?" Daniel winked at her. "For just a day? Do you need some monster killed?"

Pritus shook her head. "No, for good. Someone I trust, placed near you so you always know my thoughts on an issue. You'll be free to make any choice on matters, but this way you would know the best path forward for the Guild. Any amount you name."

Madi started to say something, but Daniel gave her a look and shook his head.

"If you pay, my party and I will take on quests for you," Daniel started. "We would also take someone along for those missions. But to what you are actually asking, no. I can't trust anyone who would pay to be near me. I'm not for sale."

Pritus stared at him for a moment like a bug beneath a magnifying glass. Then she laughed and clapped her hands. Her entire aloof and calculating demeanor disappeared, and in its place was excitement and fierce intelligence. "Good. Good. You are an actual party and not some mechanism crafted by the lords." She stood up and walked to her desk, moving books in a very precise manner. "I am sorry to test you all like that. Madeleine, I'm trusting you, as a member of the [Hero]'s party, to not betray anything I'm about to tell you. Or that I can be more than a 'cold, emotionless statue of a woman.' I have a reputation to protect."

Madi choked on a piece of her vegetables and looked startled. Orrin guessed Silas must have described Pritus as such.

The Guildmaster lifted books and placed them on stacks, clearing her desk. Orrin and Daniel came near while Madi lingered behind them.

"I received this report this morning. To be honest, I didn't care one way or the other that a [Hero] was found. Most of you end up dead or captured, or you disappear. But I do know that you are always stronger than the average adventurer."

Pritus moved the last papers, and Orrin saw the top of her desk. It had been carved and inlaid with a glistening metal design that took him a minute to make out. "It's a map."

"Yes, of course, but here—this is where I want you to go." Pritus moved her finger north of the city. By Orrin's quick calculation, she was pointing nearly eighty miles north and a little over half the distance to the elven forest.

"Why?" Daniel glanced at the map but mostly watched Pritus. "What's there?"

Pritus smiled. "A new dungeon."

"New dungeons are the domain of the Tarris family," Madi said, stepping around the boys and looking closer at the map. "We can inform them and—"

"No." Pritus cut Madi off. "Until I've completed my own audit of the other lords, the Guild will not trust dungeon subjugation to anyone else. The recent betrayal and ongoing hostilities to the north are too large a powder keg. Truly, I was about to dispatch my own team when I had another idea."

She turned to Daniel. "Is it true that a [Hero] receives twice the power per stat?"

Daniel backed away from the intense stare. "Um. I'm not sure I want to answer your questions about my class."

Pritus nodded. "So it's true. Has your party informed you what happens when you defeat a dungeon?"

Orrin knew—extra stats. They'd completed their research on dungeons before vising the Aqua Chambers.

"I know once the core of the dungeon is crushed, the party gets a set number of points to a random stat. Is there more?" Daniel asked.

"That's the gist." Pritus waved her hand. "But since one point in anything would be worth more to you than anyone else, I thought I would give you the chance first. It's a newly spawned dungeon. The outbreak was contained by members of the Guild out on patrol. Nothing more than level three appeared. Based on the statistics of dungeon growth, that means only one deca-set." She paused. "Ten levels with one boss. Any party at level twenty could take it out in a week."

"And you are going to give it to us out of the goodness of your heart?" Madi asked incredulously. She crossed her arms and glared.

"Of course not. In return, the [Hero] will agree to take on a certain number of quests for the Guild. I'd also like to fill out the other two members of your party for the subjugation."

Madi narrowed her eyes. "So that they can report all of Daniel's skills back to you."

Pritus smiled. "Naturally. I mean no harm in wanting to know the pieces on the board and their power. I can be a great ally in the coming months. Surely you don't think Odrana is done. They made a move on Dey. Dey is the Guild. They've done everything but actually declare war on us."

Orrin wanted to hit himself. He knew that Wendeln had been working with Odrana. He knew Odrana was fighting with the elves. He just hadn't realized that by subverting a lord of Dey, they obviously would make a play for power here as well.

Madi lifted her chin. "All the ambassadors from Odrana have given great assurances that Wendeln acted in his own interest and the country has no desire to provoke war."

Pritus frowned. "And here I was beginning to think you were more intelligent. It doesn't matter what they say. Wendeln's attack on the city was an act of war. The Guild will have to answer. At the least, we will be sending teams out to watch the borders and respond accordingly."

Orrin realized Pritus hadn't been filled in on who'd actually released the monster. "Um, excuse me."

Pritus and Madi turned as one.

"I think you might be operating under some false data. Wendeln's son did summon the monster, but I accidentally made him lose control of it. That's why it attacked. I don't know if Wendeln meant to attack the city in any way. He just talked about the elves and the power they have. He seemed to just be trying to kidnap Daniel," Orrin explained, his thoughts tumbling out on top of each other.

Pritus held up a finger and grabbed a notebook off a stand. She turned pages and then began to write. After a minute of scribbles, she set the notebook back down on the same spot. "That indeed is something I did not know. That makes my concerns of an imminent invasion less likely, but there is still enough for me to know the new Sanerris pup is set for domination of all the lands of enlightened races."

"Who's that?" Daniel asked.

"The leader of Odrana," Orrin answered before the others. "He's the one who started the war with the elves after he took power from his mom."

Pritus quirked an eye. "Where did you say your village was?"

Orrin smiled. "I didn't. But you still haven't told us why we should trust you and defeat a dungeon for you."

Pritus narrowed her eyes as she watched Orrin. He almost put up [Mind Bastion]. Finally, she answered his question. "With the Guild taking over subjugation for the foreseeable future, we'll be able to help the [Hero] boost his stats. Something I assume he'll need to stop the war."

"And why would he want to stop the war?" Madi asked. Too quickly.

The Guildmaster smiled. "Why else would a [Hero] be here? The timing is too appropriate. The simplest answer is usually the correct one." She turned to Daniel. "So, Daniel . . . what do you say? Should I arrange for you to get stronger?"

Chapter 4

Orrin could see Daniel was conflicted. He had promised Madi he wouldn't make any deals, but the prospect of a new dungeon was a lot to take in.

"We can give you an answer in the morning," Orrin said, saving his friend. "Even if we agree, I'm sure Madi here will want to negotiate some terms."

Madi nodded, mute. Orrin knew why, too. Madi's dream was to destroy all the dungeons in this world. They had taken her mother from her at a young age, and she was determined to make sure nobody else suffered that fate. Pritus had picked a particularly good boon to tempt her with.

"I'm afraid I must have your answer before you leave this room." Guildmaster Pritus stood to her full height. She was almost as tall as Daniel, but with her regal bearing, it appeared they were eye to eye. "If you say no, I'll not risk you rushing to subjugate the dungeon on your own. I have a team standing by."

"Then can we have a few minutes alone?" Daniel asked as he slumped into an armchair. "I'm still digesting and tipsy from your dwarf liquor."

Orrin knew his friend was not feeling the effects of the alcohol at all. [Remetabolize] would have cleared his system completely.

"Of course. Ring the bell and I'll return." Pritus frowned slightly but left quickly.

As soon as they were alone, Madi fell into the other armchair. "She's got us stuck in an alley without a knife for protection."

"What?" Daniel asked.

"It's an expression. She knows how much a dungeon subjugation could do for Daniel. We have no real political clout to throw around. Basically, we are fucked."

"Madi, I don't think I've ever heard you curse!" Orrin exclaimed in mock outrage.

"You two are a bad influence," she muttered, putting her head in her hands. "The problem is I want this. I've dreamed of crushing a dungeon my entire life. If she really can get us to a new dungeon, I'll . . ." She trailed off.

"She said she'd just want a few quests done." Orrin shrugged and started leafing through the book Pritus had left behind. "We have to do some each month anyways. Why not just make sure we have the option to decline anything crazy?"

"She also wants us to take her people with us into the dungeon," Daniel said as he put his feet up on the small table and leaned back in the armchair, stretching. "Damn, this chair is comfortable."

"Yeah, I think that might be the bigger ask, to be honest," Madi said as she also sank into her chair.

Orrin continued to wander the room, looking at the books. The majority were treatises on subjects ranging from animal husbandry to high-level magical theory. Political essays and history books were mixed in as well. There appeared to be no rhyme or reason to the stacks, and every book had a scrap of paper or bookmark in it.

"So, we refuse." Daniel shrugged. "I trust you two, but I get the feeling she isn't going to let us wait around for Brandt to return. Do you think the three of us would be enough?"

Madi shook her head. "Even a newly formed dungeon isn't going to be easy at our level. Without Brandt or . . ." She took a breath and continued. ". . . Jude, we are going to need some heavy hitters."

Orrin peeked around the jars filled with monster parts and asked, "Do you know anybody in the Guild that you would trust? We could demand certain people. The only other people I know in Dey are Tony and a bunch of shopkeepers."

He stopped in front of a vial with tiny floating red flower petals. They reminded him of someone and his eyes went wide. "Actually, that's not true. I met some Guild members once who asked me to be part of their party. I'm not saying I trust them, but at least I know them a bit."

Madi sat forward in her chair, resting her chin on her hand. "That's better than me. I may be a member of the Guild in name, but I've never been allowed to train or interact with them much."

Daniel pulled his feet off the table and let them drop. "If they wanted you in their party, they must have been desperate."

Orrin walked up behind Daniel and flicked his ear. "Don't be a smart-ass. There are three of them. Tin uses a spear and water magic, if I remember right. Emily was a fire mage." Daniel blushed a little remembering the third. "Garret is an archer of some sort, but I don't remember more."

Madi tapped her chin in thought. "The spear user would be good. We need someone to help Daniel keep the monsters at bay. Either one of the others would be fine. Of course, we need to meet them first . . . and get Pritus to agree to them."

Orrin nodded. "So, I guess we are going to do this? Should we try to notify your dad or just escape town for a bit?"

Madi smiled maliciously. "I'll negotiate the details with the Guildmaster if Daniel agrees to it. But no way are we telling anyone. I will not let this chance be taken from me." Her eyes flashed.

Daniel laughed and stood up. He grabbed the bell off the table and held it up. "I almost feel sorry for the Guildmaster. Madi is going to eat her alive."

He rang the bell.

Madi's negotiation skills needed some work.

"Five quests? And she gets to choose which of Tin's group comes with us?" Orrin asked as they left the Guild. "What were you thinking?"

Madi smiled. "But did you not realize the most important part?"

Daniel butted in as they walked back to the Catanzano house. "Madi, I'm with Orrin here. You gave away too much. And you argued too much over her supplying us for the trip. We don't need supplies. Orrin probably still has enough water and food in his [Dimension Hole] for three dungeons trips."

"I do," Orrin replied. He'd even taken an inventory of what he had and sold some of the things that were pointless to keep. His little nest egg was pushing several hundred gold again.

Madi stopped walking and looked around before pulling them into a side alley. "She said she would supply the entire team. That means the two people she chooses as well. As much as we could carry out. She probably thinks we'll take a few weapons or armor, the typical dungeoneering supplies like ropes and sleeping bags, and nothing more. With Orrin along, we can treat the two temporary party members to their pick of as much as they could ever want. That point is going to cost the Guild hundreds of gold—and their loyalty."

Madi poked Daniel's chest. "And I had her down to three quests when you butted in and asked how hard she thought the quests were going to be. Guild rules wouldn't have let her give you a higher-level quest than copper. We could have gotten away with three copper quests. She tried pushing for three silver, which would have been a death sentence for us right now. I had to go up to five."

Daniel scratched his chest where she had poked him. "I didn't know there were different quest tiers."

Madi sighed and started walking again. "Of course there are different levels. You are both copper; look at your rings. I am, too. Once you reach level twenty-five, you can request a silver ring if you want. You get control of a small group during Horde attacks and can request special quests at the silver level, and it comes with a few more small perks."

"What kind of quests are silver level?" Orrin asked. The smells from the food vendors all around still wafted in the air. Most had closed for the night, but a few remained open. Orrin even spotted a man carrying around the balloon candies they'd tried the first day in Dey.

"High-level monster kills, political assassinations, Pass explorations," Madi said as she threw her hands in the air. "Anything the Guild thinks would kill someone under level twenty-five."

A minute passed as they walked quietly. Daniel finally muttered, "Sorry."

Madi gave him a long look and huffed. "If you say you are going to trust me to negotiate, keep your mouth shut. It doesn't matter, though. We got the better part of the deal. Pritus just doesn't realize it yet."

"I still don't see how Orrin ransacking a bunch of rope and torches is going to do anything," Daniel mumbled as he pushed open the door of the Catanzano house. Orrin nodded to the guards on duty, receiving a slight nod back.

"She said we could take anything we wanted from the storerooms," Madi said with a grin. "Of course, we can take all the normal gear we need, but do you know what else the Guild keeps in their storerooms?"

"Enlighten me," Daniel said with exasperation. "You don't have to drag it out so much."

Madi frowned quickly but then shook her head. "Every monster killed, all the precious ores mined, rare plants, and even relics."

"So, you plan on looting?" Orrin laughed. "What's a relic?"

Madi's frown returned. "A relic. You know . . ."

Shit, Orrin tried to think quickly. *A relic must be something common to the world here. Fuck, I screwed up.*

"Yeah, I know. But, like, what kind would the Guild have? And would they even let us take one?" Orrin lied through his teeth. He noticed Daniel standing perfectly still as well.

Madi brightened visibly. "See, that's why I argued so hard for us to be able to take anything we wanted. Nobody knows the full inventory of the Guild's storerooms. They're huge and unorganized. Every Guildmaster tries to get them in order, but by the time they make any headway, someone else takes over and changes the system. It's a long shot, sure, but could you imagine how loyal these Guild members would be if we got them a bracelet with stats? Or a returning spear?"

Orrin's brain did backflips. Magic items! There had never been a mention of those in any books they'd picked up.

"But those must be rare, right?" Daniel asked. "I've never even heard of relics before now."

Bless you, Daniel, Orrin thought.

"Of course." Madi shrugged. "Finding something like that won't likely happen, but even if we find some Mythril or cold iron, it would be worth it. Getting proper weapons out of those is a lifelong dream of most adventurers."

Daniel smirked. "Gertrude has both and a dragon's bone."

Madi rolled her eyes. "Yes, you have a beautiful and rare sword, oh great [Hero]. For the rest of the normal folk, a cold iron sword would be the boon of a lifetime."

They stopped at the top of the stairs. Madi's room was to the left, while the boys' room was to the right.

"I honestly don't even know what the difference is," Daniel admitted. "I read cold iron makes the weapon stronger, but I didn't really study up on it much."

Madi looked over at Orrin and laughed. "He's so ignorant, I don't know how it took me so long to figure out he was from another world."

Orrin laughed along while simultaneously breaking out in a cold sweat. "Yeah, I keep waiting for him to ask me how to use the bathrooms."

Madi's smile grew wider as they picked on Daniel together. "I'm sure Orrin can tell you all about different metal types. If you want more information, some of the books in the library cover it, too. My mom dabbled in blacksmithing, so unless my father got rid of her books, there should be more in there. But back to the point at hand. If we find good materials, we can have better gear made. For us and the people Pritus is inevitably going to have spy on us."

Daniel mulled it over. "Okay. I guess you didn't totally suck at negotiating."

Madi put her hand on her hip. "Good night, you ungrateful piece of—"

"Madeleine, are you out there?" Lord Catanzano's voice drifted down the hall. "Come in here, I need to go over these numbers with you."

"Coming, Father." Madi stuck out her tongue at the boys and left them on the landing.

Daniel grabbed Orrin and pulled him toward the library. "Guess what you're doing for the next hour?"

Chapter 5

As Orrin entered the Catanzanos' library, he inhaled deeply. Despite being in a different world, the scent of the surrounding books still hit the same. It revitalized some part of him deep down and calmed him at the same time. Exactly what he needed after the minefield of a conversation with Madi they had just left.

"What do you want to look for first?" Orrin turned back and noticed Daniel backing up slowly. "Oh, no, you don't. Get back here. If I have to research different types of metal, so do you."

He grabbed his friend and dragged him into the room.

Daniel sighed in defeat. "You try to look up anything on relics. I'll try to find Lady Catanzano's blacksmithing books. I'm kind of excited to find out exactly what Gertrude is made of."

Orrin grumbled. Of course Daniel would volunteer himself for the easier task. They'd already read most of the normal primers, and nothing he could remember jumped out as a good starting point. How exactly do you look up magical items in a world where magic is the norm?

Daniel started stacking a small pile of books from a corner of the library within ten minutes. Orrin was still searching book title by book title, at least for the books that were labeled, when he had an idea.

He used [Analyze] on the next untitled book.

The first half dozen times he used the skill, all he got was:

Book

Orrin almost gave up, but he had to fulfill his daily quota for the skill anyway. After a few more attempts, something new did appear.

Book
Subject: History

Orrin pulled the unmarked book out and leafed through the first few pages. *A History of Agricultural Development Efforts in Veskar.* Flipping through a few pages, he realized it was a history book in the vaguest sense only. The book chronicled multiple leaders' attempts to develop large swaths of Veskar for better farming. It also went into detail about why each separate attempt failed, for reasons ranging from banditry to what sounded like a plague.

Orrin put the book back and then tried again. The jump in information after he read a few pages was drastic.

Book
Subject: History and Agrarian Sciences
Title: A History of Agricultural Development Efforts in Veskar
Summary: Failed farming attempts in Veskar, detailed by year and leader.

"You find anything?" Daniel asked from directly behind him. Orrin spooked and jumped.

"Don't do that!"

Daniel chuckled.

Orrin shook himself and answered, "I'm not finding anything on relics. Just farming in other countries."

Daniel gave him a look. "Why were you reading it so long, then?"

"I'm working on [Analyze]. I was hoping that if I get it working right, I might be able to just browse and see exactly what's in the book before even reading it," Orrin explained. "It's a slow process, though."

Daniel gestured to the table. "Wanna split the books and figure out what we should steal from the Guild?"

Orrin shrugged and joined him at the small reading nook. Of the six books, two were easily discarded—the titles noted they were advanced blacksmithing books. Orrin picked up the next one.

Daniel put his book down after ten minutes. "This is a dud. It just goes and on about the different methods of quenching and hammering steel and iron, but nothing about different metal types."

Orrin closed his book. "This one is the same. It's just schematics for different types of weapons, tools, and such."

They opened the last two, and almost immediately, Daniel cheered.

"Found it. An entire chapter on different metal types and the best applications for each."

Orrin waited and watched Daniel read slowly. "Are you going to read it aloud?"

"Nah," Daniel muttered. "You can read it when I'm done. It's only a few pages."

Orrin rolled his eyes and went back to searching for anything related to relics. He noticed the [Analyze] skill had evolved a bit and was still giving the subject tab on the book. Silas had organized the books in a certain way, grouping them into categories; however, [Analyze] gave the occasional different reaction. The section he'd been in before was mostly marked history, but sometimes he would also get a biography. One time, [Analyze] marked the book as fictional history. Orrin pulled that one out to check the title. *The Life of Grandmage Fauni.*

The library also had a section that returned subjects of architecture, math, philosophy, sciences, classes, magic, and politics. It was in the sciences section where Daniel had found the blacksmithing books. Mapping out the library gave Orrin a small sense of achievement, even if they hadn't found anything on relics.

"I'm done," Daniel said and waved Orrin over. "There is a lot more than just Mythril or cold iron."

Orrin read through the few pages quickly. Mythril was a rare metal mined primarily by the dwarves. It had a few different uses, but the main one was creating an alloy that strengthened any other metal. The book noted that Mythril alloys were nearly impossible to break without extreme circumstances. It also noted that working with the stuff was annoyingly difficult—it set quicker than any metal, and a blacksmith would have mere minutes to get the shape correct and beaten to perfection.

Cold iron was a black iron found in small veins in the deepest iron mines. It was rarer than Mythril but easier to work with. It could also be separated out again from a mixed metal alloy and reused over and over. The biggest use was in weapons or machinery that needed to keep an edge. A cold iron blade never needed to be sharpened. It also would slowly regrow if a piece was broken off. A new piece of another metal had to be introduced for it to work. The blade would slowly lose this ability as the cold iron percentage decreased, but a sword made with cold iron would still last decades longer than a normal steel or iron blade.

The book also mentioned Citrandish wood, from an elven tree used in the construction of their bows and wooden weapons. Harder to break and giving twice the pull to a bow, the wood was rarely found except in elven hands. The author went into detail about what had happened to the few people who had stolen bows in the past. Orrin felt very grateful that he hadn't chosen the path of an archer. He could see the temptation for a stronger bow outweighing the common sense of a person. Being planted in the ground and having a new tree grown through you while alive did not sound like a pleasant way to go.

Another was adamantine, which was so rare that only royals of the past had been able to afford a knife made with the same. It was the only metal that refused to mix with others. Small pendants or rings could still be found, but the exact nature of the advantages of the metal was unknown.

There were also irons that had absorbed characteristics from their surroundings. Skymetal was basically meteors that had fallen to the ground and been found. The owners would swear the blades moved faster. Red iron was found near flowing lava. It gave a red sheen to any blade and had been proven by the author to have a visceral reaction to cold. When pressed against ice, it cut as if warmed from within. The book noted that some ancient shields of red iron had been known to turn ice magic aside if made with a high enough saturation point of other metals; however, that recipe had been lost to time. The author theorized that other irons were possible in high-density magical areas.

"So, your sword won't break and doesn't need to be sharpened," Orrin said as he finished reading and looked over the chart of saturation points and mixture percentages for different metals. "That's handy."

"She'll also regrow if I chip her on something too hard," Daniel added. "Like if I tried to hit your head."

Orrin rolled his eyes. "Good to know, I guess. Nothing that would help either of us too much, though."

Daniel shrugged. "You need to keep learning all the things you can if you don't want to tell Madi. I can get away with the 'I'm ignorant' act, but unless you come clean and—"

"No," Orrin cut him off. "I trust her a bit, but that's too big a secret. Just pay attention. You saved me today. Keep that up."

Daniel picked up the books and moved them back to the shelves. "So, tell me more about the people we are going into this dungeon with."

Orrin leaned back in his chair and closed his eyes. It had been a long day, and using [Analyze] wore him out. He was getting better at pushing the skill further and further, but he still felt a small wave of exhaustion hit him once he used it too much. *Physical skills suck*, he thought.

"Tin is really nice. She was the one who answered my request to find you back when . . ." He trailed off. "Anyways, she invited me to lunch and introduced me to the other two, Emily and Garret. You'd like Tin. She's good people. Emily is more reserved, but smart—you can tell just from talking to her. She also has an evolved class. She found some magic item that let her upgrade from [Fire Mage] into something else that I can't remember the name of. Honestly, I think if she's on the team, she'll be the easiest to convince to use our strategy of working together."

"What's Tin's class?" Daniel sauntered back over and plopped in the other chair. "The [Fire Mage] I worked with before was powerful."

"She uses a spear and water magic, I think." Orrin looked up as he tried to remember the conversation from weeks ago. "[Waterspear], maybe? She'd be good at the front line with you."

"And the third one?" Daniel asked, pulling at a string in his shirt. He wrapped the thread around his finger once and yanked.

Orrin remembered the flirtatious archer. "Garret. He's an archer with earth magic. I didn't really get too much about his skills."

Daniel looked up. "Why are you blushing?"

Orrin stood quickly and went back to searching the library. "Not blushing. It's just hot in here. Where do you think we can find more on relics?"

Daniel followed right on his heels. "It's not hot in here. Are you sick?"

Orrin ignored him.

"Orrin, what is it?" Daniel asked with genuine concern. "You didn't cycle too much, did you? I thought you had a better handle on your limits."

Orrin sighed. "He kind of hit on me last time we were all together."

Daniel blinked twice and then laughed.

"This is why I didn't tell you," Orrin muttered and pulled another book out from the magic section. It ended up being a list of different types of obscure magic used in Veskar.

Daniel put his hand on Orrin's shoulder. "Buddy, I'm sorry. I just . . . Well, I thought you liked my sister."

Orrin threw up his hands, knocking Daniel's hand off. "I do . . . did. I don't know. I've never had someone hit on me. It threw me a bit, and I'd just rather not think about it."

Daniel gently placed his hand back on Orrin's shoulder and turned him until they faced each other. "You know I'm your friend no matter who you like, right?"

Orrin nodded.

Daniel's face turned evil. "Is he hot?"

Orrin boosted his own strength and pushed Daniel. He rolled backward and came up laughing.

"I'm going to bed," Orrin announced. He stormed out, with Daniel's laughter echoing behind him.

Chapter 6

Orrin woke up before the sun. Daniel was snoring lightly as he pulled on his clothes and made his way downstairs to the small training yard. None of the guards were up and training this early. Exactly how Orrin liked it.

Using one of the tables set out for equipment between bouts, Orrin started to clear out his [Dimension Hole]. He sorted the junk he'd accumulated into three piles: food, survival supplies, and loot.

He'd already cleared out most of the random monster parts that he had gathered since Daniel and he had woken up in the forest. He had a little food and two barrels of water as well. That pile could stay here until they left for the dungeon.

In the survival pile went his multiple vials and some penidrop clippings, along with a dwindling supply of alchemy ingredients. He had his bedroll, rope, a hand axe, and a few knives left over from Daniel's original bracer of daggers. His original clothing and a few new changes. He had a myriad of other useful items as well, including blankets, candles, torches, chalk, matches, flint and steel, a waterskin, and even fishhooks and a line. Madi had gotten him a few small jars of ink, a fountain pen, and a small blank book when he'd mentioned he wanted to make some notes and plans. Those went in as well.

He found a single arrow that had somehow missed his cleanings and put it in a quiver nearby.

For loot, Orrin had kept Samara's whip. Silas had declined to keep it, and Orrin hadn't been able to find someone to buy it yet. Everything else had been sold, and the multiple pouches of gold, silver, and copper he had were a testament that Orrin could probably retire and live quite comfortably if he wanted to. He'd split the money as evenly as possible with his friends. Daniel had spent a lot of his original gold from sharing Quests with Madi on his weapon. Orrin hadn't gone on any such spending spree, if you didn't count the small library of books he kept. He was planning on leaving most of those behind, except the bestiaries.

He slowly pulled one last thing he'd picked up out of his pocket.

The large hammer was heavy in his hand, and the damage-dealing end slapped to the dirt with a *thunk*. Jude's family hadn't wanted the weapon and had asked Lord Catanzano to sell it for them. Orrin had paid double the going price in an effort to help his late friend's family.

"What am I doing lugging you around, though?" Orrin asked the hunk of metal. He wasn't trained to use the hammer and didn't plan on learning anytime soon. He knew he would need to leave the hammer when they went to the Guild storerooms.

"I'll drop it off in my room," he said aloud.

He looked down at all his possessions and started writing in his new journal. Orrin knew Daniel would just try to wing things. Madi was intelligent, but without Brandt, there wasn't anybody to make sure they were properly supplied.

Orrin rolled his shoulders and started planning.

An hour later, he thought he'd made a good list of what five people would need to survive ten levels in a new dungeon. *See, Daniel! All those late nights playing D&D in random online groups is paying off.* He chuckled to himself.

Orrin stored away the things he didn't want to bring and then left to put in a few orders. When he got back two hours later, Daniel was just making his way into the dining room for breakfast.

"Where have you been?" Daniel asked as he grabbed a small green fruit that looked like a strawberry.

Orrin just shrugged and filled up his second cup of coffee. "Getting ready. The Guildmaster is supposed to send over somebody by noon to give us updates on the dungeon and who is going with us. Then we have a few hours this afternoon to raid the storerooms. Did you really just wake up?"

Daniel raised an eyebrow. "Orrin, it's like eight in the morning."

Orrin filled up a plate with eggs and toast. He'd cleared half his plate when Madi entered the room. Her hair was curled again and put back into a bun. Her normal battle clothing was gone, and she wore an elegant suit with a longer coat that almost doubled as a dress. She had applied some light makeup as well.

"Off to war?" Orrin joked.

Madi flinched. "Yes, actually. I have to attend a meeting with my father for the next few hours. I'll be back before lunch. Don't even try to start without me."

"Everything all right?" Daniel asked from his seat.

Madi sighed. "Yes, it will be. We've had to take over Wendeln's accounts, and the other houses are fighting over the proper distribution."

Daniel turned back around. "Sounds easy—just give an even split."

Madi sat down, pulled Daniel's plate toward her, and started to eat his food. "And what about the debts already owed to each family? Or our own debts owed to Wendeln? Should we all start from zero? What about the fact that the Timpe house is taking over most of his duties? What about the guards he paid for?"

Daniel put his hands up. "Okay, okay. I get it."

Madi smirked. "That's only half of it. Entire coffers were missing. We don't know if they were stolen by some enterprising guard or if Wendeln was cooking his books."

"Or paying off kidnappers," Orrin muttered.

Madi nodded. "My father wants to hammer that point. Wendeln used city funds to try to kidnap Daniel. We spent manpower and resources. It's going to be a long and boring meeting filled with math and lots of arguing."

"Sounds like Orrin's favorite pastime." Daniel grabbed a pastry off his plate before Madi could eat it. "Maybe he should go with you."

"I've got places to be," Orrin responded. "I ordered some extra alchemy supplies, along with a few things I thought might make our trip into the dungeon easier."

Daniel perked up. "Like what?"

Orrin started counting on his fingers. "Small tents for the rooms between floors. Nobody should have to hear you snore. A barrel with a tap, so we don't have to keep pulling water out the top with a ladle. A grappling hook in case we need to climb. A crowbar and climbing pitons. Extra blankets and bedrolls for the new members."

"Do we really need that?" Daniel rolled his eyes. "They should have their own, right? And what's a piton?"

"Climbing spike. Hammer it in and run a rope through it. Then if you fall, you won't die."

"Again, do we really need that?" Daniel asked.

"Better to be ready and have it," Orrin said.

"Well, I'll leave you boys to it, then." Madi mopped up the last of Daniel's breakfast and stood. She reached back and bobbed her bun on her head. "Do I look presentable?"

"Absolutely," Daniel said with a smile. Madi grinned and nodded at them both.

"Wait for me," she demanded again and swept out of the room.

Daniel saluted her as she left. Orrin shook his head.

"Want to spar a bit?" Daniel asked with a twinkle in his eye.

Orrin resigned himself to a long morning.

After Daniel proved to Orrin that he had in fact been letting his friend win, Orrin left to pick up the last of his orders. He hadn't gone to Jovi for the grappling hook, crowbar, and pitons. That kind of work was below the weaponsmith. Instead, Orrin had found a small forge with a new smith and placed his request. The woman had said she only needed an hour, and when Orrin arrived late, she hadn't been happy.

"Storing your purchases will cost you extra in the future," she snarled.

Orrin took his purchases and left without arguing.

He had planned on taking the main street back to the Catanzanos' house but had only walked for a few minutes before he had to take a side street. Too many merchants were in town trying to stake a claim after the chaos of the recent Wendeln trouble. Men in slightly crisper clothing with their noses in the air passed him by. Orrin's nose caught the scent before his eyes fell upon a growing line leading to a familiar corner.

Amir's father's coffee shop.

Orrin hadn't seen his friend in the prior weeks. He felt guilty and worried as he rushed to the line. He didn't really need another cup of coffee, but as he stood in line, he justified that this was another crucial provision for the dungeon.

Amir's father ran a tight ship, and the long line moved much faster than he would have expected. Soon, Orrin stood in front of an older version of Amir. Orrin almost greeted him as his friend but noticed the crow's-feet bracketing his eyes and the slight wrinkles on his forehead.

"What'll it be, young sir?" Even his voice had the same smooth calmness and patience.

"I'll need a small bag of ground beans for travel and a cup of your strongest brew to go," Orrin ordered first. He watched the man move swiftly about, turning the knobs with a utility of movement that spoke of much practice and love.

"That'll be six copper." The man was already done.

Orrin handed the coins over. He picked up the small clay cup and reached for the bag of heaven. "Is Amir here?"

Orrin's hand gripped the bag of ground beans, but Amir's father did not let go. "Why do you ask after my son?"

The shop suddenly felt smaller. Amir's father was huge, towering over Orrin. He realized that the father must know more about his son's trouble at the Hospital than Amir suspected.

"He's a friend," Orrin answered quickly, feeling the heat lift some. "We met a few weeks ago, but I haven't been around. I just wanted to say hi."

The hand released the bag of coffee, and the smile returned. "Amir is studying. He is always studying. He should take a break and help his poor father more. A friend would remind him of this, yes?"

Orrin grinned and started to back out of the shop. "Of course. Will you tell him that Orrin stopped by? He should come visit."

Amir's father nodded. "Yes. I will tell him. Here, take a cookie." He handed Orrin a dark-brown circle. Calling it a cookie would be generous. It was flat and looked like mud.

Orrin tossed out a thank-you and beat a hasty retreat.

After storing the last few purchases in his [Dimension Hole], Orrin made his way back to the Catanzano residence. He was almost to the front door when somebody yelled his name.

He turned and saw Emily the [Fireflower Mage] wave once at him. She marched toward him and gave him a small smile that barely reached her eyes. "Good morning. I hear thanks are in order." She put her hand out.

Orrin took her hand, slightly confused. "Thanks? Oh! Did Pritus select you for the—"

"The mission," Emily interrupted him. "Yes. The Guildmaster granted me the honor. I'm hoping to live up to her expectations. It is good to see you again. Tin has been beside herself since we learned you were part of the [Hero]'s group." She pitched her voice higher in mimicry of Tin. "'We almost had a [Hero]!'"

Orrin laughed. "I'm not the [Hero], though. That's Daniel. You'll meet him soon. I was just heading back. I've been out all morning getting supplies. Are you here for the dun—mission debrief?"

Emily's eyes lit up at the mention of Daniel. "Yes. We are all supposed to be there and then head out tomorrow. What kind of supplies?"

Orrin started explaining what he'd gotten and why. Emily's nod of approval as he spoke gave him confidence that he hadn't been wasting his time.

"Preparation like that is impressive," Emily complimented him. "But if you expect us to all carry a huge pack, it'll be dangerous and time-consuming."

"I've got it covered," Orrin answered cryptically.

Emily squinted at him and shrugged. "Lead the way. Garret should be along soon."

Orrin sputtered.

Chapter 7

Sure enough, Garret sauntered into the Catanzano house ten minutes after Orrin brought Emily in. He was in the middle of introducing her to Madi when the archer announced himself.

"Orrin! Where have you been hiding?"

Madi's eyes shot up as the tall man walked right to Orrin and hugged him.

Orrin stood very still as he felt the heat rise a few degrees.

"Orrin." Madi stepped closer. "Introduce me to your friend."

Orrin opened and closed his mouth multiple times before Garret bowed low, sweeping back a short cape. "Garret Bell, at your service, Lady Madeleine."

Madi put her hand on Orrin's elbow and positioned herself between the two men. "I'm assuming that you are to be our fifth member, along with Ms. Emily here."

Garret nodded and waved at Emily. Emily shook her head in dismay at her friend.

"Good." Madi gently pushed Orrin toward the front dining room. "Daniel will be down soon enough. Let's get settled. The Guildmaster sent word that her attaché will be arriving within the hour. That should be more than enough time for us to all get to know each other and set some ground rules for working together."

Orrin felt the heat in his face start to fade as they filed into the cleared dining room. *He's just a flirt. Ignore it,* he thought. But when he sat down and Garret ran a hand along the back of his chair and lightly touched his shoulder, Orrin jumped again.

"Garret, quit it," Emily demanded. She sat down in the empty chair next to Orrin. "Sorry about him. He's incorrigible but harmless. I'll keep him in line."

"Unless you want me to get out of line," Garret whispered across the table.

Emily pointed at him and a small crystal of fire formed at the tip of her finger. "One more quip and I'll burn you again."

Garret put his hands up in surrender. "I'll behave. Sorry, Orrin."

Emily waved her hand, and the fire crystal dissipated.

"After the dungeon, I'll ask you on a proper date," Garret got out before he fell out of his chair. The smell of burning filled the room. "Damn it, Emily. These are new pants."

Madi hid her mouth with her hand for a moment before composing herself. "Let's agree the first rule of this party should be to not harm or distract each other during the dungeon raid."

Garret ran his hand through his hair as he sat back down gingerly. "Agreed."

"That includes flirting or trying to get a rise out of each other," Madi said and then raised a hand as Garret started to interject. "Yes, Garret. I heard it. Don't antagonize your teammates."

"Good rule," Daniel said from the doorway. "Rule two, everybody listens to what Madi says, in the dungeon and out. She's going to keep us alive."

Madi kept herself composed at the praise and vote of confidence from Daniel, but Orrin could see the words had a great effect on her.

Emily went to stand as she noticed the [Hero], while Garret had already noticed and was starting to bow.

"Rule three, no bowing or posturing. We're a team for this mission. I'm just an adventurer like you. I'm sure I'll learn as much from you two as I have from Madi here . . . and Orrin," Daniel added after only a small beat.

"That is going to be hard for us," Emily admitted. "It's an honor to meet a real [Hero]. To meet you."

Daniel sat down at the other end of the table from Madi and waved a hand. "I'm serious. I'm just a normal guy from another world who has some cool magic and shit. A few months ago, I was just going to school and worrying about what I'd wear to prom. Please, just treat me like you'd treat Orrin."

Orrin watched Garret close his eyes and take a breath. He smirked at Orrin but nodded to Daniel.

"If that is how you'd like it," Emily said, settling back in her chair. "It's still going to be an adjustment. When Tin told us that the Guildmaster was requesting us for a mission with the [Hero], half the Guild was in an uproar. Why us?"

Daniel pointed at Orrin. "He vouched for your group, and Pritus selected two of you to fill the gap in our ranks. Don't disappoint his trust."

Emily and Garret turned back to Orrin with renewed respect. Madi clapped her hands.

"Before we get the information about the dungeon, I'd like to discuss the two of you a bit," Madi started. "Basics first, if you don't mind. Class and level? Have you ever been in a dungeon? Any notable weaknesses?"

Garret and Emily exchanged a glance, and Emily nodded. She stood, pushing her chair backward. "I'm Emily Ibarra, [Fireflower Mage], level twenty-five. I raided the Boiling Swamp before it was cleared. A two-tier, two-year-old dungeon south of Dey. We turned back after the sixth floor due to losing our main fighter to a pit trap. Weaknesses are mostly water monsters."

After her cut-and-dry speech, Orrin expected the same from Garret. Instead . . .

"I'm Garret Bell, [Earth Archer] extraordinaire. I'm level nineteen but teetering on the edge. I've not raided a dungeon, but I've helped turn back enough Hordes and fought enough monsters to know the game. I have no weaknesses unless you count a beautiful smile or good time a weakness."

Madi sighed. "Does your class allow you to take damage?"

Garret shrugged. "I stay on the edges of fights. I've got a trump card if I need to avoid a big blow, but if the party does its job, I should be able to take down any monster quicker than most."

Emily spoke up. "He's not just bragging. His arrows hit hard, and he has a knack for trapping monsters. He usually outkills me and Tin combined."

Madi nodded, taking a few notes. "We'll discuss our strategy later, but know that we don't care how hard you can hit individually. We work as a team. If you don't think you can take orders and go against the normal adventurer code of 'most damage output possible,' you can leave now."

Emily frowned but didn't move.

Garret laughed. "Are you saying you want me to not kill the monsters?"

Daniel hit the table loudly. "If Madi says to not kill a monster, you listen. If you can't do that, we can't trust you."

Garret's smile disappeared. "Whoa, whoa. I'm not saying I can't follow directions. It's just . . . why?"

Orrin raised his hand, and Madi nodded at him. He stayed in his seat, not trusting his legs while having to give the same speech he'd originally given to Brandt, Jude, and Madi so long ago. "It comes down to strategy. If every one of us just goes full out at whichever monster we want, the chances of success go down. Instead, we'll work as a team. Daniel can usually keep the attention of a few of the monsters and stay up while we take down stragglers or more dangerous prey first, depending on the situation. Madi and I have worked out a good system of giving directions during a fight. We'll explain it all later. By picking our targets, we can concentrate our damage and increase our odds with every kill . . . or escape and regroup if the enemy is too strong. We each have a few tricks up our sleeves, too, so, using those in a smart way and in cooperation with each other, we don't have to worry about anyone going off on their own and dying."

Emily's razor-sharp gaze focused on Orrin again as he finished talking. "So, Madi gives the orders?"

Orrin nodded. "Most of the time, yes. But if you hear me shouting, or even Daniel, it's likely a good idea to listen. The three of us have fought together enough that we know how to stop any gaps in each other's weaknesses."

Madi spoke next, talking about her own class and level. She even gave a short demonstration of her color-coded messages, reassuring Emily and Garret that she would go over it again in much more detail at a later point. Daniel also had a chance to give them the general overlay of how he'd fight, keeping his skills vague on purpose, as they'd agreed beforehand.

Orrin had already gone over his class with the two new members in the past, but so much had changed since that point. While his main skills were still buffing, he could also heal, track with [Map], give a protective shield of sorts with [Ward], use [Teleport], and keep the party supplied with [Dimension Hole]. He didn't get a chance to explain that he was a Swiss Army knife, though, before there was a knock on the door.

"Ma'am, a member of the Guild is here for you." A guard Orrin didn't recognize opened the door a bit more, letting the man inside.

"Thank you, Sir Perkins," Madi answered. "Come in, please."

Of course, she has already memorized all the new guards' names, Orrin thought. With the general upheaval across the city lords, the guards had been shuffled between different positions. Orrin had a hard time keeping them straight.

The man who entered was not what Orrin had expected from a Guild member. The man was old. Older than Tony. *He must be eighty at least,* Orrin judged as he glanced at the long white hair and braided beard that reached the middle of his chest. The man clutched two books tightly and gazed around with an almost dazed look in his eyes.

"Guildmaster Pritus has sent me to prepare you for a dungeon foray," the man said. "I'm Calak Ewing, Guild assessor."

"An honor to meet you, sir." Madi bowed her head. "Thank you for meeting us at my home. We hope to not take up too much of your precious time."

Orrin glanced back at Madi, who was using her politician voice and flowery language. *Who is this guy?*

"What's an assessor?" Daniel asked, still sitting. "Do you want a chair, Mr. Ewing?"

Calak glanced around and seemed startled to find Daniel sitting so close to him. He jumped back a step and almost tripped but righted himself at the last moment. "What's an assessor?! You must be Daniel, the new [Hero]. Your power level has grown, young man, but you are still ignorant of the ways of our world. You should spend more time learning, or else you'll die of that ignorance as so many before you have."

"Daniel, an assessor, like Calak, is something of a historian. They study trends and information on different topics to give us predictions on what might be," Madi explained.

Orrin itched to ask more questions. If Calak had a class geared toward information gathering, he could use that to their advantage. Maybe he could take the skills himself and figure out a way to get them home. Unfortunately, Daniel didn't ask any more questions, and Orrin felt too many eyes were in the room to risk asking what could be common knowledge.

"Please, sir, have a seat. What can you tell us of the new dungeon?" Madi motioned to an empty chair, which Calak shuffled to. He sat, still clutching his books to his chest.

They waited.

Calak watched each of them in turn.

Daniel, Orrin, and Madi watched him back. Garret raised an eyebrow at Emily, who shrugged.

"This party has a 23.2 percent chance of clearing a tier-one dungeon. As the exact specifications of the dungeon type are unknown, an extra 10.3 percent was taken off. While I would make recommendations, the Guildmaster has assured me that this is the group you have decided to stay with. Is that correct?"

Everybody took in a collective breath. *Twenty-three percent chance of succeeding?*

"This is our party, yes," Daniel said, with an edge that Orrin recognized. Daniel did not like being told he couldn't do something.

That prediction probably pissed him off, Orrin realized.

"If you fail to clear the dungeon, there is a 71 percent chance of one fatality, a 64 percent chance of two fatalities, a fifty-tw—"

"Stop," Daniel said with an authority Orrin hadn't ever heard in his friend's voice. "There is a 100 percent chance we clear this dungeon and survive. I don't want your predictions. I want information on the dungeon."

Calak's eyes blinked rapidly as he looked at Daniel. "Sorry. Sorry. Sorry. I get lost in my numbers." He looked down in front of him and realized he still held the books close. Reverently, Calak placed each book next to the other and opened the smaller one first.

"Initial dungeon break was three days ago. Fifty-odd level-two monsters of various types, including poison, water, and steel, appeared and were contained. Twenty-three level-three monsters of the same assortment were contained. One level-three aberrant escaped, type unconfirmed. Based on this data, the dungeon is tier one, with a deca-set predicted."

"Pritus said our party could take that out in a week," Daniel challenged Calak.

"Guildmaster Pritus could have meant a full party at level twenty. The recommended level for dungeon subjugation would have a higher success rate." Calak closed the smaller book and opened the larger one. The pages were yellowed, but the leather binding was pristine and polished. He also took a single piece of paper from his pocket and set it delicately on the table.

"With the combination of poison, water, and steel, it is likely that the dungeon will include moving traps, rivers or lakes of acid, and monsters of the same type. A list of possible monsters for you, if any of you care to read it, along with some historic traps found in steel- and poison-type dungeons."

Calak began to read off the names of monsters. Orrin recognized one in ten of them but hoped he could peruse the bestiaries later.

"Any questions?" Calak asked, his gaze shifting around the room.

"None at this time, thank you, sir," Madi answered after a pause. "If we have any questions, we'll reach out."

Calak shuffled his books back together and stood. "If you should succeed, please complete a full report. More data helps future generations increase their odds of survival with knowledge and proper planning."

Orrin watched Daniel. The [Hero] was still glaring at the old man as he left.

"I'm not saying I'm not willing to go, but one in four chances that we succeed isn't the greatest," Garret piped up as soon as the door closed.

"The only information he bases that off is our current levels," Madi said as she stood up and walked to the folded piece of paper left in front of Calak's seat. "We can improve our own odds by being smart."

She smiled up at Orrin as she grabbed the paper. "Ready to do some research?"

Orrin smirked. "Let's defeat a dungeon."

Chapter 8

"Useless," Orrin muttered for the hundredth time. Daniel had spent all of ten minutes trying to plan before taking Garret and Emily to the Catanzano training grounds to see what they could do.

"We do need to know what kind of fighting skills they have," Madi said, trying to play mediator again. "It's not like either of us would stand much of a chance against outright fighters like them. Daniel can at least stand his own."

That at least was true. Emily's fire magic was enough to keep Daniel back, with every additional minute adding heat to the mage's body. She let off bursts of fire so strong that the sand at her feet had been turned into a thin layer of glass. She brought out a small staff, nothing more than a walking stick, really, and proceeded to beat Daniel about the head with it when he got close enough.

Garret was an even worse matchup for Daniel. While the [Hero] liked to close in for a fight, Garret skipped back and loosed arrows that just appeared in his hands. He'd explained in between rounds that he could use magic to create an arrow out of any surface his body touched. Even his densely compacted sand arrows packed enough punch to knock Daniel back a step. The few times Daniel had gotten close enough to strike, the archer had deftly dodged every swing.

"You telegraph your attacks with your feet and the ground tells me where to move," he'd said with a shrug and a wink at Daniel's frustration. "Don't be too hard on yourself, though. You're, like, five levels below me."

Like Orrin, Daniel had gained an extra level and was sitting at level thirteen; however, all his physical stats were double boosted by his [Summoned Hero] skill. So, although his strength was at twenty-four, he hit like it was at forty-eight.

Daniel
Hero
Level 13
HP: 280/300
MP: 70/80
Strength: 24
Constitution: 15
Dexterity: 13
Will: 8
Intelligence: 10

Orrin sighed and leafed through his bestiary, reading one entry after the other. Madi had promised to look into traps and had a few books from her father's library on the small table; however, she had stopped reading a few pages in and watched the spectacle of the Daniel getting trounced.

"'Steel-Clawed Toad,'" Orrin read aloud to grab her attention. "They hide underwater and jump on a person as they walk by. They use their claws to shred you from behind and then leap off, back into the water."

"You've got [Monster View]," Madi muttered, distracted, as Garret stretched between rounds. He had taken off his shirt, a totally unnecessary move, as it was quite cold out. "We'll know where they are before they jump."

Orrin groaned. "You do realize that I can't be expected to keep watch the entire time. We should have plans ready."

Madi turned at the frustration in his voice. "Orrin, I swear I get it. I want to be prepared, too." She waved her hand at the training ground as Emily and Garret faced off against each other, letting

Daniel have a small break. "But you have to know what they can do. Garret is great at dodging close, but Daniel already figured out a quick jump throws him off. These Steel Toads would be able to get the drop on him. His skills only let him read the ground. Emily's fire would probably be weak against them, too. Which means you would be our best defense."

She put her hand on his and gently closed the bestiary. "We don't have to leave right away. We have time to plan. It'll be all right."

Orrin stared into her dark eyes and saw her concern. He let out a breath he'd been holding and felt a little of his stress fall away.

Madi smiled.

"That's match," Daniel yelled and threw a bucket of water on Garret. His pants had caught fire and had some very interesting holes.

"Damn it, Emily." Garret's normally smooth voice was hoarse from the smoke. "I liked this outfit."

Emily smirked and shrugged. "You're not even wearing half of it."

Orrin let out a laugh. Garret's eyes narrowed, and he pointed his bow. "I think it's time for some new opponents."

Daniel raised an eyebrow. "Madi isn't much lower in level than you. She's decent with her spear, too. Are you su—"

"No, Orrin." Garret winked and crooked a finger. "Want to go a round?"

The past few weeks had included a lot of downtime. Daniel's incessant need to prove himself meant Orrin had been used as a training dummy. He had started to develop his own style in battles: he ran away. His fighting was subpar, and without wasting some points on a weapon skill, he wouldn't have a chance of holding his own against his friend. So, he'd cheated. Of course, Daniel still won the fights, but Orrin counted getting away for a minute or two as a win. He didn't need to take down the things they fought, only to survive until someone else did.

"Orrin is more support," Daniel chided. "He's there to keep us going and help us hit faster, but I don't think a—"

"Let's do it." Orrin spoke over Daniel, feeling a wave of heat go down his back. "It's probably best for them to see me in action, right?" He turned to Madi. She smiled and nodded.

Daniel threw his hands in the air. "Why does no one listen to me? I'm the [Hero], right? That should count for something."

Despite his muttering, Daniel moved out of the training yard and sat at the table next to Madi. Emily stood close by and watched as Orrin moved out onto the sand.

"Weapon?" Garret quirked his head.

Orrin summoned an [Ice Sword] and held it awkwardly to his side. Garret nodded and touched his bow to his forehead, the sign he was ready to go.

"Um, what kind of training do you want to do?" Orrin asked sheepishly. "I mean, how do you want to score things?"

Garret smiled evilly. "First one to beg?"

Orrin could almost hear Emily roll her eyes. "First to incapacitate or draw blood," the fire mage yelled from the sidelines.

Orrin nodded and put his sword to his head. *Fuck, that's cold.*

Garret tapped his head with his bow and darted back, pulling a sand arrow out of the air and firing it at Orrin. Except Orrin had cast [Camouflage] and, with a hop to the side, the arrow missed.

Garret growled and shot two more arrows, one glancing off Orrin's arm. The [Ward] he'd put up swallowed the damage.

I could [Inverse] some dexterity debuffs and try to put him down, Orrin thought as he jumped back and forth, dodging arrows. Garret's skills didn't make the arrows fly any faster, and Orrin had had the foresight to boost his own stats before agreeing to the fight. His body moved quickly and he was gaining a little more familiarity with his body's increased reactions after all the practice Daniel had put him through.

"I can still see you when you land, Orrin." Garret pulled his bowstring back and waited. "Damn, that spell hurts my eyes."

"I know, right?" Daniel said from the table. He was reading the bestiary. Orrin was stunned and took another arrow to the chest.

"Hit you," Garret said triumphantly, letting his bow dip down. "That should have drawn blood. The round is mine."

Orrin canceled [Camouflage] and held his arms open, brushing some sand from his shirt. "Sorry. I'm still in it."

[Ward] was almost gone. That hit had been really strong, and with his low constitution, it was actually a bit worrying. But the shock on Garret's face was worth it.

Orrin cast [Lightstrike] and watched the archer take the hit without flinching. He frowned and pulled back for another shot.

Orrin didn't give him the chance. He ended the fight with what Daniel called cheating and inversed Garret's dexterity until the man slumped to the ground. His arrow disappeared as it fell from his fingers.

"Incapacitated, right?" Orrin looked over at Emily, who had a stricken look on her face.

"He's alive," Madi said quickly, standing up. "Orrin, can you let him up, please?"

Orrin buffed Garret until the man got to his feet. "You'll be back to normal in a few minutes. It's temporary."

Emily let out a half gasp, half cry. "I thought . . . He went down like his strings were cut and . . . what was that?"

"Cheating," Daniel said from over the book. "He cheated. He's disqualified and Garret wins."

"Shut up," Madi laughed. "Orrin won."

Garret's face, normally filled with cheer and confidence, was pale. "I couldn't move an inch. It felt like every bit of my dexterity had been drained away."

"It was." Madi's smile grew wider. "Orrin's our secret weapon. I know he told you he can increase stats, but he can also debuff them. That's what he calls it when he takes them away. I've watched him make monsters fall to the ground. As long as we are smart and don't rush into anything stupid, he can make anything we fight weaker and slower."

Emily and Garret looked at Orrin with renewed respect.

"The match is yours, then," Garret said, his smile returning. "Emily, your turn."

"I'm not stupid," she replied. "If he zeroes out my will, I'll have a mana headache. No, thank you."

Garret and Emily didn't stop asking questions, though, and Orrin ended up explaining [Camouflage] to them. Garret scoffed at his [Lightstrike], but Emily shushed him.

"It's not the strongest spell, but one that a lot of low-level mages take. Sometimes just hitting something can disrupt their concentration or a skill."

Madi was eventually dragged into a sparring match with Emily, who kept the upper hand. After Madi missed a [Shimmersight], Emily stopped the fight.

"We need to work on your aim," she said, shaking her red robe to let some of the cool air in. "You could have won. Where did you train?"

Madi squatted on her heels, breathing hard. Fighting with Emily meant a lot of running away from fire. "I've had a few tutors, but nothing formal for magic fighting. My father didn't want me to be an adventurer."

Emily put out a hand and helped her stand. "Let's leave the boys to the books. Come with me."

Madi glanced quizzically at the three males, finally worn-out and reading. Orrin waved as they left.

Daniel blinked hard and rubbed his eyes a few minutes later. "Where did Madi and Emily go?"

Garret shuffled a few pages of notes on the growing stack in the middle of the table. Orrin took a peek and saw the flirtatious man's research skills were quite good.

"Emily is probably bragging about her formal training and giving vague and unhelpful hints on how she can improve her magic," Garret said as he stretched his arms over his head, cracking his back. He smiled when he caught Orrin watching.

Orrin ducked his head back into his book, reading about the Venostamen, a two-foot-tall walking flower with teeth. It could blend into its surroundings and would strike once a target was close enough. The venom it injected could take down a level-twenty adventurer in a day.

"Why couldn't she tell us, too?" Daniel asked, completely missing Orrin's blush, to his relief. "Not that I use too much magic, but it could be helpful to know."

Garret grabbed a pitcher of lemonade from the middle of the table and refilled his empty glass. "Emily is weird about what information she gives out. She trained at the Sanerris School for four years. The rumor is Odrana will send somebody after you if you try teaching their secrets."

"Will they really?" Orrin looked up from his book.

Garret took a few loud swallows before answering. "No idea, but Emily still won't give me any help. I think she helped Tin, though."

He stood up after finishing his drink. "Listen, this has been fun, but I'm expected elsewhere this evening and I need to change." He gestured to his burned outfit with a smirk in Orrin's direction.

"That's fine," Daniel said and leaned back on his chair. "Orrin's probably going to make me read all night. You should swing back by in the morning. I think that's when we are going to hit the Guild's storeroom. I know Madi explained it, but try and think of some stuff you might want to pick up."

Garret tapped the table and let a wooden arrow appear in his hand. "I'm usually pretty sufficient on my own. See you two in the morning."

Orrin frowned in thought as Garret left. Daniel caught the look. "What?"

"I think . . . I think I have an idea to make Garret more powerful."

Chapter 9

"Spill it," Daniel prompted. "What's the idea?"

Orrin took a few scraps of paper from around the table and fanned them out. Pointing to each piece in turn, he said, "Stone. Skymetal. Red iron. Some Mythril alloys. Whatever else Garret thinks is best."

Daniel looked at the paper and then back at his friend. "Orrin . . . that's paper."

Orrin reached up and flicked Daniel's forehead. "We'll have a necklace made or maybe like a shirt. It will have all the various types of things he creates his arrows from. He'll be able to pick the right tool for the job."

Daniel's eyes lit up as he caught on. "That's actually genius. He complained during our matches that all he could really use was sand and wood. I think he wanted to show off his stone-cage thing that he brags about, but I wouldn't let him get near enough to the walls."

Orrin nodded. "This way, he can just tap his chest if he needs something specific. Of course, this all might be useless. There is probably some sort of limit or rules about what he can use, but it's worth a shot."

Daniel thumped his friend on the back. "It also gives us an idea of something valuable to look for in the Guild's storeroom—anything that Garret might make into an arrow."

"I wonder if he could make an explosive arrow if we found C-4 or dynamite," Orrin whispered.

"Nobody's around, Orrin. No need to whisper." Daniel started scooping up all the notes. "Anyways, are you really going to make me go through all this?"

Orrin glared.

"Fine. Fine." Daniel raised his hands in defeat. "But you know as well as I do that come fight time, you are going to be the one yelling the details for every monster we encounter."

Orrin crossed his arms and leaned against the table. "While that might be true, don't you think it might be a weight off my shoulders if you help out a bit more? This isn't the same thing as you writing your English paper the night before it's due and still getting an A. This is life and death. Remembering what something can do before I have the chance to yell it out could save everyone's lives."

Daniel frowned a bit. "I know it's dangerous. I'm helping, aren't I? Just because you have this need to research every facet of an issue before starting something doesn't mean the rest of us aren't pulling our weight. Madi has been putting together supplies for you to carry in your magical bag, getting recipes for items that take up less space but have double the nutrition."

He continued, standing up and leaning over the table a bit. "And while you might not have noticed, I was testing out how both of our new party members react to different scenarios and fight patterns. Did you even realize that Garret overrelies on his ability to read my attacks from the ground? He should never try to get close to me, but he thinks it's all a game. He actually laughed when I hit him. Emily's the complete opposite. Her magic is strong but takes forever to get set up. If something gets the drop on her, I'm not sure she'd have anything to react with. While you were reading about the monsters we might fight, I've been trying to figure out how to fight with the party we have. This is going to be completely different from the dungeon we did with Brandt and Jude. We don't have their experience or leadership. I'm going to be the only real front-line fighter. You heard what that guy said—there's a 70 percent chance someone dies in there."

Daniel became very quiet and let his head hang. "What if he's right? What if *you* die? We keep getting caught up in these stupid adventures. We were going to go visit the elves, remember? Madi told me they live for thousands of years. I'm sure one of them would know if any other [Hero]es had ever made it home. Even a hint that it's even possible . . ." He trailed off.

Orrin's anger at Daniel's seeming avoidance of research cooled. He walked around the table and put his hand on Daniel's shoulder. "Of course it's possible. We don't need the elves to tell us that. Plus, all I remember was somebody saying there was a 100 percent chance we destroy this dungeon and everybody lives."

He jostled Daniel and waited for his friend to look up. "If you want, we could try to make our way farther north after we crush this new dungeon back to wherever it came from. I'm not too sure visiting a nation at war and asking for their help is the best idea, but I'm willing to try if that's what you want to do."

Daniel's eyes were watery and his voice cracked as he responded. "I'm not sure what I want to do. It's too much sometimes, you know?"

Orrin nodded and, without telling Daniel, released a small [Calm Mind] spell on him. He hadn't realized how much the pressure was getting to Daniel. He had always seemed so calm and put together back in their world, too. The golden boy. Orrin began to wonder if that had been a facade as well.

"Sorry for acting like you aren't helping," Orrin said. "You know me—I get tunnel vision when I focus on something and don't think about anything else."

Daniel nodded sagely. "That is why you keep me around. You need someone to swat you upside the head."

Orrin rolled his eyes.

Daniel moved to bop him on the side of the head, but Orrin had anticipated the move and increased his dexterity a few times. They laughed together in the courtyard with the sunlight throwing shadows along the walls.

"No way." Madi shook her head and sat down at the library table, pulling out Calak's list and checking for any missed entries they hadn't investigated yet. "It's reckless, and we need a lot more supplies for a trip like that."

Daniel tried his best smile and slid into a chair next to Madi. "But we can plan all that now. Orrin can store more than enough food. We'll already have most of what we need for the dungeon raid, and we'll be heading in that direction anyways. It just makes sense to go now."

Orrin stood by the door and kept an eye out for anyone who might be walking—or rolling—by. They'd made their way into the Catanzano house proper after another hour of researching, only to find that Emily had already given a short lesson to Madi and left. Daniel was trying to get Madi on board with skipping out on the two Guild members after the dungeon was defeated and going straight to the elven forest. Surprisingly, she was resistant to the idea she had previously agreed to.

"I said no, Daniel," Madi huffed. "I think it's a terrible idea right now."

Orrin noted her reasons were changing but left the negotiation to Daniel.

"But it'll be the best opportunity we'll have," Daniel pushed. He reached out and put his hand on the book she was about to open. "Madi, listen to me. Orrin and I are going. We're going to need someone with your knowledge of diplomacy to keep us from getting riddled with arrows. Please?"

Madi squinted at his too-obvious wheedling. She pulled the book out from under his hand and then smacked it down quickly. Only Daniel's quick reflexes saved his hand from getting squished.

"Don't try that with me, Daniel. You should know better." Madi sighed and closed her eyes. "Fine. The real reason I'm not excited to run into a war zone is some news I overheard from my father. Odrana has sent a squadron from their Fire Mage Corps to start setting fire to the trees. The war is escalating."

"All the more reason to go," Orrin muttered from the door.

"What?" Madi turned to look at him. "I didn't hear you."

Orrin pushed away from the door and stood across the table from his friends. "I said that is all the more reason to go now. We need to get the [Hero] to where he can do the most good."

Madi tilted her head. "And if we get caught? Or the elves decide to shoot us first?"

Orrin shrugged. "We turn back. I'm not saying we should go walking into a trap. Just that the [Hero] has a Quest to solve. If the war really is ramping up, this might be our best chance at finding a way to end it."

Madi turned back to look at Daniel, then glanced at Orrin again. "You two have already decided. Asking me is just a formality, huh?"

"Yes and no," Orrin answered before Daniel could open his big stupid mouth. "We have decided it is necessary. If you have a real reason, other than your safety concerns, why we shouldn't go, we'll listen. You are our party member and friend."

The hardness in Madi's eyes melted when Orrin called her their friend. She turned away from them for a moment, and Orrin thought she wiped her eye once before turning back. "It really is mostly safety concerns, but if you both believe this would be beneficial somehow..."

"I do," Daniel said with conviction. "Something is telling me to go to the elves."

"But after the dungeon, right?" Madi said with an eagerness that Orrin didn't miss. She still had her dream of destroying all the dungeons she could in retribution for her mother's death.

Daniel nodded. The boys waited quietly while she stared at her hands. She fiddled with the corner of the book she held, enlarging a small hole in the leather binding a bit more.

"Fine. We'll go. I need to go add some more things to my orders, though." Madi glanced back up. "Promise me something, though. If it gets too dangerous, Orrin uses [Teleport] and gets us out of there right away."

"I promise," Orrin replied.

Madi let out a long sigh. "You two are so much work." She didn't expand on her thought, just stood and made her way around Orrin, leaving the library.

Daniel waited until the echo of her footsteps was gone and lifted his hand for a high five to Orrin. "That was beautifully done, my man."

Orrin slapped his hand out of habit. "What was?"

"Calling her our friend," Daniel explained. "She still walks on eggshells with you sometimes. You gave her the perfect line."

"I was just telling her the truth. It's how I really feel," Orrin said, feeling dirty. "I wasn't trying to manipulate her or any—"

"Exactly." Daniel stood and moved the books back to their shelves. "You can't lie for shit. That's what really sold it."

Orrin examined the conversation in his head and tried to figure out how he felt. He hadn't meant to trick Madi by using mind games. He also hadn't wanted her to feel forced to side with them. He genuinely wanted her input on whether it was too dangerous to go to the elves. Daniel's *gut feeling* that they could help end the war in some super-secret special way wasn't enough.

Orrin's stomach dropped as he had a thought.

"Daniel?"

"Yeah, buddy?" Daniel's back was to Orrin as he reached up to put a book on the highest shelf. "What's up?"

"Remember that movie that you liked so much you bought the special edition? The one that we watched over and over at your house for like a year?"

Daniel's body stiffened for only a minute before he pushed the book into its resting place and dropped back down off his toes. "Doesn't ring a bell."

"Are you sure . . . no rings at all? Not even One Ring?"

Daniel turned to face Orrin, wearing his most disarming smile. "What are you—"

Orrin interrupted his friend and asked point-blank, "Are we going to the elven forest just so you can try and sleep with an elf?"

Chapter 10

Daniel blushed as he denied the accusation. "No way. We need their help to stop the war."

Orrin stared at his friend.

"It just makes sense. They are the ones being oppressed, so they'd be more likely to accept some help, right?"

Orrin continued his dead-eyed glare.

"And you already said you'd go. You could stay here if you're scar—"

"Finish that sentence and I'll drop your dexterity to zero and kick you," Orrin threatened.

Daniel gave up and smirked sheepishly. "Jude told me they are absolutely gorgeous. If we save them and one wants to thank me . . ."

Orrin rolled his eyes in disgust. "You know they had an elf slave down at the market. You'd be saving a lot of time and effort if you just bought one."

Daniel paled. "That's not what I meant."

"It's the same thing," Orrin argued and lowered his voice an octave in a bad imitation of Daniel. "'Hi, I'm the [Hero] and saved your species. Do you want to come to bed with me or should I get mad and leave you undefended and alone for the next invader?'"

Daniel's head dropped. "That's . . . that's not . . ."

"That's exactly what it is." Orrin's voice rose as he stepped closer. "Damn it, Daniel. There's an entire section of psychology devoted to savior complexes and white knight syndrome. Do you know how often my mom complained about the paramedics who bring in girls and leave their phone number with them? It's fucked-up. That's without bringing into play the entire [Hero] aspect. You realize you are essentially a rock star to these people, right? If I find out you have groupies, I'll . . . I don't know what I'll do, but it'll be bad, okay?"

Daniel nodded along at his scolding. "I didn't think of it like that. Seriously, O. I swear."

Orrin's temper cooled at Daniel's repentant tone and he stepped back.

Daniel caught his eye and cringed a bit as he said, "I still think we should go, though."

Orrin didn't respond but pierced Daniel with another stare.

"From everything we know, Odrana isn't going to want to work with the guy they tried to kidnap. We can at least gain some goodwill with the elves and try for diplomacy if that's the way Madi thinks we should go. We can't sit here and do nothing. Silas's reports have the elves lasting another month or two before the Odranan army forces their way into the forest. We need to help them now, not after the war is over."

Orrin watched Daniel's impassioned speech closely. He decided that despite believing his intentions to be mostly pure, he wouldn't let him out of sight if and when they got to the elven forest. However, all he said back was "Fine."

Daniel appeared shocked. "Fine? That's it. You're not going to argue that we should try some other harebrained plan?"

"I trust you." Orrin shrugged. "You made some good points. Plus, I know you'd try going yourself if me and Madi said no."

Daniel at least tried to look offended but just broke back into his grin. "You know me too well."

Orrin tried to hit his friend, but Daniel's [Side Steps] activated. Orrin tripped over his own feet and slammed his knee into the corner of a chair.

Daniel laughed. "You deserved that."

Orrin groaned and rubbed his knee. "Asshole."

After Orrin felt that he had gotten all the work from Daniel he was going to, the boys gathered up their notes and returned to their room.

Daniel fell asleep, obviously worn-out from his sparring all day. Orrin rolled through his skill lists again. He had been pissed to find no [Treasure View] option for the [Map] skill but figured that would have been too easy anyway. He was still scrolling through his skill options, trying to find any spots for improvement.

All his boosting skills had grown a little more in experience from the few spars and his habit of keeping his dexterity boosted around Daniel. However, it was going to take another few weeks of dedicated leveling to hit that ten thousand mark for each. Orrin had almost used up his fourteen ability points to bring [Teleport] to the next level.

> **Would you like to upgrade [Teleport] for 10 AP?**
> **Yes or No?**

He'd decided not to yet. He still wanted to buy [Merge] as well. He had lots of interesting ideas for that skill, but at a cost of twenty AP, Orrin couldn't make himself save the points.

"I should get some new skills related to poison, water, and steel to see if I can get new wards," Orrin mumbled to himself, careful to not wake Daniel. Extra wards specific to the new dungeon would probably be invaluable. He narrowed down a few low-cost spells related to each area of magic to discuss with Daniel tomorrow.

For poison, he narrowed his options to two spells, [Venom Bite] or [Toxic Touch]. Both fell under the poison heading and only cost one or two ability points.

> **[Venom Bite]—become the predator. Coat your teeth with venom and bite your enemies. Intelligence modifier attack damage. -1 AP**
> **[Toxic Touch]—your touch becomes toxic. MP cost variable to toxicity. -2 AP**

He was leaning toward [Toxic Touch], even with the higher cost. He didn't think biting was going to become his new attack method, and although the intelligence-damage modifier sounded powerful, especially for him, Orrin couldn't see a situation where he needed to get close enough to bite someone. He also didn't think he'd need to touch someone, but [Toxic Touch] was only a point more. Slapping someone with poison sounded better than going full [Vampire]. Orrin smirked as he imagined Daniel and Tony freaking out about [Vampire] skills.

While water magic had more options, including a lot of water-attack spells, Orrin was pretty sure he wanted to get [Water Reservoir]. For one ability point, he would be able to make water. It would free up lots of space in his [Dimension Hole], letting him carry more food. In addition, the water magic would probably give him a water ward. He'd considered some sort of water-breathing spell as well, but the cost for those types of skills was more than a few AP, and the descriptions mentioned air and water magic. Spending that number of AP and risking not getting a water ward wasn't exactly a safe choice when the end goal was the ward. [Water Reservoir] also used a very small amount of mana for a gallon of water, so he wasn't worried about running out of MP.

Steel magic was the most expensive of the three fields of magic. The store had nothing that cost fewer than three ability points. He'd found a few things that made him think of Ira, the member of the Dragoon team he'd saved. The base spell [Control Steel] allowed manipulation of the metal at a basic level. Additional options were grayed out, with a notification that the base spell was required before purchase. Spells like [Sharpen Steel], [Quench Steel], [Temper Steel], [Steel Pull], [Steel Push], and many more made Orrin wonder just how many spells Ira had had to buy to get his flying, shredding knives of death. While [Control Steel] cost five ability points, each additional option cost another three AP. Orrin continued to scroll through the add-on abilities that all seemed to stem from [Control Steel], looking for anything that jumped out. He really didn't want to spend five points on something as useless to him as [Control Steel].

He'd also searched for [Lightstrikes], which he knew existed thanks to completing the Obtain Level Ten Quest. He hadn't taken the upgrade at the time. Now, he couldn't find a way to upgrade his base spell, as the system store gave no indication that such an upgrade even existed.

He kept going over different options until the day crept up on him and he fell asleep.

When he woke up the next morning, Daniel was already half-dressed. He had strapped Gertrude to his back holster and then tried to put on his pants. Orrin chuckled when Daniel's sword caught the fabric and bent him backward as he tried to finish putting his clothes on.

"Shut up," Daniel muttered, taking his sword off and putting it back on its stand before getting dressed like a normal person. "I'm just tired."

Orrin stretched and didn't make a move to get up. "Are you ready to hit the storerooms today? Anything you're looking for in particular?"

Daniel finally got his pants on and sat on Orrin's bed to strap up his shoes. "That's the plan. I'm not really looking for anything. I thought you were just going to take everything of value and we'll figure it out on the other side."

Orrin groaned as he sat up and started pulling on his clothes. "Yeah, but also, we can grab anything we might need for the dungeon. Do you have anything packed for the trip?"

Daniel patted Gertrude on his back. "What else do I really need?"

Orrin put his head in his hand and sighed. He double-checked that everything from his [Dimension Hole] was stored away in their room and headed down for breakfast, ignoring Daniel's question as they left.

Emily had already arrived and was nursing a cup of something. Orrin's hopes of another coffee-drinking friend were dashed when she poured some more tea for herself. Madi was eating a plate of eggs. There was no sign of Garret.

"Good morning," Daniel chimed in as he started loading a plate with food. Living at the Catanzanos' house always meant a free breakfast, and Daniel was taking advantage of that fact.

Emily just nodded at him. Madi waved her fork in greeting.

Orrin tried to make conversation. "Garret's late?"

"He's always late," Emily replied, sipping more of her dirty water.

Orrin loaded up a plate as well, although with much less than Daniel. He also grabbed the entire carafe of coffee and put it within arm's reach. The party of four ate quietly for a few minutes.

Orrin was on his third and final cup of coffee when Garret strolled in.

"What a fine day it is." He grabbed an orange and started to peel it as he sat near Orrin. "Everybody already here?"

"We were supposed to be here half an hour ago," Emily said with a frown.

"There's no harm done," Madi tried to mediate. "We still need to go over the final preparations. Have either of you given any thought to what sort of things you'd like to requisition from the Guild's stores?"

Garret popped in a slice of his orange and spoke around his full mouth. "I'm really not picky. Anything I can carry out and sell is what I'd like."

Madi shook her head in disappointment and turned to Emily. The fire mage shrugged.

"There really isn't anything that I could think of, either. I saw the list of supplies you're planning on bringing, and I know you explained Orrin can carry some things in his storage skill, but unless we find books on fire magic theory, I'm with Garret on taking valuable stuff. The Guild doesn't really sort anything in those rooms. I'm sure we can find some rare monster parts and make some extra gold. I still think it'll be mostly a waste of time, though."

"What if we find a relic?" Daniel asked, too casually.

Orrin rolled his eyes.

"We won't," Emily answered confidently. "Even with the Guildmaster turnover rate, anything of real value would have been found. It's more likely we find a few small scraps of red bison hide or some precious metals. Relics would mean paperwork. Paperwork doesn't just disappear."

Madi coughed. "Paperwork does disappear sometimes. If somebody wants it to happen."

Emily turned slowly to appraise Madi. "Do you have some information we don't have?"

She shook her head. "I just know how administrations work. People mess up. By accident or on purpose doesn't matter. We don't need to find a relic. A few pounds of cold iron or Mythril and we can make some amazing weapons or armor. Even a sliver of dragon bone and we can get some enchantments made."

"You can enchant dragon bone?" Daniel looked up from his plate. "Gertrude has dragon bone. Why did nobody tell me this?"

Madi turned to Orrin and raised an eyebrow. "You didn't tell him?"

Orrin was thankful he had just lifted his cup to his face. A large gulp of coffee and a shrug were enough for Madi to roll her eyes.

"Dragon bone can be etched with a rune and store mana for later use," she explained. Madi put her spear in its short form on the table. "I have a thumbnail-size flake of dragon bone in here. I can compress the length about a hundred times before it needs to be charged. Just some mana at the end of the day and it's all good to go again."

"What kind of runes? What are the options for enchantments? Where can I get this done—" Daniel asked, his food forgotten at the prospect of upgrading Gerty.

"We can worry about that later," Orrin interrupted. "At the end of the day, we get the supplies on our list and then search for anything of real value. Then we can worry about enchantments and getting stuff made."

Garret slapped his legs and stood up. "All right, everybody ready?"

Chapter 11

Daniel officially invited Garret and Emily into the party, and the five of them made their way down the streets of Dey to the Guild. It was still early enough to not be too congested, and the walk felt nice. While the sun was out and hot, a cool breeze from the south swept across the city. Orrin's cloak rippled in the wind until he pulled it close.

"Garret, Orrin had an idea about making a metal shirt for you to summon arrows from," Daniel said after a stretch of walking in silence.

"I'm sorry, a what?"

Orrin sighed. "I thought maybe if we get a few tiles of different materials, you could wear them to be able to summon arrows whenever you need them."

Garret caught on quickly and nodded along. "Yeah, it's not a bad idea. The problem is that whatever I use to make the arrow has to have enough mass to make an arrow in the first place. It's why some archers with [Create Arrow] carry around a quiver full of different arrow types. So a shirt probably wouldn't work," he said with a laugh.

"Damn," Orrin muttered, trying to think of another way to get the same result. "We could try and get you a quiver and arrows like that."

Garret shook his head. "And ruin my look? I appreciate the thought, truly. If I'm going to be fighting something specific, I'll plan ahead and bring a bar of steel, but the way my skills work, unless I had a bunch of skymetal or red iron, nothing else would really be worth my time."

"What do you think you'll use against steel monsters?" Madi asked, taking an extra-quick step to keep up with the longer legs of Garret and Daniel. Orrin found himself hurrying along as well. Emily's robes made her look like she was floating, so he couldn't tell if she was also doing a half jog to keep up with the two taller men.

"Stone works well against most types. Water monsters can usually be displaced, too. Look, it's not that it's a bad idea to have a few options. It's just . . . bringing a few bars of steel, granite, or some other materials I've used in the past would mean one more thing we'd have to lug around in the dungeon." Garret waved his hands as he talked.

"Orrin could probably make room for some—" Madi started.

"We're here," Daniel said as they rounded the corner to the Guild. "Let's get looting."

When Daniel told the receptionist they were there to raid the Guild storerooms, the man almost had a stroke. After Madi smoothed the situation out and presented the letter from the Guildmaster declaring that they could take as much as they could carry, the man sent for a Guild clerk.

A bored-looking teenager, probably a few years younger than Orrin and Daniel, walked up a few minutes later. He looked at the letter and waved his hand over the top. The Guildmaster's signature glowed for a minute, and he shrugged.

Without introducing himself, or even talking, he walked off again. When nobody followed, he finally opened his mouth. "Come on, then. I haven't got all day."

Daniel exchanged a look with Orrin and chuckled. They followed the clerk as he led them through a series of hallways, opening three locked doors before arriving in front of a nondescript wooden door without a handle. He pointed dramatically at the door and handed a small square of paper to Madi. He didn't say a word as he began to walk off.

Daniel grabbed his shoulder. "Do we just knock the door down or what?"

The boy looked at Daniel's hand on his shoulder and smiled. Daniel let out a gasp of pain and pulled his hand off quickly.

"Please don't touch Guild employees. The door cannot be knocked down. Put your Guild ring against it and it will swing open. When you leave, I'll know and be back to escort you out." Despite his age, the boy's tone hinted that he was used to being listened to.

"What was that? Lightning? That's awesome!" Daniel's excited grin disarmed the clerk's imperious attitude for a moment. The haughty smile changed quickly, and Orrin saw the young boy underneath.

"[Electric Touch], but close enough." The boy's cold demeanor warmed markedly. "I didn't really hold back, either. That would normally put a Guild member on the floor."

"I'm going to remember that one." Daniel reached up to slap the clerk's shoulder but pulled his hand back at the last minute. "Maybe I won't touch you again."

Orrin rolled his eyes. Daniel's easy nature at work, making friends again.

"Let's get to it then." Madi nudged Daniel. The clerk waved and made his way back down the hall.

"What an asshole," Daniel muttered as soon as he was out of earshot. "He fucking tased me."

"You could have just asked him how to open the door; you didn't need to grab him," Orrin said, not really trying to defend the action but still feeling some satisfaction as Daniel shook his shocked hand.

"My hand is numb."

Emily let out a snort of laughter.

Madi was reading the small piece of paper. "It's a map . . . sort of. It's really just four squares positioned against each other and an X to show this door. At least, I think that's what the X is."

She looked up and motioned for Daniel to open the door. He was still absent-mindedly rubbing his hand and didn't notice. Madi closed her eyes and took a deep breath, letting it out in a dramatic fashion. "I'll go first, then."

Her ring flashed in the air as she rapped against the door. It slid up, and she walked into a room larger than the Guildhall.

"Magic fuckery," Daniel muttered as he stepped into the room, glancing at the thirty-foot ceilings.

Orrin couldn't make out the sides of the storeroom. It had to be a few hundred feet in every direction. A space this large should have been overwhelming when he knew the entire Guildhall was smaller than this room. That wasn't what nearly broke his mind, though.

The storeroom was filled with junk.

Right next to the door was a pile of broken wooden practice dummies. Three steps in, a weapons rack had been erected; every item stored on that rack was rusted and crumbling. A broken table and two chairs were haphazardly placed against the wall.

"What a dump," Daniel said, speaking Orrin's thoughts out loud.

"How are we going to find anything worthwhile in here?" Emily moaned.

Madi smiled. "Teamwork. We're going to comb one room at a time."

Orrin and Garret groaned at the same time.

Two hours later, they finished the first room. Other than a half-burned quiver that Garret turned his nose up at, they found nothing of real value. Orrin's [Analyze] hadn't been any help, only showing him what his eyes could already see: the room was full of trash.

Madi wasn't too deterred. She'd been able to scavenge enough camping materials to save some gold, but Orrin didn't really see the point in the daughter of a lord of Dey saving pocket change.

"Let's try the door to the left first," Madi said as she piled up the extra sleeping bags and two-person tents near the door. "It's a stand-alone room. The third room has a small antechamber, so we can hit both of those last."

Daniel, eager to do anything but stay still in the room of detritus, opened the door and stepped in. His voice echoed back as if he was in a cavern. "Hey, guys. This might take longer than we thought."

Madi and Emily were on his heels and blocked Orrin's view as he tried to get through. When he nudged the women to the side and saw the room, he was shocked.

They had spent the last two hours doing a methodical search of the first storeroom. It was a big room, filled with narrow passages burrowed between the heaps of thrown-together junk. The new room was easily three times as large. Two small paths broke left and right from the front door. Mounds of pelts were stacked up to the left. A few had fallen down and blocked the small alley between the animal skins and the sagging bookshelf filled with various bottles. The right path was not better, with bones, teeth, and skulls stacked in a manner that made Orrin fear the entire thing would come crashing down. Farther in, he could just make out more shelves, stacks of what looked like weapons of all sorts, a few dummies with armor strewn about, more piles of animal parts, and what looked like cords of firewood piled to the ceiling.

"This is ridiculous," Garret whispered in awe behind Orrin. "We could spend months in here."

Madi clapped her hands. "Search for metal or anything obviously magical in nature. Orrin, I hate to ask you, but can you try going through the bones? Maybe we'll get lucky and find one that's from a dragon. Emily, can you use [Mana Sense] to pick up on any traces of magic?"

Daniel started walking down the right path.

"Daniel." Madi stepped quickly after him. "You're with me."

"Huh? Sure. I want to see what's in those jars," he said, pointing at the far wall. Orrin couldn't make out what he was pointing at.

"I can't see that far," Madi said, confirming Orrin's suspicion that Daniel was using his [Telescope] skill.

"It looks like something's floating in the jars," Daniel said, starting off again.

Garret laughed and began picking through the hides like they were rugs. "Are we really going to go through this entire room?"

Madi turned back, then glanced at Daniel as he was walking forward again. "Just . . . just do a sweep. We'll meet back here in thirty minutes and decide," she said to the archer, then ran after Daniel.

Emily sighed and tapped Garret's shoulder. They started walking down the left path. Emily winked at Orrin as she dragged Garret away. He mouthed a silent thank-you at not being stuck with the incessant flirting. He would need to concentrate while using [Analyze].

At first, the skill only returned a single word.

Bone

However, after five minutes, he started to receive additional information on the different items, but learning that this stack was femurs and this stack was incisors didn't really help much.

Finally, the skill upgraded enough to show him what he really needed.

Fillium Femur (Bone)
Torchclaw Incisor (Bone)

His allotted thirty minutes passed too quickly, and Orrin found no dragon bones. He didn't hear Madi and Daniel returning. Instead, he smelled them.

"—many times do I have to apologize?" Daniel was saying as they came into view.

"Wait there!" Orrin plugged his nose and took a step back. "What is that smell?"

Madi's entire front side was covered in a gooey blue slime. Daniel had some along the bottom of his legs but looked like he had mostly evaded whatever it was that hit Madi. She was glaring at Daniel.

"I touched something after she told me not to," Daniel said sheepishly.

Madi turned on Daniel with a fury normally reserved for charging monsters. "You grabbed the chest after I specifically told you it was trapped."

"I didn't know it was going to burst out with . . . whatever got us."

Madi's anger cranked up another notch. "Whatever got us? You have some Ichitial stink on your shoes. I'm covered!" She was screaming toward the end of her sentence, just in time for Emily and Garret to round the corner. Garret stepped back and held his nose.

"What happened?" Emily asked as she approached with a small bundle in her arms.

"Daniel decided to trigger a trap and evaded it while I took Ichitial spray all down my front," Madi said, tears in her eyes. "Damn it. It's even in my eyes. Orrin, I need some water."

Orrin paled and shook his head. "I left everything behind so I'd have more room."

Madi looked from person to person as they shook their head. Nobody had planned to take this long in the storerooms.

"Wait. I was going to get this anyways." Orrin remembered his planned skill purchase right before Madi started to cry in despair.

> **[Water Reservoir]—create one gallon of water. 10 MP. 1 AP**
> **Would you like to purchase for 1 AP?**
> **Yes or No?**

Yes.

Orrin looked around for something to hold the water and found a large, concave skull. He cast the spell. The water overfilled the skull, and he handed it to Madi.

She took the skull and dumped the water over her head. The slime washed off slowly but did start to puddle around her feet. She held the skull out in question. Orrin refilled it four times before the stink started to evaporate.

"Did he just buy a water creation spell?" Garret asked as he crept forward, smelling the air until he got too close to Daniel. "Oh, you should get his feet, too."

"No, he can keep stinking," Madi said petulantly. Orrin ignored her and filled the skull before handing it over to Daniel.

"Seriously, did you just waste ability points on water?" Garret asked again.

Orrin glanced at the look on Garret's face. "I was planning on doing it anyway. I can save a lot of room in my storage if I don't have to carry gallons and gallons of water into the dungeon."

Garret just looked stunned at the perceived waste of AP.

Orrin realized something. "Hold up, you said you found a chest? Was there anything in it?"

Daniel grinned and held up a small ring. "It was behind a stack of books that were placed differently than the rest. It wasn't bigger than my fist, but we found something at least."

Orrin tried [Analyze].

Ring

"Do you know what it's made out of?" Orrin asked when his skill failed. He tried again, but nothing changed.

"Nope," Daniel said proudly. "But, you know, if there was one trap in here . . ."

"There might be more," Orrin said with a hungry grin.

Chapter 12

Orrin pulled up [Map] and used [Trap View]. The room gleamed with yellow dots, including one on the bone pile he'd been working on.

"There must be ten traps set in this room," Orrin murmured to himself as he used [Zoom] on the nearby snare. He stepped a few feet down to a stack of monster skulls. When he couldn't get the blinking yellow cursor to get any bigger, he squatted down and peered into the empty eye sockets. "I think there is one here, but I can't figure out what it is."

Emily put her hand on Orrin's shoulder and motioned for him to step back. She closed her eyes and sank into a seated position with her legs crossed. Small rivulets of fire grew from where she sat, spreading out among the skulls. They crept along at a snail's pace, but once they disappeared under the skulls, more mini lines grew up and out to each bone. They spread at an alarming pace, and Orrin almost shouted for her to stop.

"Don't worry, it's not destructive right now," Garret whispered, having snuck up behind Orrin, who jumped. "Emily's fire only burns when she wants it to. She can explain it better later, but her fire has its own mana pool that she has to replenish by feeding it stuff. She could make everything that those little lava flows touch go up in flame, soaking it all up for her fire, but she can also use it to get a sense of what's in the next room or around the corner. I bet she'll find the trap before we—"

SNAP!

A dozen skulls filled with razor-sharp teeth, making up the middle row of the stack Orrin's face had been inches from before, suddenly snapped shut, only to reopen and slam shut again. They continued to click, like a chattering-teeth toy but much more deadly. Emily's fire flared and the moving bones were incinerated. The small avalanche of bones that fell around the party clattered loudly.

Emily stood up. "The ones I destroyed had some sort of magical trigger on them. As soon as I touched one, they all started chomping away. I felt something wooden in the middle of the pile, though."

Digging through the bones, Daniel pulled out a padlocked chest the size of a basketball.

"No key?" Orrin asked, kicking a few stray bones back toward the main pile.

Daniel shook his head.

Emily sighed and put her hand on the metal. Her hand flared, and the metal grew red before dripping to the ground.

"Handy," Daniel cracked. Nobody laughed. "Come on. Get it? Hand—"

"Shut up and open it, D," Orrin commanded.

With a long-suffering sigh, Daniel placed the chest on the ground and opened it. Inside was a red velvet cushion holding a white bone about four inches long.

Orrin used [Analyze].

> **Bone**
>
> **Come on, he thought and used the skill three more times.**
>
> **Bone**
> **Bone**
> **Tailbone**

"Tailbone," Orrin muttered. "That's all I can get so far."

"If it's a tailbone, it could be from a dragon," Madi commented hopefully. "It was guarded."

Orrin stored the bone in his [Dimension Hole]. "We can get it looked at later. Let's find a few more traps."

"Why would the Guild trap their own storeroom?" Daniel asked as they walked toward the nearest yellow spot on Orrin's [Map]. "It doesn't make any sense."

"Pritus didn't do that," Garret offered. "From what I've gathered, about thirty years back, the Guild went through so many Guildmasters in so short a time, factions started forming. Rivalries and blood feuds ran amok. The clerks were all loyal to different factions and didn't recognize the current Guildmaster as the rightful ruler of the Guild. Pranks turned to deadly traps. There's a reason nobody has fully explored these rooms in decades."

Daniel and Orrin were quiet as they absorbed that information. Orrin stopped and pointed at the next trap on his blue box. "Something is behind that bookshelf, I think. Or the bookshelf itself is the trap."

Everybody looked at Emily. She sighed. "I can't do this ten times. It does cost mana."

Orrin chuckled and cast a few [Increase Will] and [Increase Intelligence] on her, hopefully at a low enough level to not trigger any side effects. "Does that help?"

Emily's eyes widened. "You doubled my mana pool!"

"I tried to keep it low," Orrin explained. "If I boost your stat by too much, you'll get sick. We should try and find the sweet spot before going into the dungeon. I'm pretty sure that constitution affects it somehow, too. But we can get into specifics later."

Emily just shook her head and sat down again. Her fire vines grew quicker and thicker from her seated body. What had taken thirty seconds before took twenty seconds this time, and soon she pulled her vines back to her body.

"What's up? Did you not find anything?" Daniel asked, hopping from foot to foot impatiently.

"There is something on the back of the shelf, but it's in a container of some sort," Emily said as she stood and dusted her pants. "Luckily, my [Inferno Veins] didn't trigger anything."

Daniel glanced over at Madi. "Can I move the shelf?"

"How do you think you are going to do tha—"

"Orrin, buff me!" Daniel flexed his arms and waited.

Orrin didn't move.

"Come on, man." Daniel dropped his pose and frowned at his friend.

Orrin sighed and hit Daniel with a few [Increase Strength] buffs.

Daniel grinned as he double-checked his stats. Putting his hands to the side of the shelf, he pulled. The deafening shriek of the heavy wood scraping along the stone floor filled the hall. Emily and Garret covered their ears, while Orrin and Madi just grimaced.

Once he had moved a corner away from the wall enough to allow someone to squeeze through, Daniel dropped his hold, taking a step back. "Fucking hell, that thing is solid. Even boosted, that was a struggle."

Orrin ignored Daniel's whining and stepped around to investigate the back of the bookshelf. Strapped with leather and metal bands against the very middle was a six-foot-long cylinder. Orrin started to reach for it, but Daniel yanked him back.

"Dude, what are you thinking?" Daniel pushed Orrin behind him. "You just said that thing is trapped. Think."

Orrin turned red as he realized his boneheadedness. "What do you think we should do, then? It's strapped to the shelf, but the leather looks a bit worn. Maybe we could just cut that bit?"

Daniel disappeared behind the shelf and then popped back out. "The metal runs down the entire side of the straps. We might need Emily to burn the metal again like she did with the lock."

Emily groaned but stepped forward.

"Wait," Orrin said, putting a [Ward] on the mage. "Okay, you're good to go now."

"What was that?" Emily asked curiously. "I saw you cast something on me, but I didn't take any sort of damage or alert. That's odd."

Orrin shrugged his shoulders. "I've got a spell, [Ward], that gives you an extra layer of protection. You should be able to take—" Orrin paused and double-checked his mana point pool."—a little less than four hundred damage before something deals actual damage to your health."

Emily raised an eyebrow in disbelief.

"He's serious," Madi interjected. "Still, be careful, though. We don't know what kind of trap we're dealing with."

Emily took a peek around the corner and stared at the metal canister. "I'm seeing very strong fire magic on that thing. It might be best for everyone to back up a bit."

Madi, Daniel, and Garret crept back along the makeshift path, standing a few dozen yards away. Orrin cast a [Ward] on himself and ducked behind a small chest close by. Emily gave him a very unimpressed look and pointed toward the group.

"I can heal you if it does too much damage." He answered the unspoken question.

"Fire does a lot less damage to me than it would to you," Emily retorted but didn't argue further. She stepped behind the shelf and, starting at the top strap, began to burn away the metal and leather with a glowing finger.

When the fifth and penultimate strap fell away, the canister tilted and slipped down through the last fastener. Emily reached out her hand to grab it, but the metal bottom struck the stone floor before her fingers could close around the container.

BOOM!

Orrin couldn't see anything over the dust cloud. He heard coughing from Emily and assumed she wasn't dead yet, at least. He darted from behind his perch and began readying [Heal Small Wounds] at level three.

The bookshelf had been shattered and sent flying. The various books and small boxes on the shelves had been propelled off like so many pieces of detritus. Avalanches of weapons, extra supplies, and small pieces of furniture tumbled all around them. A darkened patch of soot in a five-foot radius around Emily showed the level of explosion from the trap.

The front of her robe had burned away in patches, giving Orrin a brief glimpse of her body underneath before she turned her back to him.

"Please step away for a moment, Orrin," Emily asked with a slight cough.

"I can heal yo—"

"I'm fine, I just need a minute for my robe to mend itself."

Orrin nodded at her back and went to check on the rest of the party.

"Dude!" Daniel was practically bouncing. "That was amazing. The bookcase just exploded and sent shit flying everywhere. Is Emily all right?"

Madi and Garret stood well behind Daniel. Garret's eyes were wide, and for once he didn't have anything to say.

"She's fine," Orrin answered loud enough that everyone could hear. "She just needs a minute; her robe took some damage."

Madi immediately pointed back toward the first room. "There were some old robes and clothing near the other door. Should I go get something for her to wear?"

"She said her robe can mend," Orrin said with a shrug.

"What did we find?" Daniel asked, trying to peer over Orrin's shoulder.

"We'll find out when Emily is ready," Orrin said, putting his hand on his friend's chest. "Let's try and be patient, yeah?"

A few minutes later, Emily returned with her dress still in tatters but with more coverage. She held the canister gingerly and placed it on the ground.

"I didn't want to open it until we were all here," she explained. "The magic it was giving off is gone, but I thought maybe Orrin should examine it for traps again."

With a nod, he brought up his [Map]. "Nothing showing up anymore," he confirmed.

Emily carefully ran her finger along the bottom of the cylinder. The metal dripped, and the lid fell with a clang to the ground. She looked inside and frowned.

"It's just a bow," she said dejectedly.

However, as she pulled it out of the container, Garret let out an excited squeak.

"That's not just a bow," he gasped. "That's an elven Citrandish longbow."

The archer reached out and caressed the wood, pulling it from Emily's hands. Holding it horizontally to the ground, he inspected every inch. Orrin thought it looked the same as the bow on the man's back, but he decided to keep his mouth shut.

Daniel opened his big mouth instead. "It's just a piece of wood. It doesn't even have a string."

Garret rocked the bow in his arms. "Elves use the hair of a loved one to string their bows. If this one was stringed, it would mean it was stolen. Of course, it still could be, but it's supposed to be near impossible to snap an elven-hair bowstring."

"Won't the elves want it back?" Orrin asked, remembering the passage from their research about the consequences of being caught with a stolen Citrandish bow.

Garret nodded. "But that doesn't mean I can't try it, right? Maybe even take it to the dungeon?" He glanced up at Daniel. "Just holding this is a dream come true."

Daniel shrugged. "Give it to Orrin. He can store it where nobody can see it until we get to the dungeon."

Orrin reached his hand out to take it, but Garret recoiled. "Maybe I can hold it until we leave?"

Orrin noticed Madi's grin in the background. This was exactly what she had been hoping for.

"All right," Madi said as she clapped her hands. "We've got a few more traps to disarm. Hopefully with fewer explosions this time?"

Chapter 13

Orrin counted the traps carefully this time. They had eight remaining to examine in this room. The next two hours were spent finding each trap, having Emily assess them with her [Inferno Veins], and then figuring out different ways to neutralize or set off the snares.

Daniel and Garret ended up being the best at setting off the traps. Daniel simply tanked or dodged the damage. When he took the lid off a trapped urn, he was hit with an acid that burned into his skin, letting them see the red muscle underneath before Orrin quickly healed him back to full health. He swore he only felt the pain for a second and hadn't even screamed. Despite the deadly trap, the urn was empty. Daniel kicked it, punting it against a wall, where it shattered.

"I hope that wasn't a priceless work of art or something," Orrin muttered as they walked away.

Daniel was also hit with an electric shock from opening a trapped drawer but simply shrugged it off. The drawer contained yellowed and faded paperwork that none of them could make out clearly. Orrin thought it was a disciplinary action, but either way, it had no real value to them. They left it behind.

Daniel's next go seemed easy enough. A small wardrobe had been tilted against the back wall. After they cautiously righted it, Daniel opened the doors. He only narrowly dodged the swinging axe that fell out like a pendulum. After standing up and cursing at the long-dead pranksters, Daniel pulled a shoebox-size container out of the closet.

"Wait," Orrin said as Daniel started to grab the lid. "Let me check if it's trapped, too."

Daniel ignored Orrin and popped the top.

"Clothes?" Daniel picked up a corner of the cloth and held it up for all to see. "Somebody used a spring-loaded axe to protect clothes?"

Emily hesitantly reached out and ran the fabric between two fingers. "That's dwarven silk. It's woven with strands of metal to deflect glancing blows from sharp weapons. That's worth a few dozen gold pieces to the right buyer."

Madi grumbled, "If there's even enough fabric to make a shirt. That looks like it was made for a dwarf."

Orrin glanced around at the angry faces. The trap-exploring hunt was not going well.

"Let's try one more and then take a break," Orrin suggested. "I think Daniel has a few more minutes on my last buff."

Garret spoke up from behind them. "I'd like to try one of the traps."

Orrin and Daniel looked at each other. Daniel shrugged and waved a hand.

"Sure," Orrin answered. He led them to the nearest remaining trap.

After Orrin pinpointed the exact trigger—a small bust of a bearded, noble-looking male—Garret pushed them back until they were almost out of view. The arrow he summoned was of the same stone they stood on, but when he released it, the stone dart flew with the speed and precision of a normal arrow. The eight-foot-tall block of spiky black ice that exploded from the sculpture would have been a nightmare to deal with . . . if Emily hadn't simply waved a hand, turning the entire thing to water.

"Ice magic has almost no effect on fire," she said with a grin.

Orrin almost summoned an [Ice Sword] to test that theory but figured he could always do it some other time. The group was flagging a bit at this point.

"Is there anything?" Madi asked with a sigh.

Garret picked up the bust from its pedestal. Surprisingly, his arrow had not knocked it off the four-foot marble stand.

"This is too heavy," Garret murmured before turning to the group. "The marble is a facade."

"Break it?" Daniel suggested.

Garret lifted the bust above his head, but Emily quickly stepped close and plucked it from his hands.

"Let me try first," she said, running her finger along the edge.

Orrin caught a glimpse of a fire crystal sitting on the tip of her fingernail, acting like a small blowtorch. Emily left a scorched black line along the white marble as she worked a small circle around the bust's scalp.

"That should do it," she said, taking out a knife and trying to work the edge into her burn mark. She slipped only once before the dagger caught. Emily twisted her wrist, and a skullcap of marble popped off, revealing a black material underneath.

"That's cold iron. The entire bust is cold iron," Emily said with delight. She began burning away more of the marble with a sparkle in her eyes.

"Don't waste your mana," Madi admonished. "We can clean the rest of the marble off later. Check the pedestal, too."

Regrettably, the pedestal was marble throughout.

"There are four traps left." Orrin counted them off. Two were close to each other. "Should we take a break?"

"No," all four members of his party said in unison before bursting into laughter.

"I think we've been properly incentivized," Madi said with a chuckle. "Which way to the next one?"

"Next two," Orrin corrected. "There's a pair of them close by. Over this way."

Orrin directed the party to the westernmost wall, on the opposite side of the door. At least, he thought it was the western wall . . . he'd gotten a bit turned around on the walk in. The first trap was a coatrack covered with fluffy fur jackets. About ten feet away was a couch. The area between the two traps was clear of any other items.

"A couch and a bunch of coats?" Daniel asked in disbelief. "Should we just leave these? You know there isn't going to be anything of value."

"At least Emily can reach both at the same time," Orrin commented, having gotten a better idea of the fire mage's ability. *At least I can investigate her and Garret's powers while in here.*

Emily just nodded and sat directly between the traps. The rest of them backed away a few steps.

Those few steps were not enough.

As soon as Emily's fire magic touched the coatrack, the fur jackets flew off their handles and swarmed after the party.

Madi's spear extended and tore one jacket into two pieces; however, the separated garment wrapped one half around her arm and the second circled her legs, pulling them taut. With a frustrated yell, she was swept off her feet and pulled to the couch. After a moment, her yells were muffled as several more fur and heavy fabric coats assailed her. The couch cushions stretched and morphed, wrapping her even tighter.

Orrin and Garret didn't even react. They were both watching Emily at the wrong angle and were quickly knocked down and tied up by the clothing. The couch hugged them closer, pinning their arms and legs down.

Daniel lasted longer. He swung Gertrude faster than Orrin had ever seen. He dodged and used his skills to their full effect, but in the end, ripping and cutting the clothing only made more strips of cloth. He was overwhelmed and tossed to the couch as well.

Only Emily was spared. An inferno blazed around her, making her appear as nothing more than a dark silhouette against the rising flames. Orrin caught glimpses through the scratchy wool blazer that had partially wrapped around his face as she simply burned her way through the attacks. The floating cinders of charred clothing settled around her, and within half a minute, she had destroyed the remaining foes.

As they didn't seem to be in mortal danger, Orrin resisted the urge to [Teleport] or buff his strength. He waited patiently as Emily pulled at the straps of cloth holding them all down. She pushed her fiery hands through the fabric of the couch until she reached the wooden frame. They heard a snap, and the couch sagged in the middle, broken. The cushions eased their hold and Orrin popped off the seat, stomping on a few rags that had lost their magic when enough of the garment was burned.

"I told you," Daniel huffed. He'd sliced the coatrack in two. "Total waste of time."

Emily started laughing.

"What?" Daniel asked gruffly.

"The look on your face when you were yanked back." Emily started laughing harder. "I just kept imagining having to explain to the Guildmaster how the [Hero] had been killed by a fur coat and a couch."

Daniel pursed his lips and then blew out a burst of air. He began to chuckle and then joined Emily in her full-on laughter.

Garret nudged Orrin. "They're both crazy, aren't they?"

Orrin nodded.

After confirming neither trap had been guarding any prize, Orrin pointed out the last two marks on his [Map]. Piles of broken desks and old tent canvas separated the last two traps with the waving paths carved out by past Guild members. One centered on a sword stored in the middle of a weapon rack, with no other weapons hung in the brackets. It was situated against a row of wooden dummies that had rusted armor and small buckler shields but no weapons. The second was a tapestry hung on a wall just a stone's throw away but not within sight. They examined both from a distance before heading back to the weapon.

"Even with Orrin's spell, I'm running low on mana," Emily explained when asked to examine the sword. "I can get maybe one more [Inferno Veins] off, but then I'll need to rest. With how much we've explored, I'm guessing we'll come back tomorrow?"

Madi grimaced. "The deal was a onetime entry."

Orrin added, "I have a few mana potions if you really need one."

The party glanced at the sword and weighed the options.

"We can always spend the night in the first room," Daniel suggested. "We found those tents and can put something together to be comfortable. Pritus can't complain if we don't leave, right?"

Garret grimaced. "I'm not sure I want to sleep on old monster skins."

"You can leave the bow with us when you go home," Madi said with feigned indifference at Garret's stricken look. "If Emily is up for it, that is?"

The fire mage shrugged. "This has already been a better haul than my last five quests combined. We can at least check out the other two rooms and see if Orrin finds any more traps. I don't have to use my magic the entire time, too. Daniel seems good at avoiding them. Not to mention having someone in the party who can heal is a game changer. I still don't understand your class, Orrin."

Orrin turned his eyes down and hunched his shoulders, not wanting to answer more questions. He hadn't thought of how many of his spells and skills he should reveal. Healing Daniel had been a reflex. They already knew he could buff, heal, and examine objects.

While the party argued whether to stay or not, Orrin walked closer to the sword and tried to [Analyze] it.

Sword
Sword
Mythril Alloy Sword

"Hey, it worked!" Orrin yelled and turned to the group. They all looked at him with wide eyes. "It's a Mythril sword . . . or some sort of alloy. My skill is finally starting to work a bit quicker . . . What is it? Why is everybody looking at me like that?"

Daniel had Gertrude raised with one hand and was beckoning Orrin with a slow and steady motion with the other. Emily's hands were burning bright red, and Garret had a stone arrow nocked. Madi's spear was out and extended. Orrin could see the telltale sign that she was preparing [Shimmersight], as well.

Orrin turned and observed the sword was unmoved. The five wooden dummies were also there; however, the random armor pieces had floated off and reattached themselves into four complete spectral knights. Orrin could see the ghostly apparitions of swords in each free hand, pointing at him from behind the bucklers as they took a defensive position.

"Oh, shit."

Chapter 14

Orrin tried to roll back, but his increased dexterity had worn off. Instead, he fell on his butt and scrambled to the party line with no dignity. He gathered his intent and cast a few buffs on himself, Daniel, and Garret. Their working strategy against monsters was to let Daniel take the brunt of close combat while the rest of them worked the edges. Daniel hadn't moved yet.

"What are you waiting for?" Orrin asked as he summoned an [Ice Sword]. He pointed the tip at the floating armor.

Daniel cocked his head and took a step back, which forced the rest of the party to move as well. The four armored ghosts didn't move.

"I think they only protect the sword," Daniel said hesitantly. "Are you sure it's made of Mythril? Madi, what would that be worth to us?"

Madi closed her eyes for a second, and Orrin watched her mouth move as she muttered numbers to herself. "Depending on the alloy and percentage of Mythril, anywhere from forty to a hundred gold."

Orrin knew a single gold piece was worth almost $500 in his own money. A gold piece could be earned from a solid copper-level quest, but that could take a day or two of work. The sword was worth a month to almost three months of daily quests.

Nonetheless, he asked, "Should we leave it?"

"I think so," Madi answered.

"No way!" Garret yelled at the same time.

Emily held her answer in reserve but stood closer to Garret.

Daniel turned and looked at Madi. "It's your call, Madi. I think Orrin triggered it when he passed that point"—he pointed to a nondescript stone—"but I have no idea if they'll follow us once we attack."

Madi glanced at Orrin. "Can you see what they are?"

Orrin used [Identify].

> **[Phantom Chevalier] HP 200/200 Status: Spatial restriction**

"Phantom Chevalier. Two hundred HP, and they are spatially restricted, whatever that means," he answered.

"They can't leave a certain area," Daniel answered. "Don't ask me how I know that. I just do."

Orrin shrugged and pulled out the one thing he'd left in his [Dimension Hole]—the bestiary book.

"This is totally not the time to read a book," Garret said with a quick glare over at Orrin.

He ignored the archer and swiped page after page. "Found it."

> **Phantom Chevaliers are ghostly creatures that are immune to most regular weapons and must be dealt with by means of cold iron or magic. They attack with group tactics, usually targeting one member to the exclusion of all else until defeated.**
> **If a [Spiritcaster] or similar class is present, it is possible to capture. (***).**
> **Please see Ghost (**) in Volume One for tips on capturing and using for security.**

"Only cold iron and magic will damage them," Orrin called out. "They'll pick one person and attack them only."

Daniel shrugged. "Okay. Hit me with a [Ward] and then I'll go in. Madi and Emily, do what you can from back here. Orrin, you, too. Garret, sorry we don't have any cold iron for you."

"He could use the bust," Orrin suggested.

Garret shook his head. "It needs to be longer—the length of an arrow, at least."

"Can you melt it?" Madi asked Emily.

"I could, but I can't shape it," Emily answered.

Orrin thought a minute and then began to summon another [Ice Sword] and then another.

"What are you doing?" Daniel asked.

"Give me a minute," Orrin said with a smirk. "This will either work and be brilliant or I'll look like an idiot."

He gathered six of the swords and searched nearby. He found what he was looking for and tied the [Ice Swords] together, creating an oddly shaped funnel. He stabbed the lashed-together swords into the top of a low side table.

"I say . . . idiot," Daniel said, flicking the side of one of the swords. "What use is this against those?"

Orrin tried to wiggle the makeshift mold, but it remained upright. "Emily, how precise can you be when you melt the cold iron?"

Emily glanced at the swords. "Those will melt as soon as the first bit of metal hits them."

Orrin glanced up from his work. "I'm not so sure. These aren't supposed to melt from fire." He pulled up the spell in his blue box and tossed it to Emily.

Ice Sword—summon a sword of hard ice. Does minimal damage but will not melt in the hottest of fires. Each sword lasts one hour. 1 MP per sword.

"I'm not sure this means what you think it means," Emily countered. "Do you mind if I try to melt one?"

Orrin glanced up and summoned another [Ice Sword], handing it to her. Emily inspected the blade and hilt and then lifted a finger. The now-common fire crystal sparked to life on the tip of her finger. She dragged it across the thickest part of the blade. It split with ease and fell into two pieces. A moment later, the sword disintegrated in her hand.

"Fuck," Orrin cursed and stopped working. "So, the system description is totally useless, then?"

Emily let her spark go out. "Not really. I'm sure regular fire wouldn't melt the ice, but magical fire does. It's something to keep in mind. I still might be able to melt the metal without the swords being destroyed, but if they fall apart, we are going to have an unwieldy glob of metal to handle."

"It's worth a shot," Madi said, still watching the Phantoms, which hadn't moved. "If Garret can do some damage to these things, we might be safer staying beyond their range. I vote we melt the bust."

"Seconded," Daniel added. He hadn't moved from his readied position.

Emily shrugged and took the statue, turning it upside down. She spent a second burning the rest of the marble off and then stood close to Orrin. He felt the heat radiating from her hands as they turned red.

"I'm trying a lower temperature so I can hopefully control the flow a bit more," she explained.

Orrin kept turning away, checking on the ghosts, and so he missed the first drop of cold iron that peeled away from the top of the head. He did hear the hiss as it clipped the sword and began a slow descent into the funnel he'd created.

The sword didn't appear to melt.

"This might actually work!" Orrin said with glee.

"They're moving," Daniel shouted, lowering Gertrude's tip.

Daniel's warning was in vain. The Phantoms, after finding nothing to attack in their designated assault zone, slowly drifted back to the wooden dummies behind the Mythril sword. The armor pieces settled back exactly where they were before, and the spectral monsters dissipated.

"Well, that's convenient," Garret muttered.

Emily ignored everyone and kept working. Orrin could feel the temperature turn up a bit as the slow drip turned into a more steady stream. Almost all the metal landed between the swords, but some still fell to the sides, splattering the stone floor with a sizzle. The seams of the swords weren't perfectly aligned and some of the molten iron began to leak out toward the bottom. Orrin used another sword to try and scrape the metal. That worked against them, freeing up more iron to flow.

"Let it escape. It'll cool in the air and still be a better shape for Garret," Emily demanded, her hands nearly touching as the last of the metal seeped out of her hands.

Orrin wanted to kick himself at the dumb idea as he saw so much metal piling up around the base of his little experiment. He couldn't even see the top to check if they'd made a long enough pole of cold iron for Garret to work with. Emily knelt by the contraption and began picking up pieces of splattered cold iron, dropping them directly into the top of the sword funnel.

"Did it work?" Garret asked, having let his stone arrow disappear. "It looks like a lot of wasted gold to me."

Emily glanced up with a smirk and held up her finger. The crystal appeared, and she drew a circle around all the swords, cutting them in half. As they disintegrated, they all looked back at what was underneath.

A blackened cylinder—or, at least, close to a cylinder—of iron still glowing red in small streaks stood like a melted candle. The puddle at the bottom made the entire thing appear wider with a tapered point. Garret took three quick steps and tapped the bizarre metal art with his foot. An arrow appeared in his hand.

"Good enough." Garret grinned.

Emily cut the stick of cold iron off at the base and handed it to Garret before melting the rest into a puddle. "We can grab that when it cools. Let's get that sword."

Orrin made the party trigger the Phantom Chevaliers three more times. The first two tests were to pinpoint the exact parameters within which the Phantoms would appear. It turned out that a semicircular perimeter of ten feet would summon them to defend the sword. The third test was a little different.

"Hit one and then run?" Daniel asked again. "Can't I just kill it?"

Orrin double-checked the buffs he had put on everyone. Garret was moving his hand through the air like a little kid practicing karate. His increased dexterity was approaching the borderline of what Orrin felt comfortable giving him, but his arrows were going to deal a big chunk of the damage if the current plan worked.

"Not this time," Orrin explained again. "If it follows you outside the border, we all go on the offensive and you can swing Gerty to your heart's content."

"I hope they do . . ." Daniel muttered.

Orrin sighed. He hoped the Phantoms would operate like a proximity ward and only attack within the borders of the trap. If they followed people outside that . . . well, Orrin was pretty sure somebody else would have triggered the trap before now if that was the case. He was banking on there not being bodies around to support his theory. He wanted to have Garret simply snipe the Phantoms one at a time from a distance, keeping everybody safe.

Daniel rolled his shoulders and stepped forward across the pile of miscellaneous junk they'd set along the trigger line. The four Phantoms appeared the same as before. Orrin's friend darted forward, bringing his huge sword down directly on the Phantom on the far left.

All four pivoted toward Daniel and floated with more speed than they'd expected. Daniel sprinted back and leaped over the line, turning with his sword raised. He waited as they approached and held Gertrude above his head.

The monsters stopped at the border.

Orrin let out a sigh of relief and used [Identify].

[Phantom Chevalier] HP 164/200

"You did thirty-six points of damage to it," Orrin announced. "Garret, hit the same one."

"Yessir," the archer said with a smile. He held the string of his bow to his cheek for a moment before he released a cold iron arrow.

[Phantom Chevalier] HP 146/200

"Eighteen damage," Orrin announced. "Madi and Emily, you can try casting spells at them, too. Keep at it."

The Phantoms stirred inside the bubble that contained them, with Garret's arrows striking over and over. Emily sent small bolts of fire flying along with Madi's beams of light. Orrin tossed a [Lightstrike] at each one but didn't waste any more mana, just in case. With a final arrow from Garret, the last Phantom shrieked and melted into a fizzle of lights. The armor fell to the floor with a clatter.

Experience Gained: 285 XP (60 XP x 1; 75 XP x 3)

Daniel rested his sword on the ground and groaned. "I guess I'm going to have to share all the experience."

Madi nudged him. "Don't complain. It's safer this way."

Orrin smirked and pointed to the sword. "You can get the loot."

Daniel rolled his eyes and stepped over the fallen armor pieces. With a sarcastic flourish, he drew the small sword and whipped it over his head. As he neared Orrin, he knelt and presented the Mythril weapon on his arm like a knight presenting to his liege.

"You're an ass." Orrin rapped his knuckles on the [Hero]'s head.

Chapter 15

The party appraised the tapestry. The last trap hung behind a stack of crates filled with empty potion bottles. The glass had yellowed with age, and a fine sheen of dust settled across everything.

"What's with the wall rug?" Daniel asked. "Wait! Is a dragon going to come out of that?"

The "wall rug" depicted a man and woman in full plate armor attacking a two-legged, winged monster.

Madi corrected Daniel. "It's a wyvern. See how it only has two legs and wings? A dragon has four legs."

"Does anyone know the story?" Emily asked. "It must be important to have been made into a tapestry."

"Nothing comes to mind," Madi said with a shrug.

Garret shook his head, and Orrin stayed quiet.

"I definitely do not," Daniel said as he stepped closer to examine the embroidered scene.

Madi gripped Daniel's sleeve and gently pulled him back. "Let's not trigger another trap."

Emily cracked her fingers and took up position in front of the group. Her [Inferno Veins] crept along the bottles and crates, slipping up the wall and over the fabric. Her eyes were closed in concentration, but Orrin noticed the furrow deepen as she left the veins up longer than she had before.

"Is something wrong?" Orrin asked quietly.

Emily cracked one eye open to respond. "The tapestry isn't trapped. I think there's something behind it, but I can't find a way in to see. Does anyone object to me burning it?"

"It might have some sort of historical significance," Madi began.

"Burn it," Daniel and Garret said at the same time.

Emily gave Madi a sympathetic grimace, and the fabric went up in flames.

"Madi, I thought you said there were only four rooms," Daniel said as he peered through the smoke.

"There are only four," she replied. "The first one and the double room we haven't gone in yet are the three most explored, but every record I found said this is the last room."

"And a fifth one here." Daniel waved Gertrude side to side in an attempt to clear the smoke. "Although it seems like the door is kind of small."

As the smoke finally dissipated, Madi and Emily inspected the small hatch. The tapestry had adhered to the wall in a perfect outline, hiding the door completely. It was about two feet tall and three feet wide, with a long metal handle in the middle.

"Orrin, can you check if the hatch is trapped?" Emily requested.

Orrin pulled up his [Map]. The trap light was gone.

"I don't get it," Orrin said. "It's disappeared. Did you burn the trap away?"

Madi shrugged and grabbed the handle of the hatch, pulling down. The door grated against the stone, and the hinges screamed as she opened it.

Orrin ignored it as he pulled up his skills list and found [Trap View].

"Oh, [Trap View] lets me find hidden items, too," he explained to the four backs of his party. "It's weird that I don't have some sort of different indicator between the two . . . Are you all even listening?"

Orrin put his hand on Daniel's shoulder, and he glanced back. Daniel moved to the side and gestured.

Behind the hatch, Orrin gazed into a deep recess carved out of the wall. It reminded him of an oven, with a wooden beam separating the hole into two sections, except the wood had obviously rotted. Or maybe the weight of what was inside had been too much for the simple wooden support.

Gold and silver. Ingots and bars of gold on top with silver bars under the broken beam. The stacks of precious metals merged in the middle of the vault.

Orrin's mind stuttered.

"Madi . . . how much is in there?" Daniel asked.

Madi stayed silent, her mouth open as she muttered under her breath, counting.

"If that's pure . . . and I'm not counting the silver . . . it's worth about three thousand gold, probably closer to three and a half with all the silver," she finally answered in a hushed tone.

"That's about five to six hundred gold for each one of us," Orrin whispered. He hadn't spent all his money on a big, stupid weapon like Daniel, but that much gold would still significantly upgrade his purse.

"I know I'm the one who made the deal with Pritus," Madi said, still talking in a whisper, "but shouldn't we report this to the Guild? That's a significant amount of capital they could use for the defense of Dey."

Orrin didn't miss Garret's glare at Madi.

"We should split it up before we go back," Garret murmured. "Anyone who wants to turn in their share can."

Emily pinched Garret's arm. He yelped.

"We're a party," the fire mage said with fierce determination. "We decide as a group."

Garret rubbed his arm and scanned the group. "Fine. Fine. I'm just saying, that's enough for a person to retire on."

"Exactly," Emily retorted. "I'm not looking to settle down just yet. I'm with Madi on this one. I say we turn it all over and see if the Guildmaster wants to give us a finder's fee."

Daniel picked up one of the gold bars. "It's much heavier than I would have thought."

Garret wiped his eye and turned away from his lost fortune.

"I'm all for giving over some of it," Orrin thought out loud. "Being pragmatic about it, we should keep a bar each. We did find it, after all."

They argued the merits of handing over the entire hoard or what percentage would be believable for longer than they should have. Finally, Orrin started putting ingots in his pocket, storing them away in his dimensional space.

"We can figure it out later," he said. Garret watched his actions with envy. "We've been going for hours and are exhausted. Should we move back to the first room and try to get some sleep?"

"Fine with me," Emily said. She was blinking a lot, and Orrin noticed her sway a bit as they stood there. "I used a lot of mana today."

Once Orrin had stored the last of the silver in his [Dimension Hole], the party quietly made their way back to the first storeroom. Daniel pushed a pile of chairs under a table to make enough space for five bedrolls. Everyone crawled in, but they all stayed sitting up.

Orrin noticed Garret and Emily watching him a bit more than normal.

"What's up?" he asked.

"Nothing," Emily said, too quickly, and started playing with her fingernails.

"They're worried you are going to sneak off," Madi answered his question.

Orrin was surprised. "I won't."

Madi smiled patiently. "I know that. Daniel knows that. These two"—she hooked a thumb in their direction—"don't know you as well as we do."

Daniel yawned. "Orrin wouldn't do that. He never buys anything anyways. I bought Gertrude and he complained for, like, a week."

Emily and Garret had the decency to look apologetic but didn't say anything.

Orrin slapped his head. "Gertrude! Daniel, let me see your sword."

"What? Why?" Daniel picked her up from his side and went to hand the giant sword to Orrin, despite his questioning.

"The hilt is dragon bone," Orrin explained, grabbing the sword and promptly dropping it. "Shit, I forgot how heavy it is."

"She is a perfectly normal weight," Daniel grumbled, lifting Gerty back up for Orrin.

Orrin used [Analyze].

Dragon Femur (crafted)

"Yes!" Orrin shoved his hand into his pocket and pulled out the tailbone. [Analyze]

Dragon Tailbone

"Ha! It is a dragon bone!"

"Can somebody explain what is going on?" Emily asked, pushing her sleeping bag a few feet away from Orrin's.

"My skill works on my own knowledge. The more I know about something, the quicker I can pick up what it is. But I don't really know anything about dragon bones," Orrin explained, shoving the bone back in his storage. "Daniel's sword is made from dragon bone, so once I've used [Analyze] on it, the skill learns what it is. If it kept telling me just that it was just a tailbone, no big deal. But if it was a dragon bone, my skill knows what that is now."

"And would tell you what it is," Madi continued the thought. "We should go back and check those bones again. Maybe we missed more!"

Garret groaned. "Tomorrow. Please."

Orrin agreed, "We can check it tomorrow before the other rooms. It shouldn't take too long. You did say that was the biggest room, right?"

Madi nodded. "It's also the most uncategorized. This first room is a dumping ground for the past fifteen years, with no real organization. Any good crafting materials are brought into the next room, the first one we'll explore tomorrow. I think that's where Pritus assumed we would really hit. It has a small room for random items not classified but deemed mostly harmless. I'm hoping we find something worthwhile there, too."

"I'm fine with gold," Garret muttered.

"You could take your cut and leave, but then you wouldn't get to try the Citrandish bow," Madi said temptingly.

Garret's eyes widened. "I didn't mean . . . I just . . ."

"She's messing with you," Daniel said with a laugh. "This is our party. We'll figure out the loot and destroy a dungeon. Maybe we'll find something better in there."

"If we survive and actually destroy it, a few stat points are worth more than a bow long term," Emily agreed.

"You just don't understand how good that bow is," Garret countered. "If half the rumors are true, I'll be able to hit twice as far and twice as hard."

"How are the stat points distributed in a dungeon?" Daniel asked Emily.

"You don't know?" The mage looked at Madi. "You didn't tell him?"

"He's from another world," Madi said with a shrug. "I forget he doesn't know everything."

Emily pursed her lips and put her finger to her chin. "Well . . . you know about the dungeon core, right?"

"Yep," Daniel answered happily. "Destroy it at the end and all. But what exactly is it? And what do you get?"

Emily looked at Madi for help.

"I've never destroyed one, either," Madi said. "What I've heard is it seems random. Nobody can ever predict exactly what stats you get or even how many. I know that Brandt got—" Madi went silent for a moment, then continued. "A guard I know received a few strength points from one."

"That's similar to what I've read," Emily said after a pause of her own. "Some think that certain types of dungeons are more likely to give certain stats. Fire dungeons usually have a constitution bonus, supposedly. But I've never seen any real statistics to back that up."

"That still doesn't answer my question," Daniel said, leaning on one elbow. "Does the core drop from the final dungeon boss or does it just sit there at the end? Could we sneak by and destroy it?"

Emily smirked. "No, you can't sneak by and destroy it. You know dungeons grow by ten floors at a time, right? Well, every tenth floor has a floor boss."

"That I know," Daniel chimed in.

"Once you defeat the final floor boss, the last door opens to a final room. That room has the core. As far as I've heard, nobody has been able to open that door without the boss being defeated. That's also why the Silver Vaults and Aqua Chambers are still active. Each one has a floor boss that took decades to figure out how to defeat. From what I've read, the Silver Vaults still have a floor boss that is undefeated."

"Floor 110," Madi whispered. "My mother died fighting off a dungeon break after a team tried and failed over a decade ago. The Vaults always set off a dungeon break after somebody fails at that floor."

Orrin watched quietly as the new party members absorbed Madi's revelation.

"How could somebody go so long in a dungeon? Over a hundred levels must have taken months!" Daniel shifted on the floor.

Madi blinked and appeared thankful for the topic change. "Parties that take on the Vaults have to get permission to go that far in. That expedition was likely in the sixty-level range. The first eighty floors or so probably took them a few days, maybe a week?"

"Someday we'll get there, too," Orrin whispered. Madi heard him.

"Yes, we will." She smiled, a firmness in her voice.

They chatted a bit more about the plans for the next day before Daniel yawned again.

"I'm going to sleep," Daniel announced. "Last one up tomorrow has to help Orrin sort bones."

Chapter 16

The next morning, Orrin kicked Daniel awake.

"Ow! What the hell?"

Orrin squatted and poked his friend. "Last one up. I guess you have to sort bones with me."

Daniel groaned and stretched. "Yeah, that's not gonna happen."

Madi and Emily were already up and ready to go. Madi had sorted through a heap of broken dishes until she'd found enough bowls and cups for them to drink some of Orrin's conjured water. Garret stood apart from the group, styling his hair in front of a shattered mirror against an armoire.

Garret tucked a stray hair behind his ear and glanced over at Daniel. "You were the one who set that rule."

"I'll do it," Madi cut in, forestalling the argument. "Let's map out any traps in the third room first and then we can backtrack for the bones."

Orrin pushed the party's gear into his [Dimension Hole] and followed Madi as she led them to the far side of the room. They entered through the door.

Daniel whistled.

"This is much more organized," Emily noted.

The room was smaller than the two they'd already explored. Shelves had been set up around the perimeter of the room. The left half reminded Orrin of a library, with see-through bookshelves in rows. While some had books, most shelves were covered in stacks of various monster bits—claws, teeth, hides, jars filled with clear liquid and floating bits, plus alchemy tools, smith tools, and labeled flasks.

An enormous table spanned the length of the right half of the room. A stand in the middle contained a single book and a jar of ink. The rest of the table was clear but split into small alcoves that would provide only the bare minimum of privacy from the next seat.

Madi nudged Orrin. "Check for any traps, please. This room must be the one the new Guildmaster has been working on organizing. The rumor is she tossed everything out into the main hall and had them start from scratch from here. Anything that comes in has to be recorded in her master logbook there."

While Orrin pulled up his [Map], Garret walked up to the book and flipped through the pages.

Orrin frowned and tried again. The same result.

"There are no traps or anything in here," he announced.

Garret turned away from the book. "You sure? After all the ones we had yesterday?"

Orrin shrugged. "Maybe they set off anything they found? Should I check out the last room before we go back?"

The final door was in the back of the room, the only stretch of the wall not covered with shelving.

"We might as well," Madi agreed.

The door looked no different from the others, but as Daniel pulled it open, he grunted.

"This door is heavy," he muttered. "Way heavier than it should be."

Daniel poked his head inside. "This is more of a closet than a room, Madi."

Madi and Orrin peered over Daniel's shoulder. The last room contained cleaning supplies on a single shelf against the back wall, with a broom and mop.

"We could have just finished up last night," Garret complained. "This room is organized, and we know what else we need. I could have been home in bed."

Even Emily let out a disappointed sigh and returned to the record book.

"Might as well double-check," Orrin said and entered the cupboard. He ran [Trap View], closing it out as quickly as it popped up. He paused and pulled it up again.

"Um . . . guys?"

With all four of his party members pushing into the room with him, Orrin was feeling a bit claustrophobic. After Emily had used [Inferno Veins] to search the single trap that appeared in the cleaning closet, they'd pulled the shelf out of the room, discarding the supplies on the table. She'd been adamant that no traps were present, only a concealment of some sort.

"Maybe it needs a magic word to open," Daniel suggested.

"That's the dumbest thing I've ever heard," Emily countered. "Obviously, there is a hidden latch or lever. I can't see through the stone wall, but something is definitely right behind here."

She rapped her knuckles at waist height behind where the shelving had been.

"Do you think it's more gold?" Garret pushed in again, jostling Orrin. "If we find two caches of gold, we are keeping one."

"Can everyone back out, please?" Orrin yelled. "I'm getting smashed here."

He had tried using [Analyze] on the stone, but nothing appeared. As the rest of his party had started suggesting ideas, they'd also crowded in until they all stood in the shoebox-size room together.

The other four stepped back sheepishly.

"I think the best way might be to just break the wall," Madi said, her finger over her mouth in contemplation. She snapped her fingers. "Orrin, can you boost up Daniel's strength? I think I saw a hammer back there on one of the shelves."

Garret quickly bounded over to the other side of the room and returned with a small hand-held sledgehammer.

Orrin threw his highest [Increase Strength], level three, spell on Daniel the maximum five times. With Orrin's will at twenty-eight, the plus-four increase became an eleven-point increase. Fifty-five extra points in strength put Daniel into the high seventies for strength. For whatever reason, Orrin's buffs didn't affect Daniel—or himself—as they did everyone else. Orrin had performed some testing on Madi back at the Catanzano manor, with only a few minor side effects. She could stand an increase to her stats of up to a little more than twenty points before she felt side effects. They hadn't found anyone else willing to be a guinea pig, but Orrin had his theories. For now, he wouldn't increase anyone but himself and Daniel more than fifteen points or so per stat.

Daniel's eyes glazed as he watched his status screen. When Orrin's final spell cleared, he smirked and held the hammer over his head with one hand.

"I have the power!"

Orrin kept his face very still.

Daniel smirked at him and then looked around. "You all would be laughing if you got that."

He turned and disappeared into the closet.

"Sometimes I forget he's from another world," Madi stage-whispered to Orrin, "and then he goes and says weird shit and I'm reminded all over again how strange he is."

"I know what you mean," Orrin chuckled.

"I can hear you!" Daniel's voice came from the room, along with the sound of hammer on stone.

Two minutes later, Daniel returned, covered in dust. "It's books."

Madi stood up from the chair where she'd been resting. Orrin pushed off the table he'd been leaning on. Garret and Emily were going through the rest of the room for the predetermined supplies but came back over when they heard the hammer stop.

"Books?" Madi asked, glancing behind Daniel. "How many? What kind?"

"I don't know," Daniel said. "I didn't want to pull them out in case there was another trap."

Orrin punched his shoulder. "That was surprisingly bright of you. Good job."

Daniel's mouth turned up as if he'd bitten into a lemon. "Surprisingly?"

Orrin quickly ducked into the room. "I'll just go check for traps."

The cleaning closet was covered in a fine layer of stone dust from where Daniel had knocked a hole in the wall at knee height. Small chunks of the wall lay in a pile on the floor, and Orrin could make out five, maybe six books behind the wall. He pushed his [Trap View] into the newly made alcove but picked up nothing.

"It seems all clear to me," Orrin shouted. "I'm going to grab these few."

Pulling the books out of the hole, Orrin's eyes got wide as he read the titles.

"They're all skill books!"

Ten minutes later, Daniel had finished destroying a perfectly good hidden wall and the party had spread the ten skill books out on the table.

"These are all pretty good," Madi said in a low voice. "Most are rare enough that we could sell them and make a lot of gold. Some I haven't even heard of. Personally, I'll pay for this one."

She picked up one of the spell books. The books were embossed with the name of the spell they'd teach—in this case, [Sunbeam].

"This is a direct upgrade for me," she continued, holding the book to her chest. "I didn't know that a spell book like this even existed. I could do more damage for the party and I'd be able to—"

"It's yours," Daniel interrupted her. "You don't need to pay us for it."

Madi shook her head. "No. I will pay for it. This is too much."

Daniel put his hand on her shoulder. "It's not too much. Just make sure to save all our lives a few times."

Emily cleared her throat. "If we are allowed to use these . . . I wouldn't mind taking one of the [Firebloom] spell books. I had to pay dearly for mine, and I have a sister . . ."

Daniel nodded. "Go for it. This entire thing was to make us all stronger, but family is family."

Emily's smile lit up the room. "Thank you. Really."

"Now if only there was a weapon skill book, Orrin could finally be useful," Daniel said with a laugh. "Garret, do you want any of them?"

"None of the spells or skills really do much for my build. I'm not sure what these two are, though."

The archer pointed to the two Madi had set to the side. The first had a dark-green cover with gold lettering. It was heavy and looked expensive, with the title *Life Tree*. The second was well-worn by time and had a dark-blue cover with light-blue stitching of the words *Way of the Water*.

"I'm not sure what those are, either," Madi admitted. "Those are the ones I've never heard of."

Orrin pulled up his store in his status screen and typed in "life tree."

"[Life Tree] is a druid spell. You can set up a magic tree that heals the local environment of most types of corruption or contamination. It's pretty mana heavy to start and drains as long as it's going, too. I'm not sure even I could keep that up for long," Orrin said, summarizing the spell. "What?"

Garret and Emily were looking at him weirdly. Madi also gave him a squinty look.

"How do you know that?" she asked.

"[Analyze]. I'm getting better at it." The lie came so quickly, Orrin surprised himself.

The answer seemed to placate them. Madi held up the *Way of the Water* book. "What about this one?"

Orrin stared at the book like he was going to use [Analyze], while secretly searching his interface store.

> **Way of the Water—You are adept at the Way of the Water fighting style.**

"It's a fighting style," he answered. "I'm not sure what kind, though."

"I've never heard of that one," Garret said. "But if Orrin really doesn't have any martial skills, it might be worth using. Worst case, you have a skill book–learned fighting style you don't use."

Madi shrugged. "We can get it appraised if you want. We might be able to get something better and more well-known."

Orrin shrugged. "I'll take it by Bartholomew's after we leave."

The bookstore Bartholomew's was where Orrin had purchased [Side Steps], the first and only skill book he'd used. The small selection of skill books Bartholomew's had cost a silver coin to peruse, so Orrin knew he'd likely get bilked for the information, but everybody in Dey purchased their skill books there.

Orrin swept the rest of the books into his [Dimension Hole] and looked around. "If you guys want to finish up here, I'm going to go search those bones for more dragons. Madi, you coming?"

As they left the other three behind, Madi was quiet.

"Are you okay?"

"What? Oh, yes. Sorry."

Orrin slowed his walking speed in the main room, turning to her. "Madi."

She looked up from her feet.

"What is it?"

"[Sunbeam] costs thirty ability points. It's not right that I take that," she said, still clutching the book to her chest.

"You heard Daniel—it's yours. We came here looking for good stuff. You set it up. If it's something you want, then use it."

Madi glanced up finally. "Orrin, my planned path wouldn't let me get this until I was in the midthirty range, if I made it that far at all."

"Awesome." Orrin smiled at her. "I guess you'll need to revise your plan. I should really make a plan and stick with it. I know I'm going to pick up a few more specific ward spells for the dungeon, but I keep spending all my ability points before I can save up enough to buy the ones I really want to get."

Madi shook her head. "I know that pain. Getting [Shimmersight] cost fifteen. I had to wait for two full levels without buying anything. I just . . . I'm so glad you two found us on that road. I mean, obviously, I'm glad you two saved our lives, but my entire life has been turned upside down. I'm about to learn [Sunbeam] before I hit level twenty."

"Is it really good? I didn't check it out."

"It's like my [Lightbeam], but with light and fire damage and way more powerful. It's also part of my core spells, so getting it will unlock more high-level spells I can plan around."

Orrin started walking again, checking to make sure she followed. Her eyes were still glued to her book.

"That sounds pretty cool. All I want to get is [Merge]. I'll be able to smash different spells together and make new ones."

Madi started laughing so hard that Orrin had to stop walking. "That's funny. Oh, damn. You really caught me off guard."

"What?"

"'All I want to get is [Merge],'" Madi mocked, wiping her eyes. "As if that hasn't been a lost spell for hundreds of years. Everybody and anybody would kill for that spell."

Orrin forced a laugh. "Yeah. Ha-ha. You caught me. Now can we please get back to searching for dragon bones?"

He felt the sweat dripping down his back. Madi let out a long breath.

"Okay. Thanks. I needed that. Let's see what we can find." She walked past him to the side room door and opened it. "Are you coming?"

"On my way," Orrin said shakily.

Chapter 17

While Orrin's ability to use [Analyze] multiple times in a row had increased, the number of bones in the side room ended up being too much for Madi and him to go through. When the rest of the party came searching for them, they hadn't found one additional dragon bone.

"Did you get everything on the list?" Madi asked Daniel as he pushed a rolling cart into the room.

"Almost everything," Daniel answered. "We couldn't find arrowleaf root or any ghost essence."

Emily picked up a small bottle from the cart. "I'm quite sure a competent tailor can use captured shade instead of ghost essence." She kicked the pile of bones Orrin had already worked through. "But I'm not confident enough in alchemy to suggest an alternative to arrowleaf root. We might just need to pay for those potions."

During their planning session for the dungeon, Emily suggested a few items that might help combat water and steel monsters. Potions of water breathing were expensive, mostly due to the multitude of rare ingredients needed. The plan was for them to all carry at least one at all times, in case a monster attempted to seal them in a watery grave.

Another item she'd suggested was sigil thread. A tailor could sew a specific spell or design into a piece of clothing for quick casting. Emily wanted an [Incorporeal Escape] spell for each of them. Sigil thread itself wasn't expensive, but the ingredients for each specific spell differed. [Incorporeal Escape], just like it sounded, turned an adventurer intangible for a handful of seconds, letting the person escape from situations that they deemed too dangerous. Emily was adamant the sigil was necessary in dungeoneering.

Other than that, Daniel had fully stocked the cart with the remaining ingredients for potions of healing and mana they'd wanted, along with a few better-known poison antidotes. Although they'd discussed possible armor upgrades, Garret had declined. His current leather was from a Steeltooth Bristlebear, and he doubted the Guild would have anything stronger collecting dust. Emily wore her red robe, with some tactical pieces of armor underneath during actual quests, but most eschewed more formal types of protection. Madi, of course, was outfitted better than anyone in the group, although her house colors of golden yellow and green clashed with the more muted armor Orrin, Daniel, and Garret wore. Only Emily's red robe had more color.

Orrin and Daniel still had their armor from Esme, the quietly scary seamstress/armorer Silas Catanzano had hired to outfit them. Orrin's half-sleeve cuirass appeared to be fully leather but had layers of metal under it for added protection. The cloak he wore also had metal links sewn into it to deflect strikes. Daniel would be using his magic chain mail, with a twisting design that drew the eye—and hopefully blade—away from vital areas. He rarely wore the full getup unless they were going out monster hunting.

"We'll find what we need," Madi said, turning back to Orrin. "How long until you can look again?"

Orrin rubbed his head. "I'm getting a headache. I might be at my limit for the day on [Analyze]. These bones have all been for two- to three-star monsters anyways. I really don't think I'm going to find another dragon bone in this mess."

Madi sighed. "Okay. Can you fit everything on the cart into your storage?"

He groaned as he stood and cracked his back. Picking up a potion in each hand, he started to stuff items into his pockets. His cloak had a lot of them. Each item disappeared into his [Dimension Hole].

Garret was standing by the door, flipping a long arm bone up in the air and catching it. "If we need to carry some stuff, I saw a few extra packs in the front room."

"It shouldn't be a problem," Orrin answered. He pushed the narrow end of a large flask into a cloak pocket. Items seemed to shrink at one end as he put them away, getting sucked into wherever he stored things. "I took out the water barrels so . . . actually . . ."

Orrin turned and started to pull the cart toward his pocket. The cart and all the remaining bottles, flasks, containers, and loose alchemy ingredients disappeared.

The bone clattered to the floor as Garret missed his catch. ". . . That's not something you see every day. Do you have more room? Why don't you just push all the bones in? I saw a stack of pretty decent swords and maces back in the front room. We could sell those for quite a bund—"

"We aren't here to raid the Guild," Madi cut him off. "We are only taking what we need . . . and the things of value that we found that were trapped."

"And the gold," Garret said with a smirk.

"I thought we were turning that over to Pritus?"

"Emily! Whose side are you on?" Garret cried, his hand on his chest.

The fire mage rolled her eyes. "We don't need that as much as the Guild does, and you know it. With the lords of Dey in disarray and so soon after coming off a Horde, the Guild is stepping up in a big way. Guild members are being sent out on reconnaissance of the Pass and helping plug the holes left by the deaths of so many guards. Not to mention finding new dungeons and letting nobodies like us"—she pointed at herself and Garret—"tag along with a real [Hero] to defeat it. Instead of complaining and flirting with the support members, how about you get your head out of your ass and realize how lucky we are?"

Emily's more reserved nature built throughout her speech. Orrin watched as Garret backed up from her building temper. Daniel stood back with a smirk on his face, while Madi bounced from foot to foot, ready to jump in and play peacemaker if necessary.

Garret looked at the group abashed. "Sorry. That's just a lot of gold. It makes sense to turn it over."

Daniel sauntered up to Garret and put his arm around his shoulders. "You know, we don't have to raid the Guild . . . but maybe we can pick a few choice items to resell for other supplies we definitely are going to need. I think that's fair . . . right, Madi?"

Orrin stood silently by as Daniel slowly convinced Madi to let him and Garret sell off a few of the random but rare items sitting around the main room.

"When did I become the packhorse?"

The functionary who had led them to the storerooms arrived within minutes of them leaving the first door.

"I thought your trip inside would take less time and be more fruitful," he sneered.

"I'd say we found what we came for and more," Madi retorted. "However, we do need to speak with the Guildmaster as soon as possible. We found something we'd like to give her."

The clerk's eyes rolled dramatically. "If you'd like to make an appointment with her receptionist, I can show you the way, but know that she is very busy and—what the fuck is that?"

Orrin had pulled one of the bigger gold bars from his pocket.

"Like she said"—Orrin slipped the precious metal back into his magic storage pocket—"as soon as possible."

They were ushered to a meeting room, and within ten minutes, Pritus arrived.

"Why is one of my clerks telling everybody that you found gold in the storerooms?" Her piercing eyes glanced at Garret and Emily before they settled on Madi. "The agreement was whatever you carried out was yours, but if you really want to try and steal tangible money from the Guild, then you—"

"Guildmaster Pritus." Madi stepped up and spoke over the head of the Guild. "While we were clearing out the storeroom, at your direction, of the multiple traps and threats left unchecked by previous heads of the Guild, we discovered a safe containing gold and silver behind a tapestry in the westernmost room. Orrin, if you will."

Orrin stepped forward and started slowly pulling the gold and silver bars and ingots out of his [Dimension Hole], just as they'd discussed before leaving the storerooms. He could hardly contain his smile at Pritus's shocked face.

"Of course, as upstanding members of the Guild, we immediately sought you out to turn over this small fortune for the use in Guild activities supporting Dey," Madi continued.

Pritus glanced at Madi. No words were spoken, but Orrin felt an entire conversation happen in the quick eyes of the two intelligent women.

Orrin slapped the last bit of gold down and faded back into the line the rest of the party had created. Good soldiers delivering a boon to the commander.

"Such a magnificent treasure would surely need a commensurate reward," Pritus said, testing the waters.

Madi smiled serenely. "The reward was in clearing the storerooms of traps for the Guild. Now, staff can safely catalog their contents, sell off the excess, and return that profit to helping Dey rebuild after all the recent troubles."

Pritus narrowed her eyes. "I'm assuming that Lord Catanzano would be best at distributing those profits?"

Madi shook her head. "I would trust you, as the Guildmaster, to put the people of Dey first." Madi's voice changed from her politically suave tone to a friendly and more personal tenor. "Jen, no strings here. Use it to help the city."

Pritus raised her eyebrows at Madi's use of her first name but swiftly clamped her shock down. "The Guild and the people of Dey owe you."

She opened the door and barked orders. Three of her people, one the young man with the shocking power, entered and stared at the heaps of gold.

"Now," Pritus ordered.

The table was cleared in minutes.

Daniel rolled off the wall where he'd been lounging. "If that's all, we've got a dungeon to get to."

The Guildmaster held up a hand. "If that's what you turned over, I'm hesitant to ask what else you found." She sighed. "A deal is a deal, though. When do you plan on leaving?"

Daniel glanced at Madi, who shrugged.

"Maybe this afternoon? We have a few last-minute errands, but I'd like to get there sooner rather than later."

Pritus nodded. "I'll send a portal specialist over to the Catanzano manor. Good luck to you all."

She swept out of the room.

"That saves us some time," Madi said, clapping her hands together. "So, who wants to go shopping?"

The party spent the next few hours selling a few items discreetly, paying for an [Alchemist] to make as many potions as he could with the ingredients they supplied, and spending a hefty amount on the ingredients they still needed, along with an [Incorporeal Escape] sigil for each member of the party.

Orrin fingered the thread running along the bottom corner of this cloak. "This isn't going to ruin my clothes, right?"

Emily chuckled. "No, once it's used, the thread disintegrates. Your cloak will be fine."

The final place they visited was Bartholomew's. The clerk had gladly bought three of the skill books they'd found, along with two of the spell books. He didn't have enough knowledge on the [Way of the Water] or [Life Tree] books to give a fair offer and didn't need the extra copy of the last skill book, [Artificer, Level One].

Garret and Emily went their own way around lunch, promising to meet back at Madi's house in two hours. Orrin and Daniel returned to their room, pulling Madi in as well. With all of Orrin's stuff on his bed, he dropped the rest of the loot they had on Daniel's side.

"Garret is going to want to keep that bow," Madi announced.

Orrin had no doubt she was right. The bowyer they'd visited had sold them a few of his strongest strings, but they'd decided not to bring the Citrandish bow out in front of him. Garret was practically salivating at the thought of using it.

"Should we really have given that much Mythril to Jovi's assistant to just make a few arrows?" Daniel complained.

"He smelted Mythril and cold iron bars for Garret," Madi answered. "That was a major reason we went in the storerooms, to look for rare metals for him to use."

"Lorren didn't really smelt the Mythril," Orrin said, picking up items and sorting them into "keep" and "leave" piles. "It just sort of melted into a puddle. It was funny watching him get upset when he couldn't set it quick enough."

Jovi's assistant, Lorren, had warned them that Mythril was tricky to work with. He'd barely gotten one arrow-size length of metal out of the sword into the proper shape. They'd left the rest of the metal with him to work with as payment.

"I think I have everything sorted here," Orrin announced. "The only thing left for me is to buy a few spells and hopefully get specific wards."

Orrin had already spent the one ability point on [Water Ward]. After he'd purchased [Water Reservoir], the new ward had appeared on his status page with the customary blinking cursor.

"Madi, maybe you can help." Orrin pulled up the spells he'd been looking at for a potential poison ward. "[Venom Bite] is cheaper, but [Toxic Touch] just seems like it would be the better purchase, right?"

Madi looked at the blue screens Orrin tossed her and shook her head. "You realize you are never going to be specialized if you keep buying things randomly like this?"

Orrin shrugged. "Who needs specialized? I protect you guys, you protect me."

"I told him [Venom Bite]," Daniel said. "It's not like he's ever going to need to use either, so he might as well save the extra point."

"I still think he should buy [Sword Proficiency]," Madi argued. "They even have the skill book if he doesn't want to use ability points."

"That was two hundred and fifty gold," Orrin cut in. "That's more than Daniel spent on Gerty."

"He could always use the water fighting book," Daniel suggested. "Bartholomew didn't even know how much it was worth, so it's probably really good."

"The guy who works at the store is not named Bartholomew," Orrin groaned. "That's Gregory."

Daniel shrugged and picked up the book off the bed. "[Way of the Water]. That sounds kind of cool."

Madi watched their back-and-forth and made for the door. "I'm going to get all the food set up for Orrin. For what it's worth, Orrin, I think you should go with your gut. If you don't like [Venom Bite], don't get it."

Orrin went back to sorting.

Daniel sat on his bed, knocking over the piles Orrin had been making.

"What do you think?"

"Huh? About what? Dude, you just knocked over the extra blankets. I just folded those."

Daniel wagged the book in front of him.

"I don't need to fight," Orrin said, shaking his head. "I stand in the back."

Daniel ignored him. "You said this is a fighting style, right?"

Orrin nodded.

"Do it. For my peace of mind."

Daniel caught Orrin's eye. He had his serious face on.

"We could sell that and use the money for—"

Daniel pushed the book into Orrin's arms.

"We can always make more money. We are about to go into a dungeon, where we are going to be fighting monsters and defeating a floor boss. I need to be able to worry about that and not you defenseless behind me."

Orrin looked at the dark-blue cover. The book was beat-up and had been forgotten in a false wall for who knew how long. He brushed his hand over the stitching.

"Fine," he agreed. "Just promise you aren't going to throw some monster at me to test it out."

Daniel held his hand up and visibly crossed his fingers. "Sure, buddy."

Orrin tried to hit Daniel with the book but missed. With a sigh, he sat down and opened the book, triggering the skill learning.

> **Would you like to use skill book: Way of the Water?**
> **Yes or No?**

Orrin hit yes, and the world went dark.

Chapter 18

Orrin opened his eyes. He stood in a massive, domed white room with alcoves set into the rounded walls all around him. The recesses were stacked one on top of each other, and he could just make out a presence in each one watching him.

"Where the fuck am I?" he mumbled. He tried to pull up his [Map].

Nothing happened.

He tried to pull up his status. Again, nothing.

"Hello?" Orrin yelled, the shout echoing across the chamber. Nobody answered.

Orrin caught movement from the corner of his eye and turned. While a moment ago the floor around him had been the same white marble as the walls, now a splash of color had been added in the shape of a square. The deep blue reminded him of something.

The skill book, he thought, connecting the blue stone to the book he'd opened. *I was learning that fighting skill.*

Movement from above arrested his line of thinking. Something was falling from a very high distance. Orrin's heart stopped at the speed the body had reached in its descent. He didn't have time to turn away before the person hit the floor with a splash.

"That's not right."

The body, made entirely from water the same deep color as the book and square fighting ring, pulled itself back together and walked . . . splashed? . . . toward Orrin.

"What is going on?" Orrin backed away from the watery visage.

When the watery figure flopped its way across the square fighting line, it took up a stance, its elbows tucked back with its palms facing Orrin. A slight bend of the knees with both feet pointing toward him. A wrestler pose.

Orrin kept backing away until his foot went out of the blue square.

> **Would you like to quit learning [Way of the Water]?**
> **Yes or No?**
> **Reenter the fighting square or be forcibly ejected in 10 seconds . . . 9 seconds . . . 8 seconds . . .**

Orrin stepped back in quickly.

"Why did nobody warn me about this?" he complained to the watery figure. "I'm stuck in here until I learn an entire fighting style?"

The watery man did not respond, his stance unchanged.

Orrin was stumped. In all the research he and Daniel had done, nothing like this had been mentioned. Daniel had definitely not been forced to swing his weapons even once before knowing exactly how to use them.

He also had no idea how to even begin whatever it was he needed to do. He'd been in exactly one fight in his life before coming to this world. The few people he'd needed to attack had been instances of opportunity and sneak attacks mostly.

The one time on Earth that he'd thrown a punch at somebody, he'd been beaten badly. His anger at the insult about his missing father hadn't helped him connect the punch. It didn't matter that Daniel had retaliated against the other boy a few days later. Orrin was not a natural fighter and knew it.

The water blob stepped forward. Orrin took a step toward it.

"Are you supposed to teach me?"

The head nodded.

"I'm a terrible fighter."

The figure shrugged.

"You can understand me?"

A nod.

"How long does it take to learn?"

A shrug.

"Damn," Orrin said and scratched his head. "Wave your left arm for yes and right arm for no. Does that work?"

The figure's left arm snaked out in something between a wave and strike.

"Let's start easy." Orrin walked closer to the figure. "You have to teach me the [Way of the Water], right?"

The same left-arm movement for "yes" struck.

"Should I just try to hit you?"

The left arm waved noncommittally.

"Is this going to take all day?"

Both arms waved.

"Is that a maybe?"

The right arm waved. No.

"You don't know?"

No.

Orrin thought about how quickly he'd used the [Side Steps] book. Something was different here.

"Is this a simulation?"

Both arms waved again. Orrin felt he understood this one a bit more.

"If I finish learning the book, does the same amount of time I spend here pass in the real world?"

No.

"So, I'm stuck in here until I learn an entire fighting style?"

Both arms moved, but with a delay. Yes and no.

"I'm stuck, but not until I learn everything?"

A slight delay, then yes.

Orrin paced as he thought. He needed to fight the water man to learn the skill. He was stuck until he learned whatever amount of fighting it had to teach him.

"If I quit learning before I'm allowed to leave, can I come back?" he asked hopefully.

No.

"So, I have to learn the fighting style, but it's allowed to be in parts?"

The delayed yes-and-no response appeared again.

"This is so dumb," Orrin complained. "Why? Are all skill books learned this way?"

No.

Orrin paused. He hadn't meant that as an actual question.

"What's the difference? Could I learn this fighting style without all this?" he asked, gesturing around.

The water man nodded.

"How?"

The form's shoulders slumped a bit, and its head tilted. It looked like it sighed and flicked its hand at him.

Orrin's screen appeared.

> **Bypass learning [Way of the Water] naturally and use as skill book?**
> **Yes or No?**

Orrin's brain raced.

There was something odd happening here. While he wanted to use the book to pick up a fighting skill, something new had presented itself. The only difference between him and someone else using a skill book was his admin powers.

"Mr. Watery Man . . . is learning a fighting skill naturally better in some way than learning it as a skill book?"

The figure's head nodded empathically.

"And I have the option to do this because I have admin powers. Right?"

Yes and no.

Orrin slumped on the ground. "Why can't anything ever just be easy?"

The figure shrugged.

"That wasn't a question." He sighed. "Do you have a name? Or should I just call you Mr. Water?"

No.

"No, you don't have a name? Or no to Mr. Water?"

No. No.

Orrin laughed. "Okay. I'll think of a name for you. I'm just going to need a minute to get my mind around this. You know, ever since I arrived here, nothing has ever worked like I thought it would. Why should learning a stupid fighting skill be any different?"

When no response came, Orrin slowly got to his feet.

"Please don't laugh too hard," he said, putting his fists up. "I'm really bad at fighting."

The first fight lasted three seconds. The watery man ducked under Orrin's wild right swing and lifted his own right leg in an upside-down kick that smacked into Orrin's face with the pressure of a small wave. It didn't hurt but did knock him back on his ass.

As he sat there, stunned, Orrin simply knew the name of the attack he'd just been subjected to. Scorpion Fish Strike.

"You can't talk, but every time you hit me, I'm going to learn the name of some stupid attack, aren't I?"

Yes.

Orrin could have sworn the figure laughed, its shoulders shaking.

The figure, which Orrin decided to call Styx, never attacked him. He always waited for Orrin to make the strike before retaliating in a fluid motion, using Orrin's own momentum against him. Every punch was dodged or ducked under, while every kick just missed as Styx surged back or slid into Orrin's space to push him off balance. The attacks were all named things like Returning Tide and Dolphin Blow. Not surprisingly, everything was water related.

"Styx, we've been fighting for an hour," Orrin said, pushing himself off the ground. He'd just had his foot swept out from underneath him by Crab Sweep. "Is there some specific amount of time I have to spend getting my ass kicked in here?"

Styx gestured no.

"Am I any closer to getting out?"

Styx shook his hand no. After hesitating, he pointed at Orrin again, and his floating blue box appeared. In this room, Styx had all the power. Orrin didn't even know long he'd been in here. He'd tried counting every time he'd been knocked down and counting each fight as half a minute, but after losing count at about a hundred, he'd given up.

[Way of the Water]: 0.3%

"Seriously?" Orrin groaned. "This is going to take forever. Are you going to just use every attack possible on me until I give up?"

The water in the middle of Styx's chest churned, and he swept up close to Orrin. A finger poked his head—the first attack Styx had made.

Orrin rubbed his forehead. It didn't hurt, but every attack left Orrin marked by water. His clothes would get wet from each attack but magically dry between each round.

"What do you want?" Orrin demanded. "I'm doing everything you want. I can't hit you. I didn't upload all the fight moves when I used the book. You are too quick. Why would somebody even make this an option? What point is there in getting hit over and over?"

Styx rolled his hand, inviting Orrin to continue his tirade. Somehow the simple movements of the watery humanoid were getting easier to understand.

"There isn't a point to getting hit over and over?"

Styx waved both hands, yes and no. He then pointed at Orrin.

"I'm not supposed to get hit over and over?"

Styx threw up both hands in triumph. Yes. Yes. Yes.

Orrin's thoughts drifted back to the fights. Every attack he threw at Styx was countered, with little movement or reaction needed from the defender.

"[Way of the Water] isn't about offensive fighting, is it?" Orrin said aloud. "It's a defense."

[Way of the Water]: 1.1%

Orrin reflected on the different names he'd been learning. Instead of thinking of them as attacks, he felt the movements in his body as defensive reactions. As soon as he had the thought, Styx swung his right arm in a wide haymaker.

Orrin reflexively dipped and used the first hit that had landed on him: Scorpion Fish Strike. His form was off, but his foot still dipped into the water making up Styx's shoulder.

Styx backed up and bowed. Then he started to attack.

[Way of the Water]: 4.9%

Orrin was exhausted. He was spread-eagle on the white marble, trying to count the alcoves. Each complete circle had fifty recesses. He'd been able to make out just over thirty circles before his eyes failed him. The circles started getting too close that high up for him to make out properly. Daniel with his [Telescope] skill would have been able to make out more.

"Styx, are those alcoves all the different moves of [Way of the Water]?"

Styx was standing nearby, waiting patiently for Orrin to stand again. The last spar had lasted almost two minutes before he'd knocked Orrin down. He waved no.

"What are they?"

Styx didn't respond. When Orrin's questions became too broad, his binary language broke down completely; however, Orrin could feel his teacher's frustration at not being able to answer.

Orrin pushed the question to the side and rolled over before standing back up. He situated his body into the first stance Styx had taken: Formless. Keeping his body open for whatever was thrown at him, the first form let him react to Styx's attack style. He'd also learned River, Ocean, and Rain. Mist stance was something Styx had shown him twice before becoming frustrated at something Orrin was doing wrong. He hadn't repeated the stance again.

Orrin waited patiently, edging his feet to the side and keeping Styx in front of him as they circled each other. Styx struck with two consecutive high kicks. Orrin slapped one away with Otter Tail and redirected the second with a change into River stance. He dropped low and swung his leg out in an attempt to break Styx's one-legged posture. The liquid man flipped off his single foot and pivoted his body in the air to kick again in Rain Hits the Soil. As he brought his heel down where Orrin's center was, he found Rising Wave meeting his attack. Orrin's feint had worked, and his fist shattered Styx's face, the water splashing a dozen feet behind them both.

Styx, instantly fully formed, bowed. Orrin could swear he saw a smile form in the dark recesses of the watery head.

> **[Way of the Water]: 5% (1/20 completed). Continue or save progress?**

"Save progress? Does that mean I can come back?" Orrin asked.

Styx waved his left arm for yes.

Orrin hit save and blinked.

"Did you learn it?" Daniel asked, sitting close to him on the bed.

Orrin yelled and fell off, landing hard on the floor.

"Dude, what the hell?"

Daniel frowned. "O. What's wrong?"

"How long was I out?"

Daniel reached down and helped Orrin stand. "What are you talking about? You opened the book and the words disappeared like normal. I said two words and you fell off the bed."

Orrin ran his hand through his hair. A minute ago, it had been slick with sweat from the hours of fighting he'd been doing. It was now dry, without the dirty feeling that should have been there after such a workout.

"It was different. Something happened."

Orrin explained the white room and Styx to Daniel while his friend's eyebrows rose higher and higher.

"You suck, dude! I want to learn martial arts from a secret master," Daniel complained.

"D, I was stuck there for half a day." Orrin was pacing. "I only completed 5 percent of the book."

"But you can go back, right?" Daniel asked with concern, standing up. "And you know how to fight now?"

Orrin poked the skill on his status screen, feeling the ability to reenter Styx's training room. "Yeah, I can go back . . . and I think I have the basics down at least."

Daniel stood up and gave Orrin an evil grin. "Want to test out your skills?"

Orrin returned the smirk, feeling the stances in his mind. This might be fun.

Chapter 19

Not surprisingly, Orrin lost any fair fight against Daniel—"fair" being defined by Daniel as not using debuffs against him. The difference was in how long it took.

"Stop moving," Daniel demanded as he swung the practice sword at Orrin.

Orrin, standing in Formless pose, ducked under the horizontal swing and danced away. He cast a few [Lightstrike]s at Daniel before his friend charged him again. The rules of the fight with Daniel were simple: whoever hit the other first with their sword won, unless Orrin could strike him with ten casts of the weak light-beam spell. Orrin had increased his dexterity this turn and focused solely on evading and retreating. He was up to seven hits.

Daniel jumped into the air with his sword raised overhead. The vertical downswing was easy enough for Orrin to avoid, even without his new fighting style. Despite being at only 5 percent, the [Way of the Water] was proving to be a game changer.

Orrin sidestepped the attack and pointed his finger to win the match. It had been the longest duel they'd ever had without Orrin debuffing Daniel into a crawling mess. Except when he stepped, Daniel's body twisted in the air with him. Orrin quickly moved into River pose and tried to dodge, but it was too late. Daniel bonked him on the head.

"Match!" Daniel shouted in triumph.

"You cheated," Orrin argued. "We said no spells."

Daniel smirked. "[Gravity Well] isn't a spell. It's a skill."

Orrin shook his head. "That's not what we agreed on and you know it. I had you."

Daniel shrugged and replaced the small practice sword on the weapon rack. "Someday, young padawan, you shall surpass the master."

Orrin groaned.

"Seriously, though, that fighting skill is slippery. It's perfect for you."

"What does that mean?"

"You need to be able to avoid getting hit. I only got you because you went for the attack. If you'd backed up another step or two, you would have been able to slip by me again. You did it twice before when I tried to draw you in."

Orrin paused as he put his sword back, too. He didn't use a summoned sword while sparring. "You did? I didn't even feel it."

"I've been using [Gravity Well] to change my own momentum instead of someone else's," Daniel explained. "Madi got a few tips on spells and skills from Emily and passed them along."

"Speaking of Madi," Orrin started. He explained his earlier screwup by mentioning [Merge]. "So don't talk about it. I need to figure out how to get it and keep it a secret."

"You already know my thoughts on that."

Orrin sighed. "We are not having this conversation again. You are a [Hero]. I'm not. The more people who know our secret, the bigger chance I get kidnapped to blackmail you—or worse."

Daniel shrugged. "We've dealt with that before, but I'll respect you and drop it. If you do get [Merge], I'm sure we can chalk it up to one more weird thing about your class."

As they made their way back to their room, one of the staff intercepted them with a bow.

"The lady requests your presence in the kitchen, young masters."

"Gerald, how many times do I have to tell you to call me Daniel?"

Gerald nodded with a smile. "At least once more, young master. Shall I show you the way?"

Daniel scowled and shook his head ruefully. "We can find our own way, thank you."

Orrin grinned at the man as they left and received a conspiratorial wink.

In the kitchen, Madi had the house staff scurrying around fulfilling last-minute requests. Most of what they planned to bring was to be stored with Orrin, but each adventurer was required to bring their own food supplies, just in case they were separated or Orrin died. Daniel had grown very angry when that last article had been addressed.

Breads, smoked meats, and even a small stack of grapes and oranges had been assembled. Cheese and nuts were sorted into separately labeled containers and wraps. A canvas bag was set to the side.

Madi looked up as they arrived. "Good, you're both here. Orrin, could you go ahead and start loading up on everything here? I've already separated out emergency rations for each person."

Orrin just nodded and began putting the foodstuffs away. Some of the bread was still warm and would be again later, when he drew it out. Madi's attention to detail for this foray was nearly perfect. He reached the end of the table and poked the bag.

"Madi, what's in here?"

"Coffee," she replied without looking up.

Orrin smiled. "You are amazing. I only bought a small bag. This should last us quite a while."

"I didn't get that. Somebody dropped it off for you, and I thought you'd want to bring it along. If you are going to bring it, make sure it's ground. Nobody is going to carry a bean grinder for you."

One of the cooks coughed pointedly once Madi turned around. She nodded toward a corner of the kitchen, where a small hand grinder and coffee press were already sitting out.

"Meredith, you sneak," Orrin whispered and quickly swiped the items into his storage. "How's your son?"

"Better now," the older woman whispered back. "Thanks again, dearie."

Daniel waited for people to clear away before leaning into Orrin. "How are you so friendly with everybody? I can barely get their names."

Orrin gestured at his friend. "You are the famous [Hero]. I'm just a guy who is loose with his mana and can heal without waiting in a Hospital line."

"Bribery then?"

Orrin laughed. "No. I needed a way to increase my healing experience without just parading around that I'm doing it. I overheard one rumor and asked around. Meredith's son had a broken leg, and the wait list was long enough she was worried it would set bad permanently. So, we both got what we wanted."

He turned back to Madi with a thought. "Madi, the person who dropped off the coffee. Was it an older guy or about our age?"

Madi didn't even spare him a glance. "Our age. He said to apologize to you for something? Oh, and he asked if you could stop by his shop at some point. Wouldn't give a reason."

"I'm not going to have time before we leave . . . maybe I'll send a message." Orrin turned to find some paper.

"I already told him," Madi said, catching his attention before he left again. "He said he'd expect you when you could make the time."

Daniel grabbed an apple out of a basket on a different shelf. Orrin noticed Meredith's quick frown.

"How long before we leave then?" Daniel said between bites. "We should at least say thank you to your dad for all the supplies before leaving."

Madi kept her back to them and didn't respond. She rolled up a cloth with a few knives and forks and dropped it on the table close to Orrin.

"That should be all of it," she muttered. "Let's go see if Emily and Garret are here yet."

"Madi?"

"Thank you so much, everybody. That will be all for today," she announced before trying to scamper out the door.

Daniel blocked her path.

"What's going on?"

Madi glanced over her shoulder at the people funneling out another door. Only the few main kitchen staff remained. She mumbled something too quietly for Orrin to hear.

"He doesn't?"

"What's going on?" Orrin stepped in closer.

Daniel pointed at their party member. "Her dad doesn't even know we're going."

Orrin pulled both of them through the door into the hallway. There was no use in having the conversation in front of the people who worked for Silas.

"To the dungeon or to the elves?"

"Neither," Madi murmured.

"You told us it wasn't a problem," Orrin accused. "Why does he think we need all this food?"

"I set it up myself." She looked up at him at that. "I am capable of doing things without him."

Daniel put his hand on her shoulder. "That is not what Orrin said and you know it. You didn't lie to us, but you left out some pretty major details. What's going on?"

Madi realized they were still in the hall and pulled them along to one of the small meeting rooms for important visitors. Closing the door behind her, she fell into a chair and covered her face.

"I haven't told him yet. I'm terrified of going through with it," she said from between her hands.

"We can go with you," Daniel suggested. "Explain to him the Guild gave us this opportunity. Maybe even see if he could make you an official envoy to the elves."

Madi shook her head. "It's not just the dungeon and the elf trip. I have to tell him I'm becoming an adventurer with you full-time. I'm resigning as Lady Catanzano and giving up my claim to the lordship."

Orrin was stunned. Madi had mentioned not wanting to take over for her father before, but Silas had been grooming her for the position for her entire life. If she dropped the bombshell on him now, right before they were supposed to leave . . .

"Maybe don't tell him that right before we go on a secret mission to save the elves?" Daniel said.

Orrin plopped into a chair and put his own head in his hands.

"I mean, what if he gets mad and tries to keep you here?"

Orrin groaned. Daniel was such an idiot sometimes.

"What if he tries to keep us here?"

"Are you saying that if he tried to ground me, you'd run off and leave me here?" Madi stood. Her face was calm, but her eyes were a storm waiting to crash against a ship.

"Not at all," Orrin said as he stood up, stomping on Daniel's foot. "We'd just hate to have to break you out and teleport away. I can't even get us to the dungeon, and trekking around looking for it would be a waste of time."

Madi raised an eyebrow but the smile pulling at her lips gave Orrin a moment of relief. He'd sidetracked the two headstrong members of his group before they came to blows.

"Maybe don't tell him everything now," Orrin started. "You have to tell him about the dungeon. We can't steal supplies from him and have him wondering where we are. Read the situation and see if he needs to know about the elf trip, but wait until we come back to make any big career-move announcements."

Orrin held up his hands to stall her inevitable counterarguments. "We support you; you know that. He might be fine with it . . . but let's not tempt fate right now."

Madi sat back down. "You're right. Both of you. I shouldn't have tried to run off without telling him, but he's so good at seeing right through me sometimes. Sorry for not telling you."

Daniel wisely stayed quiet and just nodded his head.

A knock at the door interrupted their conversation. "Lady Catanzano, Ms. Ibarra has arrived for you."

"Please bring Emily through to us," Madi called back. After a moment, she turned to Daniel and Orrin. "Can you stall for me? I have to find my father and explain—"

"Go," Daniel said gently. "We'll wait."

Madi punched his arm as she walked by.

"What the hell?"

Madi laughed. "Orrin does it all the time. Just testing it out."

As she left the room, Daniel turned on his friend. "You are a terrible influence on her."

Emily arrived first. She and Daniel chatted about provisions and supplies for a bit after he explained Madi was running a last-minute errand.

The teleportation siblings, Jack and Jillian, arrived early. Orrin hadn't seen them since Daniel's rescue, and he thanked them again for their help. Jack continued to be an ass, but Jillian shook his hand. After introducing them to Daniel as part of his rescue team, he thanked them as well.

"It was just a paycheck," Jack mumbled but took Daniel's hand. Being the [Hero] came with some built-in respect, it seemed.

Jillian pulled Daniel into a hug. "No, it wasn't. We are honored we got to help rescue Dey's [Hero]. If you ever need a jump, let me know."

Orrin saw her stick a slip of paper in Daniel's pocket and questioned whether she was talking about a [Teleport].

Madi burst into the room, out of breath, a few minutes later. "Sorry," she huffed. "Last-minute stuff. We're good." She held up a thumb to Daniel and Orrin.

"We're still waiting on Garret," Emily sighed. "He's always late."

"Am I?" Garret's voice echoed in from the hall before he popped in as well. "That doesn't sound like me at all."

"The Donovan job?"

"Those thugs were early. You can't blame me for—"

"The Pasquil infestation?"

"I still swear that Tin told me two hours past sunrise, not one."

"Should I keep going?" Emily asked, her arms folded.

Garret bowed to the siblings and took Jillian's hand. "Who are these lovely folks that nobody has introduced me to? My name is Garret Bell. Wonderful to make your acquaintance."

A peck on Jillian's hand had her enamored. Jack's attitude soured even more.

"All right, all right." Jack pulled out a map and spread it on a table. "Let's get this done. This is where we will be taking you."

He drew a line up the map from Dey and pointed to a small blue line south of where the dungeon was.

"We don't know all the particulars of your mission, but we've been told to keep it hush-hush. We were told you'd be able to make your own way from here?" Jillian continued when Jack took a breath, turning her last sentence into a question.

"That should be fine," Emily answered. Turning to look at the others, she shrugged. "I've got a good memory. We'll be fine."

Jack clapped. "Then let's get you to your destination and me home with a paid bill."

Chapter 20

Orrin waved to the brother and sister teleport team as they disappeared without a sound, leaving their party on the north side of a small stream.

"I can't believe she asked both of us to dinner . . . in front of each other," Daniel said, shaking his head.

"I might take her up on dinner." Garret pulled his backpack up on his shoulder. "It might be just what I need after this job."

Daniel double-checked Gertrude strapped on his back. He carried his pack like a duffel bag at his side. "What about Orrin?"

"Orrin can join us if he wants."

Orrin ignored the male half of his party and turned to Emily. "You said you'd be able to find the way? How long do you think it'll take us to get there?"

Emily pointed north by northeast. "I'm pretty sure you could use [Map] and find the guards we're supposed to meet. It's maybe an hour's hike. This is close to where the Guildmaster said the dungeon is. They usually take on some characteristics of the surrounding area." She waved at the small brook. "This might be what made it take a water bent."

Talking about the different qualities of the dungeon reminded Orrin he still hadn't made up his mind about which spells to buy. Poking around in the spell store, he went with his gut and selected the one he thought he might get some use out of.

> **[Toxic Touch]—your touch becomes toxic. MP cost variable to toxicity. -2 AP**

Would you like to purchase for 2 AP?
Yes or No?

Yes.

Orrin tagged the new icon and found [Poison Ward] for a single ability point. He bought the same.

[Poison Ward]—creates a ward around you and your party within 50 feet that protects against poison magic for MP maximum. 20 MP.

He still didn't have a steel ward, but Orrin didn't feel like spending five points—six if a new ward became available—on such a specific type of magic. Poison, ice, and water were ones he felt would be more useful in the future. Eventually, he'd need to get fire and maybe the light magic ward he'd avoided purchasing, but he felt no rush to do so. Even if he had to hide it, he still wanted to get [Merge]. Doing more with [Alchemy] also seemed interesting, but after all his research and Brandt's warnings about the prohibitive cost and training needed, that skill was pushed to the back burner.

Orrin also cast a level-one [Utility Ward] on the party. Quickly calculating the math in his mind, he realized that the plus thirty to every stat from a level-two spell would likely result in everybody needing a day off to recover from the overeffects. Instead, he kept the increase to a safer fifteen. The cost of a level-one spell also meant his spent mana would be more than half refilled in the hour it would take to get to the dungeon. He could also top off with a mana potion if he needed. The extra strength and dexterity would make traversing the terrain a little easier. Emily gave him a smile when her physical stats went up.

As they trudged along, climbing up a hill away from the water, Orrin filled Daniel in on his new purchases.

"You went with the more expensive spell even though you don't plan on using either one?"

"How often am I going to have a chance to bite someone versus touching them?" Orrin defended himself. "One point is going to make a huge difference."

"You don't know that," Daniel said, taking a big step up on a rock. "What if you have to wait to buy something now or can't even afford it in the first place? The prices of spells and skills only get more expensive the higher tier they are."

Orrin shrugged. "I can already boost your stats to the max. Everything else I get just gives us options."

Daniel reached over and tried to ruffle Orrin's hair. "My little Swiss Army knife."

After a bit of climbing up the sparsely wooded hill, Orrin pulled his [Map] back up. He stopped Emily and pointed her a bit more north. The four dots on his map were likely the guards sent from the Guild.

"It's probably going to be another ten minutes, tops," Orrin announced to the rest of them.

Garret grumbled something but was too far behind for Orrin to make it out.

One of the Guild members caught their movement before they reached the small tent set up against the hill. She moved down to them, picking her footing with a speed and grace that spoke of either a high dexterity or some sort of movement skill.

"About time you made it," she said as she jumped down to land in front of them. "Which one of you is the [Hero]?"

Emily and Orrin pointed at Daniel. He waved.

"I'm Sadie. I'm in charge of this shit show until Pritus says otherwise. She wants the [Hero] to be first through. Nobody has been in since we found the entrance and defeated the monsters from the break," she explained as she led the way up the increasingly steep hill. "I'm sure you were briefed, but it never hurts to be sure. Water, steel, and poison monsters were confirmed. Something did escape, but only Jackson got a look at it. He got thumped by a Steel Boar and had to be taken back to Dey for some healing. I didn't think he got hit that hard, but he kept jumbling up his words, so better safe than sorry."

Sadie introduced the other Guild members watching the dungeon. Jeb, with his halberd and half-plate armor, squatted near the entrance of the tent and gave only a nod before returning his gaze to the distance. Derrick wore red robes similar to Emily's. He smiled and shook their hands. Beth had green robes and a walking stick that could have been a freshly cut branch—some leaves remained still.

"Jeb is our front line, while I spend most of the time harrying stragglers back at him. Derrick and Beth are good ranged casters to help kill whatever needs killing," Sadie explained. "Jackson should be back in a day or two. If you die in there, we'll be going in to destroy it. If you take longer than two weeks, we'll be going in to destroy it. If another dungeon break happens, we'll know you're dead and come in to destroy it. Any questions?"

Emily stepped to the side to exchange pleasantries with Derrick. Madi and Daniel asked Sadie a few questions about the monsters and fighting tactics. Garret tried to break Jeb's composure by squatting in front of him and complimenting his large weapon.

Orrin stood awkwardly and silently, waiting for the group to enter the dungeon. Beth also stood off to the side, content to stay quiet.

Finally, Daniel clapped and got everyone's attention.

"I'll be going in first, but obviously we don't know what we are going to be up against." He paced in front of the tent. "Orrin, I want you to go in second. Madi, you try to stay right on Orrin's tail. Garret, you go next, and Emily, bring up the rear. Once we see what we're dealing with, we can figure out our game plan. Orrin, maybe set us all up with a regular [Ward]?"

Madi clutched her short spear tight and nodded.

"Sure, not a problem," Orrin answered as he handed Garret the Citrandish bow, already strung with the best string they'd been able to find. He quickly cast a [Ward] on all five of the party.

"Is that a—"

Sadie elbowed Beth and shushed her.

"Let's go," Daniel said and opened the tent flap.

Orrin followed close behind. The tent covered only a small part of the hill, but a crevice had formed in that spot. Orrin imagined a pit into hell would look more inviting. Daniel was already squeezing in sideways, carrying Gertrude pointed in and dangling his bag behind him as he turned.

Orrin hitched his shoulder strap up and started forward. His shoulders were just narrow enough that he could squeeze through without too much difficulty. He heard Madi close behind. Watching Daniel closely, Orrin was able to pinpoint the exact spot where his friend disappeared. He summoned an [Ice Sword] and stuck it into the soft earth just before the dungeon portal.

"Be ready. I dropped a sword to show where we enter," he threw back over his shoulder. Then, without waiting for a response, he stepped past his marker and entered his second dungeon.

Welcome to the Crumbling Waste!

As Orrin's foot hit the dungeon proper, he took three hits in quick succession to the chest.

[Ward] 500/530

"Get down," Daniel yelled from a few steps ahead of him. He was crawling along the floor. Orrin followed his lead and got on his hands and knees.

They were in a long corridor. The walls were slate and the ground was cobblestone. Orrin picked up one of the small knives that had hit him before being deflected off by his magic shield. It was shaped like a kunai. After a second, the two he hadn't touched melted into the ground. The one in his hand began to burn, and he dropped it. He noticed his [Ward] had taken another point of damage.

"Don't pick up the kunai," Orrin shouted to Daniel. Madi arrived a moment later and Orrin pulled her down before three more of the weapons flew out of the darkness.

"Wha—" Madi landed in a heap. She heard the clatter behind her as the knives hit the blank wall that was the exit. "Thanks?"

"Daniel says we crawl." Orrin pointed ahead to where Daniel was shuffling along. Every few feet, more of the kunai lodged into the wall, but always at about chest height. "Stay here and pull Emily and Garret down."

Orrin crawled forward and pulled up his [Map]. He yelped at what he saw.

"Daniel, get back. The entire room is a big trap. Only certain stones are safe and . . . oh, shit."

Every time Daniel had brushed his limbs along one of the yellow trapped stones on his [Map], Orrin watched the throwing daggers burst from the darkness ahead. Orrin could tell the long chamber was only a few hundred yards long, but when Daniel had rested his hand and Gertrude on the latest stone embedded in the ground, something new had appeared: a small panel on the wall a few feet ahead of Daniel, with dozens of red dots scurrying about behind it.

"Monsters, two o'clock," Orrin shouted.

Daniel didn't need the warning as the multitude of balding, furry rats poured out of the hole and directly at him. He swiped Gertrude as best he could, but even with the increased strength and his own [Light Weapon] skill, she was too heavy for the position he was in. Luckily, she was heavy enough to smash a few against the wall.

Orrin heard a grunt as Garret wasn't pulled down quick enough and took two hits. His [Ward] kept him from taking any damage, and Orrin threw a [Lightstrike] at the monsters. They went down with one hit. He pulled up [Identify].

[Plague Rat] HP 9/9

He cued up for another strike just before Emily arrived.

Of all the members of the party, Emily reacted the most professionally. Upon arriving in the dungeon, she ducked down and to the side, dodging the three kunai before they'd even appeared. She noticed all four of her party members on the ground and fell to her knees. Finding the [Hero] being swarmed by almost a hundred small rats, she raised her hands and attacked.

A bloom of fire spread from her hands like a lance, moving where Emily pointed. Only crispy, black husks remained of each monster she passed. The spell only lasted for two deep breaths, but Orrin watched her decimate the rats.

Experience Gained: 2 XP

Daniel slowly pulled his arms and legs back and looked over his shoulder. "Thanks for the assist, Emily."

Orrin threw out his hand as Garret made to crawl forward. "The floor is trapped. The medium-size stones send out the flying knives, and the big ones . . . well, that one Daniel touched let out the rats. At least around me, the small ones aren't showing up as trapped."

Madi took a tentative step on her toes. "These are too small for full steps. Somebody is going to fall at some point."

"We could try jumping between the bigger ones," Garret suggested. "It means some fighting, but if it's only those weak things . . ."

"How long is this tunnel?" Madi asked, trying to gaze into the darkness. "I can't see the end."

"Maybe three hundred yards," Orrin answered, glancing at his map. "I can't see those side rooms that have the monsters until they open. If Daniel can stand up, he can probably sweep any rats and you guys can all use ranged attacks. Emily should stay at the back, just in case something opens up behind us. Good save, by the way."

Emily gave Orrin a tight smile. "Do the traps reset? If we have to jump from one to the next and then fight a new wave of those things each time, this could take forever."

Orrin tried to pinpoint the exact large cobblestone that had triggered the rats but couldn't get a good read from where he was. He stood slowly and hopped from one small stone to the next. In the ten feet to Daniel, he only triggered one set of flying steel, which his [Ward] deflected.

"Shit," Orrin moaned. "I think it reset."

"Should I trigger the same one again?" Daniel offered. "We can see if we killed them all the first time."

"I think we should run for it and kill anything that gets in our way," Garret suggested. "Orrin's shielding spell is working for the weapon traps. This narrow hallway isn't the best for me."

"Or," Madi chimed in, "we could take our time and do our best to avoid triggering anything. It'll be slower, but we won't use as much mana before getting to the second room. We have to pace ourselves."

Emily turned to Daniel. "What do you think we should do?"

Daniel was the figurehead of the party, the leader in name. Orrin had watched him lead his team to victory in soccer and pep up his basketball team to come back from a losing streak. He had the natural charisma to charm others and enough belief in himself to make a decision and go with it. However, Daniel was also smart enough to know this wasn't a game. This was a life-and-death scenario where the wrong choice could spell disaster for not just himself but the people following him. Daniel's uncertainty was evident as he glanced between his party members, finally landing on his friend. Orrin shrugged and smirked.

"Fast or slow, we can always take breaks between rooms."

Daniel readjusted the bag he'd slung sideways over his back while holding Gertrude. "We could run for it, but I think the experience might be easier on the first level. As long as the [Wards] hold out, I say we move slow and fight each monster we can find. If we can get a few more levels before reaching the boss, great."

He turned to Garret. "Sorry."

The archer raised an eyebrow. "For what? It was just a suggestion. Slow is probably smart. What if triggering all the traps at once while running lets something else in?"

Daniel shook his head. "What the hell? Why would you suggest running if you didn't . . . Oh, never mind."

He turned his back and raised his foot over the bigger trap stone. "Everybody ready?"

Chapter 21

"What the hell happened?" Daniel asked from the safe room. The group was soaking wet, and despite Orrin's [Wards], each of them sported multiple small bites all over.

Emily was dancing around, hitting herself and flailing. Madi hugged her, pinning her arms to the sides. "They're gone. We made it through the floor. None of them followed us."

The party had been making good time, clearing a big swath of Plague Rats from each trap. The large stones that triggered the mini waves of monsters had a cooldown time of just under a minute. By keeping close and using Orrin's [Ward] spell, they'd avoided the flying dagger traps and killed the eighty-eight rats in each set. The fights didn't go off without a hitch, though. That many monsters meant that each person took several hits, swiftly draining Orrin's [Wards]. Orrin himself had to use an [Ice Sword] to dispatch a good number of the rats. They had set off eight different traps, including the first one twice. It was on the tenth trigger that things went sideways.

Emily, taking up the rear, was the first to notice something different. Wetness caught her heels, and when she turned to check, the moving wave of water had struck her just above the knees. If not for the increased strength and dexterity from Orrin's [Utility Ward], she would have been knocked to the ground. Instead, she only stumbled.

Garret hadn't been looking backward and the wave carried him forward, right into Madi. The two of them were slammed, spun, and half drowned as the wave pushed them down into the hard stone surface. While no kunai had appeared, the former weapon traps did set off more waves spilling at the group from behind.

Daniel and Orrin had enough warning to take the waves in stride. Maybe it was the few summers they'd spent at the beach, jumping into the surf. Maybe it was that both had learned to swim at a young age and a few feet of water didn't faze them as much as the others. With Dey having no nearby large bodies of water, they later learned that only Garret knew how to swim well.

The rats could also swim. They wiggled through the water faster than they scurried, crawling up robes, pants, and cloaks. Emily's fire spells sputtered out after a few feet. Daniel struggled to hit more than a few at a time. Garret and Madi were just getting to their feet. They might have been able to turn the tide, no pun intended, but for one little mistake.

In her haste, Emily had stepped back and triggered the first rat trap. A door behind them opened, and nearly a hundred more swamped them.

"Run!" Daniel yelled, pushing through the rodents tearing each other up to stand on top and jump at the adventurers. Emily became an inferno, which created a constant fog of steam around her. Garret was splashing away from the fire mage, more worried about the heated air than the rats biting him.

Daniel slammed against the door at the end of the hallway and heaved against it. The three feet of water suctioned the door, and Orrin quickly threw his strongest [Increase Strength] spells on him. Once Daniel pried the door open, water disappeared as it rushed into the doorway like . . . magic. He tossed Orrin and Madi, just arriving, through the door.

As Orrin rolled into the safe room, he checked himself over. His latest [Ward] had been bitten down by half. Madi's shield was hanging on only slightly better. Both had taken a few points of health damage between Orrin's reapplying his [Ward].

Garret had fallen through the doorway a handful of seconds later, followed closely by Emily. Daniel stepped through a bit more gracefully. Garret's [Ward] had survived better than anyone else's. He'd been staying back and had only really been hit on the last foray. Emily had taken the worst of it. The second door's rats had clustered on her, burning themselves to death for a bite or two. Without Orrin there to re-up her shield, the rats had been able to do some damage.

"Emily." Orrin spoke calmly as he approached her. Madi was still helping her brush her robes down. "I'm going to heal you a bit, okay?"

Emily's eyes were wide and panicked, but she nodded. Orrin cast [Heal Small Wounds] and watched dozens of small bites close up. He snuck a [Calm Mind] spell on her as well, and Emily's shoulders slumped as if she was exhausted.

"Thank you."

Madi held Emily's waist and brought her to the far corner of the safe room before they both sat. Emily mumbled an apology to the group as they made their way past.

"It must have been the tenth trap," Madi ventured. "When we triggered it, the dungeon threw something new our way. I guess we should have tried going slow."

"Everybody is alive and we passed the floor," Orrin reasoned, pulling out a small cube Madi had found in the Guild's storeroom. It was a heater cube, a magical device that put out the heat of a fire. They weren't too expensive, but having one on a trip into a dungeon was a luxury most eschewed, because they were about the size of a child's lunch box but quite heavy. He set the cube down and turned it on, closing his eyes as the warmth hit him. "We can take a small break and then keep going if you all want."

Garret and Daniel gathered close to the heater cube as well, letting the warm air dry their clothes. Emily's robes either had a self-drying feature or she could control her own body heat, because she was already dry. Madi made sure she was fine before heading over to the rest of the group.

"Emily is feeling embarrassed about setting off the other trap," she whispered quietly to the boys. "If one of you says something hurtful to her, I'll make sure you regret it."

"It wasn't just her," Daniel said, loud enough for Emily to hear. "In the rush to get to the door, I opened two more. The water coming at us like that surprised us all. We all made it through. That's all that matters."

Garret rubbed his hands together over the heater. "I'm just glad she didn't cook me. I like my women hot, but not like that."

Madi and Orrin exchanged glances and held their breath. Emily chuckled. Then she laughed quietly, the tension finally breaking.

"We've been over this before, Garret. You're not my type." Emily stood up using the wall and made her way to the group. She didn't need the heater but appreciated the warmth of their company.

Daniel tried to steer the conversation back to the dungeon. "Floor one had steel and water. No poison yet, though."

"The rats were called Plague Rats," Orrin countered. "But I didn't see any poison or conditions on my status."

"You didn't look them up in your book?" Madi teased.

"That's not a bad idea," Orrin said, reaching for the book. Daniel groaned.

"She's making fun of you, dork."

"And I don't care. I'd rather know for sure."

Orrin found the listing for Plague Rats and confirmed to the group that the monsters could carry any disease they encountered in large numbers into civilized areas, infecting multitudes if not stamped out quickly, but the one-star monsters were barely worthy of the lowest ranking in the bestiary.

After everyone had a chance to calm their nerves after the first floor, Orrin put the heater back in his [Dimension Hole] and finally checked his notifications.

Experience Gained: 154 XP (2 XP x 77)

Not too bad, he thought. He didn't have much skill with the sword, but swinging the sharp end at a mass of moving fur didn't take talent, just a little movement. Orrin knew the rats were a best-case scenario for him, even with the minuscule amount of experience they provided. If only the water trap after ten monster releases wasn't a thing, the first floor could have produced a steady trickle of experience for them all.

Daniel pushed the strap of his pack up on one shoulder and rested Gertrude on the other. "Everybody ready? Same plan for the second floor. Does anyone need a fresh [Ward], Orrin?"

Orrin had already reapplied where needed and gave Daniel the all clear. A moment later, they were stepping through the door to the second floor.

After the dark and narrow hallway that was floor one, Orrin blinked against the sun in the sky. He stood in a sparsely wooded forest with brush up to his ankles. A quick check of his [Map] showed a host of monsters in the distance and a long trek to the exit.

"At least nobody is throwing knives at us," Madi commented as she glanced around next to him.

"I'm picking up maybe twenty monsters between us and the exit," Orrin said, pointing toward the second-floor door. "That way."

Walking through the thicket was not a quiet activity, and it was only a few minutes before the party had their first encounter with the floor's residents.

"Steel Boar," Orrin announced after a quick [Identify]. He'd been able to spot a sliver of the metallic hide as it broke through two clumps of brush.

Daniel dropped his pack and held Gerty like a baseball bat. As the boar broke through a small sapling and charged him, he swung with a quick pivot. The hollow ting of metal on metal filled the air as he battered the charging, tusked pig a foot to the side.

"Shit, it's got to weigh a ton," Daniel cried out as he leaped to the side. "Madi, try to daze it."

Madi had already set up her signature spell, [Shimmersight], and released the flying ball of light. Before it even hit, a lance of fire melted a coin-size hole in the boar's side and two arrows struck the metal head, crowning it like spikes.

Orrin checked the monster's health.

Steel Boar—HP 88/200

"It's over halfway down," he yelled out. "Hit it again."

Another lance from Emily and more arrows followed. Orrin threw a [Lightstrike], and Daniel waded into the middle to hit it a few more times. When the beast fell with a shuddering gasp, Daniel kicked it with his foot to make doubly sure it was dead.

Experience Gained: 50 XP

"That thing could take a beating for a second-floor monster," Daniel complained.

"Any monster with 'Steel' in its name is going to be the same," Emily replied, poking at the dead monster with her staff. "I'd like to study this one for a minute if we have the time. I sent my first [Firestrike] at the center mass but the second at its shoulder. I want to see which one went deeper so we'll be able to know where to target the rest to bring them down faster."

Daniel nodded and retrieved his pack. Orrin followed him.

"We should probably try and pick off any stragglers if we can. Most of the boars travel in pairs, and there are five in one group, but around the edges are a few stand-alones," Orrin suggested.

Daniel grinned at Orrin. "Always thinking one step ahead. Thanks. I don't think we need to try to clear the floor. Five of those at once might be too much. Do you think you can get us through without pulling the big group?"

Orrin double-checked. "It shouldn't be a problem as long as we keep the fights short. With two, it might be harder, especially if one tries to run away."

Daniel nodded and outlined the plan to the group: Madi would mark whichever monster reached them first as the main target, and only after it went down would they turn their attention to the second.

"Of course, we are going to try and only take out the ones that are alone," Daniel announced. "If we can move through this floor by avoiding a fight, we will."

Orrin hesitated before raising his hand.

"Are you seriously raising your hand?" Daniel asked incredulously.

He lowered his arm.

"I have an idea on how we could avoid all the boars, but it's stupid and dangerous."

Daniel's eyes twinkled.

Chapter 22

"You want to use yourself as bait?" Madi glowered at Orrin. She had her spear extended, and Orrin distinctly saw her hand twitch as if she wanted to stab him.

"I can boost my dexterity, run around and create a stampede, and then go invisible while the rest of you make your way to the next room. We aren't here to get experience. The goal is to defeat the dungeon."

Orrin still felt a twinge of guilt that they hadn't shared the Defeat a Dungeon Quest with Emily and Garret. Madi, Daniel, and he had decided against broadcasting what his Quests were. Daniel hadn't cared, Orrin had voted to keep it secret, and Madi had been the tie-breaker, saying they should only give them the Quest if they were able to get something in return.

"That's reckless," Madi said, the tip of her spear swooping in an arc as she gestured. "You don't know that your spell will work against them. Some monsters can see through illusions like that. Also, you'd be on your own. If something happened to you, we wouldn't be there to help. Damn it, Orrin. We wouldn't even know you'd need help until you didn't show up in the safe room."

Daniel's smirk turned into a grimace. "She makes a lot of good points, O. We can keep that plan as a backup if we get swamped, but only if it's absolutely necessary."

"We really shouldn't have too much trouble taking one or two at a time," Garret piled on. "If we do have too many on us, maybe Orrin could pull them away, disappear, and then return to us. It'll take the boars longer to find us again, and we can move closer to the door."

Emily moved up alongside Orrin. "What kind of invisibility do you have? Your build keeps getting more and more interesting."

"[Camouflage]," Orrin answered. Sometimes the way Emily looked at him made him feel like a bug under a microscope.

"Fascinating," she whispered to herself, then, louder, she asked, "What made you take that spell? Why not go for the standard [Invisibility] build?"

Orrin felt his neck get hot. "I didn't know how to get [Invisibility]. I guess [Camouflage] doesn't eventually turn into it, huh?"

Emily gave him another look. "You really don't do any research before jumping into things, do you?"

"Most of the time, I'm reacting to things trying to kill me. Being friends with a [Hero] creates a lot of unique situations, and I'm trying to stay alive. I don't have the time to research every single thing I want to. Sorry that I'm not perfect."

Orrin didn't know why his voice raised throughout his response to Emily's question, but he almost shouted the last sentence. The rest of the party noticed their discussion, and Daniel moved to intercept.

Emily held up her hand to forestall him. Turning to Orrin, she spoke softly. "Nobody is perfect. There is no best way to approach any skill or build, just what people have passed down as the easiest paths. Sometimes I forget that not everybody has access to the books and teachings available, especially outside Odrana. I'm sorry for what I said. As far as I know, [Camouflage] does not ever turn into [Invisibility], although it may be possible. Both skills are perception-based spells, but [Invisibility] surrounds the caster with magic that deflects light and in some instances sound. [Camouflage] only blends the caster in with the background. The more complex the backdrop, the more likely you'll be seen. The one thing I remember about the two is that [Camouflage] is usually considered inferior. That doesn't mean it's true, just what I read. If you want, I can send a letter and make a few requests when we get back to Dey to see if anyone I know can dig up more for you."

Orrin felt properly chastised. He'd yelled at a teammate again and only received an offer to help in return.

"Sorry I yelled at you," Orrin mumbled. "I'd appreciate that. From what others have described, my spell makes it hard to look at me and they naturally avert their eyes. I think the magic does something to others as well instead of just making me harder to see."

Emily's eyes twinkled as she listened. "Fascinating. Some sort of disturbance field. Is it scalable? What level is it?"

"If you answer her, she'll never stop asking questions," Garret warned. He'd taken up his borrowed bow and was testing the pull again and again.

Orrin shrugged. "I don't mind. I've got it to level two and almost a fourth of the way to level three."

As Orrin explained the difference between the first level and the upgraded spell version, Emily listened intently.

"Attacking doesn't break the spell? [Invisibility] has to be at the third level for that. Once you've unlocked the spell, which requires [Mirror Shield] and a light spell as the least expensive way known, you can only use it when standing still for the first level. The second level lets you move around, but attacking or casting any other spell breaks it. Level three is when you can really move around a battlefield and do damage quietly. You're already there. Now I want to send off for some research to satisfy my own curiosity. Are you planning on bringing it to the third level? As far as I can remember, additional levels of [Invisibility] only increase the time component of the spell."

"I'm not sure," Orrin admitted. "I have so many things that I want to get still. Do you know how to upgrade [Lightstrike] to [Lightstrikes]?"

"Nope, but I can find out when we get back."

"That's enough planning for now," Daniel butted in. "Let's go kill some pigs."

Emily nodded. "The shoulders are the weak point. Garret and I should be able to hamper one enough to cripple it. Can you take care of a second if we need it?"

Daniel smiled and twirled Gerty in a wide arc. "It would be my pleasure."

With Orrin leading the way, the party was able to avoid most groups of the Steel Boars on the way to the next floor. They encountered only two fights that they couldn't avoid. The first was a set of two. As Emily promised, her [Firestrike] attacks melted the boar's shoulder, making it tip as it struggled to run. Garret positioned himself on the other side, and an arrow of Mythril seemed to sprout from the other side of the boar. Three more arrows punched into the monster before it fell to the ground.

Orrin had hit both with a [Lightstrike], doing the bare minimum to keep getting some experience. He'd spent his attention boosting Daniel again, as the last boost had worn off. With his strength maxed out, Daniel's combination of [Shooting Star] and [Gravity Strike] dented the second boar's chest so deeply that both its front legs were splayed. The grinding noise as it tried to run away was deafening until Madi hit it with a [Shimmersight]. While the monster was dazed, Daniel rained three more strikes down, ending the first half of the fight. Emily and Garret made quick work of their crippled boar.

The second was a straggler. Everybody got a hit on that one, and it went down before it knew what was happening.

Experience Gained: 216 XP (83 XP x 2; 50 XP x 1)

Daniel glanced at his blue box. "Did anyone else get a weird number for experience? The math doesn't seem right."

"Fractions are rounded down and don't stack," Emily said by way of explanation.

"What does that mean?" Daniel asked.

Emily pulled a mana potion from her bag and drank it. Orrin forgot how much more mana he had than others sometimes. He was well under half his pool, but with [Meditate], he was regaining more each minute.

"These Steel Boars give something like 250 experience per kill, but that has to be split among us. If we all get an attack on one, we'd get fifty each. But if only three of us do, then we each get eighty-three and a third of a point of experience. Except percentages of a point get rounded to the nearest point. Anything below half a point and you lose it."

"That doesn't seem right," Daniel complained. "So, an entire point of experience just goes poof?"

Emily's thirst for knowledge always shone brightest when somebody asked a question she didn't have an answer to. "I know, right? There are entire fields of leveling philosophy that argue whether that lost point was ever there to begin with versus there being some way to capture that slight bit of extra experience. Remember, we're only talking fractions of a single point of experience here, but it underpins the broader study of what experience actually is. If a monster has a set amount of experience it grants us upon its death, then why would the system not be able to handle keeping track of fractions? If the system sets that number, then why not make it so an exact amount of experience is earned, no matter the number of people who participate in the subjugation of the monster?"

Orrin shook his cloak where it had gotten stuck against his potion belt. "But it has to go somewhere, right? Something can't just suddenly not exist anymore."

The fire mage's smile scared him. "That's right. The theories behind that particular field of study get a little hard to follow without some higher-level system courses, though."

"What kind of courses? Are you talking about school?" Daniel asked as he strapped Gertrude on his back and hefted his back again. "Who has time to sit around and talk about the possible ways the system gives experience?"

"Obviously, school. And all kinds of courses," Emily answered. "Almost everybody in Mistlight takes some sort of education before selecting their class. It's expected to have a base knowledge of most of the major branches of noncommon classes before you turn fifteen and to take another year of classes focusing on your path after you've hit your first level."

Orrin felt a tickle in his mind at the mention of Mistlight but couldn't remember where he'd heard the name. Daniel and Madi were walking a few steps ahead of the other three, but Madi's pace slowed.

"I didn't know you were from Odrana," Madi said with a calmness in her voice. Orrin heard the constraint.

Emily missed the tightening of Madi's voice, as well as Daniel's hand moving up to the hilt of his sword. "Of course I am. I studied at the Sanerris School for four years before traveling to Dey to be an adventurer. I probably would have returned a year ago if I hadn't found that fire magic construct. Then I joined up with Tin and Garret here and . . . what's going on?"

Madi and Daniel had stopped walking and faced Emily and Garret. Orrin was behind the twosome, hoping this wasn't what he thought it was.

"Why didn't you tell us you were from Odrana?" Daniel asked. His voice held none of the restraint Madi's had. Being in front of him, Orrin realized for the first time the fear a [Hero] staring you down could bring.

"Why does it matter? Everybody is from somewhere." Emily shrugged and took another step forward. Daniel's sword swung out, and Emily's robes fluttered in front of her as she stopped on the spot.

"I think what Daniel is trying to say"—Madi spoke up, her hand gripping her extended spear but not pointing it yet—"is why would you not specifically state that you are from the country that recently tried to kidnap him?"

Emily's joyful nature that came out while explaining things retreated behind her cold and calculating gaze. Orrin felt her assess the distance between herself and the two in front of her. He even felt her attention fall on him a few steps behind her. Garret had wisely taken a large step to the side.

"I didn't think it worth mentioning because I'm a member of the Guild and live in Dey. I haven't been home in years and had nothing to do with the kidnapping of Daniel," Emily said, bending slowly and placing her staff on the ground. She raised her hands in the air, straightening in an exaggerated slowness. "I wasn't even certain that my country really was behind the kidnapping, despite hearing some rumors. If it is any consolation, I'm certain my family would have objected to anything of the sort."

"Your family? Ibarra . . . How did I miss that?" Madi took a deep breath. "I thought it sounded vaguely familiar. Didn't the Ibarra family support the Sanerris family when it took over Odrana? I didn't know your family was still around."

Emily frowned. "That's not exactly how it happened, but I don't think this is the time for a history lesson. Suffice it to say, right now my loyalty is to this party and the Guild. If I left the Guild and returned to my family, I wouldn't hold any position of power, nor would I be part of anything as pigheaded as kidnapping a [Hero]."

Daniel's eyes never left Emily. Garret and Madi waited patiently for whatever would play out.

Orrin caught the slight movement of his ever-present [Map] skill and cursed. "Whatever you're going to do, D, you better do it quick. We've got two groups of boars bearing down on us from either side."

Daniel lowered Gerty. He leaned forward and whispered something to Emily. The fire mage simply nodded once. She swooped down and picked up her staff, turning to Orrin.

"Which way?"

Orrin pointed to their left. "Two from that direction." He then pointed behind Daniel. "Three from there. They'll arrive first."

Emily glanced at Daniel. "I'll take the two on my own."

Daniel nodded and pointed at Garret. "You're with us. Try to take one down at least. Madi, blind as many as you can."

Orrin watched everybody move into action.

"What about me?"

Chapter 23

As Emily's hand began to glow bright red and Daniel, Madi, and Garret moved away, Orrin bristled at feeling useless once again. Nobody even thought to use his plan. He could have drawn one of the groups away and come running back. He could have drawn all five boars away and let the party continue deeper into the dungeon without being accosted.

"You always have to be the center of attention, don't you, D?" Orrin spoke aloud, but nobody was close enough to hear him. "Fuck this."

Orrin hit himself with five casts of [Increase Will] at the second level. Since his will was already at forty-three, the increase of two points became nine. His will increased to eighty-eight. He then cast two [Increase Dexterity] at level three for an increase of thirty-five per cast. He didn't reach a hundred, but ninety-four dexterity was close enough.

Orrin ran to Emily. "Don't be stupid," he yelled as he ran by her. "Go help the others. I'm going to drive these two off."

Emily shouted something at him, but Orrin was already moving away from her. He ran as fast as he could until he saw the two Steel Boars charging down at him. He summoned an [Ice Sword] and swung at the rightmost one as he drew close.

Moving as fast as he was going, Orrin badly miscalculated. He'd thought his sword would hit the boar and draw its attention. The plan had been to dart in and out, enraging the beasts, before leading them off on a merry chase until his [Map] showed him the party was ready to deal with the last two. Instead, Orrin learned what happens when two fast-moving objects collide.

The combination of his maxed-out dexterity, the momentum of the swing, and the boar's own motion sent shock waves of vibration up his arm. The sword exploded into small pieces of razor-sharp ice that quickly dissipated—but not before leaving dozens of cuts up his forearm and hand. Losing the sword didn't matter, as it only cost a single point of mana to summon. The sting of the cuts was bad but nothing he couldn't fight through; however, the vibration also shattered the bones in his arm and hand.

Orrin's scream of pain lasted only half a second before he triggered [Mind Bastion] and let the skill turn off the pathways to his brain that registered the hurt. Feeling the deep cold of logic seeping into every microdecision, he realized his growing resentment toward the minimal damage he could do in a fight had triggered his need to fight like somebody else.

I shouldn't be charging in like this. What was I thinking?

He checked his mana. Just over a hundred points after all the boosting and fighting they'd done. Orrin darted away from the mildly dazed boar he'd struck. The ringing of its metal body was proof it had taken damage, but probably nowhere as much as Orrin.

His right arm was a mess—his hand was cramped into a claw, and two of his fingers were bent in a way that made [Mind Bastion] clamp down on the bile rising in his stomach. His radius . . . or was it his ulna . . . whatever forearm bone it was had broken, and the white of the bone was sticking through the skin. He assessed the pain in his biceps muscle as well, not feeling it but knowing it was there. *A torn muscle, too?*

Using his left hand, he popped the top off one of the mana potions on his belt and downed it. As his mana pool refilled, he worked quickly.

First, a cast of [Heal Small Wounds] at the highest level he could do. It cost a little less than the normal twenty MP, but he cringed at the waste of usable mana against the Steel Boars. The bone in his arm sank back beneath the skin, and his two mangled fingers straightened with an audible *click*. He'd only reset the bones, not completely healed them. He could still feel his hand refusing to close into a full fist and his muscle felt tight, but he didn't have more time or mana to waste.

He cast an inversed [Increase Dexterity] on the boar he hadn't hit. It was almost upon him. It took two more spells before the front leg missed its step and it fell into a heap, sliding toward him.

Orrin stepped around the flailing beast and walked with deliberate steps toward the first boar. It was snorting and pawing the ground, about to charge again at the intruder that had rung its bell.

Three dexterity-reducing spells hit it before it could take a step. The drop in its coordination had it scrambling like a first-time skater on the ice. It fell with all four legs splayed out.

Orrin summoned another [Ice Sword] and went back to the other boar. He began lightly poking the monster with his left arm, keeping pressure off the freshly broken right. Small dents in the metal body appeared. Orrin checked its health and watched the slow drip of points being knocked off.

"This is going to take forever," he muttered. He struck the boar twice more before remembering his new skill.

> **[Toxic Touch]—your touch becomes toxic. MP cost variable to toxicity.**

His mana was low, but he could spare a few points to test out the skill. Reaching his right hand out, he fed five points of mana to the skill and felt a tingle along his fingertips. He brushed the cold metal of the boar, leaving deep-green fingerprints that faded away as he watched.

Orrin heard footsteps coming up behind him and fell into a crouch.

Emily was out of breath after trying to keep up with his sprint. She was also livid.

"Did you just break your arm?" she asked. "I heard you scream!"

Orrin switched back to his sword and poked the boar. He held his right arm up.

"A bit, yes. I went ahead and cured it, but it still hurts a bit. I'll need to heal it more later if I can."

Emily's eyes narrowed. "You're different. What's happening?"

"A skill I have. I needed it to turn off the pain. Don't tell Daniel."

Ding. Ding. Ding. He continued chipping away at the health of the prone boar.

Emily glanced at it. She put her hand on its head. The skin touching the boar glowed red, and she slagged the metal into its brain.

Experience Gained: 125 XP

"That wasn't nice," Orrin said stoically. "You stole half my experience."

"You need to fully heal your arm if you can," Emily said as she walked toward the other boar. "Don't waste your mana. We need to hurry back and help the others."

"I'll be okay."

Emily stopped and swung back around. Her eyes smoldered. "Heal yourself now, Orrin. Don't make me ask again."

Orrin reasoned that he'd already done damage to both boars and letting her finish them off would be quicker. Wasting his dwindling mana for some pain didn't seem like the best use of his remaining magic, though.

"I'm going to head back and help them," Orrin announced. "You've got this one, right?"

Orrin felt her movement. Before gaining [Way of the Water], the quick grab by Emily would have stopped him in his tracks. With it, he spun, took her outstretched wrist, and bobbed under with a turn. He held her pinned against his chest with her arm twisted behind her, his sword against her chin.

"Be very still," Orrin demanded. "What was that?"

Emily took a breath and released it in a huff. "You know I can cover my entire body in fire, right?"

"Before I push my sword up into your brain? I don't think so."

"What is wrong with you? Did you get hit in the head? If you don't heal your arm completely, it might not set right. Why aren't you listening?"

Orrin's brain changed gears, and he pushed her away a step, releasing his hold on her. "What do you mean? I did heal the breaks, I already told you that."

Emily turned with the utmost care, moving slowly and keeping her arms wide. She had dropped her staff when he grabbed her, and she made no move to retrieve it. "Orrin, you told me your arm is hurting and you're blocking the pain. That means something is still wrong in your arm. If you don't heal it completely, it could set wrong or leave you broken. How do you have a healing spell and not know about the time limits for fixing the body?"

"What time limit?"

Emily gave a tight frown before answering. "If somebody is hurt badly enough, you only have a small window of time to heal them. It's why Lord Catanzano is still in a wheelchair and why some people have permanent injuries. You can't seriously not know this. What kind of backwater town did you grow up in that you didn't have a healer?"

Orrin examined his body. Using [Analyze] with [Mind Bastion] running gave him more information than he'd ever gotten before. He didn't just see the normal screen of [Identify] or the slight progress for his mana regeneration that he'd developed.

He saw much more.

[Mind Bastion] kept him focused on what mattered, and he tore his eyes from the data flowing in to focus on the abnormal status of his arm.

> **Status: biceps tendon tear; multiple transverse fractures to ulna, metacarpal, and carpal bones (set without union); compound fracture to radius (set without union).**

Orrin weighed the data and nodded at Emily. He then cast two more [Heal Small Wounds] on himself, double-checking after both until the tear and fractures were gone.

"I didn't know. Sorry for all that," he said, waving his hand to encompass the scuffle.

Emily kept an eye on him as she turned and drilled her hand through the prone boar's head.

Experience Gained: 125 XP

"We are going to have a talk later," Emily promised. "A long one. Too much of your knowledge is incomplete."

"Sounds good." Orrin didn't really care about later. "We need to get back to the others. All three of their boars are still up."

Emily didn't say another word as they raced back. Well, Emily raced. Orrin tried his best to control the urge to leave her behind again. He thought about increasing her stats to the point she could keep up and letting her deal with the consequences, but wasting a few minutes now was better than a full day or more for her to recover from the side effects of overbuffing.

Garret had taken down one of the three Steel Boars before they arrived. The prone beast looked more like a metal porcupine. Emily splashed a wave of fire between the remaining two, keeping them from rushing an exhausted Daniel at once. He gave a nod to her before dashing off to swat one of them. Orrin cast a [Lightstrike] at each remaining enemy before slowing down the one trying to edge around Emily's wall of fire. His mana was absurdly low at this point, but he could always blood cycle if he needed to.

No.

Orrin shook his head. He would replenish his mana before they moved on. It might be easier to use [Blood Mana] and then heal himself back up. He could do it a few times, probably up to six full mana pools . . . well, not his current, boosted pool, but at least his normal, nonboosted amount that—

No!

Orrin slapped his face and took a deep breath. He released [Mind Bastion] and screamed as the delayed pain hit him. His arm was healed, but the nerves in his body were still messaging his brain that something was wrong. He used the last of the mana he was willing to spare to send another [Heal Small Wounds] coursing through his body.

Experience Gained: 100 XP

"Orrin? Are you all right?"

Orrin could hear Daniel talking to him, but he kept his eyes closed as the cold feeling of the skill left him. He kicked himself at his stupidity. Did he even mean to trigger [Mind Bastion] or was it going to automatically pop up anytime the pain was bad enough?

"He's been acting weird," Emily whispered to Daniel.

His friend approached him and put a hand on his back.

"O? You can drop it now. We got them all."

"I already did. Broke my arm. Pain's almost gone."

Daniel waited quietly, never moving his hand from Orrin.

As soon as the pain was gone, Orrin checked his status. He sucked in a breath.

"Are you okay?" Madi asked, stepping closer. "I've got a health potion if you—"

Orrin shook his head. "I'm fine. Better than fine, actually. Something happened when I . . . well, I guess . . . Do you remember how when I tried to use [Analyze] before on my mana usage, I'd get question marks for how much I could do a day? Well, I used it while running [Mind Bastion] and . . . this is just easier to show you."

Orrin grabbed the relevant portion of his status screen and threw it to Madi and Daniel.

Mana Maximum: 380 (530)

Mana Potion Usable: 3/4
Blood Cycle: 0/1,520

"I think I did it," Orrin squeaked. "That's how much mana I can use before it kills me!"

Chapter 24

Daniel and Madi knew how much Orrin's accomplishment meant to him. Not only would the knowledge of how much mana he could safely use give him access to more buffing for the team, but he'd be less likely to hurt himself again.

Daniel's smile turned sour as he glanced over Orrin's back and saw Emily. She was studying Orrin with her head cocked to the side.

"Orrin, let's table this for now."

"But now I ca—"

Daniel glared at his friend, cutting him off. "Later. Are there any more boars directly in front of us?"

Orrin checked his [Map]. The party had already moved past the biggest group of boars, and only two pairs remained between them and the exit. Orrin relayed the information.

"We could continue straight on and try to thread the needle between the last four, but I can't predict how they'll move," Orrin explained. "I think it might be smarter to hit one group and travel around the edge."

Daniel nodded. "That's what we'll do, then."

"How much mana do you have left, Orrin?" Emily asked.

She and Garret had stood apart from the threesome as they were talking. Her question prompted Orrin to check his full status again.

"Shit. I'm really low."

"You don't get to ask questions," Daniel said, pointing Gertrude at the fire mage. "We are going to have a talk about your country in the next safe room."

Emily shrugged, completely disinterested. "You're going to be angry at me no matter what I say. That doesn't mean I won't continue to look out for the team. He used a lot of magic to take down the boars back there. He also was acting without any self-interest while under the effects of some sort of pain-dampening spell or skill. If we are going to go into another fight, I think we should all know what's going on."

"Orrin doesn't have to answer anythi—"

Madi placed her hand on Daniel's arm. "Daniel, she does have a point. They don't know Orrin like we do, and he is low on mana."

"I could take another potion," Orrin offered.

"How did you take down the boars so quickly?" Emily saw an opening and questioned him. "Did you use [Inverse] and [Increase Strength] until they couldn't carry their own weight? Or did you use [Inverse] and [Increase Dexterity] so they couldn't move their legs? Do you try to see which will be most cost-effective before you cast the spells?"

Orrin was sure she would have continued her line of questioning if Garret hadn't pulled her away from the group and had some very animated but quiet words with her. His hands slashed through the air multiple times until she huffed and stomped farther away from the group.

"Sorry about her," Garret said with his easy smile, sauntering back to the three of them. "She gets into her learning mode and doesn't know when to stop."

Garret stopped just outside Daniel's striking range, a fact that did not go unnoticed by anyone, and tried to appear humble . . . as humble as the provocative man could, anyway.

"I know you don't trust us. I get why. Just remember, though, while we are in here, we have each other's backs. Emily might be . . . Emily, but she is loyal to a fault. I've never seen her shirk her duty or not give it her all, so maybe give her a break for not telling you she's from Odrana. At least until you all can have a nice chat. Preferably while I'm sleeping."

The archer spun on his heel and moved back to Emily. He affably put his hand over her shoulder, and she promptly elbowed him hard . . . twice.

Daniel took a steadying breath. "How is your mana? Do you need a potion?"

"I can take one if I need to, but I might just leave the fight up to you guys. No use wasting a potion if we're going to have a chance to rest in a few minutes anyways. I can always cast a spell or two in an emergency," Orrin assured them both.

"Madi, can I talk with you? I . . . I think it might be better for you to ask Emily some questions. I'm getting too angry every time I look at her. She wasn't there. She probably had no part in any of that shit, but still . . ."

Orrin cast a spell, and Daniel's shoulders sagged as the stress and rage faded from his mind.

Daniel quirked an eyebrow. "Did you just cast your calm spell on me?"

Orrin smiled. "I think it's worth it."

Emily and Garret had something to prove as they attacked the final two boars standing in their way to the next floor. Garret rained down outsized stone arrows that slowed down their charge as Emily hurled boulders of fire at the monsters. Working in tandem, they reduced one beast to ash before the second reached Daniel's swinging metal. Five minutes after, the group fell into the safe room, having successfully cleared another floor of the dungeon.

Orrin was setting up the portable heater again. Madi and Emily were arguing in a corner of the room while Daniel stood by passively. Orrin hit the switch and felt the gentle warmth spreading off the cube. He felt Garret approach.

"Think they'll get over it?" he asked, pointing to the rest of the party.

Orrin shrugged and turned to the handsome man. He hadn't realized how close Garret had gotten. He gazed up, hesitating for a second before answering.

"Imagine you were kidnapped and tied up to be delivered like a prize to Odrana. You escaped but then found out someone you were working with was from there but didn't tell you. How would you feel?"

Garret's lip pulled up into a half smile. "It would depend on how well I was tied up."

Orrin rolled his eyes. Garret had been making jokes about everything since they started off from Dey. While he didn't mind the attention from the attractive man, his inability to take anything seriously had put a damper on any other feelings.

Orrin still felt conflicted. Back on Earth, he'd pined after Daniel's sister for years. He was beginning to realize it might have started when they were younger, when she'd paid slightly more attention to him than anyone else he'd known. He knew Garret's reputation. Emily was not averse to telling him off regularly. Orrin had watched him make passes at everyone in the party—except Emily. He guessed, though, that Garret had tried in the past and Emily had told him exactly what would happen if he tried again.

He liked the attention and the feeling in his chest when Garret gazed longingly at him. However, he was beginning to think Garret wasn't a one-person kind of guy.

"Does it always have to be a joke?" Orrin whispered, turning away. "They'll work it out. I need some rest."

Garret didn't respond and left, moving to a free corner to set up his camping bag. Orrin felt something in him twist. He'd half hoped Garret would respond with something real instead of more innuendo. Silence was somehow worse and better at the same time.

Daniel blew air through his nostrils as he stomped over to Orrin. He threw his own camping bag down and sat on the floor.

"Madi says I have to be nice. Emily's fine," he said, the anger in his voice palpable.

"You seem really happy with that," Orrin commented, sitting down next to him.

Daniel closed his eyes and took multiple steadying breaths. He opened his eyes after a minute.

"I'm not, but that's just my own anger at Odrana, not at her specifically. I can't avoid the entire country and all its people just because of a few dickheads. I still think she should have told us up front, though."

Orrin pulled a few apples and a lump of cheese from his [Dimension Hole], breaking off a piece and handing it to his friend. "Maybe she should have."

Daniel narrowed his eyes and glanced sideways at Orrin. "I'm not forgetting that you ran off and did something stupid again. I'm pissed at you, too."

"Understandable." Orrin took out a knife and cut his apple into slices.

Daniel threw up his arms. "What is going on with you? One-word answers and agreeing with me on everything. What is this?"

"Just reflecting." He offered the knife to Daniel.

Daniel snatched the blade and chopped his apple into broken bits. He stared at the mess on the floor and then pointed the knife at Orrin.

"You think I was unfair to her. You think I'm lashing out because I was powerless against her country when they tried to kidnap me, don't you?"

Orrin used [Calm Mind] on Daniel for the second time in the last few hours. He waited until his friend's heavy breathing stilled. He also waved off Madi, who was still talking to Emily but had taken a few steps toward them upon Daniel's outburst.

Orrin took his own deep breath. "Do you remember our big fight? When we were clearing out those rat dens."

Daniel was dazed at the double whammy of the spell sapping his built-up anger and Orrin's recalling of their fight. He simply nodded.

"You called me a creep for liking your sister or something like that. I never really told you that I liked her, did I?" Orrin didn't wait for a response. "When my dad left and I started hanging out with you two more, I was still really depressed. You both did your best to cheer me up. Of course, you still had soccer practice or whatever it was you were doing, and your parents would bring you to all that. Sometimes, I'd sit on my front steps waiting for you to get back . . . or maybe I was waiting for my dad to come back . . . I don't know. Anyways, Zoe used to come sit with me. She'd talk about . . . Honestly, I don't remember what she'd talk about, but she'd keep me from sinking farther into myself."

Orrin put the knife back into his pocket, feeling his skill make it disappear to wherever these things were stored.

"I think that's why I liked her so much. She paid attention to me. She was there for me when I had nobody else. My mom was working more, and now that I'm starting to grow up a bit, I see that she was depressed, too. That doesn't matter right now, though. I'm saying that I never really thought I was being too obvious. I never really thought about how that must have been for you. I'm sorry."

Daniel sat quietly through Orrin's speech. When he finished, he spoke. "What happened? Why are you saying this stuff?"

Orrin nudged his shoulder against Daniel. "I just realized that I don't need to be infatuated with every person who pays me a little bit of attention. I also realized that somewhere along the way, I'd forgotten who my first friend was. The guy who dragged me out of my house in the first place. So, if he feels slighted because somebody did something, I'm going to be on his side. Rule number two, remember? We are a team."

Daniel smiled and lightly punched Orrin. Then, he slowly processed Orrin's words and glanced at Garret. Emily had made her way over to the archer, and they were chatting. Madi came over and sat by the boys.

"What are you two doing?"

Orrin smiled at her and handed her the third apple he'd pulled out. "Growing up a bit. How'd it go?"

Madi accepted the food. "She understands why we're mad but essentially didn't care enough to tell us. She was worried we wouldn't let her come along on the dungeon run and thought the risk outweighed the reward. She did apologize to Daniel and swore she'd use her contacts to find out as much as she can about the kidnapping attempt. So, at least we have a lead."

"That's not too bad, then." Orrin popped the last of the apple into his mouth. "Did we set watch shifts yet? I'm almost out of mana and need a quick nap."

"Go ahead and sleep," Daniel said softly. "I've got you."

"Thanks, D."

Madi watched them both during the exchange. She smiled.

Chapter 25

Orrin groaned as something tapped his shoulder.

"Leave me alone," he mumbled into his blanket.

"It's your shift."

Orrin opened one eye to glare at Madi. She smirked and raised her hands.

"Fine."

A quick glance at his status showed that his mana was fully replenished. Emily was settling herself down in the corner, so she must have been the other component of the all-girl watch shift. Since both the other men were asleep, Orrin figured he was on the last shift. The final watch of the night would be a single person, who would be responsible for starting breakfast each day. The extra work was the downside to getting to rest first and not having to wake up in the middle of the night for your turn.

Orrin sat near the heat cube and played with the skill store tab. It was something he'd been doing more and more, trying to read through different skills and spells. When he got bored of reading the descriptions, he'd switch over to the miscellaneous tab and start in on the random items that were generally regarded as not worth the points.

Once a few hours had passed, he put a pan over the heater and began to boil some water. Pulling a small device from his [Dimension Hole], he reverently placed the boxy item on the ground before pulling a small bag from his pocket. He took a handful of what was inside and placed it into the cylindrical funnel on the device. With a twist, he popped out a small wooden bracket from the box and began to turn the crank. A popping sound cracked across the room before dipping into a steady grind as the bag's contents were pulverized. Orrin tried to gauge how fine the powder became, but he was hardly an expert yet. He pushed the bracket back into the box with a small click and waited for the water to be done. While he waited, he pulled an assortment of breads and fruits out of his storage. When the water was ready, he had a small continental breakfast ready for the party.

He took out the single most important tool for the dungeon delve and tapped the powder into it. Holding the pan carefully, he poured the boiling liquid into the glass canister. As the water hit the ground beans, he savored the aroma that followed.

He tried to put the lid on quickly, but the smell permeated the room and people began to wake up to the wonderful smell of freshly brewed coffee.

"Are you kidding me?" Madi said in mock outrage.

"It's a necessity," Orrin answered. "Well, for some of us. You don't have to have any if you don't wa—"

"I never said that."

Orrin chuckled as he watched the party wake. Emily blinked with overexaggerated movements, trying to clear the sleep from her eyes. Daniel stretched against the wall before standing up and helping himself to the food. Garret turned over and went back to sleep.

Emily noticed Orrin's pursed lips. "He's not a morning person, but he'll be ready to go."

When the coffee was ready, Orrin pushed the plunger that strained the coffee grounds to the bottom of the golden liquid. He poured himself a small cup and sipped before letting out a contented sigh.

"You bring any sugar for that?" Daniel asked.

Orrin put on a face of horror. "Oh no! I completely forgot the sugar. How are we going to survive?"

Daniel frowned and threw a croissant at him. The pastry hit his shoulder. Orrin grabbed it off the floor and saluted Daniel with his freshly obtained breakfast.

"Thanks, friend."

After they'd eaten their fill, Orrin cleaned up the mess by shoving everything left over in his [Dimension Hole]. Daniel relented and sipped a cup of black coffee, wincing with each mouthful.

Orrin waited until everyone was awake to cast [Utility Ward] and [Ward] on each member of the party. Garret grumbled something as he drank the dregs of the coffee and ate half an orange.

"Everybody ready?" Madi asked, trying to get them in the right frame of mind.

Nobody responded.

"I'll go through first," Daniel said. "Madi and Emily follow. Garret and Orrin, behind them."

He didn't wait and ducked into the doorway. Madi threw an apologetic look back and hustled through after him.

"This is going to be a long trip, isn't it?" Emily sighed and stepped in, too.

"Do we have time for more coffee?" Garret asked Orrin. "They'll be fine for a few minutes, right?"

His smile, which had once been so enchanting, was suddenly disagreeable. Orrin shook his head and headed to the doorway.

He stepped through.

And began to drown.

The group had discussed the possibility of underwater rooms and come prepared. Such floors weren't all too rare in dungeons, especially with a water persuasion, and each of them had a few water-breathing potions ready to deploy if needed. The biggest problem was knowing if it was needed beforehand.

The problem that Orrin was facing right now.

He'd forgotten to take a breath before stepping through and knew he didn't have enough time to fully analyze what was going on. Nobody was close enough in the murky water, and even if they were, he wouldn't be able to communicate with them in any meaningful way.

He reached for his belt and began fumbling with the cache of potions he'd strapped on his hip. Luckily, he'd separated out the water-breathing potions far enough to the side that he was able to pinpoint which one he needed immediately. He disconnected one from the holder and had it halfway to his lips when Garret stepped through behind him, jostling him.

The potion slipped from his fingers and sank into the darkness below him.

Orrin willed the potion to lift back up into his hand. His chest began to burn with the need to breathe. Precious seconds wasted, he scratched at his belt for another potion in a panic.

Long tentacles surrounded him, and something pressed against his mouth. Orrin screamed as the monster attacked, barely noticing the water that filled his lungs when he opened his lips. He took a lungful of air and screamed again, bubbles rising in the water.

Took a lungful of air . . .

Garret's arms . . . the tentacles . . . retracted from around him. The archer was downing his own potion, having fed one to Orrin first. He gave a thumbs-up to Orrin and pointed above them. With a kick of his legs, Garret swam toward the ball of light blinking merrily through the water.

Orrin took another moment to steady himself and dog-paddled up after the man who may have just saved his life.

About fifty feet up, his head broke the waterline, and he felt a cool breeze against his face. Everybody was waiting, Madi's lights blinking like a beacon and illuminating the area all around them. They were treading water in the middle of an ocean, or at least a lake without edges they could currently see. Stars twinkled above them, with no moonlight to dim their shine.

"T-thank you," Orrin sputtered. "If you hadn't . . ."

Garret smiled languidly. "You'd have done the same."

"What happened?" Madi asked.

"I forgot to take a breath, fumbled my potion, and Garret had to force-feed me one of his. I thought I was going to drown."

"You idiot," Daniel cursed. "Do I need to remind everyone to take a deep breath on each floor? I thought we'd gone over this."

Madi splashed water into Daniel's face. "Not the time. Orrin, can you open your [Map] and check if there are any monsters around? I'm not liking the odds here."

Orrin pulled open his display but forgot to tread water and sank below the waves before surfacing again. He checked and sighed. "No monsters, but there are a few hidden treasures on this floor. The door is that way," he said, pointing.

"I vote that we get out of here as soon as possible," Emily offered, struggling to keep afloat in her robes. "Most of my magic is next to useless here."

"I'm with Emily," Garret chimed in. "Using my bow underwater greatly reduces my damage."

"No arguments from me," Daniel said. Gertrude was strapped to his back, and he had to throw his body forward into each small wave from being toppled backward by the weight. "Orrin, can you lead the way?"

They swam for five minutes. Five minutes of fighting the small waves that constantly battered them and pushed them away from their destination. Orrin's muscles burned, and he found himself longing for the days of running.

He stopped and pointed down. "The door is down there."

Daniel nodded and dived, the weight of his sword helping him drop faster than the rest of the party. Orrin followed as each member also began the descent back into the dark water. His potion still worked, having been promised to last up to four hours. He gulped in water like it was air, and bubbles floated past his face.

At the bottom, Orrin saw the doorway. Daniel and Emily were making frantic hand gestures. Madi was swimming toward the surface again. Garret arrived before Orrin and pushed his way past the two, reaching for the door. His hand slapped against nothing and he fell through, landing on the ocean floor.

Daniel pointed up and kicked off the ground. Emily reached down to pull Garret to his feet. The three swam back to the top.

"It's inactive, isn't it?" Orrin asked once everyone was treading water again. "The door."

"Yep," Daniel spat. "It's got little divots in the sides. Three of them. Fucking MacGuffins."

"Three holes to put something and three hidden traps or treasure on the [Map]."

Garret punched the water. "How is anyone supposed to survive this without a mapping skill? This is unfair."

"It's a new dungeon," Madi explained. "Most of the floors like this in other dungeons are well mapped out through trial and error. We're lucky we have Orrin to point us toward the keys to this door. It's not all that uncommon. I will admit, the constant need to swim and fear of drowning is not ideal."

"If the rest of you drink a potion, we don't have to worry about that," Orrin pointed out. He pulled up his [Map] and tried figuring out the best path to the three hidden marks. "We could walk along the ocean floor even."

"Let's not waste our potions if we don't have to," Daniel ordered. "Unless someone gets really tired, try to save them for the rest of the floors. We don't know if there is another floor like this, but with monsters."

Madi groaned. "You had to say it. Now a floor will be covered in water and filled with monsters for sure."

Orrin waved them on and began to swim. The three marks on his [Map] were far enough away from the doorway to the next floor that finding them without his skill would have been a nightmare. The first was only a quarter mile away, but that was swimming against the waves that seemed to turn against them no matter the direction they picked.

"Down." Orrin pointed, barely able to make a sound. "There."

Daniel wasted no time and dived. Emily, Garret, and Madi followed immediately. Orrin spread his arms and floated on his back, letting the waves carry him as he rested.

"Orrin," Daniel shouted from a few yards away. "Get back here."

He held his hand in the air, something clasped tight in his fist. A pearl.

"There was a clam the size of a horse. I tried to pry it open, but Emily just burned a hole right through the shell. This was inside."

Orrin double-checked the [Map]. Sure enough, one of the dots was gone.

He sighed. "The second one is half a mile that way. The other is way on the other side of the door. We're going to be doing a lot of swimming."

Nobody was excited, but they soldiered on with determination. After retrieving the second pearl, they all spent a few minutes resting, floating on their backs. Orrin pulled a rope from his storage and they all held on tight so as not to float away.

"You know, if you ignore the fact that we're in a dungeon designed to kill us, in a huge body of water that's fighting against our every movement . . . the sky is very pretty," Orrin said, his hand closed around the end of the rope.

"I'd rather have dry land," Emily responded quickly. "Although I will admit the stars are nice to look at."

"They're almost as pretty as your eyes," Garret murmured, moving his hand up the rope.

Orrin couldn't even see whom he was hitting on. What he did see was Emily pushing Garret's head underwater as Madi and Daniel laughed.

Chapter 26

After obtaining the final pearl and swimming back to the door, they'd all tumbled out into the safe room between floors. Daniel complained they had only made it through three floors, and Madi had to soothe his fears that they were traveling slowly.

"We've only slept once," she pointed out. "Time is murky down here, but if we count it like that, we've only spent a day and a half. It takes a normal team that long to get through one floor. We are making amazing time."

Garret and Emily nodded along. Everyone but Emily was changing into dry clothes after the prolonged swim—Emily simply used a spell and her robes were warmed and dry.

"Could you use that on us?" Madi asked hopefully.

"If you don't mind a sunburn. It literally burns the skin. I have a passive skill that protects me from it."

Orrin pulled on a dry shirt. "You know, if I got a [Fire Ward], I'm sure that would protect us. Then you could do that clothes-dryer thingy on us."

Madi flicked him in the head. "You are not wasting ability points. Stop."

Daniel grinned at somebody else getting hit.

The party rested for an hour at Madi's behest. The constant swimming had taken more out of them than they'd first imagined. But soon enough, Daniel was giving them marching orders and everyone lined up for the fourth floor.

"We've had a poison, water, and steel level, so we could see any of them again, but most likely we'll have a combination of two or even three," Emily informed them. "The deeper we go, the stronger the monsters will be, too. We were really lucky the last floor didn't have anything we had to fight off. It was too easy, to be honest."

"If we didn't have Orrin, how long do you think we'd be swimming around?" Daniel asked. "I think that floor would break most parties."

Emily chewed her lip. "You might be right, but only for the first few groups. Once somebody figured it out, everybody would learn the fastest path through. We've got the dangerous job of being first, but Orrin did save us days of swimming around."

Orrin's neck warmed.

"He's blushing," Garret said with a smirk. "I didn't think he could be any cuter. Ow!"

Emily pulled back a burning hand from Garret's side. "I've warned you already."

Garret mumbled something but didn't respond aloud.

They entered in the same order again. Orrin remembered to take a deep breath this time before he stepped through.

Darkness.

"Hello?" he whispered.

"Over here," Madi said, casting one of her butterflies of light into the air. It hovered over their heads for a moment. Then something struck it so fast it disintegrated.

"Every time . . ." Madi complained.

Orrin felt Garret appear behind him.

"Anybody have a light?" he asked.

"Every time Madi or Emily tries a spell, something attacks the light," Daniel said from a few feet away. Orrin hadn't even seen him. The darkness was so complete that he could wave his hands in front of his eyes and see nothing.

"I've got some torches we could try," Orrin volunteered. "Or should we just try to use my [Map]?"

"Map."

"Sure, grab a torch."

"I don't like this."

The voices all talked over each other, leaving Orrin with no clear indication of what to do. Making his own decision, he pulled two torches from his [Dimension Hole].

"Emily, a little fire here, please?"

The fire mage snapped her fingers, letting the spark she generated light the area for a moment. Seeing the proffered torches, she snapped again near one. It went up in flame immediately.

Orrin crouched low, holding the torch way above his head. He waited.

Nothing happened.

"You look stupid," Daniel said, walking into the small circle of light and holding his hand out. "Give me the other one."

Orrin handed the second torch to Daniel. His friend tapped the two together, lighting his own. Orrin pulled up his [Map].

"That's new."

"Hmm?" Daniel grunted.

"My [Map]. It's only showing the immediate area we're in. I can't zoom out. All I see is a circle with four of us in it. Wait. Who's missing?" Orrin twirled in a tight loop, searching.

Daniel was right next to him, holding the other torch. Madi, Emily, and Garret were nearby. Nobody was missing. Orrin looked again and glanced back up.

"Garret, step more into the light," he demanded.

The archer took a tentative step forward, and Orrin sighed in relief.

"Everyone stick close to me. If you go too far into the darkness, I can't find you. Lucky for us there are no monsters here, huh?"

Of course, that's when the monsters attacked.

"You just had to say it," Daniel yelled as he swung Gertrude overhead. He missed the small speck of darkness that careened into the halo of light illuminated by Orrin's flame.

The other four party members were standing in a loose circle around Orrin. Daniel had dropped his torch to the ground when the too-fast-to-see black monster struck him in the side. Madi and

Emily were doing their best to send spells out, but so far nobody had hit anything.

"I can only say I'm sorry so many times."

Two quick somethings came in from opposite directions. One tried to hit Orrin's flame, and the other struck at Daniel again. Orrin tried to get an [Identify] off in time but couldn't connect the thought to the monster. The skill had always triggered near instantaneously, but the quickness of the monsters was too much.

"Madi, send off as many light spells as you can in that direction," Emily ordered. "Garret and Daniel, attack that space on the count of three. Ready?"

At her barked-out three count, Emily and Madi sent flames and butterflies of different colors away from the group. Garret sent multiple arrows out in a torrent, and Daniel swung Gertrude side to side with a speed that defied the giant sword's mass.

Garret's arrow found purchase as a bat-like creature swallowed a butterfly. Gertrude changed direction midswing and cleaved the monster in two. Half a body, with no head but a still-twitching wing, slid in a gory runway to land by Madi's feet.

Shrieking from every direction rained upon the party.

Orrin pulled up [Identify] on the corpse.

Darkeater Bat

"What's a Darkeater Bat?"

"No clue," Garret responded, turning his bow from target to target. He was shooting into the dark, using the cries of the monsters to try and do damage.

"Darkness creatures? That's not good. That's really, really not good." Emily stopped sending gouts of flames into the ether. "Fire is useless against creatures of darkness, and they'll eat up any of Madi's light magic. We need to get off this floor."

Orrin finished replenishing [Ward] on Daniel. He picked up the second torch and held them both high above his head. "Which direction, D?"

Daniel wiped sweat from the back of his neck and pointed his sword. Without another word, the group moved slowly but with determination. Unspoken, the strategy was clear: Orrin, as the weakest link, would hold the light above them while Daniel and Madi took point. Madi had stopped using her magic and extended her spear. She wasn't fast enough to hit any of the bats, but waving it in one direction at least discouraged them from attacking.

Moving through the darkness, Orrin kept watch on the [Wards] he'd placed on everybody and checked on his [Map] regularly. Except for the swift-moving dot of an already-retreating Darkeater Bat, he saw nothing new.

"That's the third time I've seen one of those stones," Daniel shouted over his shoulder. "Orrin, what are they?"

"What is what?"

Madi shifted and took a step back, dropping to her knee. She patted the ground. "He's talking about this. The flagstone is different."

Orrin couldn't make out any difference at all, which he told her.

Garret reached down and touched the block that looked the same as every block around it. "You're right. I can't duplicate this—it's magical."

"A puzzle in the darkness?" Emily asked. Madi nodded.

"Will somebody explain what is going on?" Orrin begged.

Daniel swung too late at a bat. It crashed into Orrin's left arm. He felt the claws scratch his forearm but do no damage to him. His [Ward] was nearly cut in half, but he topped it off.

"Destroy it? Stand on it? Pull it out of the ground?" Madi and Emily made suggestions while Garret and Daniel continued the fight.

Orrin just stood in the middle of a sea of darkness, waving his two fire sticks like he was directing air traffic and feeling like an idiot that he still couldn't see what was different about this particular stone.

"Orrin, can you bring us back the same way we came?" Madi asked him.

The [Map] still showed darkness around them, but the path they'd traveled was a lighter gray. They'd yet to hit the other wall, or any wall, so he still didn't know if they were in an alley or a large room. He was praying it wasn't anything as spacious as the ocean floor had been.

He nodded his head backward. "That way."

"All right, listen up," Madi instructed. "Emily is going to stay here, and we are going to move back to the last stone. We are going to run for it. If nothing happens at that stone, we are going to leave Garret at that one. We're going to try touching the stones together. Emily doesn't think we can dig them out of the floor. Any questions?"

Orrin gaped at Madi. "I've got a hundred questions. Split the team? That's insane."

Madi smirked. "It's nice to be the one with a plan. I'm normally you in this situation. Move out."

Daniel barreled into Orrin, pushing him forward . . . or backward. Orrin only saw Emily for a moment before the darkness swallowed her.

"I could have left a torch for her," he tried to say, but nobody heard him as they ran. He swung his arm to the side when they went off target, until Madi stopped and pointed out . . . a slightly darker rock.

Orrin could almost see it. The stone path around them was a dark gray, but one of the pieces of the flooring was a light black instead. If that made any sense.

"Garret, you stand on this, and we'll move to the next one if nothing happ—"

Garret stepped on the block, and something did happen.

The bats went crazy.

Before, only a handful at a time would swoop in. But now Garret had to cover his head with his arms as dozens began to rain down on him.

"Run to the next one," Madi yelled as she darted off into the darkness.

Orrin threw another [Ward] on the archer and tried to keep up with Madi. He kept shouting directions to keep her on track. He didn't spare a second glance to see if Daniel was behind him. He had to trust Madi and whatever plan she had.

"Where is it?" he heard her chanting over and over as they moved away from Garret.

She slid along the floor and stomped her foot on a black stone. Orrin was sure he could tell the difference now.

"Oh, shit," Daniel muttered from behind him.

Orrin glanced back and saw Daniel had fallen well behind. The halo from the fire was too small, and Daniel was well outside it. But he was still visible. Once Madi had stepped on the third block, the darkness became only dimness. Now that he thought about it, Orrin was sure he'd been able to see a little more into the darkness after Garret's block, too.

They'd lit up the cavernous room enough to make out each other. Orrin could see a shape farther away that he was quite sure was Garret.

"We did it! We can see each other now," Orrin cheered. Then he followed Daniel's gaze up to the ceiling. Hundreds of Darkeater Bats hung upside down, blinking down at them. Most appeared to be waking up from a deep and restful sleep.

"Oh, shit."

Chapter 27

"Orrin, I want you to focus on healing me and keeping that [Ward] up," Daniel said as the bats began lazily moving their wings. "Drink a potion or two if you need to, but try and keep yourself from cycling. You know how I feel about it."

"Daniel, what are you doing?" Madi asked. His sword held up in the air, the [Hero] was focusing intently on something.

"I think it's about time that I see what this class can really do." Daniel smirked over his shoulder and nodded at Orrin. "Boost me to the max."

Orrin had replenished their [Utility Ward] when they had woken up but had refrained from overboosting anyone. Daniel and he were the only two who could get away with that kind of short-term boosting, and it wasn't worth it . . . most of the time.

He started spending his mana. First, he capped his own intelligence and wisdom with a few of his normal spells. That made the costs cheaper when he slapped all four on Daniel: intelligence, wisdom, dexterity, and strength.

The first bats dropped off their perch and began winging their way toward the trio.

Orrin double-checked Daniel's [Ward] and gave him a thumbs-up. "You've got this."

Daniel disappeared.

With his combination of the fast-moving [Shooting Star] skill that let him move in bursts of speed so fast he looked like he was rapidly teleporting and [Gravity Strike], his powerful fight-ender,

Daniel bounced between targets with a vengeance. By the time any monsters made it to Orrin and Madi, dozens of corpses already littered the dimly lit room.

"Orrin, this can't be the solution. There's always a way through," Madi yelled as she swung her spear at a swooping bat. She scored a cut along its torso, and it leaked its dark blood as it cried in pain and flew away.

"If you have any ideas, now would be a good time," Orrin shouted back. He tried casting a few [Lightstrike] spells before summoning an [Ice Sword]. He spotted a cluster of bats and threw his sword. It flipped end over end as it sailed through the air . . . missing the group of monsters completely.

"Did you mean to miss that badly?"

"Shut up, they cost nothing to summon."

Orrin found Daniel stopped and spinning like a top. Gertrude found flesh with every revolution. He topped off his friend's [Ward] and went back to throwing [Ice Swords].

"Give me a few of those," Madi demanded. The bats had started flying directly at Daniel.

"That bastard," Orrin said as he realized why the bats weren't targeting them. "He's using his [Gravity Well] and making them attack only him."

Orrin and Madi lobbed swords at the bats, getting the occasional dings from the system that indicated they had finished off a monster, which they both ignored. Orrin kept the [Ward] up on his friend the best he could but eventually had to start healing him as well. Even with the mountain of corpses surrounding him, Orrin counted hundreds more. In the distance, Garret was sending arrows up into the swarm above Daniel with such frequency that it looked more like a rope leaving his bow and connecting to the mass of monsters.

"Emily's going to be pissed. She's missing out on all the fun," Orrin quipped. He chucked another sword, nicking two but not killing either.

"She doesn't have anything that really hurts them," Madi grunted as she threw another sword. Orrin had just started summon-dumping them on the ground between them. "Neither do I, for that matter."

Daniel's spell ended, and small groups of bats peeled off from the main cluster. Orrin could see the frustration on his face as he yelled something, but the shrieking of the bats drowned him out.

As five bats descended on them, Orrin took a stance in front of Madi. She had her spear extended, ready to provide backup.

Orrin's first swing was perfect. For once, he used his momentum correctly, pivoting on his heel and bringing the blade down in a beautiful arc. The icy blade was sharp and true, splitting two of the bats in half. The warm, dark blood splashed against his face. He didn't realize he was screaming defiantly until the coppery tang hit his tongue.

Orrin bent over and threw up, missing the next three Darkeater Bats. Madi sliced one with her spear, and it veered away. She stabbed a second full-on in the face, impaling it on her weapon. The weight of the bat caused her center to drift, and the third bat landed on her with a furious shriek of talons and teeth.

Orrin wiped his mouth, smearing the vomit on his cloak. He tried to find an angle to hit the bat without risking hitting Madi, but her furious laughter at being shredded was . . .

Laughter?

Madi stood with her arms spread as the bat slammed against the air around her. She smiled and pointed. "Still think I was wrong to split the group?"

Orrin's mind raced. The three stones. The room getting brighter as they activated more. He looked over his shoulder at Daniel, who was still swinging wildly. Even with the boosted stats, his stamina wouldn't last forever. Sweat made his hair glisten as he fought savagely, killing bats with every movement.

"We need to find more," Orrin whispered before turning and shouting, "Daniel, we need to find more of the special stones. They protect against the bats."

Daniel shook his head and put a hand to his ear.

"Go," Madi demanded. "I can kill them when they get close."

She demonstrated by shaking the dead bat off the tip of her spear and replacing it with the one still beating relentlessly against the barrier around her.

Orrin darted into the melee, using [Way of the Water] to the full extent. He triggered [Side Steps] three times, which would have overjoyed him at the growth of his skill if not for the corresponding decrease in his [Ward] as some of the attacks inevitably got through his defenses.

How is Daniel doing so much better?

Orrin skidded to a halt next to Daniel. While dodging and trying to hit bats, he explained what they'd discovered: the room, the stones, and the barrier.

Daniel pointed. "Let's try on the far side, where Emily is. We'll run for it."

Orrin nodded his agreement and started sprinting.

"When did you get so fast?" Daniel muttered to no one.

They passed Garret, laughing maniacally as he did trick shots with his bow. He created an arrow shaped more like a sword and swiped one-handed through the cloud of bats in front of him before loading the same and shooting it through another four bats. Without Daniel's [Gravity Well], the monsters were attacking everyone now.

Emily was faring much worse when they reached her. Her staff was only semi-effective against the bats. The boys watched as a bat she hit rolled over in the air before launching itself back at her. With her lower strength score, the bludgeoning tool was not as effective as it normally would be bolstered by her magic.

"Are you out of mana?" Orrin asked as they raced up to her. Daniel swung a few times to clear a path.

"None of my fire magic does enough to be useful," she said through gritted teeth. Orrin could see tears of frustration behind her eyes. "They can't get to me, though. I tried to yell out, but you all ran away too fast."

"We figured that out," Orrin said, summoning another [Ice Sword] and handing it to her. "This might help. Sharp end goes into the bad thing."

Emily took the sword. "What's the plan?"

"The lights came up when we got to Madi's block. We're off to find the rest of them."

Emily seemed relieved to take a break. Daniel was going ham on the bats around her. "What if there's only three?"

"Then we kill all the bats."

Emily raised an eyebrow. "Bravado, or are you doing that thing where you don't think right again?"

"Neither. I'm scared shitless, but I have this guy and his sword," Orrin said, pointing to Daniel. Another dozen bats dropped from the darker part of the ceiling. "Fuck. D, let's bounce."

Daniel didn't wait and started his mad dash away.

"I mean, he could have waited for me, right?"

Emily shook her head at the younger boy and raised the sword he'd given her. "Ice. Why'd it have to be ice?"

"Go ahead," Daniel said. "Step on it."

They'd found the fourth block after two minutes. Running with a maxed-out dexterity took some getting used to, but Orrin thought the wind in his hair felt . . . well, actually like shit. His face was windburned and his eyes hurt.

"We should get goggles or glasses."

"What the fuck are you talking about?" Daniel roared. "Get on the thing."

"For running. Goggles for when we are running at full speed. I'm sure there is a speedster class. You know, something like the Flash. Somebody has to have invented that. Remind me when we get back to Dey," Orrin rambled. "Oh, and no. You get this one."

Daniel stepped toward Orrin. "So help me, O. Get on it now."

Orrin danced backward. "Listen. I can heal myself and cast [Ward]. It makes more sense for me to go find the last one. Even if I can't find it, I can survive a lot longer than you."

Daniel glared at him.

"You know I'm right, right?"

"Go, before I change my mind."

Orrin surprised himself and gave Daniel a quick hug. "Don't die."

Daniel squeezed back and then pushed Orrin to the side. He swung Gertrude at a bat that had almost clawed up Orrin's back.

Daniel stepped on the darker stone. The room lit up more. The hundreds of bats were ravaged. Orrin picked out Emily and Garret, along with what might have been Madi in the far, far distance.

He trekked on.

It's got to be close. Each trigger seems to be about a half mile apart, I think. How fast do we run with a hundred dex, anyway?

Orrin's thoughts continued to tumble over each other. The adrenaline and fear worked together to have him think about anything but the fact that he was alone, well away from his friends, and facing an army of flying demon bats.

Not demons. Tony had told him all about demons. These were just big, ugly bats that weren't affected by light or fire magic. Something that would have been nice to know before coming in here.

Orrin's eyes caught a small shift in the light on the ground. He ducked instinctively.

Two bats passed over him, their attacks narrowly missing.

He threw his sword. The hilt struck one but, other than a slight dip in its flight, didn't do much damage.

He pulled another one out of whatever magic factory made his icy blades and held it out.

"Come and get it."

Orrin would later tell of his artful dodges and graceful swings. The perfect symphony of battle, where he felled two beasts on his own in a moment of inspired swordsmanship. How the first bat's shriek warmed his face and small specks of spittle dotted his chest as he held it back with deft strokes of his sword. How the second bat fell after the snicker-snack of his weapon robbed it of both wings before it hit the ground.

He told these lies because he knew that nobody would believe that the two bats collided in midair in their rush to get to him. He made up the battle, because who would listen to a story where the two monsters skidded across the stone floor and stopped right at his feet for an easy poke to the head with the sharp end of his sword?

After his intense and not at all made-up battle, Orrin leaned against his sword to catch his breath and saw another dark stone on the floor only a few yards away. He made his way to the gray-black brick and stepped on it, activating a brilliant flash of light across the ceiling. The bats still in the air wailed and flew higher, toward a single dark hole in the ceiling. When the last bat fled into the darkness, the hole closed with an audible pop.

Chapter 28

Orrin watched the last bat fly into the inky-black hole in the brightly lit ceiling. As the darkness receded, the roof sparked with waves of light. The ripples centered back where the rest of his party was located. With the final flicker, a ray of bright-white light shone down in the distance.

"Is everybody okay?" Orrin yelled, hoping Daniel would be able to hear him.

He didn't have to wait long for the response.

"Come this way, O. The door is over here."

Daniel's voice carried with a slight echo, and Orrin could make out the small figure of his friend waving his hand over his head.

Orrin took a tentative step off his marker. He waited for the lights to dim or the bats to return, but nothing happened. He made his way toward his friends.

All four of them were already waiting when Orrin arrived.

"Took you long enough," Madi joked, pushing a shoulder against him.

Emily was standing by a door made of light. She spared a quick glance at Orrin before trying the handle. As soon as it turned, she stepped through and left the floor.

"She's a bit spooked at being so . . . At not having a good way to fight against those bats," Garret said by way of apology. He smirked at Orrin and opened his mouth to say something more.

"It's fine," Daniel said, pulling Garret's gaze and attention. "Go on through; we'll be right behind."

Garret's smile stumbled into a small grimace, but he listened to the [Hero] and stepped through the door.

"That was a cluster," Daniel sighed. "Before we go to the next floor, we should have a serious discussion about whether it's worth continuing. I don't know anything about darkness magic. That is what Emily called those creatures, right?"

Madi shrugged her shoulders. "It's a rare magic type, usually only found in some of the more restricted classes. Theoretically, I know it's a bad matchup for me or for someone with fire magic. That's almost half our party that would be useless against another floor like this or darkness monsters."

"That old fart who told us we were going to die mentioned something escaped when the dungeon break happened. Maybe it was something like one of these bats." Orrin took in the look on Madi and Daniel's faces. "What?"

"Old fart?" Daniel asked. Madi stifled a laugh, turning it into a snort.

"You know what I mean. He already accounted for not having all the data, and even when he gave us bad odds, we came in. My vote is we don't quit. In an emergency, I can boost everyone up and we can just pay the consequences for a few days in the next room between floors."

"The consequences . . ." Madi sputtered. "I'm not sure I want to go through that again."

"It's a fail-safe," Daniel bargained. "I also think we should keep going, but I'm not the one who has trouble against those things."

Orrin and Daniel turned to Madi. To her credit, she didn't cower or hesitate. She held her head high as she answered.

"Let's destroy this place."

Emily and Garret were setting up camp when they entered the room.

"So?" Garret asked as he rolled a sleeping bag out on the floor. "What's the verdict?"

"What do you mean?" Daniel asked in return. "What are you doing? We just slept."

Emily had a blanket over her shoulders and her eyes shut tight. She cracked one eye open to stare at Daniel. "He's asking if we continue or turn back. Either way, I used too much mana in that room and need to rest. I won't be of any more use today.

"Not that I was of any use in the first place," she finished bitterly.

"Stop that right now," Orrin thundered, surprising himself. "Nobody knew what we were heading into, but from what I saw, you kept your cool and fought on. You didn't give up and took out how many of those things?"

Emily muttered something, but Orrin didn't hear it.

"How many?" he asked again.

"She took out thirty-seven. I took down eighty-nine," Garret boasted.

"Emily, I only took out twenty-six," Madi said, kneeling beside the fire mage. "I had to use my spear and wait for them to get close. I was terrified, too, but we made it."

"What about next time?" Emily closed her eyes again and rubbed the blanket across her face. "If Orrin hadn't given me that sword, I don't know what I would have done. I broke my staff against one of those things. I'm not used to physical confrontation. I'm a back-line magic user."

Daniel sat down next to Emily with Madi and started reassuring her. Orrin realized he hadn't checked his own status since the fight ended and had been ignoring the notifications.

Experience Gained: 2,250 XP (75 XP x 10; 50 XP x 6; 150 XP x 8)

Pulling up his full status, he checked his experience.

Orrin
Utility Warder Level 13 (3,592/4,000)

AP: 9

"Damn it," he muttered. If his math was right, he'd only needed to kill three more of those Darkeater Bats and he would have leveled. He'd been so close.

"While they talk her down, want to give me a hand and start cooking some food? I know I make it look effortless, but pulling the bowstring back takes a lot of strength." Garret spoke from his side. Orrin hadn't even realized he had stood from his spot on the floor.

"Shouldn't you try to talk to your teammate? She felt useless in there."

"She *was* useless," the archer responded, emphasizing the middle word. "We run in a party, but Emily has always been cold to me. My words won't mean much to her, but I can cook something for her. She'll crash soon, and something warm in her belly will do more good than any lies I could spin."

Orrin didn't fully agree with him but still pulled out some food and the heater box. His own mana had been low but had already started creeping up. Emily had thrown a lot of fire into the swarms of bats. He forgot how much [Meditate] was worth.

When Daniel and Madi checked in, Garret took a small plate to Emily. His friends sat down and pulled together their own food. Garret stayed with Emily.

"How did it go?" Orrin asked quietly between bites.

"She wanted to leave, but we convinced her to stay and fight through. If we hit another room with darkness monsters, we'll reassess and she might leave by herself. She understands what that would cost her, but it's her choice." Madi picked up a sausage and took a bite. "These are good. Where did you get them?"

"A small stall down by the market. I'll show you when we get back. What do you mean, what it would cost her?"

Daniel ate in silence.

"Imagine that you are an adventurer with the Guild and somehow you get a spot on the [Hero]'s team to defeat a new dungeon. That's the kind of thing that could set you up for life. Not that Emily cares about that kind of thing, but leaving halfway through would be a major blow to any credibility you had as a Guild member. She'd probably be let go from her party and most likely would need to leave Dey and return home."

Orrin thought through Madi's explanation. "But she'd be leaving because her magic doesn't work against this type of stuff. If we'd known there were darkness monsters here, we'd—"

"We'd never have been allowed to come," Madi interjected. "Me or her. Our builds are the worst possible type to counter darkness magic or monsters. That means you, Garret, and Daniel have to pick up our slack on any floor like the last one. We're dead weight."

"That's not true. You both took out a lot more than I did."

Madi gestured to the food all around. "You make up for the lack of firepower with your utility. It's not even a fair comparison."

"You made the call to search out the stones."

"Daniel found them first."

"And then had no idea what to do about it. No offense, D. Madi, you help control battles. You're quick and decisive in emergencies. Don't doubt yourself over one floor."

Madi fiddled with her fork. She didn't respond or look Orrin in the eye, and he thought the conversation was over.

"He's right." Daniel put a few of the empty plates in a pile. "You and Emily are needed here. The Guildmaster made it clear this was my dungeon to clear, and you are both in my party. We'll overcome any obstacle this place throws at us and figure it out together."

"You hear that, Em? Daniel is pulling rank and making you stay," Garret yelled over his shoulder with a chuckle. He'd come back with the dirty dishes.

Daniel sighed at the archer's timing. "Everybody get some rest and recharge your mana. I'll take the first shift alone."

Orrin cleaned up and rolled out his sleeping bag but couldn't fall asleep. Madi, Emily, and Garret were snoring within minutes. After thirty minutes of shuffling around, he threw the cover away and made his way quietly over to Daniel.

"Can't sleep."

Daniel grunted.

"I can take over. Go get some rest."

Daniel didn't answer or move.

"Are you okay?"

"Just thinking."

"Want to share with the class?"

Daniel finally turned to look at his friend. "You might not like what I have to say."

Orrin had been waiting for Daniel to yell at him since the second floor. He'd half hoped he had forgotten that he'd turned on the dreaded skill that should not be named, but Daniel wasn't the type to forget something like that.

"Let me have it." Orrin hunched his shoulders and waited for the chewing out to start.

"I think we might need you to blood cycle and do that thing where you make enemies stop moving."

"I'm sor— What?"

Daniel chucked. "You did something stupid with the boars. You're an idiot, and if we weren't all just doing our best, I'd kick your ass. That last floor scared me, though. Those bats kept coming. I kept thinking how great it would be if you could make them all just fall out of the sky. If we come across another room where Emily and Madi can't do anything, I'm going to have to rely on you, and that means slowing the monsters down. We really underutilize that skill set of yours."

"Because it doesn't do any damage. It doesn't count as participation against the kill and I don't get experience for it."

Daniel raised an eyebrow. "When did you start caring about experience? If you lag behind, we'll power level you."

Orrin thought about what Daniel was saying. Orrin had started worrying more about doing damage and getting experience. He'd just been complaining to himself about how he should have killed more bats. "I should just hit every monster we find until it can't move."

"Probably best to not do it to every monster," Daniel countered. "Emily is watching you pretty close, have you noticed? Save it for emergencies or try to do it in secret. The monsters don't need to go prone. Maybe just have them moving half speed."

"That way everybody can still do damage and put up a fight, but we can coast through a bit easier," Orrin said, finishing the thought. "If I start blood cycling, though, we'll need to rest more between floors. Tony thought a single night's sleep would be good enough for a full recharge as long as I don't go over my max. Now that I know what that is, I hope I can convince myself to turn off [Mind Bastion] after the fights."

Daniel picked at something on his sleeve. "Do you trust me?"

Orrin scrunched up his face. "What do you mean? Of course."

"If I say to drop [Mind Bastion], do you trust that I have a good reason?"

"I think so."

Daniel finally got the piece of bat flesh unstuck. The blood had dried, gluing it to his shirt. "No, not *I think so*. I want you to convince yourself that logically—no matter what—if I tell you it's a good idea to stop blood cycling, you'll listen."

Orrin saw what Daniel intended to do and smiled. "Yes. I trust you. If you think I should stop cycling, it's probably for a sound reason that I just haven't figured out yet."

Daniel smirked back. "Do you think it'll work?"

Orrin put out his closed hand. Daniel quickly rapped his knuckles against the proffered fist.

"Only one way to find out."

Chapter 29

Once everyone recharged their batteries, the group got ready to move on to the fifth floor. Daniel clued Madi in to his plan to try and control a blood-cycling Orrin. While she had obvious concerns and voiced them, she eventually said she trusted their decision.

"Why do I feel like she still expects us not to do it?" Daniel muttered as Madi moved toward the other two.

"She's doing that thing my mom does," Orrin whispered back. "You know, the whole 'I'm not going to tell you not to do that but I'll be very disappointed if you do' thing?"

Daniel grumbled as he handed Orrin the last of the cleaned-up camp. Garret and Emily had been singing Orrin's praises all morning. Sleeping and eating as comfortably as they had been was not something anyone expected in a dungeon run. Emily was very clear that Garret should not get used to luxurious living.

As it turned out, the fifth floor of the dungeon was a mixture of the steel and poison categories they'd run into so far. When Orrin stepped through the doorway, fifteen-foot-tall plants with metal-coated teeth snapped at him. Luckily, the door had a safe zone just out of their reach.

The plants resembled a mix of Mario piranha plants and Venus fly traps, besides the obvious size difference. They also had waving green branches with razor-sharp leaves that tried to reach the party. The grinding noise of their steel teeth clanging together sent chills down Orrin's spine. An ichor dripped from the open green mouths and sizzled on the dirt ground.

He tried an [Identify].

[Steel-Tooth Dewdrops] HP: 400/400

Orrin ignored the party's discussion as he pulled his trusty encyclopedia of monsters out of storage and leafed through it. He didn't find the plant under "Steel-Tooth" but did under "Dewdrops." A small asterisk noted multiple variants could be found.

"Don't let the poison touch you," Orrin said over the group's talking. "Or the leaves or the teeth. These things have a neurotoxin that will make you feel tingly. You lose feeling after a few seconds and some kinds make you . . . dumb, if I'm reading this right."

"We should send you forward, then," Daniel laughed. "You can't get any dumber."

"'Some reports indicate cognitive dysfunction, including trying to climb into the plant's open mouth,'" Orrin read aloud. "That doesn't sound like something I want to try, so no, thanks."

"We could stand back and just attack," Madi suggested. "It doesn't seem like they can move."

"They're stationary, according to this," Orrin said, holding his book up before making it disappear in a pocket. "My [Map] shows only about fifty of them. Maybe we should just—"

Flames gushed up from the ground all around them. Orrin hunched, pulling his cape over his eyes at the bright light. He was about to use [Water Reservoir] to soak them all when he heard Garret's laughter.

"Damn, Emily. Those bats really pissed you off."

Emily's telltale red vines had crept out and up the nearest dewdrops. Orrin watched as the HP on the nearest dozen dropped rapidly. Daniel exchanged a glance with him and shrugged. Garret was lobbing a few arrows but mostly enjoying the flame storm of death.

In twenty minutes, Emily had cleared the entire room, mostly by herself. Orrin made sure to hit just enough with a few [Lightstrike]s to level up.

Experience Gained: 500 XP (100 XP x 5)
Level 14 Obtained!
+10 AP

When the last dewdrop wilted into dust, a door appeared in its place.

"Remind me not to piss off the fire mage," Daniel joked.

Emily turned her gaze on the [Hero]. He held up his hands in surrender. She raised an eyebrow and smirked. "Fireflower mage," she corrected.

Daniel bowed at the waist. "I stand corrected. Remind me not to piss off the fireflower mage."

And just like that, the fifth floor was defeated within the hour.

Emily declined another rest and took a mana potion. They were standing in the room between floors. Orrin hadn't been the only one to take advantage of Emily's burning crusade against plant life. Garret had finally hit level twenty and had requested thirty minutes to go over his status.

When the archer stood with a smile, Daniel asked what Orrin was thinking. "Did you get anything good?"

Madi slapped him on the arm. "You don't ask people that."

Garret chuckled and pulled an arrow out of the air. "Watch."

He shot an arrow against the wall. It struck the stone and fell to the ground.

"Did you see where it hit? Watch this one."

Garret sent another arrow flying through the air, except this time the arrow curved and scraped against the wall with a shower of sparks.

"[Curved Arrow]," the archer announced with pride. "The more I work on it, the more I'll be able to control the curvature."

"Are you trying for [Control Arrow]?" Emily asked while drinking some of the coffee Orrin had made for them.

"I might," Garret responded hesitantly. "I've got my eye on a few things."

Emily shrugged and downed the last of her brew. "Keep your secrets, it's all right."

The sixth floor surprised them all. The floor held a checkerboard pattern. Each square was roughly five feet wide and had a two-foot circle cut into the middle. Water splashed against the edges of the circle, reminding Orrin of a show he'd watched about ice fishing. The door to the next floor was within sight, just on the other side of the "board."

They entered a small stretch of unmarked ground with only twenty feet to the first checkered square. Everybody muttered their thoughts aloud until Madi pointed up.

The ceiling mirrored the floor, with the same watery holes.

"Why isn't the water falling out of the ceiling?" Daniel asked, craning his neck.

"Magic?" Orrin pushed Daniel out of the way. He was standing too close to the door, and Orrin was feeling claustrophobic.

"Orrin, check for traps or monsters," Madi demanded. Orrin was already pulling up the blue box.

"Monsters moving around underneath the floor," he announced.

Emily cocked her head up. "What about up there?"

Orrin rotated his map. "Shit. Monsters above and below."

Madi and Emily discussed plans with Daniel. Garret made his way to Orrin.

"Should I try and put a few arrows into one of the holes?"

Orrin rolled his eyes. "What good would that do? If nothing happens, no big deal, but if a monster pops out to attack, half the group isn't paying attention."

Garret held up his hands. "Whoa, whoa. I'm just making a joke."

Orrin scratched the back of his head. His hair was getting a little longer than he liked. It was curling at the end and tickling his neck. "Sorry. I'm nervous. I don't like the look of this room for some reason."

At that moment, Emily and Daniel walked over. Emily pointed to the far side. "Garret, can you hit a hole on the edge over there?"

Garret winked at Orrin. "Sure, no problem at all."

Orrin made sure his [Ward] was refreshed on everybody and tossed a [Water Ward] up as well. He summoned an [Ice Sword] and held it ready.

Emily eyed him. "You think that's necessary? Even if something comes out of one of the nearby holes, you've got all four of us in front of you."

Orrin realized the party had fanned out before him. Garret was at point, drawing an arrow back with the Citrandish longbow. Orrin noticed his shoulders and back stretched in interesting ways before he released the string.

The arrow dipped in the air and splashed into the water with barely a sound.

From the ceiling, a low roar echoed. A beast of scales and fangs fell from the corresponding ceiling tile and dropped like a stone into the same spot where Garret's arrow had landed. The blue and silver of its hide sparkled as it dived, more of its body coiling out of the hole in the ceiling. Just as the serpentine head struck the water on the floor, it stopped growing. It was the exact length of the room's height.

"Was that a snake or a dragon?" Daniel said in surprise. "Orrin, how many of those are there?"

"I can't count them. They move too fast and swarm over each other, but I think more than ten and less than twenty."

"Did you get a chance to [Identify] it?" Madi asked.

"Sorry, no. I was too surprised. It was . . . kind of beautiful, right?"

Emily, Madi, Garret, and Daniel turned to stare at Orrin. He blushed. "What?"

Daniel smiled. "Nothing, buddy."

Garret repeated the shot, but nothing happened. He sent an arrow into the ceiling tile the monster had fallen out of, but the waters stayed still. He even tried shooting a few random squares in rapid succession, but no more of the monsters appeared. Their charming tramp blew through his teeth in frustration.

Orrin chucked his sword. It turned end over end before skidding to a stop on the edge of a central pool.

"Why did you do that?" Daniel asked, keeping the smile from his face.

"I thought maybe the things are smart and realized that an arrow didn't necessarily mean foo—"

Another of the monstrosities erupted from the pool of water that Orrin's sword had barely touched. Nobody saw where the sword went. They were all agog at the forty-foot snake monster flying up into the air. Halfway through the air, it twisted and entered a different hole in the ceiling.

"It didn't go into the one directly above it," Emily pointed out.

"We all saw the same thing," Garret retorted, earning himself a slap to the back of his head. "Ouch."

Orrin was smiling. "Got it."

"What is it?" Madi asked.

Orrin was already leafing through his book. "Steel-Armored Sphacelus Wyrm . . . found it."

Orrin read aloud.

"'Sphacelus Wyrms have been hunted to near extinction due to the refined use of their scales. These monsters can grow up to twenty feet long and can bite cleanly through an adult male's arm. The wyrms have a venomous bite; however, the scales absorb the monster's surrounding toxins, increasing the overall toxicity of venom. No two Sphacelus Wyrms have the same venom, leading to crafters using the scales for a variety of uses.' It has five stars."

"Five stars isn't too bad," Daniel said, trying to lighten the mood.

"There's nothing about variants. The author thinks they get to half the size we just saw. I'm going to take a guess and say these wyrms might be a little more than five-star monsters," Orrin countered.

"He's right." Emily stepped in front of Daniel and put her hand on his chest. "This isn't a room where we want to fight. We just need to figure out the pattern."

"Huh?" Orrin and Daniel spoke at the same time.

"It's obvious," Garret said as he sat down and started scratching a grid on the stone floor. "The wyrms move through the holes in a pattern, and we need to figure out how to get through without any of them coming out."

Emily walked over and put her hand on Garret's head. "He's learning."

Garret shook her off. "I've spent enough time with you and Tin. You don't just keep me around for my dashing good looks."

Madi sat and pointed out the pool the arrow had hit and started talking with Garret. In a few seconds, Daniel and Orrin were being ignored.

"What do we do?" Daniel finally asked.

Emily glanced up. "Start throwing stuff in the pools and let us know what happens. We need more data."

Orrin and Daniel spent a few minutes throwing more of his swords. The wyrms didn't respond again. Daniel finally had the idea of throwing real food, which pained Orrin. After the first tiny piece of chicken hit the pool and a wyrm appeared, he couldn't argue against it, though. Especially when the second, third, and fourth pieces also brought out wyrms from the floor below and the ceiling above.

"There are sixty-four squares," Orrin complained. "That's going to be all our food if we have to try each one."

"No, it's not," Daniel laughed, throwing a finger-size piece of food into another pool. "I know you overpacked. I saw how much you brought. We can always throw coffee beans."

"You wouldn't dare!"

Daniel laughed again while Orrin started to think of ways to kill the [Hero] before he tried to do something unforgivable.

Chapter 30

After three hours of testing, talking, and throwing away more of Orrin's food stores, Emily and Madi solved the pattern. Orrin tried to listen to them explain but it was like watching a video on how to solve a Rubik's Cube—no matter how many times he tried to wrap his mind around the ever-revolving logic, the girls couldn't get him to understand.

"You know, it's nice that you suck at something," Madi teased.

Orrin flipped her off.

"What is the plan, though?" Garret asked. He hadn't even tried to listen to them explain how certain locations on the board had been used as predictive models to do . . . something. Orrin's brain hurt.

"What do you mean?" Emily responded. "We know how to make all the monsters go into the ceiling. Then we just walk across."

"If you think it's going to be that easy, I've got some beautiful land to sell you in Veskar. Prime real estate, truly."

"He has a point," Orrin agreed. "We don't know if only the water triggers them. Nobody has tried standing on the squares. What if they all drop out of the air at once?"

Daniel hefted Gertrude and swung her once. "Then we fight and try again."

"I'd really like to avoid fighting one of those big worms," Garret countered.

"Wyrm, not worm."

"That's what I said."

Emily rolled her eyes. "We can test what happens when we stand on the square once we get them all in the sky. Then we will send one person across at a time or maybe two. We can figure that out later."

Garret had the best long-range aim, so he spent the next thirty minutes playing a complicated game of basketball with chunks of food. Orrin was stingy until one of the small pieces of bread missed and almost rolled into the wrong pool of water.

"I need more weight," Garret complained.

Orrin relented and brought out some strawberries he'd squirreled away, as well as a bushel of apples.

"How much food did you bring?" Daniel asked incredulously. "This is ridiculous."

"Yeah," Madi agreed, her lips stained by the strawberry she was chewing.

Once every wyrm had been displaced from below, Daniel took a tentative step onto one of the squares. When nothing immediately happened, he walked the edge until he was halfway across the board.

"Follow the same path," Emily ordered, pushing Garret out as the second test subject.

Garret reached the midway point just as Daniel stepped off the checkerboard. He waved from the other side.

"All good over here."

Madi went next.

"Once she's across, I'll go. Stick to the same path and wait for me to get halfway. Don't break whatever design we've figured out here," Emily said, not taking her eyes off Madi.

"Why am I going last?" Orrin complained.

"You can make yourself fast and try to outrun those things. My fire will probably just piss them off more."

Orrin couldn't argue with her reasoning but still hated being the final moving piece of the plan. He watched Emily take her first step as Garret joined Daniel.

Everything went according to plan. His teammates were waiting for him on the other side. He joined them without incident, and they entered the doorway.

"Good job, everybody." Daniel walked straight across the room. "You all ready?"

"You don't want to take a break?" Orrin asked. "We can spare five minutes."

"No, let's just push through and take out the next floor. I've got a good feeling."

The seventh floor proved to Orrin that Daniel's good feelings were not worth listening to.

"So. Many. Spiders." Orrin fell against the wall, exhausted.

"I don't know which were worse, the big ones with the eyes or the tiny ones that tried crawling in my mouth." Garret shook his leg, trying to get the creepy-crawly feeling to go away. "I hate spiders so, so much."

"The tiny ones." Madi shivered. "I bit down on a few, and the way they burst . . . I think . . ."

She turned and puked against the wall.

The room was a maze. It wasn't particularly hard or even very large, but the swarms of eight-legged monsters with biting fangs, sticking webs, and hairy legs were overwhelming.

"We made it through," Daniel said, pointing to the doorway next to them.

"Only because Orrin could get rid of the poison," Emily pointed out. "Otherwise we would have had to hole up and recover the hard way multiple times."

Orrin's skill [Remetabolize] had proven invaluable. They had brought some antidotes, but like other potions, one could only take so many a day. The mana cost was on the high side, and he'd had to take a few mana potions himself, but the group had been able to fight into the swarms of crawling monsters as they pushed farther into the high-walled labyrinth.

"Let's just get out of here." Garret shuddered. Of everyone in the party, he'd taken to the floor the worst. Even now, his eyes were bulging out of his head as he swiveled in circles, pointing an arrow at phantom beasts. "I'm never sleeping again."

After a good sleep and a small meal, everyone lined up more or less rested. Garret still occasionally swiped at his legs but otherwise seemed halfway back to being himself.

"Was it just me or was breakfast a little scant this morning?" he complained.

"Half rations until the last floor," Orrin announced. "We wasted too much with all the wyrm testing."

Daniel snorted. "You have more than enough left, you're just punishing us."

Orrin ignored him and stepped through first.

The room was another large dome with a metal pedestal in the middle. The walls around him reached up vertically before beginning a gentle curve to the center, giving the impression of being in an egg.

"Where's the other door?" Daniel asked as he stepped in behind Orrin.

Madi, Emily, and Garret appeared and glanced around.

"No monsters. Orrin, check for traps." Madi kept her spear extended.

"I already did. Nothing."

Daniel approached the pedestal, the rest of the group pushing in slowly behind.

The pedestal looked like a birdbath that Orrin's dad had brought home once. That one had been made of stone. His dad had put it in the front yard and talked excitedly about all the birds that would soon be using it. Then he'd gone out to mow the lawn and run into it with the riding lawn mower. It broke into two pieces and thereafter lived in the garage, waiting to be fixed. Orrin had finally trashed it a few years ago.

This one didn't have water in it. Instead, a liquid like mercury nearly overflowed the top lip.

"Do we break this?" Daniel wondered aloud.

Emily and Madi joined him. Garret turned his back and watched the rest of the room. Orrin tried using [Identify] on the metal pedestal but got nothing in return.

"Let's stand back and I'll hit it with a few spells," Emily suggested. She took a few steps back and raised her hand.

"Nah, I'll just break it in two." Daniel raised his sword high.

"At least wait for us to get out of the way," Orrin said, pulling Madi away.

Daniel rolled his hand in a hurry-up motion and then regripped Gerty. He swung horizontally at the base. His sword rang against the metal with a low, hollow thrum but did no visible damage. The liquid in the cistern didn't even ripple.

Daniel frowned and raised his hands over his head, bringing his sword down hard on the surface. Orrin watched as the liquid splashed from the reverberations. Some splashed on Daniel's hand.

The [Hero] screamed.

"Daniel!" Orrin yelled, rushing to his friend.

The boy backed away from the pedestal, dropping Gertrude. The flesh was bright red, but the drops of metal had hardened and fallen off his skin. Daniel kicked the metal discs in anger and held up his hand.

"That fucking burns."

Orrin used a cure spell, and the skin went through the rapid changes of healing. He was focused on Daniel and didn't turn back until he heard Emily's gasp.

Orrin spun and saw something pushing its way out of the pedestal. A flicker of movement caught his eye, and he glanced down to the base. One of the discs of dried metal that had landed on Daniel was sliding up the outside of the metal pedestal, crawling up to meet the rising figure.

The party watched, spellbound, as the escaped liquid returned to the main pool. As it touched, the metal figure grew arms and pushed itself bodily from the pedestal, landing with a splash on the floor. It began heaving and rolling like a wave, forming a leg that splashed into a puddle. It pulled two arms and a head out before it disintegrated back into liquid.

"I'm not sure we should let that thing finish whatever it's trying to do," Emily yelled at the group. She cast her flames at what Orrin was hoping was not a Terminator.

Emily's attack was the catalyst for the rest of them. Garret launched arrow after arrow at the being. Madi tried various light magic and hit it with her [Shimmersight]. Orrin tried a few spells and even threw an [Ice Sword] at it. Everything seemed to bounce off the metal, or, in the case of Garret's arrows, go right through it.

Even as they attacked, the liquid metal formed up better with each step until it reached the height of a man. Not just any man. It turned to the group and solidified into a familiar shape.

Daniel.

The real Daniel picked up Gertrude and swung down at himself. The metal hand reached up and caught the sword easily. The fingers melted and wrapped around the blade, yanking back. The attacks from everybody stopped as the two Daniels, one made entirely of metal, played tug-of-war.

Madi took three quick steps and stabbed her spear toward Metal Daniel. Her blade separated the "skin," creating a hole where she attacked. The simulacrum yanked its hand back from Gertrude and made a swipe at her. It missed, but Orrin noticed the small drops of metal landing on her.

"Madi, don't let the metal touch you." He ran to her and used the edge of his sword to scoop the bits of crawling liquid metal from her leathers and throw them on the ground. The pieces began moving back toward the cistern.

"How do we kill it?" Garret asked as he circled for a better shot. "My arrows don't seem to be doing anything."

Daniel swung Gerty again. Metal Daniel caught the blade, but real Daniel was ready and dragged the sword down and out of its grip. It hissed as it pulled away.

Orrin's mind was racing, and he reached the conclusion at the same time as Emily.

"Only you can do damage to it," he guessed.

"You can hurt it, but we can't," Emily announced with certainty.

They shared a look and nodded.

"Madi, back up. Garret, create a few big arrows and shoot at its feet. It doesn't seem to be that great at walking." Emily barked orders.

"Daniel, I'm going to boost your speed and mine. I'll try to distract it so you can hit it," Orrin said to his friend, already casting the spells.

"Make sure you don't get any of that liquid on you," Emily warned him.

Orrin nodded and took off, swinging his newly summoned sword at Metal Daniel. It ignored him at first, watching Gertrude as she danced along its chest, but when Orrin got a little closer, it snaked an arm out. The hand turned into a flowing river of liquid metal that traveled fast up the icy sword. Orrin dropped it and retreated.

"Any other ideas?" Daniel asked, trying to push the metal version of him back with wild swings.

Orrin and Emily exchanged looks again, but he was met with a shrug.

"You might be on your own."

Chapter 31

Daniel was sweating. His metal doppelgänger was his match in every way. If it weren't for Orrin's buffs to his dexterity and strength, he might not have lasted as long as he had.

Orrin increased everybody's stats in a last-ditch attempt to make some difference, but no matter the spell cast or the arrow launched, nothing struck the Metal Daniel. The only damage it took was from the rare hit real Daniel was able to make.

He had used his skills only to find Metal Daniel could replicate them. [Gravity Strike] met [Gravity Strike]. When he tried [Shooting Star], Orrin watched in amazement as the two copies of his friend bounced off each other so fast he couldn't tell which was which.

Garret's arrow cages gave real Daniel some reprieve, but Metal Daniel would eventually hammer the metal or stone down. The [Hero] signaled for another such break, and Garret masterfully landed a dozen pillars of metal around the enemy.

"Daniel, do you need a potion?" Orrin asked, taking a step toward his friend.

Daniel held up his hand to stop him but didn't look. He was concentrating on his status screen. "No. I'm trying something. Give me a minute."

Garret took a mana potion and loaded up another arrow. Metal Daniel was already breaking free. "I can only do this two more times," the archer yelled while aiming. Two of the metal pillars cracked as the Metal Daniel slammed its fist into them over and over. It pushed one until it snapped, stepping over the obstacle. It took two steps and Garret released, sealing it in again. The metal copy showed no emotion and started whaling on the stone arrows this time.

"Almost done," Daniel muttered. He had put Gertrude on his back and was holding his hands together. His muscles clenched as he squeezed something.

Did he just buy a new skill halfway through a fight?

Orrin's guess proved right as Metal Daniel broke through the arrow cage. Before Garret loosed his already prepared arrow, real Daniel shouted something and turned his closely grasped hands toward the monster. A beam of light brighter than any spell Orrin had seen burned into his vision. The entire party blinked over and over to clear the fading afterimage.

Metal Daniel's feet and shins were all that remained. The entire top half of the monster, down to the knees, had been incinerated.

"You did it!" Orrin cheered. Then he noticed Daniel toppling, falling slowly. He bounced once as he smacked his head against the ground.

Orrin was next to his friend in an instant, pouring healing spells into him as he searched him with [Identify]. His health was fine, but his mana was zeroed out. Orrin boosted his friend's will, giving him enough mana to groggily come to.

"Is it dead?" Daniel's eyes were slightly crossed, but he focused them on the still-burning feet.

"You did it, buddy. Just relax."

"Orrin!" Madi's voice did not sound relaxed.

Orrin turned and saw the metal legs melt into a puddle. The massively depleted pool of liquid pulled its way to the pedestal.

Orrin threw a [Lightstrike] at the liquid. It hit.

"Kill it, quick," he demanded. Flashes of fire, light, and even an arrow hit the puddle, burning it out of existence.

Once Daniel was half revived, the party stood dozens of feet away from the pedestal of liquid death, discussing their options. The theory was the metal would copy anyone that touched it, creating a perfect replica with all their skills and spells. Daniel had had a stroke of insight and bought a spell, [Starfire], in an attempt to damage his metal self. His reasoning—that the metal him wouldn't have a way to copy a newly purchased spell—had been right on the money. The genius was undercut by his terrible math skills, as he held the spell going for a second longer than he had mana to maintain the flow.

"I killed it, though," Daniel said with a smirk. He was still sitting, with the telltale half-closed eyes of someone with a mana headache.

"You defeated the copy, but we killed it," Emily corrected him. After Daniel had destroyed enough of the creature that it lost its shape, the rest of them had finally been able to do damage to the thing.

Orrin pulled up his status, checking his experience again.

Orrin
Utility Warder Level 14 (1,692/5,000)
AP: 19

The creature had rewarded him with almost one thousand experience. If there was an easier way to kill the metal monster, he would have suggested farming some easy levels.

"Does anyone have any idea of what to do?" Madi said. She kept the frustration out of her voice, but she was pacing.

Nobody answered.

After a minute, Daniel brushed the ground and lay back, stretching out. "I don't think we are supposed to keep fighting our copies. I mean, I had to spend a lot of ability points on that spell. There should be a way through the floor without us all having to take on our own selves, right?"

Emily nodded in agreement. "Yes. Dungeon floors are never undefeatable. Sometimes it does take a few months for somebody to think of a way through, but even the biggest dungeons are usually defeated because it requires higher levels to defeat the enemies on the later floors. There is something we are missing here."

"We're missing the door off this floor," Daniel complained. "Wake me when you figure it out."

Emily stared at Daniel for a full ten seconds before shouting, "That's it! You're a genius. We're missing the door."

Daniel opened one eye. "What? I mean, of course I am . . . but what?"

Emily twirled, grabbing Orrin's arm. "Do you have a cup or a big spoon?"

Orrin pulled away, rubbing his arm as he dug into his [Dimension Hole]. He found a ladle and held it up. Emily snatched it and stormed toward the pedestal, everybody shouting in caution.

Ignoring them, Emily carefully lowered the soupspoon into the metal. She took a large helping of the mercurial liquid and gingerly walked toward the entrance door.

Whenever they entered a new floor, the doorway they entered through remained. It was an escape they wouldn't use except in the most dire of circumstances, as it would make them exit the dungeon. Usually, they completely ignored the door. On this floor, the frame was against the wall, but on some floors, it would be a free-floating door frame.

Reaching up to the top of the frame, Emily poured the metal on the stone outcropping that encased the wooden door.

The metal cooled instantly, hardening but covering a large portion of the door. Emily eyed the growth and returned for another scoop of the metal.

"Is this a good idea?" Madi questioned. "What if we get stuck in here and can't use the door?"

"Do you have any better ideas?" Orrin responded. "It does look like it's doing something."

Emily had to return for ten full spoonfuls of the pedestal metal before the door was covered from the top to the floor. As the last drops spread over the small circular handle, the entire metal door shivered. A low groaning sound came from the door, and Emily stepped back, raising her hand to cast a spell. Daniel was on his feet, with Gertrude already pointed toward the door.

The metal wobbled and rippled. Then the entire door frame moved. It started slowly, only a few inches, before taking off like a shot. The metal frame rocketed around the edge of the room, coming to a stop on the complete opposite end.

Everybody waited. Emily clapped her hands in joy and strolled across the room, completely unfazed. She turned back when she reached the metal door. "Well, come on, then."

Other than Daniel drinking a mana potion in the room between floors, the party continued right to the ninth level. They all sighed in relief as they stepped into the large expanse. Fields rolled into the distance, and a sun beat down from above. After the maze and small rooms they'd been encountering over the last few days, even the fake daylight of a dungeon floor was a welcome change.

Daniel was happiest of all when they found the monsters in the distance. He let Orrin sneak close enough to use [Identify], making sure to keep his [Camouflage] up the entire time. The six-legged creatures were a cross between an antelope and a really large weasel. The beasts had the slick coat of a weasel but the body and long, twirly horns of an antelope.

"They're called Spurndeeks," Orrin said as he canceled the skill. He'd been tempted to mess with Daniel, but everybody was too on edge.

"I know them," Garret announced. "They're tough and have nasty teeth and claws covered in disease but shouldn't be too much of a challenge if we play it slow and smart."

"Slow sounds like Daniel's speed," Orrin said with a smirk.

Madi hit him in the back of the head.

"Hey!"

"Anyways," Garret continued, "deeks are fast and slippery. The trick is to hit them on land from the side while somebody distracts them. How many are there?"

Orrin pulled up his [Map]. "More than thirty, less than fifty. They keep moving, and these plains are pretty big. I can't see the entire thing."

"Looks like we have a choice, then," Madi said, letting her spear hang from her side. "Fight through or try to sneak?"

"Deeks have a so-so ability to track by scent," Garret contributed. "Are you seriously double-checking what I said? Where's the trust?"

Orrin was trying to be subtle, but the beast compendium was too big to hide. "Trust but verify. Sorry. Everything he said is right, but they're also really good swimmers. I didn't see any water around here, though."

Garret shook his head.

They decided to fight whatever they came across naturally as they searched for the next door. The Spurndeeks, or deeks, as Garret called them, gave a good fight, but between Daniel's attacks, Garret's arrows, Madi's stun spells, and Emily's fire, even groups of four went down in a relatively quick fashion.

Orrin kept an eye on his [Map] and was able to point the group away from the large lake with dozens of the deeks. Garret had assured them they could take the monsters out on the dry land, but he gave them much worse odds in the water. And the Spurndeeks could transition between water and land quickly. While swimming, they used their powerful tails to churn the water and move faster. Orrin's book also warned they had some manner of water magic, so investigating the lake would be a last resort.

The party spent four hours exploring the floor. Madi was the first to figure out the unique aspect of the ninth floor.

"We're going in a circle."

Orrin checked his [Map]. "No, we're still moving past the lake. It's behind us that way."

Madi's gaze followed Orrin's finger, but she still shook her head. "That's not possible. Look ahead. Right there. Do you see the two dead deeks by that rock? Those are the first ones we attacked. I sat on that rock to rest after."

Orrin looked in the direction they were walking. Two dead monsters were torn up and burned. He checked his [Map] again and tried to make sense of what he was seeing. The only explanation . . .

"The entire floor is a sphere. We're traversing the entire world in a few hours."

Daniel slammed Gertrude into the ground. "Then where's the door?"

Orrin held up a finger and twisted, trying to pinpoint the angle they'd been walking and where they'd been. "The old door should be . . . over there."

Garret took off at a light jog. He slowed after a few hundred yards and walked back.

"The door is over there."

"You're sure it's not the way out?" Emily queried.

Garret shook his head.

Emily and Madi exchanged a dispirited look.

"The lake?"

"The lake."

Orrin groaned. They'd spent an hour trekking around the water. The last time he'd counted, there were still about twenty deeks playing around the lake.

Daniel lifted his sword and slapped it on his back. "Let's get to it."

Three more hours passed as they drew the slippery hexalegged beasts in groups of two to four. The last half dozen charged as one group, but some quick instructions from Madi and a few well-placed [Shimmersight] spells culled the attack enough that the party had no trouble taking them all down. Garret brought an extra-large arrow down through the head of the last deek.

Directly in the middle of the lake, a small arch appeared.

"Only one floor left," Daniel bragged. "Good job, team."

Chapter 32

Even though they had already rested before the ninth floor, nobody argued to move on right away. With the tenth-floor boss coming up, they would need every advantage they could muster. Daniel was feeling the drain of his fight as well. Orrin took pity and moved back to regular rations, pulling out a small cake he'd been saving for after they defeated the entire dungeon.

"I think we earned it," he explained as he laid out a blanket, plates, forks, and a knife.

Garret just stared. "I still can't believe you brought all this into the dungeon."

Orrin shrugged and cut into the fluffy white cake with small red berries and cream, handing out pieces to the girls first. He'd seen it in a shop window and spent one silver coin on it.

"Orrin, this is delicious." Madi had shoveled half her slice into her mouth.

Emily was taking smaller bites, but she leaned against the wall in a more relaxed pose. She moaned in approval after a bite.

Once everybody was fed with more than just cake, Daniel wanted to talk about strategy for the next room. Madi put her foot down, saying in no uncertain terms that they would not be moving to the next room until they'd all rested again.

"But I'm basically back to normal," Daniel argued.

"The rest of us use more mana than you." Madi put her plate in the dirty pile. "We don't all have Orrin's crazy regenerative powers, and taking a mana potion now would be one less we can take during the fight. We'll rest and then fight."

Orrin wisely stayed out of the argument. Once the other three were asleep, Daniel moved over and sat by him. They sat together in silence, listening to Emily's soft snores. Orrin checked his status. The last floor brought a lot of growth. Orrin had made sure to hit every monster he could. Even getting only part of the experience pool for each kill, he'd seen his largest growth in one go.

Orrin
Utility Warder Level 14 (4,136/5,000)
AP: 19

"When we get out of here, we shouldn't head back to Dey," Orrin said quietly. He'd been doing a lot of thinking about their next project. "If we do, something else will inevitably come up and we'll get stuck doing something else . . . again. We need to get to the elves and figure out a way to end the fighting."

Orrin pulled up his Quests, ignoring all but one.

Stop the war in Odrana
Reward: 200,000 XP and Variable
Failure: Loss of 10 levels

"Emily and Garret are great adventurers, but we need to shake them somehow."

Daniel nodded. "We could ask them to go back and report in for us."

"And if they say no?"

"You can [Teleport] us away."

"If I have any mana left after the next fight, I can. Time the conversation well."

Daniel picked at a loose thread on his pants. Wrapping his finger around it twice, he yanked it. A small seam pulled loose.

"This dungeon hasn't been easy, but it hasn't been as tough as I thought it would be," Daniel finally muttered. "I mean, don't get me wrong, it's had its hard parts, but . . ."

"I get it." Orrin started using up his daily allotment of [Analyze]. "We might have gotten lucky, or maybe it's just a good group."

Daniel shook his head. "You idiot. It's you. I was going to say it's had its hard parts, but having you here made it all a lot easier."

Daniel rolled the broken thread in his fingers and tossed it away. "I'm glad you're by my side. It's more than just the buffs and healing. I'm glad I have someone I can trust to lean on."

"You've got Madi, too."

Daniel nudged his friend with his shoulder. "Yeah, we do."

Daniel stood in front of the door to the tenth and final floor of the dungeon. They'd already discussed multiple strategies for whatever they had to fight. Emily confirmed that most tenth-level bosses were single entities, usually stronger than anything found before that point.

Orrin had cast [Utility Ward] on the party before increasing his own intelligence and will to the maximum. He'd also spammed [Increase Strength] and [Increase Dexterity] on Daniel.

Garret had his Citrandish bow out and was getting more [Curved Arrow] practice in. He'd already spent an hour sending his missiles flying at various angles around the room.

Emily and Madi were having another hurried discussion about magic. Orrin was glad Emily had opened up so much to the team, but the amount of knowledge she'd been sharing with Madi was what was showing real results. Madi's slow-moving [Shimmersight] could be launched more like a high-speed baseball now. Even her butterflies were able to move in clumps, obscuring a monster's line of sight on the party.

"Hold your breath and hope it's not a water level." Daniel saluted with his sword and stepped through.

"Why would he jinx us like that?" Orrin complained as they all walked through.

The party arrived in a forest. The trees clumped tight enough to block their view for more than a dozen yards in any direction.

Garret tapped one tree with the tip of his bow. It rang hollow, with a metallic note.

"Irontrees." Garret noticed Daniel's confused face. "Trees of iron. The dwarves made them. They usually only grow along the mountainsides, and never in this number."

Orrin already had his [Map] up. "There's something headed this direction, but it keeps skipping."

"Skipping?" Daniel raised an eyebrow as he readied Gertrude.

"It's like it's lag— Um, jumping around. Coming from that way." Orrin pointed south of the door.

Daniel nodded. Emily's hands began to glow, and Garret had an arrow nocked.

"Madi, try to blind it. Then everyone go wild. Orrin, if you can hit it, try and slow it down." Daniel rested on his back foot, ready to attack.

The floor boss flitted among the trees just out of sight. Just before reaching the party, it disappeared.

"Orrin! Location?" Daniel yelled.

Orrin frantically zoomed in and out of the [Map]. "It's gone. I can't find i—"

Something large and impossibly fast melted out of a tree behind them and slammed into Garret, pulling him deeper into the forest.

"It got Garret. After it!" Daniel charged in the direction of the archer.

They found him twenty yards away. Garret's entire body was encased in the same metal as the Irontree. Two long cuts had been sliced across his upper chest and lower left hip.

"Is he alive?" Daniel frantically turned, watching every corner and shadow.

"That's his fail-safe spell," Emily explained. "He did it to himself. He basically turns into a statue for a few minutes." She knelt and poked the gash along his side. "This is really deep to show up even after he triggered this."

"Is he going to be all right?" Madi had her back to the Garret statue, spear extended.

"He'll be pissed he missed the fight. I've only seen him use this once. He said it has too long of a cooldown to be useful in any but the most deadly situations. He must have been in real danger."

Orrin took his eyes off the [Map] to toss an [Identify] on Garret. His health had gone down by a third in the few seconds since he'd been dragged away. He tried to cast a [Heal Small Wounds], but the spell didn't trigger when he targeted the statue.

Unfortunately for the party, that was the moment the boss attacked again.

Unfortunately for the boss, it targeted Daniel.

Madi's yell gave Daniel just enough time to trigger [Dwarf Star], giving him the extra mass he needed. Even with his strength maxed out, the beast pushed him back a few inches.

Daniel loaded on [Stone Skin] as the monster started slicing at him. The beast had the general shape of a praying mantis, with two long arms ending in curved hooks. It clicked its mandibles together, trying to get close enough to bite Daniel, but the [Hero] put his huge sword between them and screamed and pushed. The monster turned in the air, kicking off Daniel's chest and sailing away.

Orrin and Emily both scored hits on it before it impacted a tree and melted into the metal.

"That looks a lot like what that druid guy could do," Daniel complained, rubbing his chest.

"Are you okay?" Madi pulled Daniel back toward the Garret statue. "Are you hurt?"

"I'm fine. Orrin, please tell me you got a read on that thing."

"Yes, and even better, I got a dex debuff on it, too." Orrin held his hand up for a high five, but nobody took their eyes off the woods. He let his hand fall. "It's a Gazzelym. Looking it up now."

"I don't know that one," Madi said as she swept her spear back and forth.

"Me, either." Emily threw a ball of fire into the darkness of the woods. "Missed it."

Orrin flipped through the pages. He turned a page back and moaned. "It's not in here."

Emily threw another spell into the trees. "It might be too rare. Not every monster can be categorized. List off anything you've noticed about it. Maybe we can figure out a weakness."

"It's strong and quick, with sharp sword arms," Daniel started.

"It has chitin all over it like a bug," Orrin chimed in.

"It melts into the trees and can move between them somehow." Madi cast some [Lightstream] spells into the forest, trying to light it up. A shadow attacked each one, seeming to drink up the magic. "Shit, it has darkness magic."

Orrin thought of Sof, the druid from the Dragoon team. He'd also been able to step between trees. How would he have fought someone like that?

"We need to draw it into a clearing and surround it. If we can take away its mobility, we'll have a better chance. It's using hit-and-run tactics to take us out one by one; it just made the mistake of going after Daniel first or well . . . second." Orrin glanced guiltily at Garret. "I'm going to focus on hitting it with as many inversed-dexterity spells as I can and then do the same for strength. If we have any luck, that will take it out."

"And if not?" Daniel asked. He'd been there when Orrin's spells hadn't fully taken down another member of the Dragoon team, Bin. They'd had a theory it had something to do with higher constitution stats but didn't exactly have someone high leveled to test the theory on.

"Then we hit it with everything we have."

In the minute they'd been talking, the Gazzelym hadn't reappeared. Emily's spell must have hurt it enough for it to be cautious.

"I'm going to release some butterflies in that direction," Madi announced after a moment of silence. She cast her [Lightshow], and twenty butterflies of light spread from her open hand. "Hopefully, it will targ—"

The Gazzelym sped from behind a tree and sliced through the flying insects. Orrin maxed out the dexterity debuffs he could cast on it but didn't have time for more.

Emily launched more [Firestrikes], while Madi tried to hit it with a [Shimmersight]. Emily scored three hits, but Madi missed. By the time Daniel reached the insectoid monster, it had disappeared into another tree. He hit his sword against the tree in anger.

Gertrude sank deeply into the iron where the monster had touched.

"The tree isn't solid where it touched it." Daniel thought out loud. He turned Gertrude and dug part of the tree out. "It's like a sludge here."

The tree still stood, but a quarter of its mass had been carved out. The part that splattered against the ground was slowly absorbed into the earth.

Emily stepped closer and reached into the puddle before it disappeared. "Fascinating. It's water and darkness magic together. It's creating portals through the trees by melting them."

"Watch out!" Daniel swung his sword directly at Emily. The fire mage wisely ducked as the Gazzelym dropped from a branch above. The flat of Daniel's blade connected with a solid hit and knocked the boss off target, but it was still able to shove one sharpened arm down into Emily's body. As Daniel struck it over and over, pushing it back, Emily curled into a ball. Flames sprouted from her, licking up the iron trees to either side.

"Orrin, Emily's hurt."

"I know that, you idiot," Orrin yelled as he ran to her side. The fire burned him, but it would take a bit to get through his [Ward]. "Emily, Emily, I'm here. I'm going to heal you, okay?"

She didn't respond with words, but the flames retreated and she moved her arms from around her center. Orrin saw the deep stab wound and almost threw up. The monster's bladed arm had hit Emily a few inches to the right of her belly button and sliced cleanly and very deeply. Orrin could see her ribs and moving slimy parts inside through all the blood.

[Heal Small Wounds]
[Heal Small Wounds]

Orrin cast his spell at level three. With his will at one hundred, each spell was ten times more powerful than it should have been. *Four hundred healing per spell is a little OP,* he thought as the extra healing hastened the closing of the wound and fixed . . . things . . . inside the mage.

Emily gasped and opened her eyes. She waved a blazing hand wildly, pushed herself to her knees and coughed. Then, with literal fire in her eyes, she screamed and ran at the monster still batting Daniel's strikes away.

"For fuck's sake, I just finished healing you," Orrin complained as Emily threw herself at the tenth-floor boss.

Chapter 33

Emily bear-hugged the Gazzelym from behind, pinning its arms to its side. The fire in her eyes grew to cover her face, spreading down her neck in a flash and encompassing both her and the dungeon boss in a searing white flame.

The monster chittered in real pain for the first time and thrashed.

"Hit it with everything you've got," Emily groaned through gritted teeth. "I can't keep this up for long."

Orrin worked quickly. He reduced every stat he could, hit the oversize insect with a few quick [Lightstrike] spells, and summoned an [Ice Sword].

"That girl is on fire," Daniel singsonged. He raised Gertrude straight up and activated his [Gravity Strike]. Motes of gray swirled around the tip of his sword.

Orrin watched as the sword moved through the air like it was honey. The slow movement doubled in speed, and when he blinked, the fight was over.

Daniel's attack cut the Gazzelym in half from the top of its head to the middle of its chest. Emily had let go and jumped back at the last moment. The flames covering her body guttered once before flickering out completely.

Orrin opened his mouth to speak. He didn't know if he was going to chastise Daniel or Emily for their reckless attacks or shout congratulations. He didn't get the chance before the ground below the dead boss began to glow.

Lines of squiggly runes circled the body. The Gazzelym sank into the ground, and a black ball rose a moment later to hover in the air between them.

"Is that the dungeon core?" Daniel stepped forward and reached to touch the ball. It spat flickers of blue, green, silver, and black, and the [Hero] pulled back.

"Should we wait?" Daniel glanced at the still-frozen party member. "How long until Garret comes out of that?"

Emily rapped her knuckles on the archer's still form. "He'll be around in a minute or two. I'm not sure what would happen if you destroyed the core while he was incapacitated. Would you all mind terribly if we waited?"

"Is touching it going to destroy it?" Orrin found himself standing closer to the ball. Something about it entranced him, called to him.

"No, you have to squeeze it." Emily was knocking on Garret's head. "Wake up, you useless . . ."

Orrin stopped listening. He reached out with a finger to brush the glossy black sphere. The colors jumped in little arcs, swirling back into the dark center. He heard voices in the background as he connected with the core.

> **Welcome, Administrator**
> **Would you like to absorb this core for ten (10) administrator points?**

"What the what?"

Orrin fell back and landed hard against a tree. His heart was pounding against his chest, and Daniel was already standing in front of him.

"Orrin! Orrin? What's wrong?"

How could he even answer? The core wasn't supposed to do that. What were administrator points? Orrin felt Madi and Emily looking at him. Nobody even noticed as Garret took a deep breath and began to slap flakes of metal off his arms.

"Orrin! Answer me. What happened?"

Daniel had both of Orrin's arms gripped tight, but he was having trouble getting his friend to look him in the eye.

"I can't explain it." Orrin looked meaningfully around at everybody.

Thankfully, Daniel caught on quickly. "Can everybody give us a minute?"

"No."

Daniel turned on Emily. "No?"

The mage shook her head. "You're the [Hero], and we were tasked with listening to you, but we've completed the mission. You don't get to send us away before destroying the core. We all deserve to get those points."

Garret, who had only half an idea of what was going on, nodded and stepped up beside her.

Daniel's chest swelled up as he took a deep breath. Orrin could see his friend was still coming down from the adrenaline of the fight. A confrontation was not something they needed.

"That's all right, Emily." Orrin grabbed Daniel's sleeve and pulled away from the group. "We'll just go over here."

"No." This time it was Madi.

"Madi?" Orrin frowned.

"Something just happened. This is like last time, isn't it? In the Aqua Chambers?" She put her spear on the ground and slowly approached them. "We're on the same team, Orrin. What is it?"

Orrin thought fast. He could tell Daniel about the Administrator stuff because they were best friends. Madi had earned their trust, but he didn't know what she would do if she learned he had these powers, too. He flashed back to the image of Tony falling to his knees in fear. There was no way he was going to let Emily know. She'd try to study him. Maybe bring him back to Odrana to be researched. Garret wouldn't care but would likely sell the information back to the Guild.

"Back off," Daniel demanded. His voice was quiet but held steel he hadn't directed at anyone in the party before. "Orrin and I need to talk. This is still my party, and I'll decide—"

"Daniel, stop threatening people. Give me a minute to think."

To his credit, his friend shut up and crossed his arms.

He could try dropping Emily, Madi, and Garret. A few debuffs to their strength or dexterity and they'd be unable to move. That would mean leaving Dey behind, along with Madi. They'd planned on her being their liaison with the elves. Orrin wasn't stupid enough to think either of the teens had a good enough political mind to negotiate with the centuries-old elves, but at least Madi had been trained in statecraft since birth. Attacking all three was out.

He could still take down Emily and Garret. Bring Madi up to speed and hope she didn't turn on them. Best case, she'd still come north with them. Worst case, they'd have to leave her, resulting in the same outcome as the first option.

Think! What's the use of all these extra points in intelligence if I can't come up with a good lie? Orrin knew the stats didn't actually make him smarter, and not for the first time, he wished they did. But he was getting off track again.

If he could figure out a good enough lie, he could fill Daniel in on the administrator points thing later. Maybe the Quest triggered when he touched the core?

Thank you for the idea, Madi.

Orrin did his best to come up with the various responses and answers he'd have to give. He was going to need to lie his ass off.

"Madi, this has to do with the you know what."

Madi quirked her eyebrow.

"It's very similar to what happened in the Aqua Chambers." *Please, please, buy it.*

Madi glanced at the other two party members. They glared back.

"Could you two—"

"Fuck off." Garret cut her off. "What are you all hiding?"

Orrin played the only card he could think of to get out of this situation. "We have a Quest to defeat a dungeon."

Emily's eyes narrowed. Garret's jaw dropped.

"You . . . all three of you?" Garret stammered. "You weren't going to share it, were you?"

Madi responded defensively. "Of course not. You two are already giving a full report to the Guildmaster on every skill and ability the [Hero] has. Why would we give you more?"

Emily blushed in embarrassment, but Garret threw the accusation to the side. "Of course we are. You knew that when you accepted us, but hoarding a Quest? That's low."

"What does the Quest have to do with Orrin, though?" Emily asked.

Damn it. I knew she was too smart.

"Orrin has a weird class. Something happened in the last dungeon we were in and he was able to . . . I don't know how to explain it. He unlocked the rewards." Madi had positioned herself between Orrin and the other two.

I need to sell this. Orrin thought before he spoke. "When a Quest shows up, I can edit the rewards a bit. Not all the time, but when I'm close to Daniel. It's one of the reasons we're in the same party. We don't know why. Maybe because I awakened my class while fighting monsters off him."

He'd never given a straight answer to Madi about where they'd met or how. He saw several wrong assumptions click into place for her with that lie—the real reason the [Hero] would keep a weakling like him around. Daniel turned his face so only Orrin could see him and raised an eyebrow.

What the fuck?

Go with it!

Daniel gave a minuscule shrug. *You're the boss.*

Everyone stood in the deathly silent forest. Orrin noticed Garret was still injured, with the cuts to his chest and hip bleeding freely.

"Garret, do you need a heal?"

"It can wait. Are you going to share the Quest with us? We fought the entire dungeon with you. Do you not think we deserve the rewards?"

They'd discussed sharing the Quest with them before leaving Dey. They'd decided against it for a multitude of reasons, but right now, Orrin only had one thought in his mind: the new message.

He turned to Daniel. "What do you say?" He winked.

Daniel bit his lip and rubbed at his chin. He'd grown a little bit of stubble in the dungeon and was looking older now. "You think we should?"

Orrin gave a slight nod of his head. "It's up to you."

"I want to know what Orrin saw." Emily derailed his entire plan.

He closed his eyes in frustration. "I think I can change the reward," he lied.

Madi's face lit up. Emily was still giving him looks of disbelief and suspicion. Garret was rubbing his hands in anticipation of getting a Quest.

Madi stepped closer to Daniel and whispered something. He nodded.

"Let's talk." Madi stepped up and grabbed the two Guild members. They were only a few feet away, but Daniel leaned over and whispered to Orrin.

"What's going on?"

Orrin pulled his friend back a few steps and lowered his voice as much as he could. "Give them the Quest. It doesn't matter. I need to be the one to destroy the core, I think. Something to do with my other ability. I'll explain later."

"What are you two whispering about?" Madi peered over her shoulder. "We all get a say in the reward."

"Well, then, let's discuss it." Daniel strode forward into the small circle, and negotiations began.

In return for the Quest, Emily and Garret would report only a specific set of information to the Guildmaster about the [Hero] and his party. Obviously, the Quest would remain their dirty little secret.

"Orrin has to be the one to destroy the core," Daniel confided.

It's too bad there isn't a charisma stat, because Daniel would have that in spades. Orrin stayed quiet during the talks, only giving monosyllabic answers to questions.

He healed Garret's wounds without a thank-you. Once everything was hammered out, Daniel shared the Quest with the other two.

Emily's eyes were bright as she read her own screen, and Garret actually jumped in the air.

"Let's do this," Daniel said, gesturing Orrin toward the still-floating sphere.

"If we get to choose our reward, can I have more dexterity points?" Garret asked in glee.

"I'd prefer intelligence." Emily was standing very close and watching Orrin.

"I'll do my best," Orrin muttered and reached for the sphere again.

Welcome, Administrator
Would you like to absorb this core for ten (10) administrator points?

Yes.

A cascade of notifications lit up his screen.

Congratulations! You have defeated the Crumbling Waste!
You have been rewarded two (2) Dexterity points!

Quest Complete
Defeat a Dungeon
Reward: Defeat of tier-one, single deca-set dungeon.
Calculating variable reward . . .

Calculation Complete.
Reward selection of the following:
Increase Strength Stat + 5
Increase Dexterity Stat + 5
Increase Constitution Stat + 5
Increase Will Stat + 5

Increase Intelligence Stat + 5

Orrin almost cried in relief that the Quest was allowing a selection. Almost like the system knew he needed it.

"He actually did it!" Garret cried out. "Emily! This kid is for real!"

Orrin had done nothing. He looked at the next notification and paled.

You have been awarded 10 administrator points.
You have unlocked Administrator Skills

A new page on his status showed new skills. Except these weren't silly spells like what he'd been purchasing up to this point. Orrin read the first half dozen:

- **Assign Class**
- **Reset Class**
- **Assign Quests**
    - **Edit Reward**
- **Unlock Ability (Select One)**
    - **Unlock Skill**
    - **Unlock Spell**
- **Edit Stats (Sanctioned)**
    - **Remove**
    - **Assign**
    - **Full Reset**
- **Edit Stats (Unsanctioned)**
    - **Remove**
    - **Assign**
    - **Full Reset**

There weren't nearly as many options as his normal purchase lists, but he didn't have time to read through the entire list right now.

"What is happening to me?"

Chapter 34

Orrin put the new, confusing part of his system on the back burner and turned to the immediate rewards.

His dexterity had gone up by two, finally breaking into double digits. He didn't feel any faster or more coordinated, but seeing the numbers go up still satisfied the gamer in him.

The reward selection for defeating the dungeon was great, too. He hesitated over his favorite stat, will, for only a moment before sighing audibly and taking the increase in constitution. His health points were too low, and even with all his wards, Tony's advice to keep constitution a priority echoed in his mind.

I can always increase my will at level twenty, he thought, trying to focus.

Emily and Garret were laughing at their good fortune. Garret was sending arrows into trees around them, trying to get a feel for his new points.

Orrin lied and said messing with the rewards for the Quest had sapped his strength. He sat with his back to a metal tree and read the system notification over and over, trying to find some new morsel of information.

You have unlocked Administrator Skills

Sitting next to his ability points was a new box.

Orrin
Utility Warder

Level 14 (4,886/5,000)
AP: 19
Administrator Points: 10
Administrator Skills:
HP: 120/120
MP: 547/1,100
Strength: 9 (100)
Constitution: 12
Dexterity: 11 (100)
Will: 28 (100)
Intelligence: 11 (100)

The twenty-minute timer for his increase-stat spells was almost up. His and Daniel's maxed-out stats would soon drop back to only the [Utility Ward] increase for the rest of the day. He didn't care. The addition of yet another thing to keep track of was overwhelming him.

Orrin cast a [Calm Mind] on himself and tried to think of anything else. When he'd absorbed the dungeon core, it had shattered into pieces like it was supposed to. Nothing he'd read had prepared him for the rush of power into his body.

"I can't wait to get back and show Tin how much we've improved." Garret was making his arrows turn arcs in the air above them. He could make his arrows go in a half circle before they fell to inertia. "Do you think I'll be able to make my arrows do a full rotation before I hit forty?"

Emily watched Orrin.

Madi and Daniel were talking about him. He could hear their whispers. Daniel was assuring her that he was fine and just needed time.

"I need a vacation," he muttered to himself. "Shouldn't I have a beach arc soon?"

He shook himself as [Calm Mind] took effect. They could deal with anything that came their way. He pushed off the ground and made his way to his friends.

"Thanks for the breather. I'm feeling better."

Madi began to say something before closing her mouth and pulling him into a tight hug. He forgot how to move and only brought his arms up by reflex. The second his arms hugged back, Madi stepped away. She wouldn't look up from her feet.

"Stop trying to hide things from me . . . please." She balled her hands into fists and turned to look him in the eyes. "If you still can't trust me after all this time . . ."

When she didn't finish her sentence, Orrin realized he was supposed to assure her that he did trust her, but he missed the moment.

"We do," Daniel said in a hurry. He nudged Orrin. "It's just weird with the others, you know?"

The hurt in her eyes was real, but Orrin watched her steel herself and adopt the persona of Madeleine Catanzano, the impenetrable daughter of a lord of Dey. "I understand."

Orrin felt like shit, but he barely knew what was going on. He feared Daniel might get angry at his new powers, too. He really needed to find out more about Administrators.

He had to cast [Calm Mind] again.

"Let's get out of here." He walked toward the exit door that had appeared after he absorbed/destroyed the dungeon core.

Orrin didn't even feel Daniel's hand on his shoulder before it slipped off.

Madi was the last to step out of the dungeon. The doorway glowed with a bright-white light before the arch cracked. The deep inner darkness that marked an open portal to the dungeon disappeared.

"One less dungeon in our world," Madi said proudly.

Jeb and Derrick, two of the Guild members sent to guard the dungeon, were speechless when they saw the broken gate. Sadie, the one in charge, simply saluted the party with a fist over her heart.

"Everyone made it back, too," she said as she inspected them all. "Pritus is going to be very pleased. Would you like an escort back?"

"Orrin can [Teleport] us back. I think we might stay out here for a day or two," Daniel explained. "We want to practice our teamwork with our new levels."

The Guild members had no further reason to wait around and began breaking camp. Garret started helping them.

"Garret, you need to return the bow to Orrin. It was a loaner." Madi climbed over a few small rocks and slid down the hill as she went after the archer. "Garret? Don't you dare ignore me."

Daniel chuckled.

"It was a pleasure working with you both," Emily said, leaning on her staff. "If you ever need more help, I'm always available to help the [Hero]."

She took a few steps away before turning back. "Orrin, would you mind if I had a few words with you?"

Orrin put his hand up to cut off Daniel's response. "Sure."

He followed Emily away from the quick breakdown of the camp. She walked a few minutes before she stopped and turned to him.

"I won't insult your intelligence," she began. "You have unique magic that I've never heard of, and I'm intrigued. However, you have every right to keep your own secrets, and I would never dare to try and force those from you."

Orrin felt a bead of sweat trickle down his shoulder.

"Guildmaster Pritus did task Garret and me to watch Daniel and his party and report back. In the past, whenever a [Hero] has appeared, bad things happened. It's usually not a matter of if but when, and she wants to be prepared. From what I've seen, you two have a true friendship. Keep ahold of that. Maybe you can keep him from destroying nations."

Emily tilted her head in the way she did when watching something interesting. "How much do you know of Odrana? Outside of the unpleasantness with Daniel."

"Not much," Orrin said truthfully. "Just the basics. A friend told me there is a big school of magic there."

Emily laughed dryly. "There are multiple schools of magic, but, yes, most people only speak of Sanneris. I went there for a few years. It . . . is very prestigious, but not the only place to learn."

Then, for the first time since meeting her, Orrin watched Emily stumble over her words.

"I . . . I want—if you are interested, that is . . . If you are ever in Odrana, my family runs a school. Stridsfall isn't as esteemed, but we accept all magic users and have a good track record for researching new magics. I think . . . you would be an amaz—would be welcome."

Orrin had spent the entire time Emily talked waiting for an attack or accusation. Instead, she was . . . recruiting him?

"Obviously, you don't have to say anything or accept. I don't technically even have the authority to grant you acceptance, but I'd like to write a letter on your behalf in case you ever do want to . . . or have the time. The things you did in that dungeon were incredible. You've shown me the value of diversifying, and I can see more people trying to take a path like yours in the future. If you ever would consider teaching the way to unlock your class, I'm certain you could change adventuring for the better. Fewer deaths and more dungeons defeated."

She took a deep breath. Emily had spoken more in this stretch than she had in the entire dungeon run. "That's all I wanted to say." She started the walk back to the camp.

Orrin held up his hand. She stopped and quirked her head again.

"Thank you. I'm not sure exactly what I could teach, but I appreciate the vote of support anyways. And we all appreciate your help in there." He tilted his head back toward the dungeon. "You really went all-out. It was amazing to watch."

Emily smiled, her teeth flashing. "It is fun to go all-out like that." She rubbed her side. Orrin had healed the deep gouge in her stomach, but he knew the phantom pains could remain even after the physical injuries were gone. "Maybe not again for a while, though."

They rejoined the group and waved goodbye. Soon it was just Madi, Daniel, and Orrin.

"Are we really training?" Madi asked playfully.

"Which way to the elves?" Daniel asked in return.

Madi handed the Citrandish bow to Orrin for safekeeping. They headed north, discussing their plans as they walked.

Madi wanted to make an announced visit, shouting that the [Hero] was visiting the elves to help with their war. She believed diplomacy would be the best route, leaning into her years of training to take over for her father.

Daniel instead wanted to sneak along the border and make a scene. He daydreamed aloud of taking out multiple groups of Odranan troops, saving elves from certain death and then being carried into the elven cities on the shoulders of those they'd saved.

"What do you think, Orrin?" Daniel asked him as he finished describing how big a feast they'd throw in his honor for saving the elven princesses.

"I think it won't matter what we plan." Orrin focused on something in the air.

"What is wrong with you?"

Orrin tripped and smacked his knee hard on the ground. Daniel bent to help him up but stiffened when Orrin whispered something.

"Are you okay?" Madi asked, stopping and turning back toward them.

"Yeah, go ahead. We'll be right there." Daniel waved her away. Madi harrumphed but kept walking.

"Are you sure?" Daniel whispered.

"They keep flitting in and out of my range, but yes," Orrin said, pushing himself to his feet. "We're being followed."

Daniel moved to put his hand on Gertrude's handle, but Orrin tripped into him again, catching his arm.

"They don't know that we know they are here."

"We don't know that."

"We don't know that they know that we know?" Orrin smirked as he messed with Daniel.

"You're an idiot. We should tell Madi and set an ambush or something."

"I've got a plan."

Daniel smiled and pushed Orrin forward. "I'm glad you're back. You've been weird since the dungeon."

"We can talk about that later." Orrin pushed one problem out of his mind in favor of the most urgent one. "Whoever it is that's following us is making a beeline for Madi."

Chapter 35

Orrin increased Daniel's speed, as well as his own, about halfway to max. He felt a momentary twinge of regret that they'd had Madi walk ahead, but the stalker had been following them for some time. He'd had no idea they would suddenly strike once one of them was alone. The tall grass to either side of the long-abandoned path they'd found heading north swayed with the wind they generated as they ran.

A dark thought crossed his mind. *Did I have an idea this would happen and send Madi ahead as bait?*

Orrin shook his head and ignored his own question. It didn't matter right now. With their dexterity boosted so much, both Orrin and Daniel were already bearing down on Madi. The enemy spot on his [Map] slowed its approach and flickered between the red of an enemy and the neutral grey of a non-threat.

That's never happened . . .

Madi peeked over her shoulder at them with a smile and eye roll. Seeing the two of them running at her in a dead sprint, she must have thought they were racing.

I mean, we do compete a lot . . .

Orrin slid to a stop and popped a [Ward] on everyone. Daniel drew Gertrude from his back and circled. He glanced at Orrin, who nodded his chin to their right.

Daniel wasted no time and bellowed, "Whoever or whatever you are, come out."

Madi's spear extended to its full length, and she set up in a fighting stance, ready to lunge or cast a spell at a moment's notice.

An elf stood up from a crouch about fifty yards from them. He'd moved closer in the moments Orrin had taken to cast his spells. He raised both hands over his head in a placating gesture.

"I would seek food, if you have any to spare?"

Orrin tried to use [Identify], but the skill fizzled. The elf turned his blue eyes to Orrin.

"I mean no harm. Are you three from Dey? Perhaps we could trade information?"

Daniel whispered under his breath, "Madi? What should we do here?"

Madi stood up from her crouch and let her spear clink down to its smaller size. She stepped in front of Daniel and waved her hand, summoning the elf forward. She spoke out of the corner of her mouth. "Be alert. I would say he's a scout, out surveying the Odranan army, but he's too far south and west unless they've pushed more than my father knows. Something is wrong with this."

Orrin nodded. "He's been following us for an hour, maybe more."

Madi's face transformed from her relaxed and happy persona to the strict and confident daughter of Silas Catanzano they'd met all those months ago on the road to Dey. If Orrin didn't know any better, he'd have bet she had a skill or spell for being so imperious.

The elf kept his hands in the air as he slowly walked forward. Orrin noticed his armor, all leather, was decorated with a leaf motif. He had a bracer of knives in different sizes on a belt around his waist and a bow that looked familiar on his back. *It's a Citrandish bow,* Orrin realized.

The elf also had weapons holstered on either hip. On the left, he wore a sword that swept out in a crescent along the blade. Orrin mistook the weapon on the right hip for a mace until he noticed that the spiked head hung from a short chain. Orrin had just made out marks down the side of the staff portion of the weapon when the elf turned his body into the tall grass a bit more to hide the weapons from view.

"That's far enough," Madi called out. "Why are you following us?"

The fake look of surprise on his face was good, Orrin had to admit. "I just caught sight of you a few minutes ago and was seeing if you appeared friendly before approaching. I'm sure you know that our forest is under attack. I can't be too careful."

"You've been following us for much longer than a few minutes," Madi said, all traces of mirth gone from her eyes. She exuded confidence and strength, and Orrin was very glad she was on his side.

The elf dropped his hands from the air, but before he spoke, Madi's spear grew out, Daniel shimmered as he activated a skill, and Orrin summoned an [Ice Sword].

He slowly raised his hands again. "Sorry. If I was following you, it was not intentional or known to me. Like I said, I just noticed you and—"

"Buddy, I've got the [Map] skill and have been watching you dance around us as a hostile. Give it up. Who are you?" Orrin spoke over him. He readied an inversed [Increase Dexterity]. This guy had the appearance of someone who moved quickly.

The elf laughed. He tilted his head back and laughed at the sky.

"Madi, try and daze him if you can," Daniel muttered under his breath. "Orrin, do your thing. You guys ready?"

"Wait. No need to attack." The intruder kept his hands up. "I'm laughing at my own failure, not you."

"What failure?" Madi asked, clenching her hands around her spear. "This is the last time I'll ask. Who are you?"

The elf crossed his arms in salute quickly before raising them high again. "My name is Leanthun. I was sent to gather information on the new [Hero]. I swear on the ancient trees of Citrand that I was only going to test your fighting prowess and abilities. I would not have left any injury to you or yours. My mistake was not fully investigating your party members. I thought the boy was a follower, not someone with functional skills."

"This boy is the same age as the [Hero]," Orrin muttered, but nobody was listening to him.

"I pledge that I will bring you no harm this day," Leanthun continued. "May I approach?"

"Madi?" Daniel didn't lower his sword, keeping it pointed at the elf.

"Elves value promises. If he says he won't hurt us, he's telling the truth about that."

"For today only," Orrin muttered, again being ignored. He'd read enough stories with supposed truth tellers who could misdirect better with a few carefully crafted words than an elaborate lie. "He won't hurt us today, but once night falls . . ."

"What's that, O?"

"He promised not to harm us 'this day.' That means as soon as it's dark, he could attack."

"Is what he says true?" Daniel called out to the elf, who had taken a few steps in their direction. "You mean to attack us later?"

"I promise not to attack you unprovoked this day or tomorrow."

"That still leaves the nighttime open," Orrin half shouted. "Promise never to attack us and stop walking forward."

"I cannot promise to never attack you, for none of us knows what the next day may bring. I will promise to not harm or cause harm to befall you until we reach the forest. Is that satisfactory?" Leanthun had moved to only thirty yards away and had his hands resting on his weapons, but in a nonthreatening manner.

Orrin waited for Madi or Daniel to answer, but when he looked at them, both were waiting for him to respond. "Seriously?" He turned back to the elf. "Accepted."

Leanthun strode through the grass like a ghost, barely making the tall stalks shift. Orrin knew his dexterity had to be higher than anyone else's they'd ever met just by the way he floated across the ground.

Once he parted the lower and sparser grass near the path, the lithe elf crossed his arms over his chest again and gave Madi a slight bow. He repeated the gesture to Daniel.

Turning to Orrin, Leanthun did his weird bow again, moving a little deeper than he had before. "I have to admit, I'm impressed you noticed me. I am not used to being caught unaware."

Orrin ignored the compliment. He definitely did not blush at the words, no matter how hot his face was feeling. Instead, he decided that if Madi and Daniel were going to make him be in charge of talking with the elf, he'd do his best.

"Why do the elves want to test the [Hero]? And why send you?"

Leanthun smiled as if Orrin was a child playing war with veterans all around. "The advent of a [Hero] is always a turbulent time. With Odrana attacking our borders, some believed it prudent to assess the situation. I was sent to do the assessment Now, if I may ask, who are you?"

"I'm Orrin. Daniel's my friend. Madi over there is—"

"The scion of a lord of Dey. I know of Lady Catanzano. Where did you learn the [Map] skill? I was under the impression you were used as a mule. Some sort of storage skill for carrying items, if I'm correct?"

Orrin gaped.

"Who are you calling a mule?" Daniel stepped in front of his friend angrily. "Orrin is a valued member of this team and offers more than—"

"Daniel, shut up," Orrin sputtered. He pulled his friend back. "So, you've been spying on us. If you know so much, why try and attack Madi?"

"I was going to incapacitate her only. Her [Shimmersight] ability could have interfered with my ability to spar with the [Hero]."

Madi's hand glimmered as she spoke. "Who is your information broker? My skills are not supposed to be well-known."

"That's unimportant. I came with a job to do. While a true fight would have been preferable, perhaps a spar will still allow me some insight into your worth."

"My worth?" Daniel's knuckles turned white on the hilt of Gertrude.

"Yes. My people would like to hire you to help repel the invaders in our home. Unless, of course, you were traveling to join Odrana. I would advise against that." Leanthun's words were an obvious threat, but Orrin felt no actual violence coming from the elf.

He wasn't sent to hire us. Something else is going on. What is he playing at?

"We were coming to offer our help, but I have no problem kicking your ass all the way to the forest if that's what you want," Daniel said with much more malice than the elf's words had. "Is there some proper and fancy method of fighting you have? Or can I just beat you into a pulp?"

"Just fight with me for a few minutes. You can simply say 'out' when you want to stop."

"Daniel, can I have a word with you?" Madi gripped his sleeve.

"Take all the time you need to prepare." Leanthun drew his curved sword and maul-on-a-stick weapon.

Madi dragged Daniel back.

"Are you insane? He's just trying to get more information on your abilities. You don't need to fight him." Madi was berating him as Orrin joined. "Not to mention, he's an elf. Not the young and dumb kind that get themselves captured as slaves in Dey. He's at least three or four centuries old. Elves don't earn their own Citrandish bow until they're at least two hundred. He's fighting with a khopesh, too. That's an elite elven weapon. He's royalty or a high-ranking military member. I'm not even sure what his other weapon is."

"He insulted Orrin."

Madi waited for Daniel to say more. He didn't. She turned to Orrin for help.

"The dude is an ass. I do agree with Madi, though. You shouldn't let him know all your skills," Orrin said. "What are you looking at me like that for?"

"You boys are such idiots." Madi threw up her hands and stomped off.

"Should I boost you?" Orrin whispered. Daniel nodded. "Try to only use basic attacks, no skills. And don't kill him."

Daniel smirked. "You have no doubt I'm going to win, do you?"

Orrin shrugged. "If it looks like you aren't, I'll slow him down, go invisible, and beat him silly."

Daniel held up his fist. Orrin rapped his knuckles against his friend.

"Go kick some elf butt."

Chapter 36

Leanthun drew his khopesh and twirled the curved sword in one hand. He reached his free hand behind his back and drew a small vial out.

"Before we begin, I don't want you to hold back during this fight. Come at me as if I was your enemy. If there is an accident and you are hurt, we will need to get this down your throat as quickly as possible. It's a very high-level healing potion and will cure almost any injury you might have, short of lost limbs."

The elf moved across the path they'd been following and placed the glass bottle in Madi's hand.

Orrin used [Analyze] and saw that he was telling the truth.

[Potion of Moderate Healing]

"It's good," Orrin said, nodding at Madi.

Leanthun's brow creased momentarily. "Of course. I've already given my word. I have no need to poison him."

"We'll make sure to heal you up, too," Orrin promised.

Leanthun's smug smile prompted Orrin to max out Daniel's stats. He used [Identify] to check them out.

Name: Daniel
Hero
Level 15 (1,385/6,000)
HP: 400/400

MP: 80/80
Strength: 24 (100)
Constitution: 20
Dexterity: 15 (100)
Will: 8 (100)
Intelligence: 10 (100)

That bastard beat me to level fifteen.

The afternoon sun was on its journey toward the mountains. Orrin knew that within the hour, the sunset would set the sky on fire with a blaze of oranges, reds, and purples brighter than any of Earth's dusks. Daniel stood in the middle of the path, with Gertrude held in a vertical guard. Leanthun stopped ten yards from him and held his sword horizontally.

"When you are ready, you may attack."

Daniel flashed across the field, bringing his oversize sword down in an overhand chop that sent small rocks and chunks of dirt flying into the air. When the dust cleared, Leanthun was standing mere inches from the sword with his own blade at Daniel's neck.

"Again."

The next ten minutes were eye-opening to Orrin. Despite Daniel's maxed-out stats, he never landed a single blow against the elf. His movements were perfect—his blade sent gusts of wind hurtling at him and Madi, and every attack seemed for all the world as if this would be the one to hit Leanthun. Yet, at the moment, Daniel was panting, with sweat dripping from his face, and the elf was waiting. No blood had been drawn, but the fight was so one-sided that Orrin was worried.

If Leanthun was an enemy, could he [Teleport] them out in time?

"Your basic attack patterns are very well-done. I'm assuming you have [Sword Proficiency] at level two? You've also put in the work to override the basic system forms. I'm impressed. You are obviously using a boosting skill, as well. We'll have to train you up with that. You have the increased stats, but you haven't grown into them enough to fully utilize the speed and strength to full effect."

Orrin opened his mouth before he could think. "What do you mean? His stats are maxed out."

Leanthun glanced at Orrin to answer just as Daniel activated [Shooting Star].

> **[Shooting Star]—Upon activation, you can move in straight lines at incredible speeds for two minutes. Speed increased by Dexterity.**

Daniel was a blur. Orrin didn't see what happened because everyone else moved so much faster.

Daniel was straining with Gertrude caught in the khopesh's curve. Leanthun had caught his attack while still looking at Orrin.

"Artificially increased stat points only grant the possibility of that effect. For instance, the [Hero]'s strength is currently higher than mine. However, as you can see, I'm holding off his two-handed attack with one arm. How is that?"

Orrin waited, thinking Leanthun was going to continue. When he didn't, Orrin realized the elf was trying to teach them something . . . while holding off Daniel's attack.

"Um . . ."

"You have a skill that negates his strength?" Madi guessed.

Leanthun twisted his wrist and sent Daniel flying into the dirt.

"No. But some do have skills or spells that can reduce stats, although that is rare. Let me ask in a different way. When you last received a stat increase, how long did it take you to learn to handle your new strength or dexterity?"

Madi gasped and nodded her head. "It takes a few days before our bodies acclimate to the boosted power. Are you saying Orrin's buffs need time for us to acclimate, too?"

"Orrin's buffs?" Leanthun's brow creased again. The smallest wrinkle on the elf's otherwise perfect skin was the only tell he seemed to have. "This is not a power of Daniel's?"

He bent down and studied Daniel, who was spitting out dirt. When he noticed how close Leanthun was, he scrambled back and got to his feet.

"I'm not done. Let's go."

Leanthun waved his hand. "We'll have plenty of time for that later. What is this buff that Orrin has?"

Madi flashed a smile. "You don't honestly think we'd give you that information."

"Hmm." Leanthun ran his free hand over the symbols on his leathers. When Daniel ran at him from behind, he sidestepped and tripped the [Hero]. "You three were traveling toward my home. Am I right to guess you have a Quest relating to the current conflict?"

Orrin was pulling Daniel out of another small crater that he'd created when tripped. He was covered in dirt. Orrin ruffled his hair and created a small dust cloud.

"We are traveling to the elves to see if we can offer any assistance," Madi deftly answered.

Thank God we brought her. Orrin had no doubt he'd have spilled the beans five times over by now.

"I'll accompany you. You wouldn't be able to reach more than the outer villages we trade with. Our forest is on lockdown until we've repelled the invaders." Leanthun announced this without any trace of doubt they'd reject his proposal. He slipped his sword back into his belt. "I've left my pack a few miles out. I'll rejoin you before sundown."

Before Madi could answer, the elf had disappeared.

"I really don't like that guy," Daniel said, spitting mud from his mouth. "I should have gone all-out and used a few more skills. I almost had him when you distracted him, Orrin."

Orrin patted his friend on the shoulder. "Yes. You were so close. He'll go down fast next time."

"Yeah . . . next time." Daniel started walking the path again.

Madi slipped close to Orrin. "He doesn't have a chance, does he?"

"Nope," Orrin answered as they followed behind.

Daniel fumed and walked ahead of them for nearly an hour. Madi and Orrin exchanged small talk as they walked, but Orrin's mind was elsewhere.

"What do you think he meant about acclimating to my buffs?"

Madi chewed her lip. "He might have been lying to get more information out of us, but I don't think that's the case. I'm not really sure how to explain it, though."

"Can you try?" Orrin kicked a loose rock, which almost hit Daniel. He scowled at them over his shoulder. Madi waved.

"I'll try." She took a minute to collect her thoughts. "We just got those new points for dexterity from the dungeon, right? Have you felt any change in the way you move?"

Orrin thought back over the day. "Not particularly. Should I? I've usually only focused on my intelligence and will."

Madi clipped her spear to her belt. It had a tiny ring attached to the base, and in its smaller form, she didn't need to carry it all the time. "That is the point. When you increase your physical stats, you don't grow stronger or faster right away. The accepted time frame is a week or two before noticeable measurements can be made. There are ways to speed that up, but that's another topic."

She glanced at the setting sun. The colors bounced off the mountains and plains stretching out from them. "I'm not an expert in this at all. My father strongly discouraged me from taking any path that might lead to a self-boosting class, so it was not something I looked into heavily. I think Leanthun was talking about synergy with the buff."

"So, I need to buff you guys more and let you practice? That's not too bad. We can do that."

"I'm not sure it'll be that easy," Madi sighed. "That will help a little, but it's the difference between living with a few extra points every minute of every day and being buffed for, what . . . ten or twenty minutes? You could use [Utility Ward] on us every morning, but then what would happen? What if you leave or something happens to you? Would we get so used to it that it could have a negative effect?"

They walked for a few more minutes. Orrin bent and scooped up a few small rocks. He threw one at Daniel, missing him just slightly. Madi chuckled. Orrin handed her half a handful.

They spent some time messing with Daniel until he turned around and confronted them. Madi's laughter cooled any anger he had before he actually yelled at them.

"Should we set up camp?" Daniel searched the area until he pointed to a divot in the tall grass. "We could set up there."

"I really wish Orrin could just [Teleport] us to his village. We could avoid camping and walking and camping and walking," Madi complained.

"It's not there anymore," Orrin said tearfully, trying his best to sell the lie. "I couldn't . . . I don't want to . . . ."

"Hey, hey. It's okay. Some light camping will be good for us." Daniel put his arm around his shoulder. He muttered, "Too much. Tone it down."

Orrin coughed and started pulling a tent out of his [Dimension Hole]. Madi gave him space and didn't mention his village again. Before long, they had set up camp and brought the heater box out. Madi arranged a few of her butterflies in a ring, lighting the area.

They ate in silence. The dungeon, running into the elf, and the full day of hiking had worn them out.

"I'll take first watch," Orrin offered.

"Rock, paper, scissors for third shift?" Daniel asked Madi. Nobody wanted the middle watch.

"What's that?"

Daniel explained the game and immediately lost to Madi.

"Good night, boys. Wake me up when it's my shift."

"How did you lose? She's known the game for exactly two minutes," Orrin chided his friend as he got into his sleeping bag.

"I think she cheated. Either she knows the game already or she has mind-reading powers."

"You're a doorknob," Madi said through a yawn. "It's a given you'd choose rock. Me crush things with big rock."

Orrin laughed, and Daniel grunted as he turned over, ignoring them both.

Madi's butterflies eventually disappeared as she fell asleep or their internal timer ran out—Orrin didn't know which. He kept his eyes from closing by rereading his new Administrator options over and over. Each new skill had a price next to it, and some cost hundreds of administrator points. He had ten to work with. He probably should have tried to walk with Daniel and talk to him about them today, but he could do that tomorrow.

A rustling from the grass in the distance alerted Orrin before he saw anything. He summoned an [Ice Sword] and stood between his sleeping friends and the noise. He approached the patch farther away from the camp.

"If you're a monster, you picked the wrong camp. If you're human, just walk away."

"What if I'm an elf?" Leanthun stepped out from the grass, hefting a bag as big as his body over his shoulder. "Can I come closer or are you going to stab me?"

Orrin lowered his sword. "Come on in, but be quiet. They're both asleep."

The elf made no noise as they crept back. He rolled out his own blanket and lay on his back, watching the stars.

"Not going to offer to take a watch?" Orrin taunted.

"Nothing out here will attack us tonight. I struck a few beasts at random intervals in a circle around us. We should be safe until dawn." He closed his eyes.

Orrin watched the elf as his breathing seemed to slow.

"Like we'd just take your word for it," he muttered.

He spent his turn listening and watching, but nothing else stirred. When he woke Daniel, he had to hurriedly explain the elf sleeping in their midst. Then he curled up and went to sleep.

The morning sun woke Orrin before Madi did. She was talking with Leanthun, who had supplied a few scrounged-up eggs and a loaf of bread with fruit strewn through it for breakfast.

"They look chummy," Orrin said to Daniel. His friend was rolling his sleeping bag up and grunted.

"Did you sleep well?"

"Didn't."

"Didn't sleep well or sleep at all?" Orrin noticed the dark circles.

Daniel grunted again and tossed his tied-up sleeping bag to Orrin for storage. "Can you make some coffee?"

Orrin's face split into a grin, and he pulled out everything he'd need. "Of course! What kind do you want? I have—"

As Orrin gave options, Daniel just raised his hand and shook his head. "I just need the caffeine."

Orrin's smile wilted. "At least appreciate the coffee."

"I want lots of sugar, too."

Orrin's lips turned down into a grimace. "How did we ever become friends?"

Chapter 37

After breakfast—and the horrible abomination that Daniel called coffee—the group started back on their northward path.

"This trail is acceptable for another three days and then I shall lead."

Leanthun didn't speak much to the party after his cat-and-mouse duel with Daniel. Orrin appreciated this—he could tell his friend wanted a rematch. Orrin had to stop himself from trying to figure out the elf's level. His curiosity about what heights Leanthun had reached was tempered only by the knowledge that the elf could easily destroy him.

The elf had a habit of drifting off into the grass only to return after ten or twenty minutes, acting as if nothing had happened. Orrin thought he might be scouting until Madi pointed out some blood on his boots. He was hunting while guiding them forward. Whether the prey was monsters or humans from Odrana was anyone's guess.

During one of Leanthun's forays, a murder of crows pivoted in the air in front of them. Orrin wasn't paying attention to the flock and only glanced up when something glinted in the sky.

They weren't crows.

The birds were black but had an iridescent sheen sparkling across their feathers. They were also getting much larger as they approached.

"Incoming, straight ahead," Orrin said, putting his friends on guard. He made sure to cast [Ward] on both of them and himself. He drew himself a sword of magical ice and got ready for the battle.

As the twenty horse-size birds of prey squawked and dived at them, something flashed from the grass and bounced between the different birds. Six of them fell to the ground lifeless before the rest realized they were under attack. Four more lost wings and spiraled to the hard ground before the remaining half took flight.

Leanthun landed in front of them. His khopesh was dripping blood. In his left hand, he held his other weapon. The wooden handle was separated from a spiked ball by a chain. Orrin watched as the chain retreated into the shaft, pulling the ball taut against the handle again.

Magical, like Madi's spear.

Two of the giant birds thrashed in their death throes, still fighting the inevitable.

"If any of you desire it, the kills are yours," Leanthun said, pointing at the remaining monsters. "The experience isn't much to me."

He left, disappearing back into the tall grass.

"Seriously, who the fuck is this guy?" Daniel moaned. He turned to Orrin and Madi. "I'm pretty early into my current level. Are either of you close to leveling?"

Madi nodded. "Just a few hundred. I almost asked if we could hunt something on the way."

Daniel looked at Orrin.

"Same, to be honest. Madi can kill one first. If she needs both, she can have it. I can wait."

Madi shook her head. "We'll each take one."

For all the back-and-forth, the actual killing was more difficult. Madi approached one and tried to stab it with her spear, but the one-winged bird snaked its head around and yanked the weapon from her hands. It then let out a screech that left her ears bleeding and required Orrin to cast a healing spell on her.

"Sonic attacks," Madi said, working her jaw as she tried to pop her newly healed eardrums. "I'm going to blind it. Orrin, can I borrow your sword?"

Hitting the bird with her spell was easy. Rushing forward to hit the beast's neck before retreating out of range multiple times was not.

By the time Madi finally ended the beast's life, she was sweating. She perked right back up when she killed it.

"Nine hundred points," she murmured. "You guys, they're worth nine hundred points of experience."

With her level confirmed, Orrin made his way toward the other bird. Daniel and Madi went to retrieve her spear.

"Sorry about this," Orrin whispered to the wide-eyed monster. It had lost half of each wing and was clawing at the ground, trying to right itself. Orrin wasted no time and debuffed its dexterity and strength. The monster slowed by half but still clicked its beak toward him each time he approached.

"Screw this." Orrin used [Identify].

[Greater Shadow Stormhawk] HP 204/1,500

"I'm not spending two thousand mana to kill you with [Lightstrike]." Orrin read through his different spells and skills. He wasn't going to throw swords at the monster, either. That seemed like a massive waste of time.

Orrin considered [Toxic Touch].

[Toxic Touch]—your touch becomes toxic. MP cost variable to toxicity.

He hadn't tried this spell yet. He wasn't even sure if it was a onetime attack or if it would make everything he touched toxic for a certain amount of time. Orrin studied the ground around the Stormhawk. With [Way of the Water], he was relatively certain he could dodge in and touch the beast once.

"What's the worst that can happen? I can always heal myself if I get hit."

He decided to spend a hundred points of mana. *I'll regenerate that in an hour and a half anyway.*

He cast the spell and felt the power build in his hands. A timer also appeared in his vision. Ten seconds.

Shit.

Orrin scrambled toward the bird. His approach was perfect if a bit hasty. The Stormhawk swung a talon at him, and he dodged underneath. The bird overcorrected its attack, forgetting the loss of its wings, and fell on its back.

Orrin placed his hand on the bird's chest and prepared to jump back when he heard Daniel yell.

"What the hell are you doing?"

Orrin turned his gaze toward his friend on instinct. The Stormhawk pushed off the ground using its wing nubs, let out a screech of pain, and snapped its beak on his leg.

Damage Taken!
HP 100/120

Orrin's [Mind Bastion] clicked on at the pain, and he assessed the situation at lightning speed. His [Ward] had been completely destroyed. He hadn't reapplied his [Utility Ward] this morning, so that was only a [Ward] of 380 points. That meant the Stormhawk had done four hundred points of damage with its beak. The talons were traveling toward him now, and with his leg being held, he was going to take another hit. His hand had left a green putrid scab against the beast's chest that was slowly spreading, but he didn't have time for another attack.

Just as the bird's talons were inches away from his stomach, Orrin threw his body back, wrenching his leg. He dealt damage to himself in the form of a sprain to his ankle, but he kept his insides . . . inside. While the Stormhawk tried to right itself, Orrin had time to blast another hundred points of mana into another [Toxic Touch]. He placed his hands directly on the bird's head.

It screamed inhumanly and thrashed for a moment before going still.

"Orrin! Orrin? Are you alive? Please . . . Madi? Get a healing potion. His leg is clamped tight in this thing's mouth. Fuck! What did you do? I'm so sorry. Orrin?"

Daniel's screams seemed so faraway and pointless. Orrin knew his health was fine. He could heal himself and everything would be all right. He was more interested in the new notifications.

> **Experience Gained: 900 XP**
> **Level 15 Obtained!**
> **+10 AP**

Daniel was still yelling. Orrin sighed.

"I'm fine, just open this thing's mouth."

Daniel paused and stared right into Orrin's eyes. "It's over. Drop it."

Orrin nodded and let go of [Mind Bastion]. He promptly passed out from the pain.

When he awoke seconds later, his jaw hurt and he was missing another few points of health.

"Daniel, that was completely unnecessary and—"

"Orrin, heal yourself. Right now," Daniel cut Madi off.

His leg hurt so much. He looked down and noticed the bone was sticking out. Orrin threw up on Daniel.

His friend didn't even try to wipe away his sick. "Heal it. You can do it."

Orrin pushed his mana into the spell and felt some of the pain retreat. Like someone dehydrated coming across a glass of fresh water, he pushed more and more healing spells into his body.

"That's enough, Orrin. Don't overdo it." Madi's voice was behind him. He recognized her hands on his shoulders. She must have pulled him back while Daniel pried open the strong beak of the very dead Stormhawk.

Taking a peek at his leg, Orrin moaned in relief. His flesh was still closing, but the bone was no longer visible, reset inside the muscle and sinew his healing had fixed.

He checked his status.

> **Orrin**
> **Utility Warder**

Level 15 (786/6,000)
AP: 29
HP: 120/120
MP: 56/380
Strength: 9
Constitution: 12
Dexterity: 11
Will: 28
Intelligence: 11

"Thank you both," he sighed, falling back into the grass. "Daniel, next time I'm beating up a big dumb monster, please don't distract me."

Orrin needed to keep his eyes closed for a minute and rest. He heard Daniel stomp away, but Madi crawled closer.

"You realize what you did was stupid, right?"

"Yep. Don't go near the big half-dead bird thing."

"You know he was terrified for you?"

Orrin nodded.

"You know you're an asshole for blaming him?"

Orrin opened his eyes. Madi was kneeling and bent over, so her head was upside down to him. "He yelled right as I was fighting it. It distracted me."

Madi flicked his forehead. "You turned away. If you are going to walk into the middle of a fight, don't let us distract you. Don't let anything distract you. You just got very lucky. If I hadn't blinded that thing and Daniel hadn't hacked half its body off, you'd be dead."

Orrin frowned. "You guys attacked the dead monster?"

Madi's brow furrowed. "It wasn't dead."

"Did you get experience?"

Madi's vision glazed over as she checked her own status. Her grip on his shoulder tightened. "You killed it? What did you even do? We just saw you dodging and standing near it."

"I tried out [Toxic Touch]. I'd say it was super effective against bird types."

"What does that mean?"

Orrin kicked himself. "Nothing. Just that the poison worked really well against that monster, I guess. I hit it twice, but the second time was straight to the face."

Madi stood up and moved around him. He sat up on his elbows as she inspected the bird's corpse.

"That . . . is disgusting, Orrin."

Orrin rolled over and pushed himself up. His leg was tender, the freshly healed skin stretching and itching. He made his way over to Madi. He had to agree. The sight was not pleasant.

The spot around the bird's chest was hard to make out, as Daniel's sword had bisected the avian monster's middle. The head was a mess. Sunken flesh on either side of the beak was bubbled, rotted, and pus-filled. The smell alone would have driven the Orrin of Earth away. Now, he just admired his handiwork.

"I think I can see its brain."

Madi left him, muttering something that distinctly sounded like *boys*.

Leanthun didn't appear again until near nightfall. No more monsters crossed their path, and after Orrin apologized to Daniel, the party had made good time. As they sat around the small heater box, Daniel was trying to get Leanthun to tell him about the ongoing war response, to no avail. Most of Leanthun's answers to any questions were a variation of "you'll find out later."

Orrin was pondering something different. Ever since their first day in this world, he'd purchased skills and spells as a reaction. He had tried a few times to plan things out, but circumstances always conspired against him. He had wanted to take up [Alchemy] and maybe even convince Brandt to do so as well. He had wanted to increase his level in [Teleport], the exclamation point always blinking next to the skill on his status to let him know he could, but he'd miss out on an entire level of skills if he spent the ten ability points for it.

Not to mention the possibilities of [Merge]. The skill that Madi had claimed had been lost for centuries. It was the one skill on his original list that he still hadn't purchased. It was the most expensive skill he had ever considered. He had never had the twenty ability points to spare. He inspected the number of points he currently had. Twenty-nine. He'd known the moment Madi told him it was a lost skill that he had to have it. Something he could use to make himself stronger.

Merge: Combine Spells/Abilities for new effects.
Caution: May lose original Spell/Ability (20 AP)
Would you like to buy [Merge] for 20 AP?
Yes or No?

Yes.

Chapter 38

While the others slept, Orrin played with his new skill.

> **Merge: Combine Spells/Abilities for new effects.**
> **Caution: May lose original Spell/Ability**
> **Select Spells and/or Abilities . . .**

Orrin pulled up his complete status screen of spells and skills.

> **Abilities:**
> **[Mind Bastion]—Individual is able to control his own mind and therefore part of his body.**
> **[Dimension Hole]—Place items into a container of your choice (pocket, bag, etc.). Store items in a dimensional chest. Retrievable from any empty container.**
> **[Identify]—You can see.**
> **[Blood Mana]—Exchange HP for MP (one to one).**
> **[Map]—See the world around you. ([Party View])**
> **[Side Steps]—3% chance to evade any attack.**
> **[Mana Pool]—Increase MP by 100 MP.**
> **[Through the Ages]—A unique skill created to pass knowledge through the ages. Only those with the skill or those deemed the chosen target can read and write information using this skill.**

[Analyze]—Monitor target.
[Meditate]—Regenerate mana at 1 MP per minute.
[Obscure]—Erase skills and spells from your status. Prevents closer inspection from [Identify], [Detect], and similar skills.
[Way of the Water]—You are adept at the Way of the Water fighting style.
[Merge]—Combine Spells/Abilities for new effects. Caution: May lose original Spell/Ability.

Spells:
[Calm Mind]—Negates mind magic to a degree. Calms the target, reducing stress, anger, or sadness. Increases peacefulness and allows logical thoughts.
[Heal Small Wounds]—Heal up to 10 HP (Level 1). Heal up to 20 HP (Level 2). Heal up to 40 HP (Level 3).
[Camouflage]—Melt into your surroundings. Increase ability to remain undetected for 10 minutes (Level 2).
[Lightstrike]—Casts an unerring beam of light that hits a target for 1 HP damage.
[Inverse]—(Spell Modifier) Modify a spell to do its opposite.
[Ice Sword]—Summon a sword of hard ice. Does minimal damage but will not melt in the hottest of fires. Each sword lasts 1 hour.
[Teleport]—Teleport to any known point within 10 miles.
[Remetabolize]—Change the toxicity and structure of a toxin.
[Water Reservoir]—Create 1 gallon of water.
[Toxic Touch]—Your touch becomes toxic.

[Increase Strength]—Increases target Strength by +1 for 5 minutes (Level 1). Increases target Strength by +2 for 10 minutes (Level 2). Increases target Strength by +4 for 20 minutes (Level 3).

[Increase Dexterity]—Increases target Dexterity by +1 for 5 minutes (Level 1). Increases target Dexterity by +2 for 10 minutes (Level 2). Increases target Dexterity by +4 for 20 minutes (Level 3).

[Increase Will]—Increases target Will by +1 for 5 minutes (Level 1). Increases target Will by +2 for 10 minutes (Level 2). Increases target Will by +4 for 20 minutes (Level 3).

[Increase Intelligence]—Increases target Intelligence by +1 for 5 minutes (Level 1). Increases target Intelligence by +2 for 10 minutes (Level 2). Increases target Intelligence by +4 for 20 minutes (Level 3).

[Utility Ward]—Maximum possible Level 1 or Level 2 Strength, Dexterity, Will, and Intelligence increase to yourself and your party within 50 feet.

[Ward]—Creates a ward around yourself or a target to protect against attacks. Protects for MP maximum.

[Ice Ward]—Creates a ward around yourself and your party within 50 feet that protects against ice magic for MP maximum.

[Water Ward]—Creates a ward around yourself and your party within 50 feet that protects against water magic for MP maximum.

[Poison Ward]—Creates a ward around yourself and your party within 50 feet that protects against poison magic for MP maximum.

Currently, he had [Blood Mana] and [Mind Bastion] grayed out, along with the skill that let him hide the skills in the first place, [Obscure]. He quickly added [Merge] to that list, based on Madi's statement that it was a lost skill. With that first order of business completed, Orrin tested out his new skill.

I use [Inverse] and [Increase Dexterity] the most to slow down enemies. It seems like the kind of thing [Merge] was built for. Let's try it.

Orrin selected the two spells. The blue box appeared.

> **Merge: [Inverse] and [Increase Dexterity]?**
> **Compatibility: 100%**
> **Chance of original spell loss: 0%**
> **Variations: 1**
> **[Decrease Dexterity]—Decreases target Dexterity by +1 for 5 minutes—5 MP**
> **Cooldown: 24 hours**
> **Accept?**

Orrin paused. He read the words, then read them again. *So, it tells me if the skills are compatible and if I might lose the original spells. What does "variations" mean? And a cooldown? Is that for the debuff spell that I'd create or to use [Merge] again?*

The debuff spell that he would create cost the same as the buff spell. So he wouldn't spend the mana price for the [Inverse] spell modifier with each cast. Less mana spent meant more mana in the tank. The spell was a direct upgrade from his current process of spending five mana points on [Inverse] and five mana points on [Increase Dexterity], for a total of ten mana for one debuff. He'd go from spending fifty points to twenty-five to maximize his level-one slow spell, as he thought of it. The downside was that it appeared he would be starting from level one with the new spell.

He almost accepted regardless. Testing the new skill out was the most important thing right now, right?

What does "variation" mean?

Orrin unselected the two spells. His spell list had grown, so he selected two that he didn't use that often: [Water Reservoir] and [Toxic Touch].

> **Merge: [Water Reservoir] and [Toxic Touch]?**
> **Compatibility: 30% to 100%**
> **Chance of original spell loss: 0% to 35%**
> **Variations: 2**
> **Cooldown: 2 hours to 6 days**
> **Review Choices**

"That's what I'm talking about," Orrin muttered.

Daniel shifted in his sleeping bag. Orrin, who was technically on watch, realized he hadn't been paying any attention. Daniel and Madi were asleep close by, while Leanthun had selected a spot a little farther away from the group. He waited to make sure everyone was breathing deeply before he continued.

> **Variations:**
> **[Moisturize]—Your touch hydrates and moisturizes the skin. 5 MP per hour.**
> **0% chance of original spell loss. Cooldown: 2 hours**
> **[Create Poison]—Learn basic poisons. 35% chance of original spell loss [Toxic Touch]. Cooldown: 6 days.**

Orrin frowned. What kind of class would use [Moisturize]? Did they have spas and salons in Dey that he didn't know about? [Create Poison] was something he had looked at before on the store list, but he'd always been more interested in [Alchemy]. Of course, knowing how to make poison wouldn't hurt . . .

The cooldown had to be for the [Merge] skill. That meant that, at some point in the future, it might be worth taking [Create Poison] at the risk of losing [Toxic Touch]. He wasn't super attached to the spell. It had served its main purpose of letting him get the [Poison Ward], and he could still smell the putrefied head of the Stormhawk.

There could be better combinations, though.

Orrin closed the [Merge] box and opened the store. He'd bought [Inverse] for four ability points and never spent much time looking at the other spell modifier choices. Now, his mind was running away with different ideas. He searched for "modifier."

> **[Boost]—(Spell Modifier) Modify a spell to perform additional effect based on MP.—4 AP**
> **[Decrease Durational Spell]—(Spell Modifier) Modify a spell to decrease duration. 5 MP–4 AP**
> **[Increase Durational Spell]—(Spell Modifier) Modify a spell to increase duration. 5 MP–4 AP**
> **[Delayed Spell]—(Spell Modifier) Modify a spell to occur after a specific duration. 5 MP–4 AP**
> **[Far]—(Spell Modifier) Modify a spell to target double normal distance. 5 MP–4 AP**
> **[Fast Spell]—(Spell Modifier) Modify a spell to move fast as thought. 5 MP–4 AP**
> **[Slow Spell]—(Spell Modifier) Modify a spell to move slowly as honey. 5 MP–4 AP**
> **[Split Spell]—(Spell Modifier) Modify a spell to split effects across targets. 5 MP–4 AP**
> **[Target]—(Spell Modifier) Modify a spell to home in on a specific target. 5 MP–4 AP**

Orrin pushed away the spells that did super-specific or ridiculous things like [Improve Growth]—(Spell Modifier), which would modify any plant spell to double harvest output. He didn't need something that would help him grow heartier beans. He wanted something that would give him more bang for his spells. [Boost] and [Lightstrike] might give him the ability to dump mana into a spell that could do actual damage. The question was whether he was willing to spend almost half of his remaining ability points on a spell modifier.

I should be more strategic with this. There is no rush. We have to get to the elves and find out the situation in the forest before we make any plans.

That didn't stop him from continuing to play with the [Merge] template the rest of the night. When Madi woke up to relieve him from watch, he made an impulsive decision despite his earlier convictions.

Merge: [Inverse] and [Increase Dexterity]?
Compatibility: 100%
Chance of original spell loss: 0%
Variations: 1
[Decrease Dexterity]—Decreases target Dexterity by +1 for 5 minutes.—5 MP
Cooldown: 24 hours
Accept?

Yes.

Leanthun had two rabbits dressed and cooking over a low fire he'd built in a shallow hole when Orrin woke the next morning.

"Breakfast." The elf pointed. "We move faster today. There are human patrols about."

Orrin ignored him and put a pot of coffee on the heater box. He also pulled out a few pastries he'd squirreled away and handed them to his friends. After a moment of deliberation, he offered one to Leanthun as well.

"May the trees shade you," the elf said, covering his forehead with his hand. "This is appreciated."

Their pointy-eared surprised companion bit into the fluffy croissant and raised his thin eyebrows. "Most appreciated."

Orrin sat near Leanthun as he waited for his coffee water to boil. "I have a few questions, if you wouldn't mind."

Leanthun continued to turn his spit of rabbits.

"I know that every time Daniel asks you a question, you tell him to be patient and wait, but we are trying to end the war between Odrana and the elves. Can you at least tell us why you two are fighting?"

Leanthun snorted. "We do not fight the humans. We simply repel them from our forest. They will continue to throw their lives away, and we will continue to defend ourselves. If the council spoke, our greenest fighters could wipe the plains of the Odranan stench in a fortnight."

Orrin noticed Madi watching from the corner of her eye. "What do they want? Has anyone tried to negotiate peace?"

Leanthun sliced a piece of meat off the probably-cute-once bunny and tasted it. He chewed and then removed the rabbits from the fire, handing one to Orrin. "If the council knows what the Odranans want, they might share such with the [Hero]. I'm not on the council and not privy to that knowledge."

"Who's the council?" Orrin held the spitted rabbit out to Madi, who scooted in closer.

"The elves govern themselves through a council of elders. One in charge of each section of elven society," Madi said as she took the proffered meat and pulled a knife from her side. She began cutting. "I believe they had a monarchy at one point, but the council is all that survived the—"

"Lady Catanzano is correct. Our council makes most decisions for our people. Within the next few days, I'll bring you to them. We will need to make one stop along the way, but they will explain much and request more. A [Hero] in our forest is better than another enemy at our border."

"Don't worry—" Daniel yawned as he trudged over. "I'm sure we can figure out how to get an army to leave you alone. That's all you need, right? One little [Hero]?"

"You doubt your own powers?"

"Brother, I don't doubt myself for a second, but what good is one person against an army?"

Leanthun frowned. "Most of Odrana's army is conscripted. They have very few adventurers, as those usually go to Dey to find fame and fortune. The majority of the men are farmers or artisans by trade. Even with your low level, you would lay waste to scores of men in minutes."

Madi cringed. "It's true. You've been so caught up with the higher-leveled groups of Dey, it's probably not obvious. Only one in a hundred people is likely to have any fighting skills or magic. The leaders of the army are definitely strong and capable, but the majority of their forces are simple people."

Daniel paled. "I have to kill people who don't want to fight?"

Chapter 39

The day passed slowly, with Daniel sulking. Orrin wasn't much help, spending his time trying to come up with new ways to use [Merge]. He also used his new spell, [Decrease Dexterity], on Daniel until he tripped. He had to quickly cast a few dexterity buffs so his friend wouldn't notice.

Madi tried to engage with them but gave up in a huff when Daniel told her to leave him alone.

The long day turned into a long night, still with little conversation. Madi took the first watch. When she woke him for the middle shift, Orrin watched his countdown, and at the exact moment he could use [Merge] again, he created his second spell: [Decrease Strength]. He had considered getting one of the magical stats first, but Leanthun had told them they had three days of walking before he would lead them off the beaten path. Orrin figured he would be able to get will or intelligence tomorrow night. He was so focused on his own planning that he didn't notice Daniel was still awake. When his friend sat down next to him, he started.

"Not doing a good job as lookout if I can sneak up on you." Daniel pushed Orrin's arm. "What are you thinking about?"

Orrin glanced at Madi on the other side of the heater box. Leanthun was farther away, still as the night air. "I got that new skill we talked about. I've been looking at new combos."

Orrin pulled up his [Decrease Dexterity] spell in a blue box and added [Merge] as well before flipping it to Daniel. His eyebrows went up as he read them both.

"You used it to make spells you already have?"

Orrin shushed him and nodded at the sleeping forms near them. "Cheaper mana costs. There's a cooldown for using it, too. Do you think they're asleep?"

Daniel peered over his shoulder and shrugged. "I don't know if elves have super hearing, but Madi's probably too far away to hear us. What's up? Are you going to try and convince me that it's okay to kill innocent people, too?"

Orrin waved his hand. "That's a problem for tomorrow. We haven't had a chance to talk since the dungeon, and I need to tell you something."

Orrin paused, trying to gather his thoughts. Daniel didn't always respond well to his new powers. He also trusted Madi a lot more than Orrin did—he trusted her, but not like he trusted his best friend, and Tony had acted like an Administrator was a god. He didn't want to freak out their only remaining party member.

Where did Brandt go, anyway?

"When I absorbed the dungeon core—"

"Destroyed it," Daniel corrected.

Orrin shook his head. "No, D. I got a weird notification that I could *absorb* it for administrator points. I've got a whole list of weird powers I can unlock now."

Orrin pulled up the list of unlockable powers and tried to turn them toward Daniel, the same way he had shared various blue boxes in the past. Only this time, the display shook and refused to turn.

"Damn it. It won't let me show you."

"Show me what?"

"I'm pretty sure it's a spell or skill list for Administrators only. I can do things like unlock spells or edit stats, but I have to unlock the ability first. I've only earned ten administrator points from absorbing the dungeon core, and I don't know if I have to spend more to use the skills."

Daniel sat silently, staring at his friend. "You . . . fucking cheat. I'm so lucky you got hit by the truck, too." A huge grin plastered across his face. "Tell me what you can do. Can you unlock dimensional travel or something?"

Orrin groaned. "Thanks, I guess? I can change or assign classes, assign Quests, edit rewards, unlock spells or skills, and edit stats. There are a few other things too, but there isn't a description of what they do."

"Like?"

Orrin sighed and pulled the purchase list back up. Some of the abilities had strange names, and he hadn't been able to figure out what they were. "[Imbue] is one. [Scry] is another, but I think that's got to be like [Identify] or [Analyze]. I didn't even mention that the edit stats have something about 'sanctioned' and 'unsanctioned.' Sanctioned by who or what? The system?"

Orrin scrolled a bit more. "Some of these are just weird. [Change Race]? That seems like a recipe for disaster. [Create Relic]? Isn't that what Madi called super-powerful old magic items?"

Daniel ran his fingers over the thickening stubble around his chin, deep in thought. "How many of these things can you unlock?"

"One. Maybe two, if I just do the assign and reset class ones."

"I don't think those are as important to us. Assigning more Quests would be helpful, especially if you can edit the rewards."

"That's two separate abilities."

Daniel ran his hand through his hair. "I guess we'll need to destroy . . . absorb more dungeon cores in the future."

"I was leaning toward the [Unlock Skill] or [Edit Stats] abilities. If I could use it on you or Madi, it would open up more versatility in your abilities. Imagine if I could just unlock [Teleport] for you or [Spear Proficiency] at a higher level for Madi? Bypass all the training and get the results." Orrin picked up a broken twig in front of him and started picking at the bark. "[Edit Stats] might let me get you guys up to max without even having to cast spells. You could be stronger and quicker than Leanthun—permanently."

"What if it isn't permanent or you can only give a few points?" Daniel countered. "Quests would let us do the same thing. We get you through another dungeon and you'll have the points to edit the rewards, too."

"Good point." Orrin pulled the last of the stick apart. The white flesh of the wood underneath shone in the moonlight. "I've been going crazy keeping this to myself. I'm glad you didn't think I was a weirdo. Stupid Orrin, complicating things all over again."

Daniel put his hand on Orrin's shoulder and squeezed. "We'll figure out what's going on with you. After we deal with this little war problem, we can go back to Dey and talk with Tony. You said he knew something about Administrators. We'll track down someone who knows more and figure out your powers. Maybe Madi—"

"Let's not involve her," Orrin cut him off. "The way Tony acted when he found out . . . I almost regret telling him in the first place. If it scared him that much . . ."

"You know you'll have to trust her at some point. That's what friends do."

Orrin threw the piece of wood into the distance. "I trust her, but you don't have to tell your friends every one of your secrets."

Daniel grinned. "I know all your secrets."

"No, you don't."

"Last year, you wrote my sister a love letter."

Orrin felt fire on his cheeks. "No, I didn't."

Daniel poked him in the ribs. "I found it on your computer when I was printing out that essay about *Catcher in the Rye*. What was the line . . . 'You make my heart sing when you walk into the room.' It was very well written."

Orrin increased his strength and caught Daniel's hand. Daniel tried to stand and pull his hand out of his grip, but Orrin ducked under the arm, pushed up, and launched Daniel into the air. His friend landed twenty feet away in a crash of dust.

"That hurt, you dick." Daniel stood up and brushed himself off.

"What is going on? Are we under attack?" Madi's butterflies rose into the night, illuminating the area.

"Daniel just volunteered to take the rest of my watch. Sorry we woke you, Madi." Orrin glared across the camp at Daniel.

The [Hero] laughed and raised his hand in surrender. "Sure, sure. Get your beauty sleep."

Orrin stomped off to his makeshift bed. It was a long time before his ears stopped burning.

I never even sent that stupid thing.

The next day passed without incident. Orrin gave Daniel the cold shoulder for a few hours but eventually cooled off. Leanthun kept monsters away from the party, and nothing attacked them outright. Toward the end of the day, they saw smoke to the northeast.

"Is that a village?" Daniel asked, pointing to the plumes of smoke.

"That's too much smoke for a bonfire. The villages up here are never that big." Madi noticed Daniel's raised eyebrow. "Villages this far from Dey aren't as well regulated as those closer to the city. They pay their taxes, but it's always too little to matter, and nobody keeps a map of where they are. If a village grows large enough to be called a town, Dey will assign someone to oversee it. I know all the towns, but villages come and go from generation to generation, and we don't keep records of them all."

She pointed at Orrin. "Like his village. I couldn't find where he came from and doubt I could unless we traveled there."

Leanthun walked out of the grass and put his hand on Daniel's elbow. "We should turn west. We can enter the forest tomorrow night if we keep a brisk pace."

Daniel shrugged the elf's hand off his arm. "What is going on over there? We can see the smoke."

Leanthun didn't turn away from Daniel's intense gaze. "Odranan soldiers. There is nothing you can do. Leave them and come with me."

Daniel reached over his shoulder and drew Gertrude. "How many soldiers?"

The elf sighed. "Too many. It matters not anyway."

"I'm not leaving people to die." He was ramping up, almost to the point of shouting.

"We can just do a rescue," Orrin suggested. "Get the people out. If you could help us distract them, I'm sure we could—"

"A distraction will not help. That village supplies us with trade on occasion." Leanthun turned and watched the clouds of smoke curling into the sky. "If I had been there yesterday, I might have . . ."

He trailed off, fists clenched to his side. Two deep breaths and the elf turned back to the group. Orrin was surprised to see tears on his stoic face.

"The village was already destroyed. The elderly and sickly were slaughtered. The rest are gone, likely with slave collars on, and headed back to Odrana to be sold. The soldiers still there are setting fire to the houses, trying to draw in anyone nearby." His teeth clenched. "They have scouts in the area. We should leave the road now."

Daniel still wanted to go after the soldiers, but Madi convinced him this was not the time. They might be strong and a few adventurers could make the difference in a large fight, but if the village was already gone, there was little point in risking it.

"We'll get revenge for them. That is technically Dey's lands, and Odrana will pay dearly for taking our people."

Orrin watched the smoke rising behind them as they walked away.

The following afternoon, Daniel announced he could see the forest in the distance.

"[Eagle Eyes]?" Leanthun tilted his head in question.

"Something like that," Daniel responded.

Orrin was glad to see Daniel keeping his secrets. He didn't need to brag about the exact nature of his skills.

"It's actually [Telescope]," Daniel continued. "It upgraded when I chose my moniker."

Orrin groaned and rubbed his eyes in frustration.

The trees were still too far away to make the distance by nightfall, so they set camp by an old and crumbling well. Madi thought the land might have been a farm at some point and searched for any hints of an old house or barn. Leanthun arrived back from his daily roaming and quickly pointed out the flagstones for where a small house had stood only twenty feet from where they were.

"The family was always pleasant," he said, looking at the broken stones with his hands resting on his weapons. Perfectly relaxed and yet ready to strike at a moment's notice. "The youngest caught sick, and they brought her north to us, as the human city was too far for them to travel. She married a farmer farther south. After the parents passed, the older child left for another town—I never found where."

"How long ago was that?" Orrin asked, setting up the heater box. The nights were still cool.

"Two hundred years and thirty-one winters. Two hundred and forty-nine from when we cured the child."

Orrin tried to imagine being that old, watching families come and go from the lands around. "Do you keep tabs on every family around the forest?"

Leanthun cast a glance at Orrin. "We know of every village and family nearby. We keep to ourselves yet keep the pledge of a good neighbor. We trade freely, offer what we can, and aid those who would seek our help."

Madi finished rolling out her mat. "Maybe you knew Orrin's village, Leanthun? Orrin, you did say you were from around here, right?"

Shit.

Chapter 40

"Madi, can I talk with you real quick?" Daniel grabbed her arm and steered her away from the elf. "Why do you keep bringing up Orrin's village?" he hissed at her.

Orrin had to jog to keep up with them. *I really need to work on my dexterity more.*

"I—I don't . . ." She stumbled then paused. Taking a breath, she turned to Daniel. "I didn't mean to overstep."

Daniel raised an eyebrow at Orrin.

Do I have to keep lying to her?

Orrin dropped his shoulders and tilted his head.

If she knows that I'm not from here, it is going to be a whole big thing. I would rather avoid that.

Daniel closed his eyes and huffed out a breath through his nose. When he opened them again, he rolled his eyes at Orrin.

You are being ridiculous. We can trust her.

Orrin crossed his arms in front of his chest and planted his feet.

It is my choice.

Daniel smirked. Orrin frowned.

"Madi, I'm not dealing with this. You and Orrin can talk. It's up to him what he wants to tell you, but if he doesn't want to talk about something, I think it would be in everybody's best interest to let it go." Daniel left abruptly, walking back to Leanthun.

Madi glanced sheepishly at Orrin. "I'm sorry I keep bringing up your village. It's just . . . you are one of the only friends I have."

When Orrin didn't respond, she rushed forward, stumbling over her words. "When I was twelve, an ambassador from Veskar brought his daughter with him. I guess he wanted to show her the world a bit. She was a little older than me, but my father thought it would be a good learning experience for me, so he gave me a job. I was supposed to show her around, keep her entertained, that sort of thing."

Madi wrung her hands and wouldn't meet Orrin's eye. "We spent the entire day together. We laughed and talked about our parents and what they demanded of us. I thought we were becoming close. We went to my favorite salon and got our hair made up. I even brought her to one of my favorite restaurants for dinner."

Orrin had no idea where this story was going, but he was glad she wanted to talk. He was weaving together a new piece of the elaborate lie that had become his past. His village was going to be located near the mountains. They were self-sufficient and rarely talked with the elves. *Why were we targeted by Odrana, though?* They didn't stay in one place and were attacked on the move? *Maybe . . . herders of some sort?* Orrin had never watched a documentary or read a book on farming practices, so anything she asked would need to hold up to further questions down the road. *I'll need to talk with someone who is an actual herder of . . . sheep? Maybe cows?*

"I didn't know that in Veskar, certain foods are taboo to eat. I ordered for us . . . It was a disaster." Madi's eyes went distant as she remembered the night. "Her father was shouting at my father that I had tried to do it on purpose. My father had to give concessions for a trade route because of me. I failed in the task he gave me, but I also lost a potential friend. All because I didn't know something that I should have." Madi raised her head and captured Orrin's eyes with hers. "I know the villages farther from Dey have customs and traditions that we don't practice. I'm scared that I might offend you in some way and lose you. It's one reason I tried to investigate where you came from in the past."

She raised a hand when he opened his mouth to ask more about that. "I found nothing. Nobody knows anything about you or your village beyond what you've told us. I said that was one reason, but I'm going to be completely honest with you. You are a mystery, Orrin. You have a class that nobody has ever heard of. You can do something to change the [Hero]'s Quest rewards. I'm not stupid. There is some secret that you have. A secret that you don't want to share. I don't know if you are the grandchild of a [Hero], if you have a relic, or perhaps your village has some lost knowledge from ages past, but I won't ask you to share your secret. I won't ask about your family anymore. Trust me, I know how touchy that subject can be, and all I can do is apologize."

She held her hand out. "I really hope I haven't messed up too badly. Still friends?"

Orrin took her hand.

All his life, he'd only had one friend. Daniel had looked past his quirks and stuck around, but he'd had partners for school projects who forgot his name before they turned in the assignment. After his dad left and his mom started working more, the only attention he'd gotten was from Daniel and his family. Half the reason he had been in love with Daniel's sister was probably because she knew he existed. He'd realized that in the dungeon when Garret's shine had started to wear off.

In this world, given a new chance, Orrin was starting to find himself a bit more. Sure, he was still just the sidekick to his best friend, the [Hero], but he'd saved Daniel. Hell, he'd saved him a few times. He'd made new friends—Tony, Amir, and Brandt.

Madi.

She wasn't the perfect friend. She'd threatened him and Daniel, played with their lives, and treated him as expendable. But she was doing her best to make up for past acts. She valued his opinions on strategy, came to him to help curb Daniel's more annoying habits, and stuck by his side when shit hit the fan. She'd stood up to the Hospital for him. She was out here with them trying to stop a war with no real plan or ideas, just the blind faith that they would figure it out. She wasn't the perfect friend, but she was his friend and she was trying to do better by them.

Maybe I should do better, too.

When Madi grasped his hand, he pulled her closer into a hug. It was awkward and quick and he let go as fast as he could.

"I'm going to trust you," he started, gesturing for her to shut up this time. "I'm going to trust you, and I don't do that often. Daniel is the only one who knows."

Orrin double-checked that Leanthun was far away, talking with Daniel. "When Daniel arrived in this world, he wasn't alone . . ."

"How much did you tell her?" Daniel asked, sitting down close to the heater box. The little device was keeping up quite well. It warmed a small area like a fire, but without the bright light to give away their position. Orrin appreciated more the lack of smoke drifting into his face every few seconds.

"That I'm from your world but definitely not a [Hero]."

"That it?"

Orrin watched Madi turn over in her sleeping bag. "I didn't think she could handle more than that right now."

After the initial laughter at his "bad joke," Madi had asked him questions about Daniel's world. She'd grilled him for five minutes before abruptly walking away and berating Daniel. Orrin realized that she was trying to catch him in a lie.

"I think she wanted me to be from here. She complained that there are no records of two [Heroes] ever coexisting at the same time. I tried convincing her that I'm not one and somehow just hitched a ride with you, but . . ."

"You know, sometimes I think you were meant to come, too."

Orrin spun to see if Daniel was joking.

"What? I'm serious. I would have died right away without you here. I don't know who or what brought us here, but it's like they knew I'd need you."

Orrin rolled his eyes. "You'd have been fine."

"I'd be stuck in a tree, getting eaten by a tentacle monster."

"Like I said, totally happy and fine."

Daniel tried to push Orrin over. "Asshole."

They sat in silence. Leanthun had left after a quick dinner, promising to keep any Odranan forces away, but the boys had still decided to keep watch. Daniel was supposed to be sleeping but had wanted to talk first.

"You think she'll be okay?"

Orrin scratched at his hair. He needed a haircut—it was starting to curl at the ends and tickle his neck. "She didn't try to hit me, and she did say thanks for finally telling her. Although there might have been a touch of sarcasm in her voice."

Daniel chuckled. "She is snarky."

Orrin nodded. "You going to sleep? Leanthun thinks we can make the forest tomorrow. You and Madi are going to have to talk with this council of theirs and figure out if we can help."

"You think I'm taking another middle shift? You go to bed."

Orrin laughed and used Daniel's shoulder to push himself straight. "Worth a shot."

The night passed and morning arrived without interruption. Orrin had completed his set of decrease-stat spells overnight and eagerly awaited the chance to try something new. The twenty-four-hour timer for his [Decrease Intelligence] spell taunted him.

"Morning, Madi." Orrin squatted by her mat and handed her a cup of coffee.

She glared at him but accepted the peace offering.

"I just wanted to check and see . . . I mean, how are . . . Are we good?"

Madi sat up and sipped her coffee. Orrin decided she wasn't going to answer and straightened up. His back was already turned when she huffed.

"We're good."

He smiled and sat down again. He pulled a few of the berry-jam pastries she liked the most out of his storage and handed one over. He winked. "Don't tell Daniel."

She snorted. "He'll smell them soon enough. Eat fast."

Orrin asked her about elven culture and listened to her answers as they settled back into their old routine.

"If you've known Daniel for so long, why did you leave him that time?"

Coffee burned his nose as he coughed. "What?"

Madi sighed and rubbed coffee off her blanket. "After you two started doing quests for the Guild, Daniel came back into town alone. My father recruited him and got him to agree to let me join his party. You had disappeared. You know when—it was right before you broke into my house."

Orrin cleaned himself up, tossing an extra blanket to Madi to use as a towel for the mess. "We got into an argument and I stormed off. I came back for him."

Madi poked Orrin in the arm. "I'm not blaming anyone. I just don't want you two to split up again. Being in a group with the two of you is . . . liberating. I was so envious of how close you became with him in such a short time, but now I know that you've both been friends for years. It makes so much sense, I can't believe I didn't see it before. It's just such a weird thing for two people from another world to be here. I'd need to ask my father if something like this has ever happened before to be sure, but I'm almost certain . . . what?"

Orrin crunched his nose as he tried to find the words. "We trust you. We . . . don't fully trust your dad. That's a shitty thing to say to a friend but . . . it's true."

The look on her face shifted between angry, amused, and disappointed, but her voice didn't betray any emotion. "He's my father. I'll always trust him."

Orrin looked into his empty mug. "Can I ask you not to tell him about me? Would that be a problem?"

He waited for her to answer, but she waited just as long for him to steal a glance.

"I'll keep your secret unless I think it would be dangerous for you or Daniel. I know he's hard to . . . deal with . . . but he is a good man."

Orrin felt the weight of the unknown lift from his shoulders. "Well, now that you know I'm actually an alien from another planet, guess what skill I bought the other day?"

"What did you get?" Madi asked, taking the last sip of her coffee.

"[Merge]."

Madi spat her coffee all over his face.

Chapter 41

"Disgusting," Orrin complained, wiping the semiwarm liquid from his face. He rubbed his hand against the grass.

"You're being serious, aren't you?" Madi placed her mug on the ground with a trembling hand. "Don't mess around about this."

"I'm not messing with you, but could you aim your spit away from me next time?" He used [Water Reservoir] and let a stream of water trickle from his hand. The spell let him create up to one gallon, but he could do it at whatever speed he wanted. Washing his hands before the coffee dried and he had to deal with sticky fingers all day was a top priority.

Madi pushed her blanket off completely and stood up. She started pacing. Orrin straightened up off the ground and waited for her.

She turned multiple times and lifted her finger to shake at him but could only mutter dark whispers.

Daniel stirred in his sleeping bag and rolled over. He opened one eye and glared at them. "Too much noise."

Madi whirled back to the plate of pastries Orrin had set out for them and hurled one at Daniel. "You didn't take the middle watch, I did. If I'm awake, so should you be."

Daniel brushed the dirt off the food and chomped down. "What's up with her?"

Orrin shrugged.

"How long have you known?" Madi stomped over to Daniel. "He's got [Merge] as a skill. I know that one of the books my father and I collected for you had a long section about it. You know what this means."

Orrin quirked an eye at Daniel. *What is she talking about?*

Daniel stuffed half the pastry into his mouth and chewed. Madi's hand was on her hip and she was tapping her foot by the time he swallowed.

"Madi," Daniel said as he stood up and stretched. "If you want a bunch of books read, give them to Orrin. I took a peek at, like, two of those books."

Madi's foot stopped tapping. "You didn't read the collection of priceless books that discussed the best ways to combine skills and spells? The cost of which could fund the defense of the Wall for a year?"

Daniel held up his hands. "Sorry?"

"When did this happen?" Orrin couldn't help but ask. "I would have loved to read those."

Madi was in his face, pushing him backward, before he knew it. "If you had told me all this before, I would have made you. I can't trust either of you to do anything right. How many more surprises are you going to throw at me?" She turned and advanced on Daniel. "What do I have to do to get you to take this seriously?"

Orrin quickly stepped in between Daniel and Madi. "Hey! Hey! What's the big deal? We'll both read them when we get back to Dey. Madi, what's wrong?"

Madi's shoulders sagged as she ran out of steam. "If he had read those . . . if he had . . . he'd know. Orrin, you can't tell anyone you have [Merge]. Ever. Don't tell my father. Don't tell Brandt, if that asshole ever comes home."

Orrin noticed she had started to cry.

"I lost Brandt. I lost Jude. I can't lose you, too."

Daniel brushed by him and wrapped Madi in his arms. "It's okay. We couldn't lose this idiot if we tried."

"Hey!"

"What's the big deal with the skill? Is it like his blood thingy?" Daniel asked her gently.

Madi sniffed and disengaged from Daniel's hug. "It's so much worse."

Orrin's blood froze. He'd taken the skill to make cool new combinations. Why would something like that be worse than a skill that yelled, "Look at me, I'm trying to become a [Vampire]"?

"Orrin, have you told anyone else about that skill?" Madi asked with dread in her voice.

"Just you two. Madi, what's so bad?"

Madi wrung her hands and glanced around to make sure Leanthun hadn't come back. "[Merge] makes new spells. The best theory is that it is completely random if somebody can unlock it. Nobody is sure how to get it, but it's well documented what happens when it's found: countries go to war over that person."

Orrin felt a chill run down his spine. "It can't be that bad. I mean, it's not like I can make anything good anyways. I've just been combining [Inverse] and my increase-stat spells."

Madi nodded. "The new spells are better, aren't they?"

"Not really," Orrin said, waving her off. "I mean, they do cost a little less."

Madi groaned. "Orrin, you forget because you are some sort of weird mana-regenerating fiend. Everybody else can only cast a finite number of spells a day. A new spell that costs less but does the same thing as before? Do you see how much of an edge that would give anybody?"

Orrin didn't see how a few extra mana points would make the difference for anybody, but he was just considering his own inverted buffs. "What kind of things do people unlock, then? Maybe we can come up with something great and—"

"You need to stop and think," Madi interrupted him. She rubbed her temples. "You remember the spell that Lord Wendeln cast when my father and the other lords stripped him of his titles? It's called [Harvest]. It summons an entire army of the type of monster the Wendeln family usually can summon and control. Only they don't control any of the monsters when they use [Harvest]. It's a last-resort option, something to use when you are surrounded by demons and need to kill everything."

She paused and made sure both boys were looking at her. "[Harvest] was the result of [Merge]. You never know what you are going to get from the combination of spells, but the ones that are written about bring death."

"Nothing I've been able to find is overpowered," Orrin countered. "One of the combinations I tried let me make poisons or moisturize your skin. That was it."

"You're at level fifteen, right? Your spells, as far as I know, are all about random things. You don't have a specific purpose like a [Fire Mage] or [Knight]. If you had two powers that were complimentary, the synergy of those spells would make the new spell that much more powerful." She put her hand on her face and tapped her lip. "Have you tried combining anything with your blood skill?"

Orrin shook his head. "I haven't really done much with [Blood Mana]. You kind of scared me from ever using it offensively."

"Try it. See what you would get."

Orrin nodded and pulled up [Merge].

Merge: [Blood Mana] and [Lightstrike]?
Compatibility: 80%
Chance of original spell loss: 10%
Variations: 1
[Mana Drain]—Connects to the target and drains 1 MP for every 1 HP you sacrifice.
Cooldown: 4 days
Accept?

"Oh, that's actually cool. [Mana Drain] would let me use my own health to drain someone's mana."

Madi shook where she was standing. "That's not a spell I've ever heard of. If you created that, there would be a chance it could populate in someone's store. A new spell that nobody knows suddenly appearing is the way most find out someone has [Merge]."

Orrin quickly exited from the skill. "So don't create new spells. Got it."

Madi frowned. "No. That wasn't the point I was trying to make. What did you combine your blood skill with?"

"[Lightstrike]."

"The most simple attack spell there is. Try something else."

Orrin sighed and tried again.

Merge: [Blood Mana] and [Heal Small Wounds]?
Compatibility: 60% to 100%
Chance of original spell loss: 0% to 30%
Variations: 3
Cooldown: 2 days to 8 weeks
Review Choices

"Wow, I've never had a spell cooldown go to weeks yet."

Madi's face went tight. "What is it?"

"I'm looking now."

Variations:
[Create Small Wounds]—Damage up to 10 HP—5 MP
0% chance of original spell loss. Cooldown: 2 days.
[Recharge]—Restore up to 10 MP on another—5 MP
5% chance of original spell loss [Heal Small Wounds]. Cooldown: 5 days.
[Sap]—Steal 10 HP from target—5 MP
30% chance of original spell loss [Heal Small Wounds]. Cooldown: 8 weeks

Orrin read the list aloud.

"[Recharge] sounds weird," Daniel complained. "Why would you spend mana to restore someone else's mana? They could just drink a potion."

"If it worked like I'm guessing it would, the only limit to how much mana Orrin could restore would be how much he cycled his own mana. You're also forgetting that Orrin's cost to cast that would be next to nothing, and he'd be giving way more than just ten mana per cast. Now imagine Orrin standing behind an army of mages. They could cast spells at an enemy for hours. All because of one spell."

"I think [Sap] would be worse," Orrin whispered.

"Why? What would be worse than you juicing up an army of fireball-slinging magic users?" Daniel asked.

Orrin closed his eyes and imagined taking [Sap]. He could steal ten points of health from someone for the cost of only five mana. And then he could turn himself invisible with [Camouflage] and nobody would know where he was. He could boost his intelligence and will to a hundred, making the spell cost half a point of mana, probably rounding up to one MP. He would also do one hundred points of damage per cast. If he ever ran out of mana, he could always blood cycle with no need to heal himself. He'd be stealing one hundred points of health each casting. He wouldn't need an army in front of him.

He could decimate the army himself.

"You see it," Madi said quietly. "You see some way it could be exploited."

Orrin nodded.

"Could it help us?" Daniel asked. Madi hit him. "Ow. What? We are about to fight in a war."

"It wouldn't be a war. It would be a slaughter," Orrin murmured. "If I created that spell, would someone else be able to get it right away?"

Madi nodded. "Most likely. The exact combination of prerequisites wouldn't be known, but within a year or two . . . yes."

"So I need to be careful with what spells I make."

"It could be those are spells already known, with ways to counter whatever you are thinking of. We can search through my father's books when we get back and see."

Orrin didn't want to wait that long. It was a small secret anyway. "I'll see if they're in the store."

"There's no way you'd have them in your store. These are combinations of spells that would require the exact right class, and certain spells already known to unlock—"

"[Create Small Wounds] is already there." Orrin talked over Madi, not even trying to explain. "[Recharge] is as well."

He scrolled more. "[Sap] isn't there."

Madi spluttered. "How many available spells do you have in your store? A hundred?"

"Thousands. Maybe more."

Madi sat down hard. "What are you? Not even a [Hero] has that many options."

Daniel sat down next to her. "His class is [Utility Warder]. I think whatever brought me here as the [Hero] brought him here to be a problem-solver. He's my secret weapon—the friend that can find a solution to the problems I can't just beat down. None of that matters, though. What matters is he's our friend. I'm sorry I didn't read those books. Tell me everything. I can't protect him if I don't know what I need to protect him from."

Madi started laughing. "Himself. The world. Everyone? Daniel, he's creating new spells with the handful of random things he's collected from his first few levels. If he wanted, he could spend maybe thirty or forty ability points on specific skills and spells and end the world. If someone captured him, it wouldn't be a matter of if that happened but when."

"So don't tell people I have [Merge] and try not to make too many new spells," Orrin said, crossing his legs as he sat down, too. "And definitely don't blow up the world. I think I can handle that."

Chapter 42

Further discussion of blowing up the world was put on hold when Leanthun did his magical appearing act. The elf could simply materialize from the grass as if he was teleporting and did so at the most inopportune times.

"Good, you have eaten. The way to my home is clear. We can be among the trees by midday."

Without waiting, he set off again, expecting them to follow.

"You know, I'm half tempted to ignore him and walk off in a different direction," Daniel complained as he began rolling up camping supplies and throwing them to Orrin for storage in his [Dimension Hole]. "Seriously, I'm glad we have a guide, but the dude is seriously uptight."

Madi tried to talk about Orrin's skills more as they walked, but he shut her down, promising they'd have all the time they needed once out of earshot of Leanthun.

"We're going to be in the middle of the elven forest, surrounded by elves, tonight." Madi was walking backward and talking to him. Daniel was up ahead trying to get Leanthun to agree to another duel. "Then we are probably going to be fighting Odranan forces in coordination with the elves . . . unless they did something to start this war. I'm thinking we could probably still complete the Quest if the elves lose."

Orrin pulled up the Quest.

Stop the war in Odrana

Reward: 200,000 XP and Variable
Failure: Loss of 10 levels.

"I don't know how much influence the [Hero] has in making the elven council explain what's going on," Orrin started. "But if we offer to share this Quest with a few members of the council or even with some leaders from Odrana, it can't be hard to get them to stop fighting."

Madi pulled a face and almost tripped. She caught herself and turned to walk next to him. "That is the stupidest idea I've ever heard . . . and it might work, since the reward for doing it would give them so much experience."

Orrin tried to do the math. He currently needed a little more than five thousand XP to level and would need seven thousand XP for the following level. Each additional level would cost an extra thousand XP. "If my math is right, that much experience would push me and Daniel to level thirty."

"I think you're right. My father would lose his mind if I came back with that kind of growth."

"Keep up," Leanthun said, turning and rejoining them. "And please keep this one from bothering me anymore." He nodded toward Daniel, who tried to look sheepish and failed.

The rest of the trip was uneventful, with no real discussions of all the major shocks Orrin had dropped on Madi. As they neared the forest, Orrin realized why it had taken so long for them to get there, despite seeing the trees days ago.

"They're huge." He tilted his head but couldn't make out the tops. The foliage blended together so high that he couldn't make out the individual branches. "It would take like ten people holding hands to reach around the trunk."

"These are some of our youngest trees. It would take twice that number to go around the smallest tree in the forest," Leanthun corrected.

"How big do they get?" Daniel was also looking up, his eyes squinted against the sun.

Leanthun put his hand against the "young" tree on the outskirts of the elven forest. "The forest matriarch is approximately ten thousand years old and houses the entire elven population during festivals. It would take two hundred hands to link around her."

Orrin felt tiny standing beside the trees. There were no other trees for miles before the start of the forest, a clear marker that this was almost a sacred land. The trees blocked his vision when he tried to see farther in.

"When we are stopped, put your hands on your head like so." Leanthun demonstrated, placing his palms against the roof of his head with his fingers interlaced. "Do not respond or talk. I will get you through."

"What are we, prisoners?" Daniel muttered.

"Something like that," Leanthun said with a smile. "Let us go."

Daniel grumbled as they followed the elf into the dark woods. Orrin was surprised that the path they took was well lit. He followed the beams of sunlight that broke through the canopy overhead.

"Do you climb up these trees and cut sections out so the sun shines down on this path?"

Leanthun stumbled for a step and glanced back at Orrin with an appraising look. "Perceptive."

He continued to walk forward.

They followed in relative silence, broken only by Daniel complaining he had to pee . . . and that he was hungry. They'd walked for another two hours before Orrin stepped closer to the elf.

"There are six people approaching. Four from in front and one from either side."

Leanthun nodded. "I hear them. Please stand back and stay quiet."

Orrin never physically saw the two elves on their flanks, and Leanthun left them standing on the sun-dappled forest trail as he talked with the four elves who bristled at seeing humans in their forest. Two held bows like Leanthun's, and one wore a dark-brown robe of what looked like deerskin. The fourth elf was taller than Leanthun and had two of the khopesh-type swords strapped to her back. Their whispers and furious gestures made him nervous, but he, Daniel, and Madi stood with their hands on their head, trying to look as non-threatening as possible.

"They will come with us to the council." A female voice, belonging to one of the elves with a bow, broke the silent whispers.

Leanthun appeared to argue back, but the tall elf put her hand on his shoulder. He ducked his head and strode toward them.

"I'm sorry. You must go with them. Don't resist or fight. Try to stay out of trouble until I return."

"Leanthun, you promised us safe passage," Madi said loudly, making sure her voice carried to the other elves. "Does this mean you intend to kidnap a [Hero] and the daughter of Lord Catanzano of Dey?"

Leanthun smiled and winked at her. "My promise of safe passage is still true, young Catanzano. I had hoped to bring you to my mentor first, but our approach was noticed by others quicker than I anticipated. You are free to turn back from our forest, but if you leave, you must not return here without an escort. Our lands are currently infested with attacking humans, and though you have come to give aid, I would not want any accidents to befall you while in our forest."

Madi bowed, keeping her hands on her head. "We will wait for your swift return. We are sorry that we slowed you down so much. The strength and longevity of elves is well-known to outpace humans', and we have exhausted ourselves trying to keep up. Please ask your brothers and sisters if they would let us rest and perhaps eat an early dinner. We would appreciate the opportunity to experience the legendary elven hospitality."

Daniel leaned in toward Orrin. "What the hell is going on?"

Orrin stomped on his friend's foot. "Shut up and let her do her thing."

Leanthun left after a few hurried words with the tall female. She was the only one to introduce herself to them.

"My name is Filauria. You will follow and not speak."

Thankfully, Madi's political savvy convinced their new guards to handle them with care. The elves kept them surrounded in a loose circle, leaving the way back seemingly open. But Orrin knew the two watchers were trailing behind.

After another thirty minutes of walking, the trees began to show more signs of being cultivated. Branches connected and rope bridges spanned the distances between the large trees. Orrin saw windows and doors carved into the trees high above and pointed them out to Daniel.

"No talking," the elf on their left commanded. Orrin dropped his hand and shrugged at Daniel.

The outskirts of the civilization gave way to more movement, and between one tree and the next, the trio found themselves standing in a city among the trees. Where the forest behind them had been closed, dimly lit, and sparsely populated, the view in front of them made Orrin realize the elves had carefully groomed the path and outskirts to guard this gem.

A clearing that spanned miles surrounded the largest tree of the entire forest. The matriarch tree did not need an explanation or introduction; while the trees around it stood as tall as any sequoia or redwood, the matriarch tree would likely stand out if someone flew over the forest. It had to be closer to twice the height of any other tree. Orrin estimated the trees behind them were close to three hundred and fifty feet in height, making this one closer to seven or eight hundred feet tall.

The huge tree rested on a slight hill with roots that spiraled away from the base into the rolling meadow around it. The sun broke through the branches between the rest of the forest and the matriarch, so a halo of light surrounded the old tree. A city of buildings made from wood had sprouted in that light and shifted between the roots that reached almost to the edge of the clearing itself. Looking closer, Orrin realized the wooden buildings might be trees themselves.

"Look well, humans, for rarely are any of your kind gifted the sight of our matriarch." The same elf who had yelled at Orrin before waved his hand at the giant tree.

"It's beautiful," Orrin said truthfully. "What are all the lights?"

"No talking," the elf muttered. He was silent as they continued down the packed-dirt road that had suddenly appeared but then spoke quietly. "The lights you see are from the rooms inside. Windows are rare but necessary for air movement between floors."

Orrin almost asked how many floors they had carved into the giant tree but decided to keep his mouth shut. *Leanthun can tell us later. I wish he'd told us more about who we are supposed to meet, though.*

Madi, Orrin, and Daniel were shuttled quickly through the growing streets. Smaller trees lined the path, and it took him a while to realize these trees were actually homes, shops, and restaurants. An entire city made of hollowed-out trees. He had so many questions and had to physically bite his tongue to stop himself from opening his mouth.

Filauria, the tall female with the two curved swords, opened the door to one of the small tree abodes and ushered them inside. The house was small inside, with a spiral staircase that led up to another floor. A small stove was pushed against the back, and a table that would comfortably seat two had four chairs around it in the middle of the room.

"This is reserved for visiting emissaries. You may rest above. Do not leave until I return for you in the morning." She spoke with a calm detachment, as if they were barely worth her time. "Your weapons are to be left here. Do not attempt to bring any weapon in front of the council or you will die. Do not try to hide your weapons using skills and do not summon a weapon by spell. You will die."

Orrin had the sudden urge to tell her "I am the weapon" but somehow resisted. He did remember something from all her talk of weapons, though.

"Filauria, thank you for the hospitality and all that," he said, pushing his hand into his pocket. "We found this before we set out for your beautiful forest and planned to give it to you all."

He pulled out the Citrandish bow from his [Dimension Hole] and held it out to her. "We don't know where it came from or—"

"No talking." Filauria's voice, so dead and robotic before, flared with a new edge. "You will bring that with you to the council tomorrow."

"I thought we couldn't bring—"

Before he could finish his sentence, the elf swept from the room and slammed the door shut. Orrin heard the distinct clunk of a bar being placed on the door outside.

"Well, shit."

Chapter 43

Madi did her best to sketch out a plan for them, but she admitted dealing with the elven council was well outside her expertise. Leanthun hadn't given them the tools they would need, and the situation didn't look good when the invaded country locked you up in an embassy.

The rest of the day passed without event. The small home was stocked with food, which Orrin quietly swiped. Things kept fresh in his [Dimension Hole], and if the elves were going to keep them prisoner, he was going to be as petty as he could be. He even considered stuffing the bedsheets in as well. They were the nicest material he'd ever slept on in his life.

Filauria appeared in the early hours of the morning and knocked until Daniel stumbled down the stairs. He opened the door just as Madi and Orrin joined him.

"Let's go. The council will see you now."

Daniel grumbled as Orrin unpacked a small armory of weapons onto the table. He set Gertrude on top of the last of it and glared at Filauria.

Guards surrounded them again as they moved through the city toward the big tree in the middle. The large roots of the matriarch created a natural maze in the clearing around the tree, and Orrin was quickly lost as they climbed steps carved into the wood, went over bridges built to span deep and narrow crevices between close roots, and moved quickly through caverns built under parts of the tree that had risen out of the ground completely.

Even if I had [Map] running, some of these things are too high to scale. It's like a living fortress with defenses naturally built in.

As discussed, he kept his mouth shut and didn't ask more questions. Madi had asked the same of Daniel, but Orrin doubted his friend would be able to let her take the lead completely.

When they finally climbed the last set of the carved steps, complete with handrails, the group found themselves at the top of the hill where the matriarch sat perched over its domain. Ornate doors had been carved into the trunk of the tree and stood wide-open. The interior room of the tree itself was a simple circle with stairs leading up on both sides. Nine chairs sat in a semicircle on a raised dais overlooking the entrance. Filauria and the guards bowed at the door to the seven elves seated in front of them but did not enter.

"The [Hero], Lady Catanzano of Dey, and party members are here seeking an audience with the council." Filauria's voice echoed into the room and came back louder than it had entered. "They were granted passage by Leanth—"

"We know, or else we would not have summoned them here. You may send them in. Close the doors and let none disturb us."

Of the nine seats in front of them, only seven were filled. The chair in the middle was a throne, but it was empty, as was the seat to its immediate right. On the right side of the room were four elves, two men and two women. On the left side sat two more women and one last man.

It was the woman sitting closest to the throne on their right who had spoken. The left hand of the throne, so to speak. The three of them entered as the guards outside began pushing the thick wooden doors shut. As the room was sealed, the same elf stood and lightly stepped down the single raised step to stand in front of them.

"A [Hero] . . ." She let the word sit in the air, tasting how she felt about it as she studied Daniel. Madi had placed him in the center and stood upright on his right side. Orrin was to the left and a step back. The elder female elf continued, "Brought to our forest to bring us aid, no doubt. What boon would Dey ask of us in return? What could a mere child give that we could not take ourselves?"

She put her face directly in Daniel's personal space. Orrin saw her nose crinkle with disgust as she asked, "What makes you think we need your help at all? It might be easier to simply kill you. Never does a [Hero] come but with consequences far outstripping their use."

Daniel's hands flexed, and Orrin noticed his shoulder twitch as if he wanted to reach for Gertrude. The elf smiled and turned her back on the [Hero].

"So young and brash. I half expect he'll attack us before we even begin our discussion."

Madi placed her hand on Daniel and muttered something. Daniel chuckled.

The elf trying to instigate a fight whirled around and moved close to Daniel again. "You dare laugh at me here in the heart of our power?"

Daniel kept the smile on his face as he bowed a little. The action brought his face closer to hers, and the elf backed up a step as Daniel gave respect to the other elves with his bow.

"I'm not laughing at you," he said, straightening up again. "It might be easier for you to try and kill me than simply listen to reason, but no matter how young I might be, I've dealt with bullies before. I won't be baited."

"Well done." The woman nodded, and the anger that had been on her face smoothed away. She smiled warmly at them. "I apologize for testing you, but I've always found a good opening skirmish tells me more than words alone."

She climbed back on the dais and slumped into her chair. "My name is Gwynnestri Ralodove. I am the elder of defense for our forest. We have been told you have come to help us win a war. Please know we do not consider ourselves at war at this time. You may make your case."

Orrin's mind raced as Madi stepped forward. "Honored elders of the elves, we thank you for your hospitality and time. The news of fighting among your forest's edges has spread throughout the human lands. You may not consider yourselves at war, but I promise you that Odrana believes it is."

Several of the elves squirmed in their seats at hearing the country named in their hall.

Madi continued her speech, walking back and forth in front of them. She explained that the [Hero], Daniel, had received his Quest and tried valiantly to help. She spoke of Odrana sending kidnappers for him, implying the Quest might be the reason.

Make them curious. Make them doubt. Make them ask for help. That had been Madi's plan. Offering to end a fight for them was beyond what they could do at their level, but the system had given Daniel the Quest to end the war. That meant something.

Except the system really gave me the Quest, Orrin thought as he watched the other elders. Madi had finished explaining that they were not here as a conquering force but rather to give whatever aid the council deemed necessary. He pulled his attention back to her.

"We traveled this far to ask your side. No one outside the forest knows why Odrana has attacked or what they are after. It may be there is something we could help with in ending the aggression."

Gwynnestri raised her hand, and a barrier formed around the raised platform. The elders turned in and began talking, but no sound carried to the trio.

"Well done, Madi," Daniel praised her as she stepped back, letting him be front and center again.

"Why wouldn't they think they're at war?" Orrin asked quietly. The elf sitting next to the elder of defense was staring at him. "Also, who's the guy next to Gwyn?"

"Don't give them nicknames, Orrin," Madi warned. "I don't know who is who. Why is he looking at us like that?"

"He's looking at me." Orrin waved, and the man shook himself, as if rousing from a stupor. He promptly ignored them and began talking with the others.

The discussions went on for what felt like forever. Orrin tried to find anything to distract himself. He studied the different shapes carved into the elves' seats. He was tempted to use [Analyze] on the barrier, but his little remaining good sense prevailed.

Finally, he couldn't take it anymore. "Madi, are they going to argue all day?"

Her glare pierced him. "It's been ten minutes, Orrin. Be patient. They're elves."

When the barrier finally came down, Orrin and Daniel were playing slaps. Daniel had his hands on top of Orrin's. Orrin had increased his dexterity slightly so he could beat his friend and the top of the [Hero]'s hands were bright red.

"Children," Madi muttered.

"We have discussed at length the benefits of having the [Hero] attempt to stop the humans from invading our lands," Gwynnestri announced.

"I'll say," Orrin mumbled to Daniel.

"Excuse me?"

"Sorry, nothing." Orrin ducked his head as the eyes of all seven elves bored down on him.

"As I was saying, we have agreed that the [Hero] may in fact be of some use. We will accept this Quest from him and declare the elves are at war with Odrana. At that point, our forces will—"

The doors behind them began to move, and Gwynnestri's eyes bulged. She hurriedly continued, "Our forces will then sweep the invading forces from our land and put an end to this scourge once and for all. All those in favor of this resolution?"

"Oh, Gwynni, you know you can't send our people to war without a royal decree." A voice rolled over them from behind.

Orrin peered over his shoulder as another elf walked into the room. Leanthun was behind him but stayed outside. The elf they'd traveled with looked exhausted but triumphant.

The elf that entered had eyes so pale blue that Orrin thought he was blind at first. The wooden headband he wore might have been a crown. While all the elders appeared to be . . . well . . . elderly, this elf teetered on the line of being ancient. He had actual wrinkles.

"Arandir, what are you do— It has been some time since you've entertained yourself with council work," Gwynnestri said, her eyes flashing at the man.

"It has been some time indeed," Arandir whispered, stopping by the trio of humans and examining them each in turn. "A [Hero] and a scion of a lord of Dey appear in our forest, offering us support in a time of need, and they are waylaid from their path."

"They were brought to us as soon as we found them," Gwynnestri said, but Arandir simply waved his hand in her direction.

"They were on their way to see me, not a full council that would take a Quest. Did you not even think of what that would do, Gwynni? You were my student, after all."

"That was long ago, illustrious one. This is council business. The humans have continued their encroachment into our forest and—"

"Yes. Yes." Arandir paused in front of Orrin. Their eyes connected, and Orrin felt himself falling. The elf blinked and turned away. "As they always have. That does not give you power beyond what has been given. This council does not have the right to send our people to die."

"Then do your job and anoint a successor," Gwynnestri hissed at him. "Or will you be as inept and pompous as the fools who came before you?"

Orrin stepped closer to Daniel and Madi, laying a [Ward] on them both. Gwynnestri was standing and pointing at the elderly elf.

"These humans are bold, setting fires to our trees. We've lost a handful of our scouts to them, either dead or forced into slavery. How much longer will you hold out and not do your duty to our people?"

"Not do my duty?" The words were quiet, but each syllable rang with such emotion Orrin put his hands on his friends and readied a [Teleport] spell.

The male elf that had been looking at Orrin earlier stood and put his hand on Gwynnestri's shoulder, pulling her back and whispering to her. She shook her head multiple times before she hung her head and sat.

"Arandir, old friend. Are you here to take your seat? We are in the middle of a vote."

Orrin immediately didn't like this guy. His voice was silky and perfect, his hair coiffed just so, and his stance both unworried and poised at the same time. A politician.

Arandir sighed. "Devdan, must you force it?"

"The council has already heard arguments for and against. Only the vote remains."

"Then, as is my right, I will lead closing remarks before we vote."

Devdan scowled. "Closing remarks are for matters of judgment, not something so trivial as accepting the [Hero]'s request to aid us."

"But you are not accepting aid, you are seeking to force a decree on these three young humans. Once you force them to give you their Quest, we all know what you will do. Every elf will receive the same and the rewards will be diluted. You seek to steal and in doing so cast judgment. This, therefore, falls well within my rights. All agreed?"

Four of the elders who hadn't spoken yet raised a hand and slapped the arm of their chair. Devdan's lip curled at them for a moment, but then he smiled prettily and sat back down. He tapped his chair's arm with a finger. "So be it."

"Don't worry." Arandir smiled at Madi. "We'll all be sipping tea in my house by lunch."

Orrin groaned.

Arandir shook hands with a few of the elders before moving to the empty seat. He settled into the chair next to the throne and closed his eyes.

When he opened them again, he spoke with passion. "These humans have come to us asking if we require help in facing the aggression of other humans. We do not need their help. They have seen two decades and fewer levels, while our youngest warriors could outkill all three of them in battle. That is not why they are here, though. We could take their Quest and use it as justification to skirt our laws on war. But that is not who we are. They do not know why Odrana is at our door and have come with half the knowledge needed to make sound decisions. We will tell them what Sanneris is after. All those in favor?"

"You can't be serious!" Gwynnestri shouted. The other elves started shouting, and Arandir winked at Orrin before waving his hand. The sound barrier reappeared.

"Great," Orrin muttered. "More waiting."

"Don't you dare start playing that stupid game again," Madi demanded.

Chapter 44

The barrier came down just as Madi landed a resounding slap on Daniel's hands.

"You're getting the hang of it," he praised her.

Arandir coughed loudly.

Madi scowled at Daniel and bowed her head at the council. "We apologize. Please, go ahead."

The old elf smirked but didn't comment more. "The council has agreed to a trade. We will tell you why the leader of Odrana is trying to force his way into our lands. In exchange, a small number of carefully selected elves will receive the Quest from the [Hero]. The council does not and cannot declare the fight is a war, but we can accept that Odrana believes it is such. Those we select will be able to leave the forest in an attempt to complete a Quest. They are not fighting a war but will work to end one."

Orrin grinned. *Semantics. They can't fight a war, but they can send some elves to complete a Quest. The new guy gets to make them stick to the rules and the angry chick gets to send her people off to fight.*

"I suppose the terms are acceptable?"

Madi gave a half bow and began to negotiate. First, she asked for veto power if the [Hero] felt someone wasn't worthy of the Quest. Orrin thought that might be going a bit too far, and the council agreed. They'd hold the power of choosing who got the Quest. Gwynnestri did most of the talking while Arandir chatted with the other elders.

Madi also wanted a specific number of people that Daniel would have to share with. Gwynnestri wanted twenty. Arandir turned from his conversation and unilaterally reduced their ask to ten. Daniel didn't want any more than to help stop the war, but Madi told them five was acceptable for the information they were offering. Additional concessions could be given for more sharing.

"You have no bargaining power." Gwynnestri preened on her high-back chair. "We accept the five."

Arandir sighed. "The Quest will not be shared further. If you agree to five, that is all that will receive it."

The female elf stared daggers at him but resumed negotiating. Daniel had given Madi free rein in what she asked for. Mostly she was requesting trade negotiations with Dey for the future.

Orrin ignored the women talking and watched Arandir. He was laughing at something the elder on the farthest corner was saying. Something about him felt off. Orrin just couldn't put his finger on what it was.

"Gwynni, let them be for now. You can finish that later. Would you please put the sound barrier around us all? I do not think we need another leak, do you?"

Gwynnestri's face was stone, but Orrin could see the anger bubbling underneath. What was the point of living hundreds of years if you couldn't learn to control your emotions better? Orrin wasn't even eighteen and he felt he'd be able to hide it a bit better.

"Could you stop staring at her like that?" Daniel whispered to him.

"What?" Orrin averted his gaze and missed whatever Gwynni did, but he felt the magic roll over them. All the sounds nearby were being reflected and echoing while the small sounds from outside the tree that he'd been accustomed to were suddenly cut off.

"You've been glaring at the mean elf lady like you want to kill her. Quit it."

Maybe I have a little bit of work to do.

Arandir sat back down in his seat. He glanced around the council once, letting his gaze linger on Devdan before he turned to Daniel.

"You are a [Hero] and not from our world, correct?"

Daniel nodded and mumbled something. He cleared his throat and tried again. "Yes, sir."

Arandir smiled. "I am not interrogating you, son. I simply need to know what your base of knowledge is about certain things. How much do you know about our history? Have you heard of the Calamity?"

"Arandir, what are you doing?" Devdan hissed. "The boy doesn't need a history lesson. Just tell him and be done with it."

"And if the boy does not understand what it means? Would you have me backtrack later or do the job that I have been doing since before you were born, Devdan?"

The well-coiffed elf waved a hand in surrender and fell back into his chair.

"I've done my best to learn about Asmea. Is the Calamity what you call the thing the [Hero] did when he blew up your world?"

Arandir's smile shifted. While before it was like an old grandfather telling a story to a favorite grandson, now Orrin could see hints of a teacher who had found an answer just slightly off.

"It is for our purposes. What you might not know is that before the Calamity, all races lived together. Not in perfect peace or anything unattainable like that, but well enough. Each race had its own power structures. We elves had our monarchy and council. The dwarves had their democracy and a voting system. Even the orcs had a chieftain above chieftains. The humans, of course, had many different versions of each type of governance."

"And the demons?"

Arandir's smile disappeared. "What do you know of demons?"

"They tried to kill a bunch of people in Dey. When I'm around them, I kind of lose track of myself and go after them. You can get experience from killing one. That's about it, to be honest."

"Arandir, this is outside what we agreed on. You do not get to give these children all the secrets of our world," Devdan drawled from his seat. "Be very careful, oh illustrious one, that you do not break the tenets you keep. It would be a terrible day if we had to—"

Arandir raised a hand and pointed at Devdan. The elf was blasted backward, shattering his chair and smashing against the wall of the tree. Arandir didn't say a word, and not one member of the council jumped to Devdan's defense.

Daniel, surprisingly, spoke first. "Um . . . you don't need to kill him. We came to stop Odrana, not demons."

Arandir dropped his hand, and Devdan fell with it. The eldest elder studied his fingernails as the now thoroughly despoiled elf crawled to his feet and made his way back to his chair—now a stool. Devdan didn't meet any other elf's gaze, but Orrin once again felt the waves of anger coming from the dais.

"As I was saying, the people of that time had many different ruling powers. Even the elves had a few small sects that did not bend the knee to our king. Of all the races, the humans fought wars over who should rule which plot of land more than anyone else. But for all the differences, each race had one thing in common: one person in each race was born with a gift to help their own. A gift from the system meant to help nurture and grow as many people as that person could help. They were called Administrators."

Orrin felt the walls of the tree go fuzzy with his vision. The tingling pinpricks behind his ears traveled down to his fingers, and his mouth was dry. They were stuck inside a tree with guards outside, not to mention the eight elves sitting in front of them, each centuries old. He readied a [Teleport] and prayed that Daniel wasn't looking at him.

"There is much history, many secrets, and more unknown questions about Administrators, even among our people, than I have time to go into . . . or, as members of this council would be sure to remind me, would be allowed to share with you. After the Calamity, no more Administrators appeared."

"My father doesn't believe they ever existed," Madi muttered to Orrin, leaning close. "He thinks they're make-believe stories."

"Except for one."

Orrin put his foot up against Daniel's heel and began to reach for Madi. He was going to [Teleport] them out of here. He'd jump them multiple times, all the way back to Dey. He'd cycle if he had to.

"That elf spent his entire life figuring out a way to give the powers of an Administrator to another. It is why Odrana is at our door. For the first time in millennia, the information this council holds as one of its most secure secrets was discovered. I am an Administrator."

Wait, what?

Orrin's stupefied face was saved only by Madi's snort of laughter.

"I'm sorry. You expect the [Hero] to give you a Quest for the assertion that you are a mythical class that has never been proven to exist?"

Arandir frowned. "You do not believe me, and yet the Odranan army has been stationed around our forest for months. They probe and try to enter our forest, the only place that our laws dictate we can protect, and you think they do it for what? Land? Gold? We have not attacked them in force. It is clear we are not the aggressor here. What else could they possibly want?"

Madi waved her hand in the air. "I thought you would tell us. Nobody in Dey knows why Odrana is attacking you. If they have a reason, they aren't sharing it."

"Likely because they think they can get my powers for themselves."

"Your Administrator powers? With which you can strip a man of his class or create a [Hero] with a snap of your fingers?"

"No. I am not sure any Administrator has those powers. What I can do—yes, Devdan, I know what I am saying—what I can do is not up for discussion, but as with any other Administrator of the past, I can only use my powers on elves. Something that Sanerris refuses to believe. He came here himself to request I be turned over for the betterment of all Asmea. We sent him away, and he returned with his army."

Madi was about to continue arguing when Daniel gave her their preapproved signal—he stomped on her foot.

"Mr. Arandir . . . let's say I believed you were an Administrator but that you couldn't use your powers on anyone other than elves. Let's say I believed you and gave you the Quest anyways. What would you want to talk more about what you can do?"

"What?" Madi yelped in surprise as she rubbed her toes. "What are you doing?"

"I'm curious, and we were always going to help them however we can, Madi," Daniel stage-whispered to her.

Daniel, don't you dare do it. Orrin tried to catch his eye.

Gwynnestri exchanged quick and heated words with Devdan. Orrin distinctly heard the words *useless* and *pointless* but couldn't make out the actual conversation. She turned to Arandir and nodded her head. "Defense and Justice are amenable to a closed-door conversation regarding Administrator powers only in exchange for the full ten shared Quests. No additional topics or history without our express approval and additional compensation."

The council held a speedy vote, with Orrin finally learning that they didn't go by names during a vote but what part of elven society they represented. From left to right, Agriculture, Labor, and Health voted with Arandir, who called himself simply Admin. Gwynnestri was Defense, and Devdan was Justice. The two on the far right voted as State and Treasury. A unanimous vote for Daniel's offer was tendered, and the motion passed.

Madi was pissed at the lost commerce with Dey but shrugged it off, telling Daniel he better know what he was doing. She still believed the elf was lying. Gwynnestri dismissed them, telling Daniel he would be expected to come and share the Quest when summoned.

Arandir climbed down the dais and shook Madi's hand. "I know you do not believe me, but I was impressed at your negotiating skills with Gwynni. I have heard good things about your father. Please send him my regards."

The elf seemed to age as he left the tree, pulling them with him not with words but with his expectation that they would follow. He had a magnetism that felt irresistible to Orrin.

"We can go to my apartment in the city here. My home is too far away. Leanthun barely made it to me in time, and I am afraid I quite outdid myself traveling down here with such speed."

"Why would the all-powerful Administrator need to hurry to help a lowly [Hero]?" Madi asked bitterly.

"Not just a lowly [Hero]." Arandir turned his head and smiled at her. "I think there is much more to this young man than meets the eye."

Chapter 45

Madi sulked as they traveled to Arandir's apartment. Leanthun trailed behind, now acting as a bodyguard for the elder. Orrin bumped into Madi and nodded toward the old elf, then Daniel. She sighed and hurried her step, asking Arandir a question about the economy of elven pottery or something else that Orrin was too busy to pay attention to.

Instead, Orrin grabbed Daniel's elbow and slowed their stroll so they were directly in between Arandir and Leanthun. He pointed up toward the tree line, acting like he'd noticed something cool in the elven forest.

"What's the plan?"

Daniel smirked. "It's nice when I'm the one calling the shots and setting things up. Is this what it feels like for you?"

The smirk disappeared when Orrin slugged him in the arm. "Ass."

"Jerk."

Daniel rubbed his shoulder. "Did you really need to increase your strength to hit me? That really hurt."

Orrin scanned his friend with a quick [Identify] to make sure he hadn't actually taken off health. Daniel was fine.

"Don't be a baby. I shaved a single point off your health."

Daniel tried to look offended but grinned again when Orrin rolled his eyes. "I want to learn more about what he can do. If he's really the last Admin or whatever, like he claims, he can teach you. It looks like he's on our side—to a point. He did just piss off his own council."

Orrin considered Daniel's plan. From what he'd seen, Arandir had appeared at the last minute to offer a good compromise to the elven council's original plan of simply taking Daniel's Quest and going to war. The timing was convenient. It would be a good tactic to play good cop, bad cop with the [Hero]. The council still got what they wanted, and all it had taken was showing the first offered extreme option of taking the Quest and having the coolheaded elderly elf soften it up with some esoteric knowledge. If the leader of Odrana knew Arandir was an Administrator, he'd probably told people. The knowledge that there was an all-powerful person who could make you stronger wasn't something people would be able to keep the lid on.

Arandir's offer to tell them more was appearing less valuable with each thought.

"He might have staged that all to make us like him. If the guy from Odrana knows about him, his generals or whoever will know, too. It's not like he can just say, 'Hey, let's go invade the elves' and everybody listens for no reason. I'm not sure we traded the Quest for anything of real value."

Daniel raised an eyebrow at his friend. "You remember we were just going to give it to them anyway, right? Having either side incentivized to end the war was your idea. It's not like we can go fight on the front lines and make a difference. Your trust issues are showing again."

Arandir turned back and waved them forward. Orrin dropped the conversation as they approached where he had stopped. He pointed to one of the larger trees near the perimeter of the city.

"This is my apartment. Are any of you afraid of heights?"

Along the side of the tree was a small box that Orrin had thought was somebody's slightly large trash can. He hadn't noticed the smallest cut in the tree behind it, thinking it was simply a natural gash in the bark. He also hadn't noticed the rope attached to the open-lidded trash can or the latch that opened the door.

It wasn't until Arandir had ushered Madi and Daniel into the pen that he'd realized they were all squishing into an open-air elevator. An elevator on the outside of a tree that would easily fail any OSHA testing. It was already failing Orrin's testing.

"I think I grabbed this rail too hard. It broke." He held out a piece of wood that had been a guardrail a moment before. Orrin had forgotten he'd just increased his strength when he squeezed the railing in a panic.

"No worries," Arandir said as he took the proffered stick and threw it deeper into the woods. "It will regrow in time. Leanthun, we will be above. Did you have someone set out tea?"

"Yes, illustrious one. Everything is ready for you," the younger elf said from his bowed position. His entire demeanor was subservient when around Arandir.

"See that we are not disturbed."

"Never . . . again," Madi moaned as they exited the lift.

Daniel threw up over the edge and turned back with a smile. "That was better than any roller coaster I've ever been on. Can we do it again?"

Orrin felt somewhere in the middle of his two friends. He hadn't hated the rush of air as the lift ascended into the sky with such speed the air itself had pressed them down into a crouch. He also hadn't loved the way Arandir had watched the ground shrink as he leaned over a waist-high rail he could easily break.

"Let's give it a few minutes, D."

Arandir invited them in and set about playing host. Off what was his private elevator—because of course it was—the tree door opened into a surprisingly airy and open sitting room. Cushioned chairs and sofas were arranged in a small circle with a slight opening toward the one window in the tree, which boasted a magnificent view of the matriarch tree and most of the city below.

Orrin noticed that while most of the cushions, the tables, and the floors had been scrubbed clean, a few of the smaller tables and a single bookshelf had a layer of dust. He ran his finger through the grime.

"My apologies. I rarely visit here anymore." Arandir smiled when Orrin turned around. "Tea?"

His staff of servants had set out a porcelain tea set painted with blue and green swirls that evoked the ocean. The elf elder poured each of them a cup. Orrin took the dirty green water that he had no intention of drinking.

He threw a quick [Analyze] on it, just in case.

Green Tea

Daniel and Madi were already sipping their drinks. Madi made small talk, complimenting the rare offering. Orrin learned elven tea was a commodity traded only in small amounts. He set the cup down on an end table.

"This is nice and all," Daniel, said, interrupting Madi's attempt to secure a small amount of loose-leaf tea for herself. "But maybe you can tell us more about your powers?"

A small smile pulled the corner of Arandir's mouth as he sat back in his chair. "What would you like to know?"

"What sort of things can you do?" Daniel asked as he copied the elf's movements. Except when Daniel sat back, he almost spilled the tea across his lap and had to hurriedly sit back up.

"A trivial number of things that an actual Administrator could do in the past. I can reset a fellow elf's stats if they have the need. I can also reset a class if they choose poorly, but that only brings them back to a classless state. They would still need to find their own class again. However, we do have a large library of books and scrolls on different classes, along with the best way to obtain the same."

He finished talking and took a sip of his tea.

"That's it?" Daniel asked dejectedly. "Just reset stats or a class? If you can't give out Quests or give classes, why would Odrana try and invade you?"

The elf didn't respond, continuing to drink his tea. He simply raised an eyebrow.

"If you told the Sedaris guy—"

"Sanerris," Orrin corrected.

"—that you could only do that, and only to elves, why would he still be trying to get to you? Could he even make you use your power?"

Arandir put down his cup. "He could try. I have lived a very long life, but even I would eventually break under torture or certain mind magics. What I am curious about, though, is how long have you known about the other powers of an Administrator—and how you know at all."

Shit . . . what? Orrin flinched.

"What?" Daniel looked confused. "You just told me."

"I did not tell you that past Administrators could give Quests. I also did not tell you they could assign classes."

Daniel knit his eyebrows together. "Assign classes? Is that another power you have? I just figured if you could take one, you should be able to give it, too, right?"

"Very well-done deflection for a human of your age, but not good enough for me."

Daniel set his tea down on the table and leaned back against the cushions. He crossed his legs. "I'm not deflecting. One of the first things I did when I got to Dey was read a lot of books. I found a few mentions of Administrators. One of them must have said something about Quests."

Arandir smiled like a snake cornering a mouse. "You know, I am one thousand, two hundred, and thirty-seven years old this upcoming year. I am the fourth of my line to carry the Administrator role. My grandfather took the duty from his father, the last full Administrator of our world. Do you know what they both spent their time doing for centuries after the Calamity?"

He paused for effect.

"They searched for every piece of knowledge about the world before. They brought as much of that knowledge as they could to our forest for safekeeping. It's a mission that my family has taken seriously for millennia. We do not edit or change any information—except for knowledge relating to Administrators. As my father loved to remind me, if anyone could piece together what really happened, they might be able to piece together that one Administrator survived. That would be the end of our line. No books with real information relating to Administrators exist in Asmea. I am quite sure of it."

"You can't kill oral histories, though," Orrin piped up. "People will always tell stories. Even if you think you've eradicated all knowledge of something, eventually people will put together enough clues to find some parts of the truth. Maybe you just missed something recent. Daniel did read a lot of books when we got to Dey."

Arandir stood and poured more tea into his cup. He offered a refill to Madi, who accepted, and Daniel, who did not.

He didn't offer more to Orrin and gave a small frown at the wasted liquid in his cup. "That may be true, but the chances are slim. The chances that the new [Hero] found that same information where my people did not is lower. It does not matter, though. I will answer your question. You asked why Sanerris would still invade. He found a relic in an excavation, buried for so long that it took him years to figure out what it does. When he was able to activate it, he learned how useless the item was. It would only activate if I used my powers, but I have not used them in decades. Our people have not had the need, and we have known of what he had in his possession long enough to take safeguards."

Arandir sat and stared at the ceiling. Orrin glanced up and noticed the ceiling had been carved into swirls around the natural knots of the tree, giving the impression of a pond rippling out from each imperfect spot in the wood.

"I am walking a line in what I say next, so pay close attention. I will not repeat myself." He took a deep breath. "When the world had Administrators aplenty, those with power schemed and plotted . . . including those with Admin powers. Those who were afraid of what could happen created a relic, or maybe more than one, that could read the twists of the system. An early-warning system of sorts that could tell when someone had interfered with the system itself. Something that was normally reserved only for Administrators. Sanerris has that item. It activated a few months ago."

"Administrators can tell when someone messes with the system?"

Arandir smiled at Daniel's interruption. "Of course. Even a partial one such as myself can tell when something feels off. I was searching for the source of the recent waves in the system when Sanerris suborned an elf, learning of me. Naturally, he thought I was the one who activated his new toy. It does not matter that he arrived at the right conclusion with the wrong information. He knows an Administrator exists and found what he believes to be the only one in Asmea."

The elf leaned forward, the his gaze hungry again as he stared Daniel down. "Only, he does not know that I had already seen the system reacting. He does not know what I know. I am not the only Administrator. Another exists, and he is playing the [Hero]."

Chapter 46

Orrin didn't know where to look.

Arandir was sitting back in his chair with a jubilant expression on his face. He seemed so pleased with himself that Orrin wanted to laugh. He thought Daniel was an Administrator like him. He was sitting across from Orrin, an actual Administrator—or a budding one—and had reached the wrong conclusion.

Daniel wasn't laughing, like Orrin thought he might. Daniel knew Orrin was probably the one who had created the ripples in the system. Orrin had somehow created a Quest the same day they'd arrived. Sure, it was all Daniel's fault for getting caught by a monster, but Orrin's powers had activated, granting him a "Save the [Hero]" Quest. Daniel was one of two people who knew of Orrin's powers, with Tony being the other. Even Tony, who somehow knew something of Administrators, hadn't been able to figure it out on his own.

Daniel's face remained stoic. It was an expression that Orrin had seen before. Usually his friend only concentrated this hard when they were in the middle of taking a test or if Daniel was writing an essay and trying particularly hard to phrase something just so.

Orrin was almost ignoring Madi completely when he felt something very wrong from her direction. He turned and blanched.

Madi was glaring at him. Not at Arandir. Not at Daniel. Her eyes were on Orrin with a mix of emotions. Hurt and betrayal seemed prominent. Fear was there as well.

Orrin twitched his head to the side. *Later. Not now.*

To her credit, Madi schooled her face and turned back to Arandir.

"That's not possible. I've seen Daniel's status. He is a [Hero]. There is no such thing as an Administrator. I'm half tempted to pull the entire deal. I think if we went to Odrana, we could easily get them to pull their army back in exchange for the Quest. You've given us nothing of value. While I appreciate the tea, I think we should be on our way."

Arandir didn't take his eyes off Daniel.

When Madi stood up, Orrin joined him. Daniel kept his seat.

"D. Let's go. This guy is just trying to rattle you." Orrin rested his hand on Daniel's shoulder. His friend peeked up at him. His hair was getting long, and with his stubbly face, he was looking much older than his seventeen years.

"Orrin . . ."

"The elves can make up any story they want, but I think it's time we went and talked to the other side," Madi said. "Our only objective is to end the war. Maybe Lord Sanerris will be honest with us."

Daniel crossed his arms, brooding.

Orrin bent close and whispered to his friend, "Leave it. We should go."

Daniel shook his head. "If what he says is true, there might not be another chance."

"Daniel, no."

"Arandir, can you give me a few minutes with my friends?"

The elf stood up. "Not a problem. I will check with Leanthun. The council should have made a selection by now. Would you like to share the Quest with them today or wait until we finish our talk?"

Daniel shrugged. "Whatever you all want. It doesn't matter to me."

"Very well. I will return in a few minutes." The elven Administrator crossed the room and opened the door. Orrin caught a glimpse of the elevator cart before the door swung shut again.

"What the fuck are you thinking?" Orrin rounded on Daniel. "You aren't an . . . whatever he thinks you are."

Madi stepped forward and slapped Orrin across the face.

"What was that for?"

"It's you, isn't it?"

Madi raised her hand to hit him again, but Daniel caught her wrist. "Friends don't hit each other like that, Madi."

"You knew, didn't you?" The anger and hurt Orrin had seen before splashed across her face. "You both had another secret and you kept it from me, again. What do I have to do to get you to trust me?" She pointed at Orrin. "You *just* came clean with me about being from his world. You trusted me with that but not this?"

"Madi, you . . . I . . ."

"You're an Administrator. I'm not an idiot. So many things fell into place when that asshole accused Daniel. But he's not the one who changed Quest rewards or did something weird to the dungeon core. I bet none of his Quests are even his, are they?"

"Some of them are," Daniel answered before Orrin could. He groaned and slapped his forehead.

"Madi, please listen to me."

"No. You listen to me. We are in a foreign country, dealing with one of the oldest political powers in the world, and you two just blindsided me. I'm supposed to be here to help. You *said* you brought me to help. Was that all a lie?" Madi managed to keep a straight face, with only her anger leaking through, but Orrin heard the quiver in her voice.

They hadn't trusted her. To be fair, they'd had no reason to believe Orrin's Admin powers were something that would ever come up here. He'd kept this last secret from her mostly because of the way Tony had acted when he'd found out. He was scared his only other friend would look at him differently.

She was looking at him differently now, but instead of fear, Orrin was more worried she was going to attack him again.

"I'm sorry," he whispered. "I could come up with any number of reasons why I didn't tell you, but none of them would matter."

She huffed and glared at Daniel.

"Hey, don't get mad at me. It wasn't my secret to share."

"But it's your secret to steal?" Orrin cut in. "I know what you're trying to do."

It had taken him a while, but he'd figured it out. Daniel was letting Arandir believe he was an Administrator to protect Orrin. He was still the [Hero], and the elves already had one army knocking at their door. Dey had made a claim to this [Hero], and trying to keep him here would result in Lord Catanzano sending forces as well.

Orrin had no such protection. Unless he counted Daniel as his protection.

"I'm not letting you protect me from this," he muttered.

Madi pushed Orrin, hard. He fell back into his chair.

"What was that for?"

"I told you that friends don't—"

"Shut it, both of you." Madi whirled on Daniel and got in his face. "You think you are being all noble, letting Arandir think you are the Administrator, but you are doing the exact opposite. You're using me and my father. If the elves try to keep you or turn you over to Odrana, Dey would go to war against the other nations for the first time ever. You would be leveraging our friendship—you already . . .tried to do it . . .to keep Orrin's secret."

"And you—" She turned back to Orrin. He scooted back into his chair. "Putting aside how mad I am at you right now, putting aside how you kept everything from me, again, I'm going to ask this once, and you better give me the truth. Did you know there was an Administrator here? Is that why you wanted to visit the elves?"

"I promise, I had no idea. I just thought if we could finish off this Quest, we could score some easy experience."

Madi held his eyes, searching. She found whatever she was looking for and flicked him quickly between the eyes. "You're forgiven, but only because you're going to tell me everything later. Let's figure out a plan. What's the downside of letting him know Orrin is the one with powers?"

Besides the fact that we are in the middle of their stronghold with no way out, surrounded by elite warriors who have trained with weapons and magic longer than our parents have been alive, and completely at their mercy? Orrin thought bitterly.

"They won't try to kidnap a [Hero]," Daniel offered. "Yes, I get that it's a dick move to leverage Dey and a potential war, but I think the old guy is just lonely. He's like the secret prince of the elves with this cool mysterious power. If he wants to believe he's in the same league as a [Hero], I say let him."

I love you, Daniel, but you are so pretentious sometimes.

"And if he finds out that we've lied to him?" Madi asked, finally sitting back down. Daniel plopped back into his chair as well. "You can't turn to Orrin every time Arandir asks you a question. Do you even know what Orrin can do?"

"*Orrin* doesn't know what Orrin can do. That's the beauty of the plan. He's as clueless as I am."

"I wouldn't say that," Orrin muttered darkly.

Madi pushed some hair behind an ear and rubbed at her forehead. "You two are so frustrating. Orrin, what all can you do? I'll admit, I have next to no real knowledge of what an Administrator can do. It's myths, and not even the good kind. In the stories, they're the bad guys from eons ago that would show up to punish you before eating your soul. I'm guessing that's an exaggeration based on you having this power."

"What does that mean?"

"She's saying you're a teddy bear." Daniel smirked.

Orrin flipped him off.

"Can you two focus?"

Orrin sighed. "I don't really have any control over what I can do. Sometimes, Quests will appear. Usually in stressful situations like this one . . ." He trailed off and looked around hopefully. "Damn. Worth a shot."

Daniel rolled his eyes. Madi gestured in a "continue" motion.

"I was able to steal constitution points from Samara, Wendeln's kidnapper person. I traded points of mine to do that. I guess *steal* isn't the right word. I just . . . obliterated them?"

Madi's jaw dropped. "Permanently?"

"Until she died, but yeah, I think it would have been permanent. The points I spent to activate the skill were gone until I replaced them in the dungeon. Oh, I can sometimes change Quest results, but you know that. I also absorbed the dungeon core, which gave me something called administrator points. That gave me a new list of powers I can unlock. It's like ability points, but for skills not in the store. Things like assigning or resetting a class or assigning new Quests. I'm guessing I'd be able to do it at will? I don't know. I haven't unlocked anything."

Madi was frozen.

"Dude, you broke her," Daniel teased.

She shook herself. "Start again. From the beginning. What's the first thing you remember that said 'Administrator'? All the way to the things you can unlock."

Orrin sighed. "Remember how I told you I arrived here with Daniel? Well, the system thought I was an error or something. It like . . . debugged . . . that's a computer term. The things with all the information in them, remember?"

"Orrin, I don't care about that right now."

"So, anyways, the system unlocked Administrator Access and let me select my own class. That's how I got [Utility Warder]. I just kept asking it for what I wanted and bam."

"Orrin, that's not how the system works," Madi argued, running her hands through her hair. She was growing more frazzled the more he talked.

"It does for me." He shrugged and continued. He recalled as much as he could about the circumstances of each Quest, chuckling as he recalled how Madi and her father had basically forced the Stop the War Quest from spawning. By the time he'd pulled up the Administrator powers list and read them aloud, Madi's eyes were huge.

". . . and that's why I didn't want to tell you. The last person I told flipped out and begged me not to kill him."

Madi dropped her eyes to the floor. "You wouldn't kill me. I know that. But Orrin, this . . . this is a lot. You've just upended everything I've ever been taught about the system and how it operates. The stories I have heard about Administrators describe them as powerful people, sure . . . but not able to rewrite a person so completely. It's a lot to take in."

Orrin crossed his arms.

"Don't pout." Daniel put his feet on the small table. "We still need to make a plan. I can tell Arandir everything you just said and get him to explain things to me. I'm sure he'll have good advice, being a centuries-old Admin himself. We can fast-track Orrin getting us more powerful."

Madi shook her head. "Some of the powers Orrin mentioned don't sound like anything Arandir talked about. You said [Imbue] costs fifty points? That's ten times some of the other skills and almost double what [Create Relic] costs. If we got you through two more dungeons and you took [Create Relic], you could do anything you wanted. If Arandir had that, I'm sure the world would have more of them. I think we have to be careful—and that isn't your forte, Daniel."

"What does that mean?"

"She's trying to be polite, D. Don't make her call you an idiot to your face."

Madi laughed.

Orrin felt the pressure release from his shoulders. The entire talk, he'd been tense, waiting for the other shoe to drop. Madi was going to be awkward around him. She wasn't going to be able to joke around. All the negative thoughts that he'd spent a lifetime cultivating had come crashing back as soon as she found out this newest secret, but that one laugh erased them all.

They could still joke and rib each other. She was still a part of the team. She was still his friend.

Chapter 47

They settled on a strategy, letting Madi handle the negotiations . . . again. Only this time, she had all the cards and wasn't hamstrung by lack of knowledge. Sure, Arandir was centuries older, with experience leading a nation. He was likely at a level unseen by normal humans in their lifetime. He also knew more about exactly what an Administrator was.

Orrin sat with his feet up on his chair, eating some snacks he'd brought out for the group. Strategy talks made him snacky. "Remind me again why we aren't just hightailing it out of here? He's going to figure it out. Daniel can't play poker to save his life."

"And you can?" Daniel threw a grape at him. It bounced off his shoulder and rolled under a couch. "I seem to remember you losing all your chips whenever we played."

"I didn't say I'm good," Orrin countered. "We both suck."

"You've both kept secrets from me, so just keep acting like the idiots you are. It helps people underestimate you." Madi picked a few slices of melon from the spread Orrin had put out. "At the end of the day, it doesn't matter if he thinks the Admin is you or Daniel. We know what we want. We just have to figure out his angle."

"Kidnap us and force us to give out Quests until we die." Orrin crunched on a cookie. The small bakery in Dey made some great pastries, but the cookies were too hard. *I should give them a few pointers when we get back.*

A knock on the door interrupted them. Arandir let himself back into his apartment. He carried a wicker picnic basket in one hand and an overly large glass bottle in the other.

He held up both hands, showing off his wares. "I have brought lunch, but I see you have brought your own food. Perhaps we can share?"

Madi stepped forward and took the basket. She pushed some of Orrin's food to the side, setting up the cheeses, warm bread, and bowl of meat that Arandir had brought into the new space. "This smells amazing, sir. What is this?"

"Nothing too special. A few select cheeses I prefer when I am in town. The meat is from a Ghostboar. We cook it underground and soak it in a sauce we make from local fruit. I prefer it spread on a piece of bread, but it goes well by itself."

Daniel tore off the butt of the loaf and dipped it in the saucy meat. He chewed. "This tastes like barbacoa but . . . sweet. I love it. Thanks, Arandir."

With that, they lost Daniel to the food. He began making small sandwiches.

Arandir smiled. "You are most welcome." He paused and put the bottle down on the table before sitting himself. "Something to drink as well. Before we begin, please let me explain something. I am an elder of my people, the elder of administration. Most do not understand what that means. Even my own people think I handle the boring paperwork. While that is one part of my job, I have people who deal with the day-to-day. My true job is working to perfect my Administrator powers in the hope that, one day, my people can regain what was lost."

"What was lost?" Madi also sat, pouring from the bottle into a few cups that Orrin had set out. A dark-red wine filled the cups. Orrin frowned and waved the cup away.

"The full powers of an Administrator. While I have only heard the stories from my father, a true Administrator would help propel their people to the brink of perfection. I procure knowledge, study, and experiment in an attempt to unlock more power so that I can help the elves of today regain their lost glory."

Arandir took the cup from Madi and sipped it politely. "Sometimes, in my pursuit of knowledge, I overstep. I have done so with you. I apologize for forcing the issue, Daniel. I assumed that your party knew of your powers. Leanthun told me that you had been having whispered conversations frequently, and I incorrectly jumped to conclusions. I cannot take back what was done, but hopefully I can remedy the situation."

He placed the cup on the table and steepled his fingers under his chin. "If you do not accept my offer, I will keep your secret. I will also continue to help you with the council, no matter your decision. You are the best chance that anyone in my family has had since the Calamity, and I fear I may have started off on the wrong foot. Please accept my apology."

Orrin peered suspiciously at the old elf. He found himself believing in the guy. Which meant either he was telling the truth or he had a skill to help with lying. Either way, he didn't trust him.

"Apology accepted," Daniel answered, ever the golden boy and teacher's pet. "I really don't know what you expect from me, though."

Arandir laughed. "Trust and fair play once you reach a higher level. Now that I know you are an Administrator, we can discuss topics not sanctioned by the council. My role as Administrator holds different responsibilities."

"What kind of responsibilities?" Daniel asked, taking another mouthful of Ghostboar sandwich.

"Keeping the world from ending."

Orrin was slapping Daniel's back to dislodge the food that had gotten stuck.

Madi took over. "Maybe you can understand our skepticism. What exactly is it you want? And what are you offering?"

Arandir appeared bemused at Daniel's predicament. "Am I to assume that you speak for him?"

Daniel choked but nodded, waving his hand at Madi.

"I do not know what Administrator skills he has, but I do know how those skills were unlocked in the past. I also know enough of what happened during the Calamity that I can make some very educated guesses at how he might further evolve his power. My hope is that, someday, Daniel might become powerful enough to fix the system and reinstate Administrator powers to all races."

"And naturally, you would want him to give you the power if and when that ever happens?" Madi smirked.

"Not at all. I would have him choose. I would suggest Leanthun. He is my nephew and next in line to take my power if I should die. I have trained him to the best of my ability, and I believe his temperament is what is needed for my people. He is strong but kind, knowledgeable but open to learning."

Madi crossed her arms. "That's all it takes to have the type of power you described?"

Arandir met her gaze without flinching. "Daniel, what knowledge do you have of the Calamity and its cause?"

Daniel finished coughing and took a deep breath to steady himself. "A [Hero] destroyed the world, right?"

Arandir shook his head with a frown. "He did it because the Administrators of his time forced him to."

"Does this have something to do with what the council warned you not to talk about?" Madi cajoled the elf. "We really don't want to piss off the entire elven council."

"How much do you know of that [Hero], Lady Catanzano?"

"He shattered our world after going crazy. You didn't answer my question. Is this what you were forbidden to talk about?"

"If humans lived maybe half as long as we do, perhaps you would not have lost so much of your history. I can understand the orcs; they never kept much stock in the past. The dwarves, at least, know some of it."

Madi rapped her knuckles on the table. "Arandir, I'm specifically asking you not to disclose anything to us that could get us in trouble."

Arandir took a slice of the melon on the table and bit into it. "This is good. I will have to have some purchased for myself."

"Arandir, please don't ignore her. She's the person I trust to navigate all this," Daniel said, waving his hand in a circle. "Are you about to tell us something dangerous?"

"The truth is always a dangerous thing. Those who know the truth can wield it, twist it, or warp it to fit their needs. The truth, bare and untouched, is also a beautiful thing. We can learn from it and become better despite it." Arandir paused and lowered his voice to a whisper. "Truth can be different for each person. What Quest did Asmea give you when it summoned you to our world, Daniel?"

Orrin's internal alarms began to ring. Arandir knew. He knew the Stop the War Quest was not the real reason Daniel had been transported to this world. He knew the [Hero] was hiding something larger. Every conversation with the elf elder only helped him learn more about them.

"Truth is not subjective," Madi cut in before Daniel could respond. "Just like justice. Something is either true or it is not. You are still avoiding the question, Arandir."

Laughter filled the small room. Arandir wiped his eyes and held up a hand to forestall Madi's rage at being laughed at. "I apologize. Sometimes I forget the surety of youth. Truth *is* subjective. Anyone can twist facts to set their own truth. You agree that murder is wrong, correct?"

"Of course," Daniel answered quickly, trying to reestablish his footing. The Quest question had thrown him a bit. "You're going to ask, 'What about war,' aren't you?"

Arandir shook his head. "If I were to kill Lady Catanzano or your friend Orrin, what would you do?"

Daniel bristled but spoke in a calm voice. "I would end you, then I would tear down this entire forest tree by tree."

"Would you be in the wrong?"

"I would be getting revenge. You would be the one murdering."

"What if I thought that by killing your friends, I would be unburdening you to reach your full potential?"

"You'd still be dead."

Arandir sighed. "A poor example. If a mother finds a mugger holding her child at knifepoint and kills the thief, is that murder?"

Madi was looking annoyed. "Obviously not. She's protecting her child. We know what murder is."

"What if the thief was not a thief at all but only trying to recover medicine stolen by the child in the first place?"

Orrin said, "You're just adding facts to change the scenario. That doesn't change that truth is truth, only that you can change the underlying details to fit what ending you want."

"Yes!" Arandir pointed at Orrin and smiled. "The mother who does not know the underlying details will think she has saved her child from a mugger, while the child knows she is now a murderer. What I want to tell you is dangerous to the council because they want to keep the knowledge hoarded. I want to tell you so that you know the entire picture. The truth. Only with all the facts can you make a decision based on truth."

Daniel rubbed his eyes. "Madi, please tell the nice elf that I absolutely hate this kind of thing."

Madi smiled. "Daniel hates when people talk in riddles."

Arandir rolled his eyes. "The council does not wish me to tell you the story of the Calamity because it involves knowledge lost to the world. With that knowledge, our people have been able to exist in a world intent on keeping us in our forest. Our youngest travel outside the safety of our tree line in an attempt to see the world, and they are captured as slaves. We must travel in groups to trade with other countries. I believe I should tell you. I believe you did not travel to our forest to give us a Quest that allows us to bypass our rules about war. I believe you were drawn here to right a wrong made by the last [Hero] to know Administrators."

Orrin was on the edge of his seat. He'd been ready to [Teleport] them out for most of the conversation. Arandir was dangerous.

"The last [Hero] to know Administrators and the last to fight a true [Demon Lord]. The one who ended our world when the Administrators betrayed him."

Chapter 48

"Why would anyone betray a [Hero]?" Madi queried.

Orrin and Daniel turned slowly to her and then glanced at each other.

"Seriously?"

"I mean . . ."

She frowned and hushed them both. "There's a difference between testing someone and straight up betraying them. It's a common trope in stories. If you betray a [Hero], they always come after you, and it never ends well. Even the few leaders in the past who succeeded in capturing their own personal [Hero] lived to regret it."

"It is a recurrent theme for a reason." Arandir leaned back again. "We wish for history to never repeat that mistake. As for those few leaders who have made the unfortunate mistake of thinking a [Hero] is a resource to use, I will only say they did not live as long as they perhaps thought possible."

It was Orrin's turn to frown. "You're admitting to murder, altering history, and fabricating stories to do—what? Protect future [Heroes]?"

Arandir sighed. "Young man, there are different versions of [Heroes], just as there are different versions of Administrators or [Mages]. Every person is unique and holds powers truly unique. Study two [Fire Mages] and you will see small differences in the same spell. The [Hero] of the Calamity destroyed our world and displaced millions of people. He is not the most powerful [Hero] to ever live; he just had means, opportunity, and a reason. We do not protect [Heroes] from the people so much as we protect the people from their own shortsighted agendas that at the end of the day would result in their deaths, or worse."

Daniel stood and paced, something Orrin knew was due to his growing frustration. "Arandir, I'm going to try and say this straight because I'm about to lose my patience. You want to tell us a dangerous story so I'll trust you more and maybe give you or some other elf a power in the future?"

"Yes."

Daniel almost missed a step when the elf answered directly, but he regained his composure. "But you are not demanding anything in return?"

Arandir leaned forward and checked his teapot. He must have found it too cold, as he rubbed his hand along the bottom. Orrin noticed his hand glowed like Emily's had when she used her fire magic. "I demand nothing, but I humbly request that you do not share this story outside these walls. At best, you will be labeled a heretic or crazy. At worse, you will incite a war greater than you can imagine."

Daniel crouched next to Madi and had a quick conversation. He glanced at Orrin.

Orrin shrugged.

"I guess it's story time. We agree not to repeat it."

Arandir poured a cup and waited for Daniel to sit back down. "Please keep in mind that what I tell you has been handed down in my family. There are doubtless other details unknown to them or perhaps not shared from generation to generation for any number of reasons, but I will do my best to tell the history of the Calamity as I was taught."

He took a sip before he began. "The world as you know it is but a small sliver of what used to be. From Dey to the farthest reaches of Veskar is but a generously sized kingdom of the old lands. One kingdom of dozens. The elves had multiple forest groves but also sailed the seas and lived in towns with humans. Most recognized our king, but some branches did not and ruled in different ways. The dwarves claimed the mountain ranges but farmed as well. Even the orcs did more than travel in nomadic tribes. Some even built cities. The world was far-flung and diverse, but dangerous. Each race had an Administrator. Any king or dictator could claim greatness, but until an Administrator was born in your lands and worked to raise your people up, the rulers of other races would not recognize you. Over time, the Administrators created a loose coalition to exchange tips on how best to use powers, to discuss best options for class reassignment, and other things lost to time."

Arandir placed his cup down and waited until all three of them met his eye. "This next part is something you should never repeat. Demons lived among us freely. They had their own Administrator. While wars were fought with them, it was no more than against any other race. They were one and part of us. Again, I cannot stress enough that saying this to the wrong group could result in your immediate death."

He sighed and took a long pull on his tea. "Demons, despite popular myths, do not look all that different from you or me. Some have horns or tails and some have a red tint to their skin, but most could pass for human or elf. The other races can procreate with demons as well. Sometimes their children would look more like the dwarf mother than the demon father. But every demon, full-blooded or with a single drop of demon blood, has a special ability: they gain experience from killing the enlightened races."

The old elf paused. "This terrified the other Administrators. Century after century passed with the demon race slowly spreading this ability. Meetings without the demon Administrator were held to discuss the problem, for the elves, the humans, the orcs, and the dwarves saw this as a problem. Every child born with the power of a demon would fall under the demon Administrator's purview. If a human and an elf had a child, the child had a chance to fall to either side. The odds were not perfect, but it was not 100 percent. In their fear, the Administrators gathered together. All but the demon. They altered the system together. They did something to alter or take away the demon Administrator's powers."

Madi's eyes were huge. Daniel seemed to be absorbed in the story, too.

Orrin kept watch for whatever trick Arandir was trying to pull.

"They assumed that if the demons did not have the power of their Administrator, they would flounder. Instead, the old Administrator used the last of his powers to become something new—a class never seen before. Demon Lord. Instead of having the powers of an Administrator, this class gave the demon vast authority over all demons. He could command them or sway them . . . The details are vague to me. What the Administrators had tried to stop, they sped up. The new Demon Lord sent his people out to conquer and kill. War swept the entire world, and hundreds of thousands died in months. The Administrators, including my great-grandfather, summoned a [Hero]. They tasked him with defeating the Demon Lord. They lied to the man and told him the demon was the original aggressor. They promised things they could never give and sent him on his way. Then they began saving up their power to summon another, because they had only summoned the first as a diversion. They had no hope the man would pull it off."

Arandir reached for another piece of melon and caught Orrin glancing at the door. "You are free to leave if you so desire."

Orrin shook his head and sat back in his chair, resigned. "Go ahead."

"When the [Hero] returned, having struck down the evil demon, he was surprised to find them about to summon another [Hero]. The human and orc Administrators had usurped power from their king and tribe leader, respectively. So many of every race had died. The dragons had fled the lands . . . The [Hero] demanded the rewards he had been promised. They laughed him away. They thought they had won."

Arandir smiled in pride. "My great-grandfather went to the [Hero] and apologized. They talked and he let slip enough that the [Hero] figured out the rest. My great-grandfather learned what none of the Administrators knew: the [Hero] had collected friends to fight by his side on his way to the Demon Lord. He had lost most of them in his final fight and was grieving. He was nearly broken. Finding out that the great evil he had been sent to destroy was actually the one originally wronged . . . finished him."

Orrin imagined that happening to them. What if Silas had sent them on a mission to kill someone, telling them this theoretical person was evil, then they returned and found out it was all a power play? He shivered. Silas wouldn't last long.

"The [Hero] asked my great-grandfather why. Why would they go through all the trouble of outing this demon, a person they had once called friend and exchanged ideas with? My great-grandfather told him it was to keep the fighting between races to a minimum. If the demons overtook the world, anybody could kill anyone, just for the chance at some experience and levels. He laughed . . . the [Hero] laughed until he began to cry. He thanked my great-grandfather but said something cryptic that he didn't understand until later."

Arandir spoke slowly, and Orrin was certain that this was the part of the story each generation made sure to get right. "'I pray you get the world you want but never get to affect it again.'"

"My great-grandfather left, and the next day, the [Hero] unleashed a spell that destroyed the world. Every human, elf, dwarf, and orc that had fought with the Administrators was transported to this small crop of land we call Asmea. Every Administrator, save my great-grandfather, was dead. He never knew for sure why he was spared. It took him only a few years to realize something was wrong with his Administrator powers. It took him longer to realize no new Administrators were being born to the other races. He spent the rest of his life trying to figure out a way around it. The [Hero] disappeared or died, I do not know which."

He downed the rest of his tea and poured himself another cup.

"Those bastards," Daniel muttered. "They made a mess and then had him clean it up. I get why he blew up the world."

Arandir reached across the space and placed his hand on Daniel's clenched fist. "That is the part that my great-grandfather did not learn for many years. The [Hero] did not blow up the world. He reshaped it and placed those he found deserving in this prison that is Asmea, a peninsula surrounded by dangerous waters. Every person who found themselves on that plot of land that is now Dey had hatred in their hearts toward the demons. The rest of the world is alive; they just live on the other side of the Pass. The demons have spread, and most everyone is at least part demon now. However, despite the Administrators' worst fears, there is no rampant bloodshed for experience."

Orrin was reeling. "How could you possibly know that?"

Arandir smiled at him. "Where do you think I got this delicious tea?"

Orrin frowned. His [Analyze] had only told him it was green tea but not where it was from. He'd missed that. He'd spent time using the skill with Tony's small collection of tea and could trigger at least the region it was from.

"You trade with the demons?" Madi hissed.

"As do the dwarves," Arandir responded without any guilt. "There are a select few on this side who have realized the errors of the past. My great-grandfather wished until his dying day that he could have undone what he did to the demon Administrator."

"You mean turning him into a Demon Lord?" Daniel spat. "I wouldn't have let any of my enemies live. I'd say he got off easy."

Madi rolled her eyes. "Daniel, the poor man lived for centuries with the guilt of what he did. I think he suffered."

Orrin smirked at Daniel's comment. "That's the hole in your story, Arandir. If they took the demon Administrator's powers, how did he change his class?"

"I do not know." Arandir's face showed no hint of frustration. "My grandfather told me the system self-corrects, but I was not there. Nor was my great-grandfather to learn what happened to his betrayed friend. Let me give you a piece of advice that comes with age. Something that you likely will not learn for decades but maybe you will take to heart. You cannot know everything, but that does not make the things you do not understand untrue."

Daniel and Madi continued asking questions, but Orrin pulled up his Quests.

> **Defeat the Demon Lord—In the southern lands, the Demon Lord has risen. The dark armies have been assembled. Seek out and defeat the Demon Lord before the Dark Horde attacks.**
> **Reward: 1,000,000 XP and Dark Essence Unlocked**

"What about the other Demon Lords?" Orrin asked, cutting off whatever Madi was saying. "There have been others. The [Hero] who created the Sea of Fire fought one, right?"

Arandir's eyebrows furrowed for a second. "Yes. A class that we know next to nothing about. Why do you ask?"

"Where do they come from? If the system created it in response to those dicks abusing their authority, why are they still around?"

Arandir sighed. "You ask very clever questions. I am beginning to see why you are part of the [Hero]'s party. Again, I do not know the answer to your question. Every great while, a [Hero] and Demon Lord appear. I am old and knowledgeable but not omniscient. What I do know is that no new Administrator has been born into this world or across the Pass since the Calamity. You might be the key to reuniting the world and helping the people on both sides grow strong again."

"You want Daniel to go around and bop some Admin powers on each race?" Orrin asked incredulously. "You don't think the system or that [Hero] messed with things so that's not possible?"

"It might not be possible." Arandir smiled. "But I have to try. The Administrators failed the people at the end, but that was after thousands of years of peace and prosperity. All fruit rots, but I hope we can harvest the seeds and grow something new and better."

He turned to Daniel. "Would you like to help me change the world for the better?"

Chapter 49

Daniel's eyes flickered to his friends before he answered. "I think the idea you are pitching is noble. I'm not sold that the people of this world really need an Administrator, though. What's to keep them from turning out like the old guard? We have a saying in my world—absolute power corrupts absolutely. I can think of only a handful of people I've met in my life that I would trust with that kind of power."

"You are putting the cart before the horse," Arandir said, waving his hand. "We can discuss the people best suited for the job and safeguards to protect from abuse if we can even succeed. I am not even sure how we could unlock more powers for you. In my predecessor's time, an Administrator could unlock points to use in a special store in the system for Administrator-only powers. These points could be earned from helping a certain number of people discover their best class or giving out a certain number of completed Quests a year. Every Administrator had their own unique threshold, and no patterns were ever established. Unfortunately, my great-grandfather was never able to earn another point after the Calamity. My grandfather and father, as well as myself, have a bastardized selection of powers, but none of us were able to gain any points, either. We are talking about years of work to figure this out."

"We don't have years," Madi interjected. "We need to stop Odrana and get back to Dey. We have more to do than be subjects for you to study."

"Then I will need to ask questions. What sort of skills do you control?"

Orrin frowned. He didn't have any Administrator powers that he controlled. Sometimes things just happened.

Daniel's thoughts were taking the same track. "What do you mean? I don't have any powers. Sometimes things just happen."

"Like what?"

Daniel tapped his foot in frustration. Orrin could see he wanted to answer but didn't know how far to go. He saved his friend.

"Sometimes when he's in danger, he'll tell us he has a new Quest."

Madi nodded. "Once, during a fight that we thought we would lose, he was able to take away someone's constitution points."

Daniel nodded with each sentence. "Once he— I was able to change the Quest rewards."

"But you have no control over these things, correct? That is how it was for my great-grandfather. His system unlocked skills once he had enough points to spend, but he did not know the full extent of what was possible to unlock before his death."

Daniel raised an eyebrow at Madi and Orrin. *Do we tell him we've unlocked the Admin store?*

Orrin moved his head to indicate no with the smallest movement he could muster.

Madi shrugged.

"You know something." The elf's eyes were old but still sharp. "You have unlocked administrator points."

"Why—" Daniel fidgeted. One small movement of his foot.

"Please do not lie. There is no need. You do not need to tell me the specifics." Arandir rubbed at his eye. "Just to know that a way forward exists . . ."

When he trailed off, silence took over the small room. Madi spoke to break the silence. "Arandir, we don't know for sure that we can unlock more of these points or what good they would even do. You said it yourself, Administrators can only affect their own race."

The elder elf blinked. "Lady Catanzano, Daniel is not from this world. A [Hero] may look human, but he is most assuredly not the same as you. It is one of the reasons they are so powerful. They absorb ambient mana in a way that baffled the greatest minds of our people. Besides, an Administrator can give Quests to any race. It is only class selection and stat edits that are locked to race. If we can recreate the circumstances that led Daniel to gain those points, we might be able to unlock skills that only an Administrator would have."

Orrin rolled his eyes at his friends. They kept giving the elf everything he wanted. The more information the man had, the more trapped Orrin was feeling. *Am I being paranoid in wanting to keep the information from him, or are they just being too trusting?*

"Maybe we should discuss that another time," Orrin suggested. "You gave us a lot of new information to digest. Maybe Daniel should share his Quest and we can meet again for dinner?"

Madi almost said something, but Daniel grasped her knee with his hand. "Yeah. I think that's a good idea, O."

Arandir's lips pulled into a tight line, but he nodded. "Acceptable. I apologize if I overstepped. You are the best chance my family has ever had to reclaim our station and right a wrong we should never have allowed. I will have Leanthun bring you back to your rooms. Let him know if you want to speak with me or need anything. I will have the council send their selected team to you for the Quest."

He bade them farewell.

The elevator ride back down was just as quick, and Leanthun was silent on the walk back to their prison home. Only this time nobody locked the doors. Once Daniel was sure they were alone, he turned to Orrin.

"Why did you want out? He seemed like he wanted to help."

Orrin couldn't explain it. Whenever Arandir spoke, he didn't feel bad so much as slightly off. Orrin had run a gambit of spells during their conversation. [Calm Mind] did nothing. The tea wasn't poisoned. As far as he could tell, there were no spells or skills coming off the old elf. Orrin simply felt uncomfortable around him, but that wasn't a good enough reason to tell Daniel and Madi.

"I can't explain it," he muttered. He was letting them down again, holding back the party because he had some weird issue with trusting people.

"Orrin." Madi stepped in and wrapped her arms around him. "It's all right. You don't have to explain it. If you don't want to trust Arandir, we can give the elves the Quest and leave. We can figure things out on our own."

Orrin hugged her back and then disengaged. The room was still too small for all three of them, and he sat on the stairs leading up to the second story. "I don't think that's the best course of action. He knows more than he's telling. Does he not give either of you a weird feeling?"

Both his friends shook their heads.

"It started small in the council's room, but once we were in his house . . . I got this sense of something being off. Like when you are going down the stairs and miss a step. Not even that bad, to be honest. I can't put it into words."

"You don't like him," Daniel said with a shrug. He was restrapping Gertrude to his back. "That's fine. The question is, should we use him to get into more dungeons or leave the forest? I personally think the guy is all right, but I'm not a big fan of that council."

Orrin shook his head. "No, I like him. That's what is so weird. At first, it was nothing but an itch, but the longer we spent time with him, the more I felt something was wrong. This is so annoying." Orrin punched the banister. "I can't even figure out what my problem is. He did nothing wrong. The tea wasn't poisoned and he wasn't using any skills on us, I'm almost certain. Why don't I trust him?"

Madi knelt close to him. "Orrin, it's fine. We trust you even if you can't say why. We'll leave."

"No." Orrin stood suddenly. "No. We should use his help. We can play it smart and stay close to each other. That way, I can [Teleport] us out if I need to. Maybe he can get us access to another dungeon. Maybe he'll let us read through those books that he's been pruning from the world. If nothing else, I want to learn more about what is on the other side of the Pass."

Madi frowned. "That is the part I'm not sure I believe. If there is an entire civilized world on the other side of Dey, my life . . . my father's life has been a lie. I wanted to ask him more about that."

"If a [Hero] really did send everybody who didn't like the demons to one part of the world, it would be impossible to hide that sort of thing."

Madi nodded at Orrin, grabbing his words like a lifeline. "Exactly. If the elves were somehow trading with the demons over the mountains, we would have caught them at some point. The dwarves barely trade with Dey and do so grudgingly when they have to. I can't imagine them doing anything with demons. They attack us regularly. They've killed hundreds of people in the last decade alone. His story doesn't make any sense."

"We can make a list of things we want him to talk about." Orrin took her hand and pulled her to her feet. "What should we ask him?"

Over the next hour, they hammered out the specifics. They only stopped when Leanthun knocked on the door. Daniel met the selected elves and shared the Quest.

"I think we made a good start, but the real question is, do we tell him about the dungeon cores?" Madi tapped her pencil on the paper.

"It depends on if he'll answer more about what his powers are and if he could get admin points himself," Orrin responded, biting into an apple. He'd already restored all their weapons in his [Dimension Hole], including the Citrandish bow they'd never gotten around to turning over. "I don't think giving him a way to increase his own power is a smart move."

Madi quirked an eyebrow. "You can learn. Good job."

Orrin flipped her off. Daniel chuckled in the corner.

"I'm going to ask Leanthun if we can head back over. It's time."

Orrin nodded at his friend. Daniel pushed off the wall and opened the door.

"Hey, Leanthun. Can we chat with your uncle some more?"

The elf sighed. "If you just needed a break, he could have stepped out again. This back-and-forth is exhausting."

Orrin pulled the elven bow out of his storage and held it up. "We could give him this as an apology."

Leanthun rolled his eyes. "He doesn't need that kind of leverage, but do what you will. Are you ready?"

Leverage? Orrin pondered Leanthun's words as they made their way back. *Why would a bow give Arandir leverage?*

"Can I ask a question?" Orrin jogged to catch up with Leanthun.

"You just did."

"Another one. Where do Citrandish bows come from?"

Leanthun pointed to the large tree in the center of the forest. "The matriarch tree sheds a branch every dozen years or so. If we are lucky, the wood is not rotted and we can create bows from her wood."

"And they're good bows?"

The elf didn't deign to answer.

"I guess you really value your bows, then?"

"This is more than one question." Leanthun gave Orrin a look that let him know the elf knew what he was doing. "Our bows are bonded to us individually—each bow belongs to one elf for life. I could use another's, but it would never feel right . . . be right. To return a lost bow to our people is like bringing home the body of a fallen elf. I'm glad you didn't hand it over to the council. They would have taken it without giving you anything. You could give it to my uncle, but that would have complications. Better to find the family it belongs to and ask for compensation. They'll pay well."

Madi and Daniel were close enough to hear Leanthun's explanation. Orrin didn't hesitate and pushed the bow into the elf's hands. "Can you find out who it belonged to?"

Leanthun kept walking, holding the bow as if it were fragile. "I can. Would you like me to set up a meeting with the family later?"

Orrin smiled. "Nah. Tell them the [Hero] sent it and wishes it to find its way back into the hands of the family it belonged to. If that's not possible . . . send his condolences."

Leanthun turned and looked at Orrin, drawing to a complete stop. "You want to give it to them? At no cost?"

"What good would it do us? It'll be like a homecoming for the guy who lost it, right?"

"Or give a family closure if he or she is dead," Leanthun said quietly. He turned to Daniel. "Are you fine with this?"

"Seems like the right thing to do," Daniel said nonchalantly.

Leanthun studied them for a moment longer before quickly stowing the bow on his back, joining his own Citrandish bow. "I'll see to it."

When they reached Arandir's tree, Madi hesitated before stepping on the elevator.

"It'll be fine." Daniel pulled her on. "Let's go talk about demons."

Chapter 50

Arandir didn't seem surprised to find them back in his apartment. To Madi's delight, he also had no problem answering more questions about demons.

The reason being . . . he knew very little.

"I am not trying to be obtuse," he apologized. "We have some drops among the mountains where we leave a list of purchases. If we pay, the items arrive within a month. At one time, during my grandfather's rule as elder of administration, some elves would travel to their lands. That is where my information comes from. However, there was an incident over three thousand years ago. Our king visited and did not return. He was young and did not have an heir, so the council took over, and as their first act, they forbade further travel of elves through the Pass."

He also had little reluctance in telling them more about his Administrator powers. He had already told them he could reset stats or a class. That was the extent of his powers.

"My grandfather could also move stats around, but I can only do a full reset."

"How do you get administrator points?" Madi asked their last question. Everything else had hit a knowledge roadblock.

"I do not know. Since my great-grandfather's time, I know of no administrator points being found or earned. It might be that the [Hero] altered the system to no longer allow them. Until his death, my grandfather spoke of how his father had tried to find a way to earn more. He spent every moment giving out Quests and altering classes. It was all in vain."

Orrin wanted to ask if Arandir had ever defeated a dungeon, but asking that was too blunt. The elf was intelligent and would put the bread crumbs together. He couldn't figure out why he had earned his administrator points from a dungeon when the Administrators of the past had earned theirs through deeds and actions.

"Something had to have changed, then," Daniel said slowly. "After the Calamity, did anything else about the system change?"

Arandir stood and moved to a small desk on the far side of the living room. A bookshelf holding only a dozen books was placed against the side of it, and he knelt to run a finger over the spines of his books.

"My grandfather took detailed notes of all his father would tell him. My great-grandfather did not take the time to write everything down, always thinking he had more time. A curse that most of us fall for. Here it is."

He took a dark-green book with faded lettering on the front. Orrin could just make out the word *Journal* but nothing else. Arandir flipped through the book.

"If I remember correctly, the system did not change much, if at all. Then again, this was still during the first few hundred years after the founding of Asmea. Most of our people were trying to tend to the few trees we could get to grow. We had the matriarch seed, but we still had to protect her from the dungeons cropping up. It was years before we figured out how to destroy them and keep them from spawning near her. Of course, our king immediately sent the information to the other races. They were plaguing everyone. Once we had the matriarch sprouted, we spent time—"

"Wait, dungeons weren't a thing before the Calamity?" Orrin cut off the rambling.

Arandir held a finger on a page and glanced up. "No, dungeons are part of the Calamity. Broken parts of the world left to punish us."

He continued reading, and Orrin's mind raced. From everything he had read, the system wasn't omniscient or omnipotent. This wasn't a world of gods but something more like a really complicated computing system. If the [Hero] had wanted to punish the Administrators of the past by taking away their power, he could have just killed them. Instead, he had somehow prevented their abilities from being reborn into the world. At least until Orrin came along . . .

Orrin doubted the system would allow for wholesale deletion of the powers it gave to one select person of each race to further the perfection of itself. Because, from everything he'd heard, that was what an Administrator was supposed to be—someone who worked hard to make sure everyone could make the most of the system for themselves. If the [Hero] wanted to stop Administrators, he wouldn't have been able to destroy the power, but he could misplace it. He had already done something similar by putting all the demon-racist people together and sealing them away from the world. What if he did the same with the Admin powers, sealing them away underground? Whether he thought the powers would stay dormant or he'd known something like dungeons would appear was irrelevant. Orrin felt in his gut that he was right. He had already proven that he could gain administrator points by absorbing the dungeon core.

"Madi, can I talk to you?" He took her elbow and walked her to the elevator. They had left the doors open for the slight breeze. The room got stuffy quickly without an open window or two.

"I'm not riding that thing down if that—"

"No, just needed some privacy," Orrin whispered and told her his theory.

Madi scratched behind her ear. "That . . . makes sense, actually." Her hand fell to her side, and she clenched her fist. "If the [Hero] did that, he's responsible for every death from outbreaks for five thousand years."

Orrin didn't respond. Dungeon outbreaks were a sore topic for Madi. She wanted to destroy all the dungeons and had since she was a small child, when her mother had died during an outbreak.

"Arandir, how do you keep dungeons from spawning near the matriarch tree?" Daniel asked, keeping the elf's attention on him while Orrin and Madi talked.

"The same way every major city does. We have mages who search for dungeon seeds, the small bit of chaotic magic that creates a core. If we can spike that with any sort of magic, the seed is destroyed and no dungeon core can be born. It is a noble profession and one that every elf works for a time," Arandir explained and then held up his hand. "Here is what I was looking for. My grandfather wrote that, according to his father, the last true Administrator, the system before the Calamity was a rolling ocean. It was wild, strong, and unbridled. He complained that after they arrived in Asmea, the system was rigid, timid, and constricted. Before, he could feel the system work through him to help find a person's best class or skill, but after the Calamity, each individual was a struggle."

He looked up from his book. "I wanted to make sure the wording was correct. Does that help, Daniel?"

Orrin had already forgotten Daniel's original question, but he tuned them both out. The last Administrator had complained the system felt constrained. He nodded at Madi. She punched him in the shoulder.

"Ow, what was that for?"

"You just worked out something that nobody else did for five thousand years." Madi was grinning like she was crazy. "Do you know what this means? We have double the incentive to—"

"To do what?" Arandir had moved close to them in near-perfect silence. "What have you discovered?"

Orrin glared at Madi. He couldn't think of a way to lie his way out of this. "I think I should run it by Daniel. He might be able to—"

Arandir held up a finger, and Orrin felt himself float in the air toward the elf. His grandfatherly visage disappeared, and the powerful de facto leader of the elves took on the grand air of state. "I have been very forthcoming, I believe. We made a deal to work together, did we not?"

Orrin could feel Arandir's power invading his body. The elf's magic was holding his limbs still. He couldn't even move his jaw. Underneath everything, he felt something else—a feeling that tickled his memory.

"Arandir . . . put him down," Daniel demanded. He had Gertrude drawn. "Please."

The elf blinked twice and dropped his finger, setting Orrin down gently. "I apologize, Orrin. I forgot that you are not . . . I should not have done that."

The elf sighed and slumped into the chair Daniel had just vacated. "Being in charge and responsible for so many lives draws my temper thin at times. Please accept my apology. I have not slept in three days. It is not an excuse, but I am also excited beyond measure. Of course you should speak with the [Hero]."

Daniel returned his sword to his back and gestured for Orrin to get behind him. Madi followed as well.

"What the hell was that?" Daniel hissed. "I just almost attacked him. What were you guys talking about?"

Madi glanced at Arandir and put her hand on Daniel's ear. She quickly and quietly whispered the outline of Orrin's theory.

Daniel smirked. "You know what's funny?"

Orrin hadn't taken his eyes off the elf elder. "What?"

"I was thinking it was weird that dungeons didn't appear until the [Hero] ended the world. Great minds think alike, huh?"

Orrin rolled his eyes again. "You reached the first step while I was at the top of the stairs."

"I'd have gotten there, too."

"Boys . . . this isn't the time. What should we do?" Madi nodded toward Arandir.

Daniel crossed his hands over his chest. He frowned as he thought. Orrin could almost hear the hamster wheel start spinning. A hamster wheel that needed oil . . . a lot of oil.

"He attacked Orrin. You guys want to leave? We did what we came here for, and I'm not—"

"D, he just made me float to him. He didn't actually attack me."

Daniel blinked in surprise. "You want to trust him? He might have some more nuggets of info, O, but we can figure it out for ourselves. We already gave them the Quest. We don't owe the elves anything."

Orrin shook his head. "We don't owe them, but remember how he threw that other elf? He could have done that with me but just tried to be a little intimidating. I never felt danger from him. That's not why I want to tell him, though. Whatever spell he used to pick me up was powerful. He had complete control of my body."

"Like a [Mind Mage]?" Daniel reached over his shoulder and touched Gertrude's handle. "Fuck. I hate this world sometimes."

"No, not like that." Orrin gently touched Daniel's hand and brought it away from his weapon. "The spell isn't what matters. When he touched me with his magic, I could feel . . . him, I guess. I know why I feel so weird around him. He's an Administrator, but he's not. Whenever I've triggered an Admin power before, I could feel this power rushing through me. I thought it was my own power, but after all this talk about Administrators being like an autocorrect for the system, I realized it was the system itself. I don't actually have any usable Admin powers yet. Arandir does, but they are weak. It's like he has a regular class skill instead of an Admin skill."

"What are you saying? He told us he's not a true Administrator."

Orrin nodded at Madi. "He did, but I still thought he had the ability to gain more points. He can't. It's like . . . he looks like a tree and moves like a tree, but he's actually a wooden pole."

Daniel glared at him. "I hate riddles, O. Say it straight."

"Arandir can't use administrator points. I don't know what happened, but when his magic touched me, I felt it. He's forever limited to what he has."

Orrin felt bad for the man. Sure, he didn't have any purchased Administrator powers yet, but he had the points to get them whenever he wanted. He had figured out where the power behind the points came from and knew how to get more. In one afternoon, they had solved a problem plaguing this elven family for five millennia.

Now, we just have to make sure he doesn't kill us.

Chapter 51

Daniel stood in front of Arandir, his arms crossed and a scowl on his face.

"If it was up to just me, I'd put this entire forest in my rearview mirror and go back to Dey," he started.

"What is a rearview mirror?" Arandir asked.

"That's not important," Daniel said, flustered at being interrupted. "Madi and Orrin think you might be some help with these Administrator powers. I'm not entirely sold on the idea, but first things first. If you or any elf attacks me or my friends again, I'm going old-school [Hero] on your entire city. Understood?"

Arandir let out a bark of laughter before suppressing his smile with his hand. "Please do not take this the wrong way. I do apologize for my earlier action and agree to swear no violence will be done to you and yours. You must understand, though, [Hero] or not, you are a kitten roaring at a dragon. While I do not care for such matters, the council would take offense at your words."

Daniel kept his arms crossed and glowered.

"I am glad that you have decided to stay. I would like the opportunity to make up for my actions to Orrin. I would not have it said that I do not honor my debts, and attacking someone in my own home unprovoked is a slight on my honor." Arandir turned to Orrin. "If there is anything I can do to show my regret, please do not hesitate to ask."

Orrin nodded but kept his mouth shut. They'd agreed to let Daniel handle Arandir. He'd promised Madi that he would manage the situation with tact and, so far, he hadn't attacked the elf. He was improving.

"We know how to get more admin points."

Maybe he wasn't. Orrin rubbed his eyes. He listened as Daniel told the story of the dungeon core but as if he was the one who'd absorbed the core. Arandir remained unnaturally still.

"If what you say is true, the people of Asmea will be forever in your debt." Arandir stood up and paced the room with the nervous excitement of a small child. He began pelting Daniel with questions. "How many points did the dungeon give you? How many floors was the dungeon you defeated? Is there a trick to absorbing the dungeon core versus destroying it?"

Daniel held up his hand. "Have you ever destroyed a dungeon, Arandir?"

"Of course, every elf spends time clearing the blasted things. Why do you ask?"

Daniel shifted his weight to his other foot. "When you used your magic on Orrin, I could feel your power. I don't think you can absorb a core. If you destroyed one before, it would have given you the option."

Arandir's face flared with a flurry of emotions: disbelief, anger, loss, suspicion, and acceptance, all in rapid succession. "But you do not know for sure."

Daniel shrugged. "It hardly matters. If you want to go destroy a dungeon, I'm all for less of the things in the world, but—"

"That is a great idea. We can test out your claim in a dungeon."

"Yeah, no." Daniel held up his hands. "We just left a dungeon, and I'm not in the mood to go traipsing through another ten floors of—"

"Of course not. I will see you to the last room. Let me get Leanthun to find the nearest dungeon. We keep a few cultivated for training purposes." Arandir walked to his elevator and stepped off the ledge before Daniel could argue.

"They cultivate dungeons?" Madi said with a low burn of anger.

"Madi . . ." Orrin put his hand on her shoulder.

"Why does he think we would agree to another dungeon run?" Daniel stomped over to his friends. "We just left one. Besides, he's obviously at a much higher level than us. Wouldn't that hurt any experience gains?"

Orrin rolled his eyes at Daniel. "That's not the issue, D." He nodded his head at Madi. "They keep dungeons as training grounds."

Daniel finally caught the look in Madi's eyes. "Then we should totally take them up on the offer and destroy every single one, huh?"

Madi smirked at that. She stretched her neck. "I'm fine. I think it might be a little soon to go—"

"Wonderful news. Leanthun has informed me we have three dungeons currently, with one at only twenty floors." Arandir appeared by the door.

He must have jumped or flown up. Orrin was more concerned with how stealthy the old elf had been in reentering the room.

"It took us forever to get through ten floors," Daniel complained. "Plus, we didn't agree to do a dungeon run for your people."

"Nonsense, we use these dungeons to train up our forces. We cull them before they get too large." Arandir walked toward his desk and rummaged in a drawer. "Leanthun and I will do all the work while you rest by the door. Lady Catanzano and Master Orrin can relax here or anywhere within the forest, really. We have some wonderful restaurants."

"I'm not going anywhere without my friends."

"No matter. They are welcome to come as well. The experience returns for all three of you will likely be abysmal, but twenty floors should only take a day or two at most." He pulled a key from the drawer and tossed it in the air, catching it again. "Daniel, if you could push that couch toward the wall?"

A day or two? Either he is overpowered as fuck or he's cocky. Orrin watched his friend simply pick up the edge of the three-seater couch and move it with ease. *Then again, Daniel's strength is stupid high and we haven't been here half a year. What kind of power would he have after a thousand years?*

Arandir knelt and threw the rug up. Hidden by the couch and carpet, and easy to miss even when Arandir was running his finger around it, was a small hole. It could have been a knot in the wood, but when the key sank into the crevice, Orrin realized Arandir was opening a hidden safe.

A plank of wood pivoted and opened to reveal a bow and staff, nestled together in a bed of velvet. Arandir picked both up slowly and whispered softly to the weapons before strapping the bow to his back.

"Are you ready or do you need supplies?" Arandir stood, using the staff to straighten up. For the first time, Orrin felt the power radiating from the man. "The dungeon is not too far away, but it is on the eastern front of the forest. I can have us teleported there and we can be back for dinner tomorrow."

"Arandir," Madi said, stepping forward. "We haven't agreed to this. Even with you and Leanthun taking point, a dungeon isn't something we should or can just rush into."

He paused and tapped his finger on the staff. "If it is a matter of safety, I have already promised you no harm will come to you. If you require payment, this will be a free run. Even with the level-disparity penalty, you will likely gain at least a level. If that is not enough, I can offer gold. What is the problem?"

Orrin inspected the staff more closely. The wood looked the same as Arandir's bow, obviously Citrandish. However, while the bow was polished and smooth, the staff was gnarled and pockmarked. He wanted to know more and tried [Identify].

Intense pain smashed behind his eyes. He was screaming as he fell to his knees, holding his head. Blood poured from the corners of his eyes and his ears as he slowly fell back.

He blinked. He was standing in the same place as before. Daniel was saying something to Arandir. The elf wasn't listening but frowning at Orrin.

Orrin touched his ears but found no trace of blood. He rubbed his eyes, but his fingers came back clean.

"It is settled, then? We can leave as soon as you are ready." Arandir nodded to Madi and Daniel. "I will send Leanthun ahead to tell the council where we are going."

As the elf swept by them, he leaned close to Orrin. "Some things are better left unknown. It can be dangerous to use [Identify] on others and their belongings."

Orrin shivered.

"What did he say to you, O?" Daniel asked, grabbing some food from the table.

"Nothing," Orrin muttered. "Did we just agree to go defeat another dungeon?"

"No way." Daniel tossed a grape in the air and tried to catch it. Madi snatched it before it landed in his mouth. "We agreed to get carried and get free experience. We get to be the ones who are sneaky and learn all his moves. Plus, we get paid."

Orrin rubbed his eyes again. "You're too blinded by gold, dude."

"Arandir and Leanthun are both at an extremely high level," Madi chimed in. "Possibly two of the highest-leveled people I've ever met. If they think it will only take a day or two, I think that's time we can spare. But if you didn't want to do it, you should have spoken up. You seemed like you were just out of it."

Orrin groaned as he recalled the backlash from whatever anti-[Identify] skill Arandir or his staff had. "I kind of messed up and tried to see what his staff was all about."

Madi froze with the grape halfway to her mouth. "You didn't?"

Daniel laughed. "Yeah, he totally did."

Madi shook her head in disbelief and ate the fruit. "You are lucky. Some skills cause real damage. Did it knock you out or just confuse you?"

"When I tried to [Identify] his staff, I had a vision of me dying. Blood was coming out of my eyes and ears. I fell down and darkness was creeping in. It felt so real."

Daniel clenched his fingers hard on the back of the chair he was standing behind. "But you're okay, right?"

"Yes, Mom. I'm fine."

Daniel smirked but then got serious. "If you don't want to go, we can still call it off. If we don't go through with it, I think we should head back to Dey. What do you both think?"

Madi didn't hesitate. "I'm for crushing another dungeon. We're going to need to figure out a way for Orrin to be the one to absorb the core without them noticing, but he can always use his invisibility spell."

"It's not invisibility, and we don't know whether Arandir would be able to see through it," Orrin countered.

"I guess you're against it, then?" Daniel came around the chair to stand by him. Orrin noticed him glance at his ears, checking for any damage.

On one hand, they'd accomplished what they'd set out to do: Daniel had given the Quest to the elves. They could be using it as a workaround to their no-war policy and going after the Odranan forces right now, for all he knew. He hadn't used his administrator points, but with the few hints he'd gotten from Arandir, he knew enough to figure out what path he'd want to take. There was absolutely no reason for them to stay.

On the other hand, free experience and more admin points. Orrin didn't care about the gold as much as Daniel or about destroying dungeons like Madi. It would be cool to see Leanthun and Arandir operating. From what Orrin had read, having a party member twenty levels or more above you would result in an experience penalty, but they would still be getting twenty floors' worth of experience. That was not even counting the dungeon stat bonus or the admin points he would get. It would be difficult to pull off, but the worst-case scenario was Arandir finding out they'd pulled a fast one on him. They could still escape as soon as they left the dungeon.

"I'm not against it," Orrin said slowly. Madi pumped her fist in the corner. "I just needed a minute to think it through. I guess . . . we're going to defeat another dungeon."

Chapter 52

Twenty hours later, Orrin stood staring at his status in disbelief.

Orrin
Utility Warder
Level 17 (5,286/8,000)
Ability Points: 39
Administrator Points: 10
HP: 120/120
MP: 380/380
Strength: 9
Constitution: 12
Dexterity: 11
Will: 28
Intelligence: 11

"Once you have recovered sufficiently, we will go to the next floor. The floor boss is much stronger than any of you, so please continue to only hit it from a range." Arandir was sitting cross-legged on a small pillow he'd brought for the express purpose of resting between floors. They were in the in-between room after the nineteenth floor of the elven training dungeon Falling Leaves.

Leanthun and Arandir had cajoled Daniel into joining together in a group and teleported the small entourage to a nondescript part of the eastern forest edge. The two elves took turns defeating the dungeon floor by floor.

Orrin, Madi, and Daniel were sent into each room ahead of the two elves. As soon as they did any damage to a monster, Leanthun would cut the beast down or Arandir would simply make the creature explode with his magic. According to Leanthun, they were receiving a quarter of the experience they would gain from doing the dungeon on their own. The first ten floors had given the three of them half a level of experience. Not much but still a nice boost on the way to completing their Reach Level Twenty Quest.

Floor eleven had been a puzzle room, with nothing to defeat. It was floor twelve where Orrin learned how much harder the second deca-set made a dungeon. There was a reason they'd only been allowed to go after a tier-one dungeon before.

The monsters in Falling Leaves had used mostly earth and life magic. Earth magic wasn't anything too new, but the life magic had some interesting quirks. Each monster they encountered had more health and could cause conditions with their attacks. It reminded Orrin of the aftereffects of using his [Utility Ward] on too high a level.

The trio hadn't been in a single prolonged fight since they entered, with the two elves doing massive damage to anything nearby. Leanthun had even brought a plain bow for each of them in case they had no long-range spells or attacks. Daniel had played around with his for a while but still preferred to rush in with Gertrude. The first ten floors had contained nothing the three of them wouldn't have been able to take down together, and that included the defensive and very tanky tree that was the tenth-floor boss.

Yes, they'd cut down a tree to pass the tenth floor. It was the most ridiculous boss that Orrin had ever seen.

The twelfth floor had spread out in front of them, looking almost the same as many floors before. A small forest that used some sort of spatial magic at the edges made the entire room feel like it went on forever. In actuality, if one of the party members just walked in a straight line, they'd eventually run into the back of those who remained stationary. This floor looked no different.

Until the trees attacked.

The actual monsters were tiny deer no taller than Orrin's knees but with serrated edges along their antlers.

As the beasts appeared, two swiftly became six, then dozens rushed into their line of sight. Daniel was grinning and laughing like an imbecile as he swept his sword back and forth, punting the small animals into the air.

Their life magic had two main properties. One, they could heal any damage at an insanely high rate. Second, each attack the little beasts made had a chance to give them a condition that froze them in place. Orrin's [Ward] seemed to block it on his friends, but he had to keep it fully charged. The one time a deer hit Daniel with a completely empty [Ward], he froze in place for only two seconds, but the number of attacks they got off on him kept Orrin healing for longer than he wanted to.

"From here until the end, attack the trees as well," Leanthun said, standing behind Orrin, who was spending his mana to keep his wards going on his friends. Daniel was back in the fray.

Orrin used his [Toxic Touch] on trees while Madi and Daniel damaged the level twenty-two [Fear Fawns]. Leanthun finished each damaged fawn while Arandir touched each tree behind Orrin. His poison hand melted the wood, and whatever Arandir was doing left the stink of smoke drifting on the wind. Within minutes, the floor was deathly silent and suffused with the faint smell of burned wood, each tree a dried husk.

They received as much experience on that floor as on the ten previous floors combined.

They saw good gains on the next seven floors as well. Without Arandir casting spells that seemed to destroy things from within and Leanthun's quick-moving attacks, Orrin would have turned back after the first fight. He ended up spending more time keeping his wards going on his friends in the last room than actually damaging things. Daniel's gloating was proof.

"How are you only at seventeen? I hit that three floors ago." Daniel bounced in place, ready to continue to run. "You've got to get in there more and attack. Could you imagine how much experience we'd get if we brought a regular group in?"

Orrin didn't even try to explain why that would be a bad idea . . . again. Madi was sitting next to him, rolling her arm in circles. She'd taken a direct hit and been thrown to the side. While she hadn't taken any damage, thanks to Orrin's [Ward], she had twinged her shoulder from the force of hitting the ground and was trying to work out the kink.

"It is time." Arandir stood gracefully and handed his sitting pillow to Leanthun. The younger elf had a small backpack stuffed to the top with items, mostly for the elder. "Let us destroy this dungeon."

Stepping through the last door, Orrin looked around. The trees still surrounded them, but in the distance, a break in the tree line revealed a cave nestled against a hill. Orrin's senses wouldn't let him take his eyes off that location, which had a powerful aura emanating from it.

"Stay behind us and attack from a distance," Leanthun directed, moving in front of the party. "We didn't come this far just for one of you to die."

Five minutes later, Daniel was rolling on the ground.

"A bunny. A cute little white bunny with pointy fangs and you made us sit back. I can't believe it got an attack off on you, Leanthun. That was so much fun to watch."

The elf glowered at Daniel until Arandir chuckled.

"It did get a solid blow on you, nephew."

Experience Gained: 850 XP

The aforementioned beast was dead, and Orrin could feel the dungeon core present itself inside the small cave. *A core in a cave in a dungeon. How original.*

"Daniel, if you would not mind, I would like to attempt to absorb the core," Arandir said, leaning on his staff. "If I cannot do so, I will call you in. Would that be acceptable?"

Daniel waved his hand. "While you try, the four of us can start cooking something. I'm starving."

Orrin tried to catch Daniel's eye, but his friend was looking everywhere but at him. *How am I supposed to absorb the core? Stop giving me useless tasks.*

Arandir left, walking into the darkness of the cave.

Orrin pulled out some food and equipment, including a few chairs from the elven prison villa.

"These . . . look familiar."

Orrin smiled innocently at Leanthun.

"Hey, O," Daniel said nonchalantly. "Why don't you go and check the perimeter for anything else?"

"We already killed the floor boss."

"Yeah, but you never know what could happen in a dungeon. Just a quick check."

"Daniel, did you hit your hea—"

"Orrin, I'll come with you," Madi said, standing up.

Orrin figured it out a second later and just shrugged.

"There is no need for that," Leanthun started, but Daniel pulled him into a conversation about his fighting techniques and Orrin and Madi were able to slip away.

"You almost blew it," Madi ribbed him as they walked in the opposite direction of the cave. "How thick can you be?"

Orrin rolled his eyes. "I didn't think he'd want me to go in while Arandir is trying to absorb the core."

"That would be stupid. We'll wait until he leaves and then have you go in. I'll be your alibi after you sneak in and absorb it."

"My alibi?"

Madi turned away. "You don't think Leanthun really believes we're checking the perimeter, do you?"

A beat later, Orrin blushed. "But . . . then they'll both think—"

"We'll get the points and keep your secret," Madi stated. "That's what's important."

Orrin wisely kept his mouth shut.

They walked a large circle and ended up to the northeast of the cave. Orrin pulled up his [Map] and waited. As soon as Arandir walked out in a huff, Orrin activated [Camouflage] and dashed inside.

The core hung in the air in the back of the dank cave. The dungeon had generated bones of multiple races that had fallen to the bunny, and Orrin stepped carefully around them until he reached the dark orb.

> **Welcome, Administrator**
> **Would you like to absorb this core for twenty (20) administrator points?**

Not yet.

Orrin waited until Daniel walked into the cave, with Arandir close behind.

"You didn't even get the option?" Daniel's voice echoed loudly in the cave. "I told you."

"I am thankful you let me try first, but as long as you can gain more administrator points, this will all have been worth it."

Daniel stopped a few feet away from the core. "Stay back while I absorb the dungeon core. We might need to get out of here quick after."

Arandir stood still, watching the [Hero] move the last few steps.

"I sure hope this works," Daniel muttered to nobody in particular.

Orrin reached from the darkness, concealed with his [Camouflage], and triggered the core absorption.

The notifications came in fast.

> **Congratulations! You have defeated the Falling Leaves!**
> **You have been two rewarded (2) Constitution points!**
> **You have been awarded twenty (20) administrator points.**

Orrin sighed in relief and backed into the corner of the cave. *I have thirty points now. I can create relics or pick a few of the cheaper skills outright.*

He had talked with Madi and Daniel about the possible skills he could get as an Administrator. Daniel wanted him to unlock more Quests so they could power level their way to the top. Madi had told him they could basically retire if he took Create Relic but she was more interested in the Edit Stats skills. Of course, she wanted to ask Arandir more questions about those skills before he took one. Neither cared about Assign or Reset Class, and the other skills were too vague to fully understand what they could do.

Orrin was more interested in Unlock Ability or Assign Class. He could fulfill Amir's dream of becoming a [Healer] or just give him the spells he needed in the first place. He could give out the [Hero] class and let those others deal with the impending Demon Lord attack. Instead of waiting for higher levels and more ability points, he could unlock any spell he wanted.

Arandir was pestering Daniel with questions as they headed out. They knew the dungeon was defeated, having received the constitution points. Orrin waited before sneaking out and joining Madi. They made their way south and approached the party from the opposite direction of the cave. Daniel was about to pull his hair out.

"Arandir, please stop. I've told you over and over I don't know how it works, just that it does."

The older elf frowned but didn't push again.

Leanthun gave the slightest smile to Orrin as they rejoined the group and nodded in his direction.

Great, now he thinks something is going on between me and Madi. How many lies can I keep straight before I fuck one up?

Chapter 53

Orrin woke to someone shaking him.

"What?" he asked, rubbing his eyes. "Madi?"

After defeating another dungeon, they had made it back to the middle of the forest and promptly passed out. Arandir promised to bring them over once they woke up. The way his eyes glinted whenever he spoke to Daniel let them know whom he actually wanted to talk with, but the [Hero] had made it clear the three of them were a package deal.

Orrin guessed he'd had only an hour or two of sleep, since the heaviness behind his eyes still hammered into his skull. He pushed the pain down and woke up fully at what he saw.

Tears were in Madi's eyes.

"What happened?"

Madi's fingers on his arms tightened. "They took Daniel."

Her voice continued making noise, but Orrin didn't listen. Things had been calm for too long and the shoe had finally dropped. Part of him was relieved, but the vast majority of him roared in anger and hurt. He'd never believed the elves were going to act any better than the Odranan forces that had tried to kidnap Daniel or the lord of Dey who had tried to kill them all. The cynicism that he had kept from spilling over crawled up his throat.

"Orrin, why are you laughing? You're scaring me. We need to—"

Orrin understood why that [Hero] of the past had cut these people off or destroyed the world or whatever it was he'd done. His friend had come here to help stop a war. He'd tried to convince Orrin how much good an Administrator could do for these people. Before they'd fallen asleep, Daniel had been so excited at the idea.

Ignoring Madi, Orrin pulled up his new menu and checked the options. He was going to become an Administrator in truth and walk through this city to rescue his friend again. If anybody tried to stop him . . .

Assigning or resetting a class wouldn't help him. He could make new Quests, but that wouldn't do anything. Imbue, Scry, Change Race, Create Relic, Unlock Ability . . . pointless for attacking right now. He'd debated with Daniel over Edit Stats (Sanctioned) versus (Unsanctioned). They'd agreed the (Unsanctioned) meant without permission from the recipient. Like what he'd done to Samara, Lord Wendeln's right hand, the last time Daniel had been kidnapped.

You have to stop getting taken. I do not have a specific set of skills, dude.

Orrin hovered his finger on Edit Stats (Unsanctioned). He and Daniel had argued over what the cost would be. To take ten points from Samara, he'd had to give up one point of his own constitution. Arandir had hinted that an Administrator could use any power in moments of danger or high emotion. Logic dictated that he'd have to pay the same cost.

Logic . . .

Orrin activated the skill that had given him so much power and so many problems: [Mind Bastion]. He felt the power spread out and took a breath. He cast [Calm Mind] on himself, feeling the burning feeling in his gut get pushed farther down.

"Who took him, Madi?"

Madi, the daughter of a lord of Dey, had been raised from a young age to handle situations with calm and poise. That she was crying now meant she had tried and failed to protect her new friend. Orrin could see the pain and shame she was feeling. He also saw the disappointment as she heard the change in his voice.

"Daniel said if you're using that skill to remind you that you promised not to."

Orrin began to buff them both. He kept Madi's stats at an acceptable level so she wouldn't fall into a stupor after the spells wore off but maxed out everything he had.

"We don't have time. Who took him, specifically? Was it Arandir?" Orrin cast [Ward] on them both and hesitated for a second before casting the full complement of protections: Ice, Water, and Poison.

I should get all the different wards and mash them together in [Merge]. Orrin plucked the stray thought out of his mind.

"How many types of elemental magic are there?"

"It wasn't Arandir. Some guards came and asked to speak with him. He went outside and they got into an argument. I heard them, but when I got outside, they were gone," Madi answered. "What are you thinking?"

"I don't know what they're going to throw at me when I get him back. I might try to make something that protects against all magic," Orrin responded. He was already searching through skills and spells, trying to find the cheapest options for what he wanted to do.

He stopped when Madi pushed him back on the bed and straddled him.

"Madi?"

"You are going to stop and listen to me," she said, holding tight with all her strength. "Daniel said you are getting better at controlling yourself. Stop and listen to me, please. You cannot win against an entire city of elves."

Orrin knew exactly what her strength was at right now. It was laughable that she would even try this. She had to know that his strength was higher than hers, but . . .

She wasn't acting with logic but trust. Trust that he wouldn't simply throw her across the room but would stop and think because she was asking him to.

The cold retreated from his mind.

"Yeah, killing them all would be bad, huh?" Orrin chuckled. "Madi, you . . . can get off me."

She smirked and punched him in the chest before rolling off him. "Daniel told me to stay inside. I could only hear their voices, but it wasn't Arandir or Leanthun. Like I said, we should get them."

"When did you say that?"

She flicked him between the eyes. "When you started using your dumb skill. Is it still on?"

Orrin stood up and pulled his shirt on. "I'm in control of it right now, though. It lets me process my thoughts better. You're sure Arandir wasn't there?"

She nodded.

"Then let's go rescue Daniel, again." Orrin paused. "Madi, thank you."

She smiled and pointed. "Don't forget to bring his sword. He's going to be pissed if we get into a fight and he can't swing that hunk of metal around."

As Madi guided them through the city streets she had memorized, because of course she had, Orrin decided it was time to make a few purchases he'd been putting off.

First, he found the cheapest spells he could find.

> **[Fire Sword]—summon a sword of pure fire. Does minimal damage but will not be quenched in the bitterest of cold. Each sword lasts one hour. 1 MP per sword. -1 AP**

He had also looked at [Firebolt] and [Fists of Fire] but decided dual-wielding swords of fire and ice would look badass. *Take that mind logic. I can still make stupid decisions.*

He immediately purchased the corresponding [Ward].

> **[Fire Ward]—create a ward around yourself and your party within 50 feet that protects against Fire magic for MP maximum. 20 MP. -1 AP**

Wind magic was a bit easier to find, as there was only one option that cost a single point.

[Gust]—push the wind toward your target. 1 MP cost minimum. Variable strength cost. -1 AP

It wasn't something he could ever see himself using, but he'd seen Leanthun using some wind magic with his bow. The resulting [Ward] would be useful if this devolved into a fight.

[Wind Ward]—create a ward around yourself and your party within 50 feet that protects against Wind magic for MP maximum. 20 MP. -1 AP

Earth magic had too many options. Most had to do with farming, while the few offensive magic types cost more than he wanted to spend. He was also a bit confused about the difference between Earth and Plant magic but settled on one he hoped would give him a [Ward] for both.

Tilth—rework soil for better crop return. 5 MP per acre. -1 AP

Orrin wasn't a farmer but crossed his fingers he'd get the [Ward] for at least one type. Luckily, the system seemed to be on his side today.

[Earth Ward]—create a ward around yourself and your party within 50 feet that protects against Earth magic for MP maximum. 20 MP. -1 AP
[Plant Ward]—create a ward around yourself and your party within 50 feet that protects against Plant magic for MP maximum. 20 MP. -1 AP

I have Earth, Wind, Water, and Fire now. Orrin chuckled to himself. *Daniel would make a joke about finding Heart.*

He brushed off the idea of summoning a blue superhero and searched through his past options as well, selecting two he'd passed over before.

> **[Camouflage Ward]—create a ward around yourself and your party within 50 feet that mimics [Camouflage]. 50 MP. -5 AP**
> **[Light Ward]—create a ward around yourself and your party within 50 feet that protects against Light magic for MP maximum. 20 MP. -1 AP**

Thirteen ability points down. He'd spent a third of what he had but felt good about his choices. He had ignored Steel and Lightning magic for now. He knew Steel would be too expensive, and by the time he was about to search for Lightning, they had arrived at Arandir's elevator.

"I'll go up. You can stay below," Orrin offered. Madi hugged him. "Be quick."

Orrin rode up and knocked. Leanthun answered the door.

". . . what are you doing here? You should still be sleeping."

Orrin peeked around Leanthun and found Arandir sitting on his couch, reading a book. He spoke over Leanthun's shoulder. "If you don't want this entire forest to burn to the ground, you better not have anything to do with it."

Arandir placed a bookmark between the pages and set the book on his side table before rising from his seated position with the fluidity of a cat stretching. "Please do tell me what I have done."

"Somebody took Daniel."

Arandir didn't move so much as appear beside Orrin. "When?" The intensity of his stare made Orrin step back on the elevator.

"Not long. Madi woke me and we came straight here."

Arandir kept his eyes glued to Orrin's. The stare became awkward, and the elf tilted his head. "He is not here, and yet I still feel . . ."

"Are you going to save my friend or not? I'm only here first because Madi convinced me I shouldn't make an enemy of the entire elven community."

Leanthun rolled his eyes, and Orrin caught him doing it. He was tempted to hit the man with a boosted debuff to wipe the smirk off his face but caught himself. *[Mind Bastion] keeping me level. Small blessing, I guess.*

Arandir hadn't moved, and Orrin felt a tingle across his skin.

"Don't do it."

Arandir continued his probe, and Orrin felt a skill like [Identify] roll over him.

"How did I miss it this entire time?" Arandir stumbled back. "You are not from this world, either. You are the Administrator. I am correct, yes?"

"We don't have time for this. Somebody took Daniel. The last time that happened, I had to kill a lot of people. Are you going to help me?"

Arandir raised a hand, and his staff jumped across the room, slapping into his palm with a satisfying smack. "Leanthun, find him. Whoever took him, let them know I am on the way and will put the full weight of the council against them unless the [Hero] is released immediately."

"Yes, Illustrious One." Leanthun bowed in answer and jumped off the tree.

"I hate it when you guys do that."

"He will find your friend. Let us follow."

Arandir rode the elevator down with Orrin. Madi sighed in relief when she saw them both.

"I thought for sure you'd get in a fight," she said, closing in for another hug. "I saw Leanthun. Is he going to save Daniel?"

"He is," Arandir answered in Orrin's place. "You keep high company, Lady Catanzano. Would you like to accompany us to find your friend?"

Orrin had missed Madi's spear in her hand before but didn't when it extended. "Oh, I would like that very much."

Chapter 54

Leanthun returned before the elevator hit the floor. He whispered into Arandir's ear. Orrin clenched his fist as the older elf grew angrier the longer his nephew talked.

"They would not dare."

Leanthun bowed his head and spoke toward the ground. "What should we do? He'll be here within an hour. There isn't enough time to—"

Arandir gestured, and Leanthun stopped talking.

"Arandir, what is going on?" Madi asked.

The elf held up a hand to forestall her, mumbling to himself with his eyes closed.

"Sir, we're trying to be polite here, but if you keep us in the dark . . ." Orrin threatened vaguely, as he didn't quite know what he could or would do, but Arandir had agreed to help.

"Leanthun, tell them what you told me. I need a minute to think." Arandir rested his forehead against his staff and began to murmur too softly for Orrin to hear.

"Either part or the full council, minus Arandir, have assembled and are holding court over whether to turn the [Hero] over to Odrana in exchange for leaving the elven forest alone. They have decided that Arandir is too biased and voted him out of the decision. They are using one of the council's other meeting locations to discuss the fate of your friend."

"What?" Madi and Orrin shouted at the same time. Madi continued while Orrin pulled up his [Map]. "Why would they do that after he gave them the Quest? Does their word mean nothing?"

"How many places could they be at?" Orrin asked instead. "We can check them all if we have to."

"There are hundreds of fallback locations and meeting places. We couldn't search them all."

Orrin tuned him out and began scanning for Daniel. They had disbanded the party when they got back, mostly to kick Arandir and Leanthun out of receiving any group system announcements. He tried sending a party invite to Daniel again, with no response.

"All but one of those who received the Quest are dead," Leanthun continued explaining to Madi. "Lord Sanerris took to the field with a cohort of his best and slew them all. He sent one back with his demands. He wants either the [Hero] or my uncle. The council would never turn over an elf, but they might turn over Daniel."

Arandir groaned and went to one knee. Leanthun rushed to his side. "Uncle, that is enough. Do not push yourself."

"It is worth the cost," the elf got out through gritted teeth. "Almost . . . there."

Orrin felt the same weird energy he'd always felt from Arandir coming off him in waves. He was playing with the system in some way. Orrin wanted to use [Analyze] but remembered the last time he'd tried. Something inside told him it would be a very bad idea to use it at this particular moment.

Madi turned to Orrin. "Pull up your [Map]."

He had to dodge her spear point when she moved to grab his arm. "Watch out. I tried that already. I can't find Daniel in a sea of people."

"The council is now an enemy. Imagine them turning Daniel over. They are no longer friends or random people—they are monsters trying to attack your friend."

"Huh?"

"Try it, please," Madi begged.

Orrin zoomed out of his [Map] and focused his thoughts. White dots spread out everywhere, too many to count. He focused on the man Arandir had tossed across the room and imagined his smug face throwing Daniel to the wolves.

A white dot flickered on the far side of the matriarch tree. It only moved for a split second, but Orrin kept his eyes on the location.

"Leanthun, there is a row of houses near what looks like a fountain or spring of water about a mile northwest of the big tree. Do you know it?"

Leanthun looked up from his uncle and frowned. "You haven't been to that part of our city but yes, I know what you are talking about. There is a communal pool built out of the remains of—"

"I don't care about what it is. There is a building or tree house, I don't know. It's . . . two streets north of that pool and one street over. Behind a building that looks bigger than the others and is shaped like an X. Do you know it?"

"That would be the holding area behind the Justice Hall," Arandir groaned. "I do not know if that is where Daniel is being held, but that is where the council is meeting."

"How do you know?" Madi spun back around, almost clipping Orrin again.

She is dangerous with that spear. I need to have a talk with her about proper weapon safety.

"I have lived a long time, dear. I have many powers, but this is not one I will share."

"Argue about it later." Orrin threw out a party invite to them all. "Accept the invite."

"We will need to be swift." Arandir pushed himself taller using his staff. He accepted the invite, as did Madi and Leanthun.

"I can use [Teleport], so I'm going to bring us up into the matriarch tree's branches," Orrin explained, pointing to the big tree in the middle of the forest clearing. "One of you needs to point out which building I need to target, and then I'll do it again and land us right on the roof."

Arandir's look of surprise was almost worth all this hassle. "You can what?"

The four of them stumbled as they landed on the roof of the Justice Hall, the elves' version of a courthouse. Well, Orrin and Madi stumbled. Leanthun and Arandir appeared to be out for an afternoon stroll. Orrin drank a mana potion. Teleporting himself and three people twice this close together was a drain on even his large mana pool.

"We will speak with the council while you get your friend," Arandir said, waving his staff in a circle. The air around them swirled in a haze of lights, and a cloud of fast-moving wind coalesced in front of them. He beckoned them onto the floating cloud. "Good luck to you."

Madi held tight to Orrin until they landed on the ground.

"Don't wait. If you get a chance, all three of you need to get out of here," Leanthun whispered as he unhooked his weapons. "We will do our best to find you if we survive."

"Hold up." Orrin slid to a stop. "What do you mean, if we survive? You aren't going to fight your own people, are you?"

Arandir smirked. "It will not be much of a fight, I am afraid. I trained most of the council myself at one point or another. Nonetheless, it is never wise to believe everything will go according to plan. Rescue your friend and return to Dey. We will find each other again, fellow Administrator."

For the first time since meeting Arandir, Orrin realized his distrust and strange feelings regarding the elder elf were from the weird powers they both had. He was actually good people, trying to do what he believed was best for the elves, but not at the expense of his own honor. Arandir was going to help them rescue Daniel and hadn't asked for anything in return.

Orrin stuck his hand out. "I'm sorry I didn't trust you sooner. When this is all over, maybe I can help you figure out a way to bring Administrators back."

Arandir took Orrin's hand and squeezed. "Keep your skepticism, but trust yourself. I believe you will do what is best for the world."

Madi hip-checked Orrin. "Buff us up."

Orrin cast his spells, drinking a mana potion to top himself off. He was still running [Mind Bastion] but didn't want to blood cycle unless it was absolutely necessary.

"Everybody ready?"

Leanthun answered by kicking in the door to the holding area behind the courthouse and rushing in. Arandir followed close behind with his staff held out in front of him.

"They could have just said yes," Orrin complained. He and Madi ran inside.

Orrin was prepared for anything. When Madi had told him that Daniel was taken, he'd begun having flashbacks of finding his friend tied up in a tent. He wasn't sure how many of the elven council members were going to be waiting for them or if the Odranan leader, Lord Sanerris, would be there already. He summoned a [Fire Sword] in one hand and an [Ice Sword] in the other, ready to take on everything they threw at him.

What he did not expect to find was Daniel sitting all alone in the middle of twenty holding cells. He was tied to the chair, but nobody else was present.

Leanthun and Arandir were searching corners for the elders.

"Hey, O, took you long enough," Daniel said with a grin.

Madi tackled Daniel, knocking the chair backward.

"Ouch, watch it," he complained as she began pulling at the knots to untie him.

"Why did you go off with them? What were you thinking?"

Daniel frowned. "Sorry, Madi. One of the elves who so politely asked me to come meet the council threatened to firebomb the house if I resisted. I knew you were awake and could probably get out, but I also knew this shithead was probably sleeping."

Orrin sighed. Daniel was calling him names. He was worried about the situation he was in but still felt comfortable enough to mess around.

"Orrin, take Daniel and leave. Now!" Arandir yelled from the back of the room.

Orrin made it two steps before the back door exploded, flinging wooden shrapnel at all of them. Orrin was knocked to the ground. Madi covered Daniel with her body.

Orrin had already cast another [Ward] on all five of them before the dust settled, crawling over the debris toward his friends. He reached out his hand and grabbed Daniel before casting [Teleport].

It failed.

"They have a teleportation ward," he croaked around the dust in his throat. He swallowed to clear it. Instead, he started coughing.

"Arandir and Leanthun. Why am I not surprised to see you here?" A voice spoke from the door.

Orrin glanced up and saw a handful of elves come through the broken door frame. He recognized Devdan and Gwynnestri, along with two of the other elders. He hadn't caught their names before. The one who spoke wasn't an elf but a human man. He stood tall but stayed behind the council members.

"Sanerris, I will kill you for this," Leanthun threatened but did not move. The four members of the council stood waiting between them, each holding weapons or staffs of their own.

"This would have been so much easier if you had simply agreed to help me," Lord Sanerris said, pushing his fingers back through his golden hair. His clothes gave no indication of his class and he wore no weapons, but Orrin felt the distinct aura of a predator on the leader of Odrana. "Now it has come to this. Kidnapping the [Hero], yet again. I knew you would come running once I trapped your new little pet."

"What are you doing, Arvin? I have told you before, my powers would be of no use to you." Arandir sighed, leaning on his staff and ignoring the traitor elves surrounding him. "Gwynni, what have you done?"

Gwynnestri wore heavy armor and held a two-handed sword that looked like it could stand up against Gertrude in length. "Arandir, my job is to protect our people. A human, especially a human [Hero], is no concern of ours. Let Lord Sanerris have him. He agreed to pull back his forces if we do."

"Oh, Gwynni, do you believe him so easily? This man will not be appeased. He will always seek more."

Sanerris's smile grew larger. "Oh, but it is true. Why would I need you when I can have him instead? He gave you a Quest to defeat me, didn't he? Is he really a [Hero] or something else? I have heard so many interesting rumors about him. It is one reason I wanted him so badly in the first place. I can wait for you to come to me, and you will, once you learn what I know."

Gwynnestri glanced over her shoulder. "Sanerris, take the idiot [Hero] and go. Pull your people away from our forest and never darken our trees again."

Daniel stood up from where he had been lying. He stretched his arms over his head and cracked his back with a loud yawn. "I think that you are all forgetting something very important here."

He snapped his fingers, and Gertrude appeared in his hands. "Do you like that little trick? I haven't had the chance to try it yet. [Summon Weapon] is cheap, but I thought I might need it someday. Like if I ever wanted to convince a bunch of idiots that I'm helpless and then kill them all once they rounded themselves up for me."

Daniel bent his knees and took a ready stance. "Oh, wait. Is that what I did here? I guess this [Hero] is a little smarter than you thought."

Chapter 55

Daniel's words pierced the fog of Orrin's thoughts. Too many people were in the small holding room. They had rushed in the front door and found Daniel tied to a chair. Ten empty cells to either side of him and only one other entrance. The sudden betrayal of the council in forcibly taking Daniel was a surprise. Finding them siding with their enemy was a completely separate issue.

"Daniel, we should run." Orrin sidled up alongside his friend and felt his body take a natural defensive position as [Way of the Water] flooded his mind with knowledge. He didn't know what skills or spells the four council members could use, but the aura coming off Lord Sanerris alone was enough to set his neck hairs tingling. "This isn't a fight we want to be part of."

Despite his words, he quickly made sure to buff Daniel and himself to the max. Madi, Leanthun, and Arandir were already holding the top increased stats Orrin felt comfortable giving.

"O, you didn't meet all those volunteers I gave the Quest to." Daniel spoke through gritted teeth. "When they were tying me to that chair, the other elven chick there said she blamed me. She said it was my fault they all died."

Behind Gwynnestri, the other female council member hissed at him, "It is your fault. You escalated everything by coming here."

"Sariandi, calm yourself." Devdan held an arm out to keep her from charging forward. The elder Arandir had thrown across the room before looked calm as he turned back to the party. "Arandir, surrender him. You and your nephew cannot hope to take all four of us."

Daniel stood up straight and let Gertrude dip. "Is . . . is he ignoring us?"

Orrin closed his eyes and dropped his head. "Damn it. You'd think they'd learn, right?"

The female council member Sariandi raised her staff and pointed it at Daniel. Orrin swept his [Ice Sword] along the tip of Gertrude, pushing Daniel back a half step. A bolt of green light twisted by his face.

"Andi!" Devdan knocked her staff down. "Incapacitate, not kill."

There was a split second after the word *kill* where nobody moved. The flurry of movement, magic, and mayhem that followed surprised Orrin with its intensity and violence.

Gwynnestri and the other male elf advanced on Arandir. Leanthun dashed in front of the older elf and caught Gwynnestri's downstroke with his khopesh, twisting the longer sword to the side as it slid along the metal.

The other elf swung his two hammers in opposite directions, aiming to hit Leanthun's outstretched left arm and his right knee at the same time. Leanthun's spiked mace head detached, letting out a few feet of thin metal chain. A quick loop of his hand and Leanthun tangled both weapons. Hammer elf had to move to the side, as his own attack swung the spiked tip of the mace into his path.

Arandir ignored the two attacking him. He sent magic flying at Sanerris, which fizzled out as it closed in on the human. Sanerris leaned on the broken door frame and faked a yawn as the various spells failed to hit.

Daniel had ducked under Orrin's guard and attacked Devdan and the female with the staff. Madi was jabbing with her spear and sending her own spells at both in an attempt to disorient them. Devdan was waving his hands like he was at a rave, throwing her spells into the ceiling and deflecting Daniel's attacks with bursts of air and ice.

Orrin cast inversed increase-stat spells on the elves. He got Devdan and Sariandi with both will and intelligence before hitting Gwynnestri with dexterity and strength. Her sword dipped for a moment, but she powered through and caught Leanthun's counterattack.

"That looks like a fun spell," Sanerris said, tilting his head. "I must have it."

Orrin felt a spike of pressure behind his eyes for a moment before [Mind Bastion] sealed his brain up tight.

"Oh, Arandir. What is this one?" Sanerris pushed off his bored perch and began to hop through the battlefield, avoiding the skirmishes going on. "Did you teach him some tricks?"

Orrin's fighting skill was telling him to run. Run and not look back. Sanerris's nonchalant attitude in the middle of a fight this intense was disconcerting.

Daniel activated his speedy skill and pushed the two elves back. Devdan used his air magic to push himself back, sliding on ice to avoid the strikes. The woman dodged two strikes but grunted when Daniel stabbed when she expected a swing. Daniel's sword came back red, and she fell to the ground.

"You're next," Daniel threatened, pointing at Devdan. He activated [Gravity Well], trying to pull the elf in.

Daniel's skill also caught Sanerris. For the first time, something affected him. Sanerris tottered to the side and made his first move.

He simply flicked his fingers at Daniel.

The [Hero] was thrown across the room. His head struck the metal bars of one of the cells with a clang that echoed across the room. Daniel did not get up.

Orrin was moving before Daniel landed on the ground, sliding on his knees to grab his friend and pour healing spells on him as he checked his health.

"Itsh all good," Daniel slurred, blinking with one crossed eye. Several teeth were missing, and the side of his face was crushed. His cheekbone was caved in but popping back out, making crunching noises as Orrin's healing set the injury. "Jush need a minute or few . . ."

Orrin felt Madi at his back, holding the rest of the attackers off with her spear. Daniel's health was leveled, but the injury would take a minute or two to fully correct itself. Time they didn't have.

Orrin had dropped his swords as he rushed to his friend. He turned as he stood, taking in the room in a glance. Leanthun, bleeding, was fighting Gwynnestri, while Arandir was standing over the still form of the man who used the hammers. Sanerris was smiling at Madi and holding the tip of her spear between two fingers. Devdan cast a spell that caught her under the ribs and lifted her up before slamming her to the ground.

Orrin knew this was going to end badly. He was not built for up-close fighting. His [Way of the Water] skill was about avoiding attacks. The best he could do was use [Toxic Touch] to do some damage, but it was a cheap skill for a reason—it didn't do much damage at all. Strangely, as the sleazy-looking elf advanced on him, he felt the calm in his mind still trying to find options.

He could use the Administrator powers, but against this many people, it would cost him everything. He needed to be stronger. He needed to hit these people for everything they'd done. They were trying to hurt his friends, and he was NOT going to stand for that. He would do it. Whatever the cost. Orrin moved to pull the skill up and spend the points.

A sensation that he'd felt only once before reared its head. [Blood Mana] darkened his vision, making everything he saw look as if it was far away, down a tunnel. Instead of pushing back, the logical side of [Mind Bastion] embraced the darkness. Something clicked in the skill, and Orrin's vision came back in a rush. A new understanding of [Blood Mana] surged into his mind, connecting multiple thoughts into one possible chance.

Orrin's smile froze Devdan, who was advancing on them. Orrin pulled the stopper from a small glass vial he kept on his belt and downed it.

"Wha—?"

Orrin didn't try to hit him; he simply reached out and touched him.

[Blood Mana] activated, pulling Devdan's health and turning it to mana. The elf's constitution was high. High enough that such a spell should have done negligible damage. Orrin used Devdan's own health as mana to activate [Toxic Touch]. Then, while keeping the cycle going, he pulled harder and used [Remetabolize].

> **[Remetabolize]—change the toxicity and structure of a toxin. 50 MP**

Orrin spent all his mana. He'd downed one of his regen potions and blood cycled. He had a blue screen up, watching his experimental attack in the middle of the battle.

The screen displayed his new chart from [Analyze], showing him how much more he could blood cycle before he killed himself. The numbers were moving much faster than he'd thought possible.

Devdan tried to hit him, but Orrin used [Way of the Water] to move around the elf, keeping a hand on him when he could. Every time he had to let go, Devdan tried to run, but Orrin put himself back in front of the man.

"What are you?" Devdan screamed as black skin cracked where Orrin's fingers touched. Spindly veins rapidly darkened from each spot he touched. The poison was only going so far within the elf, but each tiny bit of contact exacerbated his condition.

"I'm the one you don't fuck with," Orrin said, feeling cocky. He reached and slapped the elf across his face.

Devdan opened his mouth and then started to seize. He stayed upright for a moment before falling back. He landed hard and coughed up blood. Orrin turned to Sanerris.

"You're next."

Daniel was getting to his feet and pulling Madi up. She gasped in pain and held her arm at a weird angle but slide-kicked her spear into the air and caught it with her other hand. Arandir and Leanthun didn't speak or give Sanerris a chance. They'd taken out Gwynnestri and attacked the man from behind.

"Maybe next time." Sanerris smiled and stepped gracefully around the elven attacks. "Come visit Odrana. Both of you. We should talk."

Daniel pointed Gertrude at the man. "You think we are going to let you out of here alive?"

Sanerris tilted his head. "If I wanted you dead, I would kill you. You need to train harder, little [Hero]. You know what's coming for us."

Orrin felt a chill run down his spine. *There is no way that he knows.*

"I'm the one coming for you. Do you want to surrender or should we chop you up, too?" Daniel was talking a big game, but Orrin could see he was still hurt. In fact, Orrin was the only one who hadn't taken a lot of damage in the fight.

"I can leave whenever I want. I'm still here because this tactic seems to have failed. While it has been fun bringing these sniveling scum down a peg, I never cared for this forest. I wanted Arandir to help me, but he refused. Now I'll ask you. Come to Odrana and let us find a way to end the demon threat before it is too late."

Daniel swung Gertrude at Sanerris. The man moved at the last second again, dodging like he knew where the sword would hit. He sighed and raised his hand.

"If you attack me again, I'll put you down. It would be nice if you would come of your own volition, but I do not have forever to play."

"Daniel, please step back," Arandir asked politely, leaning heavily on his staff. "Lord Sanerris, you have driven a wedge into our leaders' hearts and destroyed relationships older than your family. Have you not done enough? Leave our lands and never return."

Sanerris ran his fingers through his hair again. "Done enough? Old man, I told you. This isn't about just me and Odrana. Everyone on Asmea will suffer."

"You leave me no choice, then. I will force you to go."

"I'm not going yet. This young man here has some interesting new magic. I want it."

Orrin couldn't believe the audacity of this asshole. "Never going to happen."

Arandir smiled at Orrin and smacked his staff down on the ground twice.

Sanerris glanced around, becoming more concerned as he looked at something only he could see. "What are you doing? That . . . that's not possible. How?"

He turned and fled out the back door. Daniel chased after him, cursing him. Orrin chased his friend, cursing him as well. The back door led out to another street. Daniel was close on Sanerris's heels.

A rumble in the streets caught Orrin's attention, and he stopped running to watch in awe as a tree root the size of a train came barreling toward them. It undulated as it broke free of the ground holding it captive, reaching for its target: a small blond human against the matriarch tree.

The tree root swung in the air and came down, smashing into the ground and lifting back up. A crater remained where it had hit, but as Orrin came up beside his friend, he didn't see a body.

"Where is he?" Orrin tried to catch a glimpse of the root as it pulled back and began to make its way back, sinking into the ground.

Daniel slumped to the ground. "Too late and too weak, again."

"Daniel, where is Sanerris?"

His friend waved a hand in the air. "I was so close, O. I could almost touch him." Daniel sighed and hung his head. "He teleported out right before the tree hit him."

Chapter 56

The following two days were a flurry of activity for everyone. Orrin had healed Madi and Daniel to the best of his ability, or at least to the best that his [Heal Small Wounds] could perform, but Madi's arm had been badly fractured and Daniel was missing several teeth. Orrin also believed his friend had a concussion. He kept looking around in a dazed fashion until an elven healer that Arandir trusted showed up and cast a few spells.

Orrin's resolve to take more healing spells doubled while he watched Madi's arm bubble and twist as the bones reset correctly under the skin. When Daniel shouted in surprise as new teeth grew into the blank spaces of his smile, Orrin pulled up his own spell.

[Heal Small Wounds] Level 3 (7,840/10,000)

Just a bit more. From what little Amir had told him about the healing spell's progression, level three was as far as [Heal Small Wounds] could level. Completing all three levels opened up an entirely new tree of healing magic, and Orrin was tempted to ask the elf healing his friends for some pointers.

Arandir had the surviving elders restrained. Devdan was dead. Orrin learned he had been the elder of justice, magic, and education. The elf was considered one of the foremost authorities on wind magic and had been known to be a master duelist. He was also the head judge of their legal system . . . something that Arandir didn't seem to be as worried about as Orrin was.

"He underestimated you," Arandir had said, clapping his hand on Orrin's shoulder. "Learn from his mistake."

Sariandi, the elder of healing, had been in charge of the elven Hospital. Madi had concerns about letting the healer in to see her dead body, but Leanthun had assured them their version of the Hospital was not as corrupt as the human variant. Sariandi was a healer, but she'd been in an administrative role. Those who performed the work of healing were valued more in the elven nation.

The two elves Leanthun and Arandir had fought had been taken alive. Gwynnestri and the elder for agriculture, housing, and development would be spending the next few weeks answering questions from the other elders. Those who had not been present all swore to Arandir they had not been party or privy to the betrayal with Lord Sanerris.

Leanthun was taking the lead on keeping the council in check and working hard. Arandir sat back and let his nephew step up, and Orrin caught him smiling a few times when Leanthun was particularly harsh with an elder or two who questioned him.

Orrin spent time relaxing with his friends and discussing the future. Daniel and Madi wanted to leave and go back to Dey. Daniel even offered to share the Stop the War Quest with the elves again. Running off the leader of Odrana from the heart of the elven forest apparently didn't count as ending the war. None of them were particularly sold on going to the front lines. They agreed the only way the war would stop would be if Sanerris got what he wanted or died.

Daniel had pressured Arandir about Sanerris, but the elf was cagey about giving more information on the human leader of Odrana. He gave an excuse that an Administrator shouldn't betray the knowledge gained from their skills, but Orrin thought maybe the old elf just didn't know.

Madi was lying on a cot in the elder elf's apartment. She was under strict orders not to move her arm for a week. Daniel was in much better shape but was keeping her company, teaching her how to play checkers with a spare Kala board and a handful of cherries. Madi kept absent-mindedly eating the pieces. Daniel had been more wary of all elves and a little pissy to everyone. He'd even snapped at Orrin once about something trivial.

Madi eviscerated him. Orrin hadn't realized Daniel was angry that he'd needed saving again. He'd thought his friend had done a good job fighting a centuries-old elf and surviving. Madi's final words had been eye-opening for them both.

"Daniel, stop being a dick. It doesn't matter that Sanerris got away or that he kicked our asses. We all survived another attempt to kidnap you. You were even conscious for most of this fight. There isn't a competition between you and Orrin on who can fight best or contribute more. We work best as a team. You take the fight to our enemy, and Orrin supports us. I cover our blind spots."

Orrin had thought about her words a lot. He was so used to feeling useless in a fight. He hadn't told Madi he'd used [Blood Mana], only telling everyone that his [Toxic Touch] had been super effective against the wind mage for some reason. The rush of knowing he could fight and throw down with someone with more experience than him was intoxicating.

He knew why Daniel loved it.

He felt powerful. Even after he had turned off [Mind Bastion] and realized another person was dead because of his actions, he hadn't felt as bad as he thought he would. The Orrin from before, the one that would stand behind Daniel, not exactly hiding but not making himself known, was gone. Devdan had come after him and his friends. If the guy couldn't handle the price, he should have stayed in his lane.

Madi's words, that he was support, had hit him hardest. He knew he couldn't stand up to a powerhouse like Daniel unless he somehow debuffed him to a snail's pace. Yet, he still remembered the thoughts he'd had during his class creation.

I want to be in the background, quiet and away from any main battles.

Orrin glanced at his hands. *What if I wanted to be the one taking the fight to our enemies? What if I want to protect my friends?*

Orrin had even tested out putting his fighting skill, [Way of the Water], and [Toxic Touch] into his [Merge] slots. The error screen hadn't told him no, exactly, but he was still a little disappointed.

> **[Way of the Water] cannot be used until 100% integrated. [Merge] failed.**

Orrin had been too scared of Styx and too busy to work more on the skill—something he was going to make damn sure he had the time to do in the future.

If I was at 100 percent integration, could I have taken out Sanerris?

He spent most of the morning of the first day fussing over Daniel and Madi until they'd shunted him away. Sitting around doing nothing didn't appeal to him. Instead, Orrin found a small corner of Arandir's apartment and sat down, activating [Way of the Water].

Styx, the watery trainer, waited in the same spot, as if Orrin had never left.

"Hey, Styx. You been well?"

Styx didn't respond at first, but when Orrin activated the "continue" option, the yes-and-no answer game began again. Orrin still couldn't get any real information from the magical construct, but he did get the absolute shit beaten out of him.

It took him ten hours before Styx was satisfied and Orrin gained the next 5 percent increase. When the blue box had appeared, Orrin waved to the watery man and gladly exited the training session.

> **[Way of the Water]: 10% 2/20 completed. Continue or save progress?**

Now he remembered why he hadn't jumped back in to train. It was fucking exhausting. He nestled back up near his friends.

He'd been dozing on and off since returning, watching Daniel beat Madi at their game, when his name being called repeatedly broke him from his reverie.

"Orrin." Arandir waved off a group of runners and approached the trio. "May I speak with you?"

Madi clucked her tongue as Daniel jumped several pieces of fruit. "You didn't say we can do that."

Daniel popped her pieces in his mouth and chewed. "I'm sure I told you about double jumping."

Orrin stood from his seat and moved toward Arandir, leaving his friends to their squabble. "What's up?"

Arandir glanced up for a brief moment. "Ah. A greeting, not a literal question. I believe Daniel and Lady Catanzano are planning a return to Dey. I would like to extend my personal invitation for you to come study with me at my home."

"No offense, but why would I ever do that? Your people are in disarray, half your elders are dead or imprisoned, and I would have to leave my friends."

Orrin wasn't trying to be rude, but that Arandir even asked seemed a little nonsensical. Arandir chuckled and raised a hand. A bubble of air surrounded them.

"Now we may speak without others listening in," the elf said. "What I am offering is not for you to help with my people. Leanthun will be my proxy here and help the council regain their feet. I want you to read my great-grandfather's books. I want to help you train your spells and skills. I want to help you unlock your Administrator powers so that when Sanerris returns—and he will return—you can put him down so hard that he never gets back up."

A flash of anger gleamed in the old man's eyes at the last.

"I still don't want to leave my friends," Orrin countered. "I appreciate the offer and don't mean to sound ungrateful, but—"

"They are invited as well. My house is isolated, located near the northern ocean and away from the fighting near the border. A wonderful place for the [Hero] to train. Lady Catanzano has taken a very well-researched path for her class. One that I may be able to help her with. At the very least, ask them."

Orrin considered but didn't bring it up right away. Daniel and Madi were still licking their wounds, and he wasn't sure himself. He thought maybe heading back to Dey was the best idea and had not mentioned anything.

"What did he want?" Daniel asked, making it clear he was still pissed at Arandir and all the elves.

"He wants us to go with him to his house to train . . . Mr. Miyagi style." Orrin moved his hands in a circle.

Madi connected a chain of attacks and cleared half the board. "This game is simple. Are you sure you don't want to play Kala? I can teach you."

"Not interested." Daniel made a few more moves before scooping up the fruit and eating it. "You win."

"I'm guessing by you ignoring me, we aren't going?"

Daniel paused and turned to Orrin. "Are you seriously considering it? They just tried to kidnap and kill us."

"Just the bad ones," Orrin argued. "I'm not saying I want to go, but he's super old and knows stuff. Every story has an old wise man who teaches you how to use magic or swing your sword."

Madi grunted as she twisted. The sling they'd put her arm in was bulky. "I want to get home, Orrin. I need to convince my father to send some troops to help push back Odrana. They've played with the political leaders of two major factions in our world, and I know Lord Sanerris isn't going to stop until he captures Daniel. Dey will be the safest place for us."

"Fuck safe, I want to attack Odrana directly." Daniel stood up from his seat and swayed. The healer had told him to take it easy and not make any sudden movements for a few days. Brain injuries weren't an exact science . . . or magic. His concussion would likely linger for a while yet. He sat back down gingerly. "I hate it when the room spins."

"I don't disagree," Orrin said, holding up his hands. "I only mentioned it because you asked, D."

"How many houses does the guy have, anyway?" Daniel grumbled. "I thought this was his place."

"I think this is his city apartment," Orrin teased. "He was inviting us to his beach house."

Daniel went silent as he moved a few cherries back on the board. "Madi, does your world have surfboards?"

Chapter 57

Daniel sulked as they packed.

Packing consisted of throwing everything they wanted to carry on Orrin's bed as he shoveled items into his dimensional space.

As for why the [Hero] was sulking? Surfing did not exist in Asmea. After a brief bout of disappointment, Daniel had been more than excited to try recreating the sport in a new world. Those hopes were dashed when Leanthun overheard them talking and confirmed that the ocean didn't have waves large enough for what Daniel was describing.

Instead, they packed and planned their trip back to Dey. Arandir was disappointed but simply said they would be welcome back anytime. He had convinced Daniel to share his Quest with a few senior warriors. During the investigations, the elves had found out that Gwynnestri had picked some of the weakest members of her forces the first time around. The layers of betrayal were still being discovered.

Orrin waited for the inevitable attack or kidnapping that would pull them back into the war, but as Leanthun waved to them at the edge of the forest, he found himself a bit sad. He'd grown used to the sun flitting between the trees and the slow and peaceful mood of the elven city.

"Should we [Teleport]?" Orrin asked after a few minutes.

"We discussed this," Madi answered. "We can walk for a few hours, then you can get us back home. Better to be safe."

Orrin had grown up in the information age, with the internet at his fingertips. He'd argued that he'd used so many powers in front of so many people that surely any enemies they had could compile a full list of what he could do. Madi's explanation of information brokers, spy networks, and disinformation had boggled his mind. He was surprised to learn that Silas had been working for him and Daniel, spreading false narratives about their skills and spells to better protect them.

As they walked, Daniel and Madi discussed what they wanted to do back in Dey. Daniel wanted to meet up with the Guildmaster again. Madi was trying to get her story straight for her father. She wasn't going to lie to him, but she still had to select which pieces of information to give him while withholding Orrin's Administrator powers and otherworlder status.

Orrin started doing math.

Dey was well over a hundred miles away from their current location. Something that would have taken a few hours in a car was going to take them much longer on foot. The elves hadn't offered horses. The plan to use his [Teleport] spell would cost a lot of mana as well. Even with his buffs, fifty mana per person for every ten miles was going to eat into his mana pool quickly.

Orrin slapped his forehead. He stopped walking and pulled up his status. Specifically, he clicked the [Teleport] spell.

> **[Teleport]—teleport to any known point within 10 miles. 50 MP per person (5,000/5,000)!**
>
> **He selected the exclamation point that he had forgotten about.**
>
> **Would you like to upgrade [Teleport] for 10 AP? Yes or No?**
>
> **Orrin checked the upgrade.**
>
> **[Teleport] Level 2—teleport to any known point within 50 miles. 25 MP per person (0/10,000)**

Orrin currently had twenty-six ability points. He double-checked the rest of his skills. [Heal Small Wounds] was getting close, as was [Increase Will]. He used [Increase Will] more than any of his other buffs, usually keeping himself topped off throughout the day.

I should try to do that with all my buffs. Faster leveling.

Orrin pulled the trigger and spent the points.

Madi glanced back at him. "What are you grinning like an idiot about?"

Madi, Daniel, and Orrin landed in the square a few yards from the Catanzano household. Orrin noted that the guards leveled their weapons a little quicker than they might have a few months ago. Silas had instituted a lot of changes after Daniel had been kidnapped on his front steps.

Speak of the devil. Orrin grimaced as Madi's dad wheeled himself out the front door before they could sneak inside.

"Madeleine Catanzano." Silas's voice echoed down the streets with the volume only a parent could project. "Where. Have. You. Been?"

"Hello, Father." Madi dashed forward and ducked behind him. She grabbed the handles of his wheelchair and turned him quickly. "Let's discuss this in your study. Orrin, can you drop my stuff in my room? Thanks."

Silas sputtered as his once-obedient daughter ignored his complaints. She manhandled him back into the house while his own guards watched helplessly.

Daniel waited for the door to shut before he started to laugh.

"We've been a bad influence on her, haven't we?" Orrin chuckled.

"Our little Madi is growing up. Did you see Silas's face?"

Daniel accompanied Orrin to Madi's room, dropping off her spare clothes and the few knickknacks she'd brought. They were still sharing a room at the Catanzanos' house and found all their things where they'd left them.

Daniel jumped on his bed and stretched. "It's good to be back."

Orrin pushed stuff off his bed and fell facedown.

A comfortable silence settled as the constant stress of the last few weeks dissolved. Orrin thought back to the dungeon they'd defeated, the new Administrator powers and information he'd learned about, the elven forest and second dungeon, and the still-ongoing war between Odrana and the elves. Everything was behind them. No need to get out of bed for days. He could drift off to sleep and ignore the world for a bit.

"We should tell Madi about the other Quest."

Orrin groaned into his pillow. Something bounced off his back.

"Turn over and listen. I think she's earned it, don't you?"

Orrin grabbed a sheet and pulled it over his head.

"Don't be a dick. If you have a reason we shouldn't tell her about the Demon Lord, let me know. You're the one who has a better idea of what we're going to be facing."

Orrin finally turned on his side. "Why do you still think that? Have I been able to predict anything that's happened? I'm hanging on by my fingernails here, too, man."

Daniel threw his feet off the side of the bed and sat up. "O. I think it's time we go all in and trust her. She knows all about your weird powers, and nobody is here breaking down the door to steal you away."

He knew Daniel was right, but sometimes his stubbornness flared for no reason. "She's going to punch me."

Daniel threw his head back and laughed. "That's what you're afraid of?"

"She might try to stab me?"

Daniel laughed harder. Orrin smiled a bit and sighed. He put his face back in his pillow and mumbled something.

"What did you say?"

"Mur ma mad."

"Did you say, 'Go ahead'?"

Orrin held up a thumb but didn't move his face. The pillow was nice. The bed was warm. He was sleepy.

For all his bluster, Daniel was also too scared to tell Madi about the Demon Lord Quest by himself. He shook Orrin awake when she came by after talking with her dad.

"I told him the highlights and hinted that Arandir was going to open some new trade routes with our house. That old shit better after all we did for him." Madi pulled a chair away from the wall and sat. "Do you still want to go talk with Guildmaster Pritus? I'm sure she's gotten a full report on us by now."

Orrin eyed her, looking for her spear.

"Why are you looking at me like that?"

Daniel was sitting on his bed while Orrin was still stuck under a sheet. He realized his predicament and hurriedly began to untangle himself.

"We've agreed to tell you something, Madi," Daniel started. Her eyes flashed, and Orrin fell off the side of the bed. "For fuck's sake, Orrin."

"If you two have another secret, so help me . . ."

"Daniel has a Quest to defeat a Demon Lord," Orrin nearly shouted from the floor. "His secret. Not mine."

"Traitor." Daniel hopped back over his bed, waiting for the incoming attack.

But Madi didn't swing at them. Instead, she turned from one boy to the other, a lost look on her face. "That's not possible. You're not serious. Tell me that's a joke." Her voice got higher with each sentence.

Daniel moved his hand and flicked toward her. Orrin knew he'd just shared the Quest.

After a minute of silence, Orrin crawled over his bed and reached toward her. "Madi, are you okay?"

"It's just a Quest," Daniel added. He kept his distance, though. "We've completed almost all of the ones we originally got." He paused, then said, "Well, except for the war one, but that doesn't count."

"Why doesn't that count?" Orrin risked a glance at Daniel.

"How are we supposed to stop a war? That's not fair."

"We have to warn the lords," Madi whispered. "I thought it wasn't even possible for a . . . This changes everything."

Orrin and Daniel exchanged a quick look.

"What do you mean?"

The scared look in her eyes told Orrin more than her words. He'd seen her stare down Arandir and fight monstrous beasts without breaking a sweat. She was terrified.

"The Quest says the Demon Lord has already assembled his armies. We have to defeat him before he moves through the Pass and attacks. That's our only chance."

Daniel finally stepped around and moved within striking range. "What are you talking about? There isn't a timer on this Quest. We can find out where the southern lands are and go defeat him once we level some more. He's not going to come to Dey."

Madi read the Quest language. "'The dark armies have been assembled. Seek out and defeat the Demon Lord before the Dark Horde attacks.' Do you know what that means? A Demon Lord is going to attack Dey. A Dark Horde is what we call it when a bunch of demons attack all at once. There hasn't been a Demon Lord in over a thousand years."

Daniel's brow creased with worry. "How many demons are you talking about?"

"Hundreds, if not thousands."

Dey had struggled against two demons during the last Horde attack. If it hadn't been for Orrin and his [Utility Ward] buffs on the entire Dragoon team, the second demon might have escaped anyway. Orrin tried to imagine the people of Dey dealing with hundreds of the same.

"They wouldn't all be the same level as the Fogbinder, would they?"

Madi shook her head. "I doubt it, but every demon who gets through the Pass has every incentive to kill as many people as it can. They get experience from killing us. It would be a bloodbath." She shuddered. "That's not even the part that scares me. A Demon Lord is supposed to be just as powerful as a [Hero], guys. We have to tell someone so we can get more scouts into the Pass. Odrana and Veskar need to be warned so we can put together some sort of stand against them."

Orrin was confused about one thing. "Madi, there were Demon Lords in the past, right?"

"Yes," Madi responded, but he could tell her thoughts were running away, chasing every plan they could implement.

"Why is Dey still here, then? It should have been destroyed the last time a Demon Lord rose up."

"Questions like that and I never figured out you weren't from here. What is wrong with me?" She shook her head. "A [Hero] always went through the Pass and defeated the Demon Lord before they got that far. You got this Quest when you arrived, didn't you? Whoever the Demon Lord is has had this entire time to move and get ready. They'll know you're coming, and we've been spending time doing nothing important."

She stood and started pacing.

"Even if we could get an expedition together and send Daniel through the Pass, he wouldn't survive at his level. What we should do is—"

Orrin stopped listening and pulled up the Quest.

> **Defeat the Demon Lord—In the southern lands, the Demon Lord has risen. The dark armies have been assembled. Seek out and defeat the Demon Lord before the Dark Horde attacks.**
> **Reward: 1,000,000 XP and Dark Essence Unlocked**

"Madi, when do the dark armies become a Horde?"

"What?"

Daniel put his hand on Madi's shoulder. "Orrin's using his teacher's voice. I've found it best to just answer. He's trying to figure something out."

She pushed his hand away and answered, "I don't know for sure, but we never call a group of monsters a Horde until they enter the Pass. Maybe then?"

Orrin nodded. "If what she says is right, we have to get to the far side of the Pass and defeat the Demon Lord before his armies enter it."

"That would be suicide," Madi argued. "We wouldn't survive the Pass at our level."

Daniel cracked his knuckles and grabbed Gertrude from his bedside. "Then we better power up."

Chapter 58

Silas fumed in his office. His daughter, Madeleine, was going to send him to an early grave.

He tapped a pen against the mostly blank piece of paper in front of him, thinking. *Lay the problems out one by one and solve them in order.* That was the way he operated. He took a breath.

First, his only remaining family member—his own daughter—had left the city and his protection to play adventurer with the [Hero] Daniel. Silas knew without a doubt that Guildmaster Pritus had engineered that on purpose. Silas could respect her moves while still retaining the desire to tear out her throat. She had used Madi, even if his daughter couldn't see it now. The Guild had long requested the rights to destroy dungeons around the countryside. Those rights belonged to the lords of Dey and had since the first dungeon had been found. By having the daughter of a lord of Dey defeat a dungeon at the Guild's request, Pritus had appropriated those rights in the eyes of the people. Silas had been too busy dealing with the aftermath of everything else to see what was going on until it was too late. The Guild had relinquished the rights back to the lords, but it set a precedent. If the Guild found a dungeon before his own guard did, they would report they had taken care of the danger to Dey. It had been done before, so it shouldn't be a problem the next time.

An annoyance for sure, but one that would only cost the lords some small concessions. The Guild was usually contracted to defeat newly appeared dungeons in any case. He could set up a standard price that the Guild had to pay for lost training opportunities.

Perhaps a quiet deal with Pritus to split new dungeons between the Guild and his guard. Guildmasters didn't last forever, and he could tighten the restrictions with each new appointee.

Silas pushed away the letter he was writing and grabbed up another. He'd already signed it but considered whether he should tear it in two. Madi had drafted it for him, a small contract offer for the elven council. The terms were quite good, and if it had been the only item his daughter had returned with from the forest, he wouldn't have given it a second thought beyond congratulating her on a job well done.

Except it was addressed to Arandir, the elder of elders. Any person of power in Asmea knew the authority behind the elven council. He thought he'd completed Madi's education in whom to avoid in the world at large. This was the second problem his daughter had brought to him when she ran off to the elven forest to meddle in political maneuvers he would be hesitant to try himself.

Opening a line of dialogue with Arandir would benefit Dey in the short run, most likely even for Silas's entire life. A true lord of Dey didn't consider just his own interests, though. The elf was trouble, and at some point, he would ask for more and more to keep the lucrative trading open. Silas brought the issue up with Tarris and Timpe. Both thought more with their purses than their minds. The signed letter of intent was proof of that.

Either of these problems alone would have created a nightmare of issues to deal with in the coming months. Arandir would have to wait for his contract.

Silas pulled the sheet of paper back in front of him and tried to write the sentence again.

Upon my honor, with indisputable and actionable evidence, I have learned that a Demon Lord . . .

Silas sighed and rubbed his eyes. The next year was going to be difficult.

"How did he take it?" Orrin asked. He'd stayed behind while Madi and Daniel approached Silas.

"He made Daniel share the Quest with him," Madi answered, throwing herself on Daniel's bed. She sniffed the air. "Daniel, when's the last time you had the maids change your sheets?"

"That's Orrin, not my bed." Daniel pushed her feet to the side and sat down on the foot of the bed. "Have you been training?"

Orrin nodded. He'd gone to the courtyard and practiced some [Way of the Water] stances. A few guards chuckled at the strange movements, but he just ignored them, moving through the different katas. "I couldn't sit still while you were talking with him. What's the plan?"

Daniel shrugged. "We train. Silas is going to pressure the other lords into getting me more dungeon time. They're going to see if Dragoon team will train me up a bit, too. Supposedly, what Leanthun said about stats applies to skills as well."

"What do you mean?"

Daniel scratched the back of his head. "I . . . Well, the way he . . . I think . . ."

Madi rolled around so she was sitting next to Daniel, the two of them across from Orrin. She sighed as she explained, "If Daniel just gets his skills from Quest rewards and doesn't put in the work, he isn't using the skill to its full potential. My father is going to have a few teachers out to help put Daniel through the paces and iron out any rough edges."

"That'll be good for him. He thrives when he's being pushed."

Madi and Daniel gave him a look.

"What? It's true. He gets lazy unless someone taunts him or tells him he's doing it wrong."

Madi's incredulous look turned thoughtful. Daniel snapped his fingers in front of her. "Hey! Stop that. Don't agree with him."

"He does have a point . . ." Madi trailed off softly. "Anyway, I will be helping him prepare for an assault. We're putting together a full battalion to try and clear the Pass."

"Is that even possible?" Orrin smiled at Daniel's betrayed look. "When do we leave?"

Madi exchanged a look with Daniel. Orrin got a worried feeling in the pit of his stomach.

"Madi? Daniel?"

"Hear us out before you bite our heads off, okay?" Daniel shifted on the bed.

"It's not set in stone, either," Madi hurried to add. "So, if you are totally against it, we'll find another way."

Orrin sat silently.

"My father believes—"

"Pass."

"Shut up, dude. He wants to make you, like, an ambassador or something."

Orrin frowned. "What?"

Madi smirked. "Orrin, you upgraded your [Teleport], didn't you? You can get to the elves and back in the same hour. You are on a first-name basis with Arandir. The lords of Dey—all three of them, not just my father—have offered you the post of delegate of Dey. You can help us recruit them. A battalion of our guards and Guild members is only three hundred people. Most of those won't be at a much higher level than we are. If we can get Arandir to send even a dozen elves, we'll stand a better chance at succeeding."

"You still haven't told me what the plan is," Orrin grumped. "I'm not going to be a glorified messenger."

"Can you stop being impatient and let me talk?" Madi shot back. "On the far side of the Pass, there is a small outpost. It was never more than a place for scouts to spend the night, but it's stood for centuries. We are going to try and expand the outpost into a full Wall. If we are successful, then any Horde that attacks would have to push through that Wall before going through the Pass."

Orrin considered the strategy. It wasn't half bad. They wouldn't need to defend the new Wall to the last man and could always retreat through the Pass if they were overrun. But . . .

"How long would that take? Building something like the Wall must have taken years. From what you said, we don't have that kind of time."

Madi rolled her eyes. "We have [Stonemasons] and [Builders] who can have it up in a day or two. The main point of bringing an entire battalion is to protect them while they work. We can't afford three hundred people to watch the Wall once it's built. We would have to create entire supply chains, people wouldn't be near family, and the logistics of it just wouldn't work. The new Wall would funnel the majority of any attacking force through the gate system, giving us time to prepare."

"Why not build a bunch of Walls and defend each one in a fall-back pattern? Don't fight to protect the Wall but take as many out from the top as you can until you are forced to retreat to the next one. All the way back to Dey."

Madi rubbed her eyes. "Daniel suggested something similar. What was it you said? Draw them in and blow them up?"

"I said we should build a few Walls and line some with explosives. When they get through, we blow it up."

Orrin grunted in appreciation. "Not a bad idea, D. If we—"

"We don't have the time or resources to do that. Getting one Wall built is going to cost a fortune. Those people we will have to draft to put up the Wall will need to get back to work. They don't have unlimited mana or stamina to build Wall after Wall. Even if we could get it done, the city would see it as a failure if we simply destroy it as we retreat."

Orrin forgot sometimes that this world operated with a different set of values. They sent groups of five into dungeons without a healing class because each person wanted as much glory and experience as they could get. High-level adventurers went on suicide missions for the chance they'd be talked about as heroes after the fact.

"Silas promised to bring it up, but they're still down one ruler," Daniel added. "But if we could get a few elven archers on the Wall, we could hold them off longer. Maybe Arandir could grow a few trees together into a mini wall or something."

Orrin hated the idea of leaving his friends, even for a day or two. "Why me? There must be other people with [Teleport] who could do it. Sure, I know Arandir, but that's not enough reason to make me deliver letters."

Madi shook her head. "You wouldn't be just delivering letters. You would be the voice of Dey in the forest, in Veskar . . . and in Odrana."

Orrin stood and walked to an end table holding a pitcher of water. He could have pulled a waterskin from his [Dimension Hole], but he needed to walk away from what he'd just heard.

"Orrin," Madi said quietly. She had moved up behind him without his noticing. "We are not sending you away to protect you or because we don't want you around. You really are the best person for the job. Talk with Arandir. Get him to send a letter to Sanerris. A Demon Lord means the end of the war if Sanerris has any sense. You'll be completing the Quest."

Orrin doubted that very much. Lord Sanerris had had the glint of crazy in his eyes that spoke of a spoiled upbringing and getting away with whatever he wanted. Orrin was under no delusion the man would remain dangerous no matter the circumstances.

"It's not like you'll be gone all the time," Daniel chimed in, standing up as well. "You need to get back here and train with me. I need my sparring dummy."

"I haven't agreed to this," Orrin retorted.

Madi laid her hand on his arm. "Take the day off and rest. Or go explore the city a little. My father won't have finished getting things settled until tomorrow, anyway."

Daniel leaned in as if to say something more, but Madi gripped his sleeve and dragged him out. Orrin's fingers trembled around the pitcher handle. His mouth was dry, but no matter how hard he tried, he couldn't lift the glass to pour.

You're not being left behind, he chanted over and over. *They are not leaving you behind.*

Chapter 59

Small waves crashed against Orrin's feet as he gazed at the horizon. Arandir's retreat was half a mile beyond the tree line, but the elf spent much of his free time at the rocky beach. The older elf stood by Orrin's side, content to wait patiently.

When Orrin had made his first trip as an official delegate of Dey two weeks ago, Arandir had been delighted. Although he was still dealing with the war with Odrana, the fallout from half the council turning out to be traitors, and the surprise announcement from the lords of Dey that a Demon Lord had risen, Arandir had left the main city and brought Orrin to his home. Leanthun was put in charge in his name.

Orrin could not think of Arandir's home as anything but a tree house, no matter how beautiful it was. Despite its small size, it had windows and balconies to spare. Orrin half wondered if the house had been built as an excuse to simply watch the surroundings and escape to the ocean. Not that he minded it at all. His trips to Arandir's home were a welcome respite.

Although Orrin had fought against it, Silas convinced him that he was the best person for the job. Arandir and Silas had negotiated various small trifles over the last week, with Orrin's ability to jump from city to city making the normal back-and-forth negotiations seem laughably slow. Silas had recently offered to double the stipend the delegate job was paying him due to the progress they'd made.

Silas had even let Orrin train with the teachers brought in for Madi and Daniel. He seemed to have accepted that his daughter was going to be an adventurer, so he'd hired the best he could find. Madi and Daniel spent their days drilling with weapons and their nights doing magical theory homework. There was even a history teacher for Daniel so that he would understand more about Asmea. Orrin had been able to do some weapon training, but the [Swordmaster] tried to kick him out after he kept dodging the attacks. [Way of the Water] simply wouldn't let him parry when he could duck.

The lord of Dey also had spotters out, looking for any high-experience, low-threat monsters for him, Madi, and Daniel to kill. They'd only gone on two outings, but Orrin was so close to leveling he could taste it. Another thousand points and he'd be at level eighteen.

"Orrin, did you hear my question?"

Orrin snapped his attention from the sea, giving a guilty smirk to Arandir. "Sorry. What did you ask?"

The elf kicked the water and smiled gently at Orrin. "How much more time do you believe Lord Catanzano will waste?"

Orrin turned his mind back over the conversation they'd been having. The latest missive had been about sending elven archers to train the guards.

"I think he doesn't want to ask for too much from you. You are still at war and have to protect your people."

The war with Odrana was a technicality at this point. Silas hadn't wasted time and sent runners to both Lord Sanerris of Odrana and the current various leaders of Veskar telling them of the Demon Lord. He was attempting to rally as many of the nations and people of Asmea as he could. Orrin would call it fear-mongering, but since he had the Quest from the system to defeat the Demon Lord, he wasn't going to decline any help they could get.

Odrana hadn't attacked the forest since that time. A few soldiers, not even a hundred, had been left to guard the elven forest, but the majority of Odrana's forces had been recalled. Silas hadn't told Orrin or Daniel what was going on with Sanerris yet. The fact that the Stop the War Quest hadn't been completed was enough for Orrin to guess that the leader of Odrana wasn't giving up just yet.

Arandir knelt and picked up a few small shells. He handed half to Orrin before he chucked one into the distance. "There will not be anyone left if the Demon Lord is coming for us . . ."

Orrin knelt as well and felt the water, resting his palm against the surface. Still in a squat, he twisted his body and launched his own shell, skipping it across the small waves until it launched high. *Almost as far as he got it.*

Arandir laughed. He laughed more out here by the sea than he had in the city. "Did your skill do that or did you?"

"Didn't you say that a skill is just a manifestation of your potential?" Orrin countered.

"I might have. I do occasionally say something wise."

The other benefit of the new job was that Arandir was teaching him. There wasn't a curriculum or even a linear set of topics. They'd converse for a few hours while Orrin's mana refilled for his jumps back to Dey, discussing spells, stats, and skills. Orrin didn't divulge any more specifics, but Arandir had an uncanny way of steering a conversation toward ground that bore fruit for Orrin.

"The [Swordmaster] that Sila—Lord Catanzano hired for Daniel doesn't want to train me. He despises my fighting style. Your suggestion that I should train in water gave me a little insight, though."

"You used a fighting skill to throw a shell?"

When Orrin had activated his fighting skill while wet, the movements of each form had seemed clear and easy to follow. Once Orrin activated the training room, Styx's teachings had felt second nature. He'd breezed through the last two sessions but hadn't tried for the fifth. The normal "Continue or save progress" bar had been replaced. Orrin checked his status.

> **[Way of the Water]: 20% 4/20 completed. Test your progress and unlock the first gate?**
> **Warning: Failure three (3) times will result in all progress being lost.**

He hadn't found anything about his skill in the books of Dey, but Arandir noted that his fighting style seemed to be related to water. He told Orrin about elven monks from before the Calamity who had trained their bodies under waterfalls, moving through their stances with the water crashing down all around. Orrin did the same—not in a waterfall, but while standing in a shower.

He stood up from his crouch. "I understand the water a little bit better if I focus with it. But honestly, the waves aren't that big, and I've skipped stones before."

Arandir sorted the remaining shells, dropping all but one, which he held in the palm of his hand. "Lord Catanzano can have ten elven archers to train his guards. We will not supply any bows."

He raised the hand that wasn't holding the shell and pointed his palm toward the horizon. "Tell me, Orrin. How far do you believe this shell will travel?"

Two weeks ago, Orrin would have guessed. He'd tried the first few times that Arandir had posed these types of questions.

Arandir's magic was based on life concepts. In the dungeon, he had simply reversed the life of monsters, making them explode from the inside. He could manipulate the internal workings of monsters but also was a sort of healer by profession. He'd told Orrin that every magic had two sides, even if you couldn't find it right away. Fire could destroy a forest but cauterize a wound. Orrin thought of firefighters creating backfires to stop the spread of a wildfire. Literally fighting fire with fire. The examples were endless.

That type of magic wasn't good for something like throwing a shell far, and the old Orrin would have simply guessed the shell would land approximately where the last one had. He'd learned his lesson, though.

"That depends." Orrin answered with Arandir's favorite response to nearly any question. "Tell me more."

Arandir laughed again, and Orrin noticed a dozen small minnows swimming closer as he did. The magic within the elf drew life to him.

"What would you like to know?"

Orrin had been playing these games for weeks. Arandir was trying to get to a point, but the conversation had been taking a few turns today. "Are you going to throw it with or without magic?"

"You are asking the wrong question."

Orrin frowned for a minute and then smiled. "Do you mean how far would it travel if you throw it or how far will it travel with the tide and movement of the ocean?"

Arandir nodded and held the shell up between his fingers. "If I dropped this shell here or threw it, the waters would move it by nightfall and your answer would be incorrect."

Orrin let out a groan, dramatic enough that Arandir knew it was fake. "You're saying the question has no right answer?"

"Remember what I told you. When someone asks you a question, they also give you a glimpse into themselves. Why would I ask you this question?"

Orrin shrugged. "To confuse me? I'm not sure."

Arandir was quiet. Orrin checked his status and saw his mana was nearly full. He could make it back to Dey and meet up with Amir for some afternoon coffee.

"I asked the question so you would know there are times when no answer is correct," Arandir said softly, breaking Orrin from his daydream of hot java. "Lord Catanzano tiptoes around the question he wants to ask: Will the elves go to war and fight the invasion in the Pass with the humans who have ostracized us for centuries?"

Orrin wasn't stupid. He'd heard the nervous talk of the guards around the Catanzano house. He knew how stressed Silas appeared each day and how hard Daniel and Madi were training. The fact that Odrana hadn't attacked the forest in weeks meant even Lord Sanerris was worried about the impending Demon Lord attack—to some extent. At first, he'd been sure that everyone would travel to Dey and put up a united front against the attacking demons. Two weeks later and Odrana wasn't responding to missives. A third of the leaders of Veskar had sent money—a pittance—to help with the effort, the second third had demanded proof, and the last third hadn't responded at all.

He tried to put himself in Arandir's shoes. The entire world had stood back and watched as Odrana attacked the elves. The elves who had been corralled into this forest and were routinely snatched up as slaves. "I'm not sure I'd be able to do it."

Arandir's brow furrowed. "Do what?"

"Forgive all the humans and fight with them," Orrin said, taking his remaining shells and dropping them at his feet. "I'm pretty sure I'm not supposed to say this, but I don't think it would change your mind. Silas . . . I mean, Lord Catanzano, wants a dozen elves to help defend the Wall. That's what I've heard. I don't think anybody in Dey expects you guys to leave your forest and fight. From what I've seen, even your weakest warriors could take out a hundred of our recruits. We have bakers training with spears and florists practicing with bows. They'll have a few months if we're unlucky, maybe a year if our luck holds out."

Orrin waded to the shore and sat down on a rock they'd sat and chatted on before. He needed his feet to dry before he put his socks and shoes back on. Arandir stayed in the water.

Once his mana was topped off and his shoes were back on his feet, Orrin waved to the old elf. "I'm heading back. I'll meet you here again tomorrow, all right?"

"Orrin, wait a moment." Arandir made his way out of the water, dropping his robes as he finally cleared the waves. "I want to send my own request to the lords of Dey."

"Do you have a letter?" Orrin glanced around but saw nothing. Everything was usually conveyed through letters. "If it's important, I don't want to mess up the wording or something."

Arandir shook his head. "I don't think you will forget it. I want to request lodgings for a thousand elves be made available on the northern outer Wall."

It took a minute for Orrin to realize what he meant. "You're going fight with us?"

The elder held up a finger. "On one condition. You have told me that you still have not spent any of the administrator points. Is this still true?"

Orrin felt the noose tighten. "Yes . . ."

"I want you to tell me everything about the available Administrator abilities, and I want your promise that you will consider rebuilding the Administrators if you can."

Chapter 60

Orrin thought over the offer. He'd tried to discuss his Administrator powers with Daniel and Madi over the past few weeks, but they'd both individually told him to wait.

"We can research more when we have the time, O," Daniel had said, covered in sweat. Orrin had only been able to talk with him between melee practice bouts. "Everyone is a bit focused on getting ready for the Demon Lord, in case you haven't noticed."

Silas had told him getting in Arandir's good graces was of paramount importance in his position as a delegate. The lords of Dey needed elven archers for training. Raining arrows from the Wall was the easiest and safest way to thin a Horde, and nobody was better at archery than the elves. He confided in Orrin that they'd scoured the slave pits for elves but found none. Silas's greatest hope was that Arandir would relinquish ten or so archers to train the humans.

The reason was simple once Orrin thought about it for the first time. The normal way of getting a skill like [Archery] or [Bow Proficiency] was using the weapon over and over until you were rewarded by the system. The more you practiced, the higher you could level your skill. Humans could spend a decade shooting arrows and reach the third or fourth level. Elven adventurers didn't leave the forest until they'd reached the fourth level of [Archery], with most being significantly higher. To be trained by someone with such a mastery of the weapon could jump-start the advancement of your own skill.

Arandir was offering a thousand elves. That many bows would save more lives than Orrin could imagine.

"If I said yes, you aren't going to send your sick and elderly, right?" Orrin tried to think of what Madi would ask. "You have to send one thousand elves who can use [Archery] and are willing to train humans. Plus, they have to help defend against any Horde that attacks, including the Demon Lord."

Arandir nodded. "No tricks. We cannot send our best, but nobody under two hundred or over eight hundred will be sent. Every elf will swear to defend Dey until given the order to retreat. I will be up front and tell you that we plan on sending reinforcements no matter your answer, but the number will not be as high. I cannot risk elven lives for nothing."

"If Dey falls, the Demon Lord and his Horde will come after you in time."

Arandir looked past Orrin at the forest behind them. "Our lands have not fallen since we settled here. We may be better protected inside our forest than you would be behind the Walls of Dey."

Orrin tried to act cool and collected. "Who would be in charge? Would your people take orders from Silas . . . I mean, Lord Catanzano?"

Arandir brushed the rock next to Orrin and sat. "I am considering Leanthun as our captain. He would need to be given an equal say among the lords of Dey in the distribution of troops against attacks. From what we have been told, the lords of Dey do not believe the Demon Lord will attack immediately. Therefore, he would have training sessions for all interested in learning. I do not plan on sending just [Archers], though. I will send those skilled in different weapon paths and magic as well."

He paused, "You may not believe me, but I want to use this as an opportunity to create closer ties with the people of Dey. Perhaps if we can bring our people together, Odrana will be less likely to attack again in the future."

Madi's lessons on diplomacy popped into his mind, letting Orrin read between the lines. If the elves cozied up enough with the people of Dey, they might defend the elves when Odrana came knocking.

Orrin dug the toe of his shoe into the sand, dislodging a shell. Legs spilled out and an angry crab skittered away, hiding behind another dune. A flurry of movement as it worked its arms and the shell was half-buried again.

"I have to run it by Lord Catanzano," he finally answered. "I'm not sure what I'll tell him, but I'll ask."

"He does not know? But his daughter?"

Orrin almost laughed at Arandir's surprised face. "Madi is my friend. I have a history with her dad. He doesn't know about the Administrator stuff."

Arandir didn't respond, content to let Orrin tell him more if he wanted.

He didn't want to get into it.

"I'll try and get back tomorrow with an answer. Do you have those supplies we ordered?"

Arandir let the issue rest and directed Orrin back to his tree house. At the foot was a cart filled with an array of different goods—rolls of cloth, rare foodstuffs, and ingots of metal. A few boxes marked with numbers sat to the side.

"Lord Catanzano has the list of what goes to whom." Arandir pointed. "The rest should arrive by next week."

He paused and watched Orrin push the items into his [Dimension Hole]. "I hope he is paying you well for the shipping. A cart this full would cost multiple gold pieces to transport to Dey and would take over a week's time."

Orrin pushed a box into his pocket, still enjoying the way the large wooden cube shrank to fit. "If it saves a few lives or makes somebody's life a little easier, I'm happy to do it. See you tomorrow."

Arandir waved as Orrin teleported back to Dey.

Silas stared at Orrin.

"Explain it again, and this time don't lie to me."

Orrin sighed. "I'm not lying. Arandir wants to send a thousand elves to help with the Demon Lord invasion and wanted me to ask about accommodations and command structure."

Silas sat behind his desk in his office. Whereas before it had been a chaotic but orderly mess, in the past several days, unopened letters had begun to pile up. Orrin could smell Silas from where he sat . . . not that he was much better.

The lord of Dey wheeled himself out from behind his desk and approached Orrin. He grabbed a paperweight as he moved closer.

"Hold on a minute . . . It's just . . . right . . . there." Silas rolled the stone weight around in his hand before pressing a hidden depression in the rock. "We have five minutes before the [Sound Seal] wears off. What does he really want?"

"What's a [Sound Seal]?"

Silas threw the rock at Orrin, who barely caught it. "Answer me. What. Does. He. Want?"

"He wants some information about my skills," Orrin hedged. "I'm pretty sure he also wants to get on Dey's good side in case Odrana comes back. Has Sanerris responded yet?"

Silas didn't answer, peering at Orrin.

"We did send a letter to Odrana, right?"

Silas blinked and rubbed his eyes. "Yes, we have sent multiple warnings to them. *Lord* Sanerris hasn't responded." He pulled his wheels back, retreating from Orrin a bit. "How . . . What can I offer you to give him what he wants? With a thousand elves . . ."

"I want to stop being a gofer for you," Orrin answered quickly.

"A gofer?"

"You tell me to 'go for' this and that," Orrin explained. "I just want to get back to training with my friends."

Silas waved his hand. "Done. We have others who can [Teleport], even if they can't move as far as you or as quickly. You will have to go back and give Arandir what he wants. Are you willing to share that kind of information? Your class must be unique if he offers so much for it. Maybe you would like to share more details with me? I can offer you much."

Orrin saw that glint that Madi used to get in Silas's eyes. "Madi already knows most of what I can do. I think Arandir wants to know how I boost stats. It would make his borders safer if one in five elves could make all five have maxed-out stats."

Silas nodded. "When you get back, I may have you sit with Lord Tarris. His magic is a bit one-track, but he has a quick mind. Perhaps we could recruit a few people to take your class as well. [Utility Warder], correct?"

Orrin nodded. He felt both a little honored that Silas thought his class should be replicated and jealous that anyone else might get his skill set.

"I'm going to have to go and meet with Tarris and Timpe. They aren't going to like giving an elf this kind of power but . . . a thousand elven troops to help and train. You've done well, Orrin. I'm glad you haven't died. Stay alive and keep my daughter safe, will you?"

Orrin was taken aback by the sincerity in his voice. Silas had always been cold and calculating with him. He tried to remember if he'd ever heard the man compliment his own daughter.

"I'm pretty sure she's the one keeping us out of trouble most of the time," Orrin joked, but Silas didn't smile. "I mean, of course. I wouldn't let anything happen to her. Neither would Daniel."

"Good. Dismissed."

Orrin pumped his fist as he left. It wasn't that he didn't enjoy his visits with Arandir, but he was falling behind. He barely had time to spend visiting his friends around Dey. Tony had stopped by for a few words but knew he wasn't exactly welcome at the Catanzano manor.

Orrin had been heading for his room. Instead, he turned toward the front door. There was another friend he hadn't seen since he was back, and with no direct orders right now, it was time to get a coffee.

Picking his way through the streets was easy by now. He tried not to [Teleport] inside the city too much, as it tended to startle people, and startling people with dangerous magic was a bad idea, as Orrin had learned the hard way. Thankfully his [Ward] was always up nowadays. He made sure to stop by and cast it on Madi and Daniel before leaving the city each morning as well.

The line at Amir's family coffee shop was out the door. That wasn't saying much, as the small interior had enough room for only a few people to wait, but it was nice to see his friend's family business was doing well. About twenty people waited in line, and more joined as Orrin crept closer to the building's entrance.

"Orrin!"

Orrin had barely made it through the door when a body came flying around the counter to grab him in a hug.

"Hey, Amir. How are you doing?"

"Amir, we have customers. Get back to the coffee. Welcome, Orrin. Black with no cream, correct?" Amir's father was also behind the counter in the small alcove, twisting knobs and pouring bags of coffee beans into the weird contraption.

"Sorry, Father." Amir squeezed Orrin's arm and moved back to his station. "You must stay and tell me how you have been. Where you have been." His words were not a request but a demand. Orrin smiled.

"Black would be perfect," Orrin answered his friend's dad. "How long until Amir can have a break?"

"Ten . . . twenty minutes. Unless you want to help, then ten minutes and your coffee is on the roof."

"On the house, Father."

"That is what I said." He shook a finger at his son. "Orrin, can you pour the beans into this hopper? It must be kept at this point or the coffee runs watery."

Orrin rubbed his hands in anticipation. The work was demanding but not outrageously so. Amir moved cups through a progression of different spigots while his father checked gauges and pulled handles. Knobs were twisted and steam whistled. The entire time, Orrin had to run from one side of the shop to the other, pouring dried beans into the small container that ate the poured beans and spat out wet slop underneath.

"I can take over for now. Amir, you have five minutes."

"Orrin has just returned; I need at least twenty minutes."

"You may have ten."

Orrin turned away to hide his smirk at the bickering. He took his mug of coffee and sat against the wall outside. All the tables were full.

"You two are doing well," he commented when Amir walked out. He accepted one of the cookie sticks Amir offered.

"Business has been good recently," Amir said with a strange twinge in his voice.

"That's a good thing, right?"

Amir shrugged. "Father is happy."

Orrin dunked his cookie in the coffee, waiting for it to get soggy enough to bite. "What are you not telling me?"

Amir sighed. "I've officially been relieved of my position at the Hospital and my class."

Orrin scanned Amir.

Amir Fallah
Brewer
Level 4

"Dude, that sucks. Do you want me to put in a word with Sil—Lord Catanzano? Maybe we can get you back in."

Amir shook his head. "It wouldn't matter. Even if he threatened them, I would be an outcast still. I will find another way to be a healer."

Orrin chewed on his cookie and sipped the delicious nectar his friend had made him. "Give me a few days. Maybe I can do something about that."

Chapter 61

The next day, Orrin sat in one of Arandir's comfy armchairs explaining the different names of Administrator skills to an increasingly agitated elf.

"You are sure? None of the skills has a description?" Arandir paced as Orrin lounged. "The system does not obfuscate. It wants us to have the information needed to succeed in our selected path. There is not any reason for it . . ."

Orrin tuned out Arandir's rambling. He had already read the full list of Administrator powers to the elder. He hadn't told the man about the cost of each skill, but that was mostly because Arandir was more upset that there was no description of what anything did.

- **Assign Class (5 Administrator Points)**
- **Reset Class (5 Administrator Points)**
- **Assign Quest (10 Administrator Points)**
    - **Edit Reward (10 Administrator Points)**
- **Unlock Ability: Skill (10 Administrator Points)**
- **Unlock Ability: Spell (10 Administrator Points)**
- **Edit Stats (Sanctioned) (10 Administrator Points)**
    - **Remove**
    - **Assign**
- **Edit Stats (Sanctioned) (10 Administrator Points)**
    - **Full Reset**
- **Edit Stats (Unsanctioned) (10 Administrator Points)**
    - **Remove**

- Assign
- Edit Stats (Unsanctioned) (10 Administrator Points)
  - Full Reset
- Imbue (50 Administrator Points)
- Scry (20 Administrator Points)
- Change Race (15 Administrator Points)
- Create Relic (30 Administrator Points)

"Orrin, we will simply have to unlock every skill. I will have my scouts search for dungeons. While I believe that Assign Class is unlikely to be the skill that helps us, there is a small chance. Or perhaps Assign Quest or Edit Reward would allow you to create more Administrators . . . I am going in circles."

Despite Arandir's words, the elf was more animated than Orrin had ever seen him. The hope of fulfilling his family's greatest wish, restoring Administrators to the world, coupled with his enthusiasm at the new puzzle in his life was the greatest gift Arandir had ever received. He was acting like a child on Christmas morning with so many presents to open he was frozen still.

"I was sort of hoping to use some of my points on Assign Class," Orrin interrupted his constant stream-of-consciousness talking. "I have a friend who wants to be a [Healer], but the Hospital has kicked him out."

Arandir frowned. "What did he do to deserve that? I would not suggest going against them if they had cause."

Orrin felt his temper rise a bit as he thought of the unjust treatment of his friend Amir. "When I first met him, he was passed out from disobeying orders and trying to heal more people than allowed. He was bullied by other healer wannabes for no reason. He's a good person and a friend but didn't want to play the games the Hospital plays. You know, technically, I think the Hospital would try to have me arrested. I healed a bunch of people during a demon attack a few months ago while all their *healers* stood around watching people die. I know nothing about being a healer—I just have [Heal Small Wounds], which has come in handy a bunch of times—but my friend has studied his entire life to be able to help people. So, no. I don't think he did anything to deserve it. If I can help him, I want to do it."

Arandir's frown grew as Orrin spoke, revving him up more.

"Also, stop talking about me like I'm some sort of experiment. I agreed to tell you the skills, but I never said you could pick what I end up spending my points on."

The older elf pulled a chair up to Orrin and sat, reaching out his arm. Orrin hesitated before clasping the man's hand.

"Orrin, forgive my words if they offended you. Our Hospital would never allow those sorts of things to happen. Our [Healers] view their powers as a gift for all." Arandir spoke softly. "Whatever path you decide to take is your own. I will make suggestions and perhaps at times beg you to consider my words, but only you can make your own choices. If you want to take Assign Class and help your friend, do it. I will send for a friend who knows the different healing classes so that you can help him."

Orrin felt his face go red as Arandir spoke calmly, making him feel like he'd thrown a tantrum. "I'd appreciate that. I don't want to give him a class that gets him in trouble somehow."

Arandir laughed. "Somehow, I think that is exactly what would happen if I let you stumble your way through this alone." He paused. "Go ahead, then."

Orrin smirked and selected his first Administrator skill.

> **Unlock the Administrator Skill: Assign Class for 5 Administrator Points?**
> **Yes or No?**

Yes.

Orrin caught Arandir's eye for a moment as a well of power rose up inside him. He couldn't figure out why the elf was bending sideways and moving so fast.

"Fuck," Orrin was able to mumble as he passed out and slid off the chair.

". . . wrong with him?"

"Arandir, if you don't back off, I'm going to put you in a coma," a stern female voice said close to Orrin's face. "You drag me up here without any explanation and force me to examine a random human child who is sleeping on your floor. I appreciate your vote, but if this is the kind of treatment I'm going to get from you, I'll gladly resign as elder."

"Lyra, please."

"He appears to be in completely ordinary health for a human. Perhaps he is faking his sleep to avoid more of your stories."

Orrin could hear the voices but focused instead on his body. When he'd used the administrator points for the first time, he'd felt something inside burst. Warmth spread to each fingertip and toe just before he passed out. Now every last part of his body tingled.

He felt like he had the day he and Daniel had discovered energy drinks for the first time. They'd smuggled a case into Daniel's room during a long weekend, playing video games and drinking can after can. They'd made it over twenty-four hours before the first signs that this was a bad idea had shown their faces. The crash had been the worst part, with the tingling of his extremities making Orrin promise to never drink another drop of the stuff. Until he'd found coffee, that was.

He clenched his fingers.

"See? He's moving. One hundred percent alive and well. I'll be off, then. Leanthun lied to me about the paperwork. If I end up a bureaucrat because of you, Arandir . . ."

Orrin opened his eyes. The voice that was threatening Arandir belonged to a rather pretty and very short elven woman. She was leaning over him and used two fingers to pull his eye open more. Even while she threatened to leave, she was performing a full exam on Orrin, poking and prodding him until he finally spoke.

"I'm fine." His voice came out in a croak. He swallowed twice. "I'm fine. You can take your hand out of my shirt, thank you."

She ignored him and pushed her hands up to his chest. Orrin felt a gentle vibration from her palms. "His lungs are clear. No problems with the heart that I can detect."

"Arandir?" Orrin glanced up at the man. His hand was covering his mouth, but Orrin couldn't tell if he was worried or amused.

"Orrin, this is Lyra, the newest elder of healing. Lyra, this is Orrin, friend to the [Hero] and delegate of the lords of Dey."

Orrin glared. Arandir was definitely amused.

"What made you pass out, Orrin?" Lyra moved her hands south. "Are you ill, or was I correct in my assessment that Arandir was boring you to death?"

Orrin slapped her hands away and crawled backward, climbing onto the couch. He sat with as much dignity as he could with his shirt half undone. "I— I'm better now. Thank you, I guess."

"Better manners than most of the humans, I suppose." Lyra slapped her knees as she stood. "Arandir. Never a pleasure, but you keep it interesting."

"Before you leave, Lyra—" Arandir moved in front of her. "Orrin has a passing interest in healing. If you could—"

"Ary, I'm not a teacher. I'm not wasting my time answering questions from a child. Find a novice trainee from the Hospital to satisfy his questions. Now, if you'll excuse me?"

Arandir did not excuse her. He stayed planted in her path. "Lyra . . ."

"Arandir . . ."

Orrin couldn't help it. He laughed. They both turned on him with their hawkish eyes. Arandir's blue and Lyra's green stopping the laughter in his throat.

Orrin held up his hands. "Sorry. Sorry. I just haven't seen anyone stand up to Arandir since I met him. It's good to see him told off a bit."

Arandir continued to glower, but Lyra held out her hand to shake. "It's my pleasure. Someone has to keep him from getting too big a head. He might be in charge but not really. He's still such a child at times. Honestly, trying to tell me what to do."

Orrin shook her hand. He'd met a few different important people who felt they had to meet the Dey delegate. Some had soft hands from working in the government and some had hard-callused hands. Lyra's hands reminded him of his mom's—they were hard from constant work but the way she held his hand was soft and kind. These were hands that treated patients and soothed loved ones. The hands of a healer.

"He meant well. I have a friend who wants to be a healer, but the Hospital in Dey isn't what it is here, so I hear." Orrin released her hand. "He's just looking for a few pointers on the best path."

Lyra frowned. "The Hospital in Dey has always been a bit backward, but they usually do well enough with the training. If he can't get through the basics, I'm not sure he'd be able to handle most of the usual healer classes. What exactly are you looking for?"

Orrin explained Amir's situation, watching as Lyra became more agitated. She muttered under her breath, and Orrin distinctly heard "kill them all" more than once.

"They took away his amulet and effectively killed his dream of becoming a real healer," Orrin finished. "He lost his class and is helping run his father's shop. I have [Heal Small Wounds], but I'm not a healer and thought there must—"

"You have [Heal Small Wounds]? How? What is your class?"

Orrin glanced at Arandir, who shrugged. He was still pissed.

"[Utility Warder]. It was available and I thought it would be helpful, so I bought it."

Lyra scoffed. "You just bought it? How many times have you almost killed yourself overdrawing and trying to heal someone?"

Orrin thought back to healing in the square outside the Hospital and the backlash he'd suffered at Tony's after. He relived the moments of healing himself, Daniel, and Madi. All the lives that would have been lost if he hadn't taken this one spell.

"Enough to learn the risk is necessary sometimes. I'm getting better, though," Orrin answered truthfully. "Is there any recommendation you could make for my friend?"

"It's unlikely he'll ever be a healer," Lyra answered bluntly. She stood in front of him with her arms crossed. "As the elder for healing, I'm the head of our Hospital now. I'm only saying what I'm about to tell you because Ary asked, and even if he's a bit uptight, he's an all-right guy. Our trainees use the amulets because it's the safest way to get [Heal Small Wounds]. There are some old records of classes that came preloaded with healing spells, but over the years the best of the best kept their secrets to themselves. They wanted to create demand for their unique skills—a healer who could regrow a limb or one who could make you see again. Slowly, our ancestors lost more and more. The Calamity was the final straw that crushed our profession. Using an amulet until a trainee can purchase [Heal Small Wounds] was all that was left to start the process. Depending on what branch of healing you want to go for, and there are a lot, you can apprentice with someone who knows a few auxiliary spells and skills, but it takes decades to reach a high enough level to evolve the spell into something better. Humans usually take [Heal Moderate Wounds] if they reach that stage. There is a way to get small wounds without the amulet, but your friend would need to treat injuries with potions and bandages for several years."

"What are the classes of the Hospital? Are they all just [Healer]?"

Lyra glanced at Arandir again. "The questions you ask are well protected. We don't give that information out to anyone who asks."

"Tell him, Lyra," Arandir commanded, standing straight and looking regal.

Lyra stuck her tongue out. "After an [Acolyte] passes a certain threshold in training and gets [Heal Small Wounds] on their own, they are promoted to [Healer]. Some people stick with that their entire life, moving from small to moderate wounds, then to [Heal Great Wounds]. Those are the people who make up the rank and file of the Hospital. Mana for health, as the trainees say. There are other paths. Too many to count, really, and we do try. When [Heal Small Wounds] reaches its maximum improvement, a few other skills and spells are unlocked. The most important is [Diagnose], but there are also spells like [Purify], [Calm], or [Excise]. If an [Acolyte] takes moderate wounds, the others disappear. As long as you don't take [Heal Moderate Wounds], more skills and paths open up. We teach our apprentices enough to figure out what they want to do, but some want the easy path. Different classes can evolve with different combinations. [Mind Walker] sounds like a mind mage, but nothing could be further from the truth—they help patients wrestle their traumas into manageable parts of their mind. I've seen raving men calmed to gentleness again by our [Mind Walker]. Others experiment and see what classes they can unlock."

"But it all comes down to having the spell first?"

"That's correct. You have to prove to the system that you want to be a healer. The amulets jump-start that process."

"Where do the amulets come from?" Orrin asked. He noticed both Arandir and Lyra tighten at the question.

"There is a finite amount. We lose a few every decade as well. Someday, I fear we'll have none left."

"But they weren't around forever, right? There must have been a time before amulets."

Lyra unfolded her arms and poured herself some water. She sat down. "I already told you. You have to treat people with standard first aid. Nothing special about it, just the slog of the work. There is no direct timeline for it, either."

Orrin considered the information. "So there isn't a class that would just be the best for him to go for?"

Lyra shook her head. Orrin felt the frustration rising. He'd already spent the points to buy Assign Class. He'd wasted points on something that wasn't going to help him solve his friend's problem.

"Shit."

Chapter 62

"Am I going to pass out every time I unlock another Admin skill? Because that would really suck." Orrin had convinced Arandir to let him haul a few chairs down to the beach. Orrin missed the ocean. His parents had brought him to a beach a few hours away for vacation growing up. After his dad left, his mom had continued the tradition until Orrin was too old to go to the beach with his mom. Now, he would give anything for one of the warm peanut butter and jelly sandwiches she always brought with them.

"I have no evidence that you will not." Arandir wiggled his toes in the wet sand. "However, I think you will not faint again. On occasion, a person will drift for a moment when they take a skill or spell that is too powerful for their level. I believe that your body was shocked by the Administrator power coursing through you for the first time."

Orrin considered his words. In the distance, something splashed in the water, but it was too far away to see clearly.

"Maybe I should use all the points now. It's not worth letting the power sit unused. We're dealing with a war on one side and a possible invading Demon Lord on the other. Do you think Sanerris would leave you alone if I gave him a few Quests?"

Arandir shook his head, his blue eyes glittering as he stared at the same spot where Orrin had seen the splash. "The whales are migrating. It is far too early in the year. Something must have disturbed them."

Orrin had noticed the elder elf would play deaf and focus on something else when asked a hard question. Most of the time, he let it go. He was still supposed to be representing Dey until the final paperwork was drawn up. He couldn't wait to get back to Daniel and Madi, although they were probably getting drilled in weapon training right now.

"Arandir, if you don't answer, I'll take the Assign Quest skill and go to Odrana."

Arandir gave Orrin side-eye, pressing his lips into a tight line. "Never coerce with senseless threats. You may take whatever Administrator powers you want, but we both know that you would not travel into that man's grasp willingly. To do so would be folly and put not just you but your friends in danger. Would the [Hero] stay in wait for the Demon Lord if Lord Sanerris held you captive?"

"I wouldn't go to him. I'm not a complete idiot," Orrin said, scratching his neck. He had been thinking exactly that. He had [Teleport] and [Camouflage]. He could probably escape if he needed to, but thinking about what Daniel and Madi would say if he tried it alone . . .

They sat in silence, Arandir pointing out the shapes in the distance. Orrin learned more about whales and finally took his leave. Arandir had given him the signed papers for Silas. This would be his final outing as a delegate of Dey.

"Please do come visit still," Arandir said, placing his chair back in its rightful spot. "I would like to help train your friends. We have many [Swordhands] that would jump at the chance to train with the [Hero], and I could make arrangements for Lady Catanzano as well."

"I'll tell them." Orrin shook his hand. "Daniel might not want to visit just yet."

Arandir sighed but accepted the response with dignity. "Be well and return to our shade when your journey is over."

"I said *Daniel* might not visit." Orrin chuckled. "I have no problem hanging out at the beach with you. I'll be back."

Orrin gathered the last of his things and waved as he used [Teleport] to go back to Dey.

"You should have waited," Madi complained. "My father would have been happy to get a Hospital official to tell you all that. You shouldn't have wasted your points on Assign Class. Now you don't have enough points to get the Create Relic power."

Orrin, Madi, and Daniel sat around a fire just outside Dey. They'd been given the rest of the day to search for a monster that had been sighted to the south. [Juntha Rabbits] were ruining crops. Too fast for the average farmer to catch, the beasts were high experience and low danger. The exact recipe of monster that Silas was sending the [Hero] out after.

He had finished telling them about the power he'd unlocked and his adventures over the last few days. Madi was pissed about the lost chance at making more relics, but Daniel was unusually quiet.

"Nothing to say?" Orrin prodded his friend. "Do you think I fucked up, too?"

Daniel pushed a stick into the fire, making one of the logs drop. Fire motes escaped into the air as he responded, "I think you made the best choice. Assign Class is going to be what we use to beat the Demon Lord."

"Huh?" Madi and Orrin said at the same time.

"You can turn every [Farmer] and [Merchant] into a fighting class. Think about it. How much more will the elven training do for an [Archer] compared to a [Baker]?"

"Daniel, that would be announcing to the entire world that I'm an Administrator."

Madi sat forward, getting way too close to the fire for Orrin's comfort. "What if we set up a room with a divider so the other person couldn't see you? Do you have to see the person to use it?"

"I . . . I haven't actually tried using it."

Daniel and Madi gave him the look. The one that meant he was an idiot.

"I can try now." He scrambled to pull up the new skill.

Choose Target

"Um, Madi."

"What?"

"I'm going to try and assign a class to you."

"I like my class where it is."

"I've probably got to confirm the selection. Just give me a minute."

Choose Class:

Orrin gasped as the list spread out.

"Orrin?" Daniel sat forward.

"I'm fine." He waved his friend off. "The list is still loading, but I can see [Healer] toward the top here. Maybe I can just assign the class and Amir would be able to get [Heal Small Wounds] afterward . . . Yes! D, the [Archer] class is on here. I wonder if this list responds to my thoughts like the system did when I first . . . yep. It does. Madi, I found your class, [Prism Conjurer]. That's interesting . . ."

Orrin muttered his thoughts as he read, not realizing his friends' frustration with him.

"We can't see what you're reading, dumbass." Daniel poked him with the pointy stick.

"Madi, I think there are a few variants of [Prism Conjurer]. At least, I think these are versions of your . . . That one, [Prism Wizard], has to be for sure. What's the difference between a conjurer and a wizard? Oh, there's a class called [Optical Conjurer], too. Then . . . oh, shit."

"What? What did you do?" Madi was understandably nervous. Orrin was essentially holding her class hostage right now. "I swear, if you did something to me . . ."

"[Superior Prism Conjurer]. Have you ever heard of that?"

Madi didn't move. "That's not a real class."

"I'm looking at it right here. I don't get any descriptions of what the classes are. I feel like this could be dangerous to play around with."

Orrin kept scrolling. "It is cool, though. There are so many different options."

"Is [Utility Warder] available?" Daniel asked. Madi was still staring at Orrin.

"I'll check." Orrin scrolled . . . and scrolled some more. "It isn't there. Why isn't it there?"

"Orrin, are you sure you read that class right?" Madi's voice was brittle.

"Um . . . Yeah. It's here. [Superior Prism Conjurer]. It was actually near the top of the list. I wonder if the skill automatically gives me options geared to the person. That would be re—"

"Can you change my class?"

Orrin jolted out of his thoughts and really looked at his friend. She was shaking despite being so close to the fire.

"Madi, what do you mean? We don't even know what the class does. He's just checking if the—"

"Can you do it or not?" Madi interrupted Daniel.

Orrin scrolled to the class and rolled over it. The class highlighted, and a new prompt popped up.

> **Replace [Prism Conjurer] with [Superior Prism Conjurer]?**
> **Yes or No?**

"I think so. Madi, I don't feel comfortable doing this, though."

She blinked hard and turned away. Daniel stood up and crossed over to sit near her.

"What's going on? What is it?"

Orrin dropped the skill, watching the list that was still loading disappear from his sight. Madi was muttering something to Daniel. She was being too quiet for Orrin to hear. A few minutes later, she stood, keeping her back to the boys.

"I'm going to clear my head."

As she walked away, Daniel shook his head.

"What was that about?" Orrin asked. He was surprised when Daniel turned with a huge smirk on his face.

"Do you remember that story she likes? The one about Denna? She based her entire class around her hero from a fairy-tale story. I'll give you three guesses what the stories say her class was."

"Is there some difference between Madi's class and the 'superior' version?" Orrin asked, putting air quotes around *superior*. "If she didn't even think it was a real thing . . ."

"That's why she's clearing her head," Daniel explained. He pointed to his own head. "She knows here it would be reckless and irresponsible to just change her entire class." He moved his hand to his heart. "She still wants to try."

Orrin thought it over. "We need to do some research."

Daniel groaned. "Why do you take the fun out of everything?"

Madi returned ten minutes later. Nobody spoke until Orrin shot to his feet. "Five of them just appeared to the east. Let's go."

The race to the [Juntha Rabbits] let them all blow off some steam. Orrin increased everyone's dexterity to what he felt comfortable doing. Daniel tried to use his skills to boost forward, but he had to return to keep on track. Only Orrin could tell him where the rabbits moved. They approached from separate directions, making sure to get a single hit on each cute bunny rabbit before Daniel bounced between them in a series of vicious attacks.

Experience Gained: 1,000 XP (200 XP x 5)
Level 18 Obtained!
+10 AP

"About time," he muttered.

"Did you finally get your level?" Daniel asked. "I thought you were going to be behind us forever."

Orrin glowered. Daniel and Madi had been hunting without him. He'd kept up his routine of using as much of his mana each day as he could, but gaining experience to level was hard to squeeze in between all the teleporting he'd been required to do.

Daniel was already halfway through level eighteen. Madi was on level nineteen. She would likely reach the level-twenty Quest before either of them.

"Some of us have to do work," Orrin shot back. Daniel raised his hands in surrender.

Orrin checked his status.

Orrin
Utility Warder
Level 18 (786/9,000)
AP: 36
Administrator Points: 25
HP: 140/140
MP: 825/1,100
Strength: 9 (100)
Constitution: 14
Dexterity: 11 (100)
Will: 28 (100)
Intelligence: 11 (100)

His skill and spell list had become too long to read through outside of bed. He'd created a smaller list of the powers that could be leveled.

Abilities:
[Side Steps]—Level 3 (34/300)
[Way of the Water]—20%

Spells:
[Heal Small Wounds]—Level 3 (9,840/10,000)
[Camouflage]—Level 2 (5,980/10,000)
[Teleport]—Level 2 (1,225/10,000)
[Remetabolize]—(700/1,000)

[Increase Strength]—Level 3 (5,160/10,000)
[Increase Dexterity]—Level 3 (5,105/10,000)
[Increase Will]—Level 3 (9,550/10,000)
[Increase Intelligence]—Level 3 (6,985/10,000)

Madi was squatting by the rabbits, working hard at skinning them. Daniel was standing over her watching as she described the process.

"Did anybody take any damage?" Orrin asked eagerly. "I'm so close to finishing off [Heal Small Wounds]."

Madi and Daniel shook their heads. Daniel's face split into an evil grin.

"No, I'm not going to let you beat me up so I can heal myself." Orrin flipped him off.

"When did you stop being fun?" Daniel pouted.

Madi pushed her spear between Daniel's feet as he talked and then kicked him in the knee. He fell back and landed hard. She smiled innocently up at Orrin. "Oh no! I think Daniel needs some healing."

Chapter 63

The next twenty days were some of the longest of Orrin's life. Silas had brought in the best teachers he could find for Daniel and his daughter. The training was intense.

A handful of the weapon masters turned up their noses at Orrin joining at first, but each accepted him after a demonstration of [Way of the Water]. His ability to dodge nearly any attack vexed and intrigued even the most stubborn of fighters.

After breakfast, the trio would spend a few hours drilling with different weapons under the watchful eyes of one or more teachers. Madi worked almost exclusively with a [Spear Dancer]. The tiny man made even Orrin feel tall. He had been the only person to actually strike Orrin during their spar. He was also the only teacher to give immediate advice to Orrin after their fight.

"That was well-done," he had said, leaning against his spear, which towered over his head. "If you had kept yourself inside my range, I would not have been able to touch you. Work hard and learn the range of each weapon. Your skill is impressive but not infallible."

While Madi labored at thrusting and stabbing at a straw dummy, Daniel fought with a different sword user. Originally, Silas had brought a [Swordmaster] in to train the [Hero], but the lord of Dey had dismissed the man after he refused to work with Orrin. The new trainer, Sasha, was a [Swordhand], one of the predominant classes for a sword wielder. She refused to let Daniel use Gertrude, drilling him with different swords of regular size. Orrin had joined for a few lessons, learning to use his summoned swords for more than just an overhead slash.

Daniel threw the iron shortsword on the weapons table angrily. "This is stupid. I should be using the weapon I like, not these pieces of shit."

Orrin sighed and caught a staff that had begun to roll off the table. "You have [Sword Proficiency]. You can use any sword with ease and know the exact way to hold and thrust and all that. I have to learn the hard way. Shut up and stop complaining."

Daniel took a cup and dunked it in the water barrel used in the training yard. He drank the full cup and slammed it back down. "Exactly. I already know how to use swords. They should be teaching me how to push myself farther, not making me use swords I'll never use."

Orrin saw the shadow coming up beyond them and kept his mouth shut.

"I mean, what's the point?" Daniel continued, oblivious that the [Swordhand] was standing behind him with her hand on the pommel of her longsword. "I'm not going to fight without Gertrude. I'm going to tell Sasha she needs to let me train with my own sword or I'll get Silas to get another trainer for me."

The sound of steel being drawn rang across the yard. Sasha tapped Daniel with the flat of her blade.

"Pull out your big sword then, [Hero]. No skills or spells. Sword on sword only. Three touches or drawn blood to win." Sasha never raised her voice during training. She would put a finger in the air and wait for all sound to cease before she gave instructions, and she carried herself with an air that Orrin had first thought was disdain. It was only when he'd fought her that he'd realized she was just bored. She had come alive when he dodged more and more, trying to find a way to hit him. Her laughter when she had conceded was the loudest Orrin had heard her be.

"Teacher." Daniel turned and ducked his head. He had been beaten into the ground over and over. "Gertrude is dangerous to use in a sparring session. I could hurt you."

Sasha's eyes widened. "Oh? Then perhaps it should be three touches for me and one for you. Stand ready."

The ass beating that Daniel received was astounding.

Sasha disarmed Daniel almost immediately, his giant sword falling to the dirt a few feet away. He moved to pick it up, and Sasha slapped his back with the flat of her blade.

"One."

"I'm not armed. Can you at least wait until I pick up my sword?"

"An enemy will not wait so kindly." Sasha did, however, let him pick up Gertrude and settle back into his ready stance.

The second time she disarmed him, Madi left her training behind to come watch with Orrin. "Two silver on Sasha."

"I'm not taking that bet. Daniel isn't going to win," Orrin rejected her.

This time, the [Swordhand] moved between Daniel and his sword, holding him at point. Daniel smiled and held his hand up, activating [Summon Weapon]. Orrin hadn't had time to study how the skill worked last time. Gertrude faded between blinks, reappearing in Daniel's outstretched hand.

"The rules were no skills or spells. Do you forfeit the match?"

Daniel frowned. "How else do you expect me to fight? You disarmed me, so I'm using what is at my disposal to win the fight. Isn't that what you said?"

"Do not use your skill again or it is a forfeit. A resourceful attacker may have countermeasures against you. If you could not reach your sword after being disarmed, what should you do?" Sasha advanced on Daniel, striking with testing feints against his larger sword.

"Run away?"

Sasha tapped Daniel's sword, drawing it to the side a fraction of an inch. He overcorrected and she darted in, pushing her blade along the hilt. Daniel was forced to drop his sword but avoided her hit.

"You are surrounded by other blades. Your teammate can summon more. You have a knife on your hip. You have many options." She smiled a bloodthirsty grin. "But yes, running from me might be your safest choice."

Orrin was enjoying the cat-and-mouse game. Daniel ran to the weapon table and grabbed the shortsword he'd abandoned. Sasha disarmed him again, pushing him in the opposite direction. He pulled a longsword from a weapon rack, and she disarmed him. He dashed to where Gertrude lay on the ground, but she stood on the blade and pointed the tip of her sword at his chest.

"Do you see why we train? You might be best with your big sword, but you will know how to use all swords. All blades have similarities. All blades are one. When you can use all of them proficiently, your skill will increase with each individually as well. Do you yield?"

Orrin expected Daniel to keep fighting, but his friend used his big brain for once. He bowed his head deeper than before toward Sasha.

"I yield to you, Teacher. Which sword is next?"

After the first week of swinging his sword around didn't result in gaining his own [Sword Proficiency], Orrin skipped out on morning practice. He waited until everyone was gone and stepped into one of the bathrooms at the Catanzano manor. Specifically, the one that had a shower. A cistern on the roof filled with water, either from rain or hired [Water Mages]. The pipes ran into the room and through a magic-activated piece of equipment that could heat the water.

Orrin had given this a lot of thought. He was going to try to level [Way of the Water] again. After the last training season with Styx, he could feel the movement of water if he concentrated. Like a drop of liquid crawling down his neck, it tickled his thoughts if he focused. He was hoping being in moving water would help.

He turned on the shower, stepped in, and quickly pulled up the prompt. There was no reason to waste time or water.

> **[Way of the Water]: 20% 4/20 completed. Test your progress and unlock the first gate?**
> **Warning: Failure three (3) times will result in all progress being lost.**

Let's go. Orrin accepted.

When he blinked, he found himself back in Styx's white marble arena with the alcoves. The watery form of his teacher waited in Formless, the initial stance of Orrin's fighting style.

"Hey, Styx, how are you?"

Orrin didn't expect a response and wasn't disappointed when the watery figure didn't so much as move. Unless he asked something important, Styx wouldn't answer . . . Actually, sometimes he wouldn't answer even if Orrin thought it was important.

[Way of the Water] was a defensive and reactive fighting style. As soon as Orrin took the Formless stance, Styx would attack. Orrin felt that he had fully mastered the other stances: River, Ocean, Rain, and Mist. Each stance had its own movements. While in River, Orrin would focus on his footsteps, moving away from an attacker. His hands would flow in circles, brushing attacks to the side with only the smallest margin for error. He knew by now that he could use River to wear an attacker down until they were frustrated or made a misstep.

Ocean stance focused more on meeting the attacks of an enemy. He still would throw the attack to the side, but like the tide, he would rush in to fill the space left by the attack. It wasn't quite offensive fighting, but Ocean was what Orrin used the most when fighting monsters or people trying to kill him. He needed to be able to attack, and the moments when he surged forward gave him the opportunity to do so.

Rain and Mist were stances that Orrin had mastered but still didn't fully understand the use of. Rain was all rapid movements, almost in an unpredictable pattern. It had elements of both River and Ocean to it, letting him retreat and advance on a target but with none of the strength of either. Except in fights against Styx, he had never used it in a real battle.

Mist had taken Orrin the longest to get. Styx had seemed reluctant to continue training in the stance until the last training session. It had been Arandir's suggestion to train in water that helped him figure it out. The movements themselves didn't seem hard, but Styx had never accepted the stance from Orrin. Feeling the water along his back, Orrin had had a moment of inspiration. Like the beads of water running along his skin, he slid his feet between the movements, never stopping. He skated along the ground in constant motion. The water that made up Styx's body had positively vibrated in glee, and Orrin had learned more of the moves of Mist.

He still felt like there was something about the Mist stance that he hadn't fully grasped, but Orrin couldn't progress with his training until he unlocked the first gate . . . whatever that was.

"How do we do this, then?" Orrin asked as he stepped into Formless.

Styx didn't move, waiting silently.

"Are you going to attack me?"

No response from the man of water. The lights from nowhere that lit up the arena splashed through his body, leaving fractal rainbows on the ground.

"Should I attack you?" Orrin asked but didn't expect an answer. He felt the shower in the real world hitting his back in exaggerated slowness. *I bet if I activated the training in the middle of a fight, I could control time.* He banished the thought for now.

Styx remained in the neutral waiting stance of Formless.

Orrin lasted four minutes standing still opposite Styx.

"I need to unlock the gate, whatever it is. How do I do it, Styx?"

When no response came, Orrin moved forward and threw a punch. Styx splashed into a puddle of water all around.

> **[Way of the Water]: first gate failed.**
> **Warning: Failure two (2) times will result in all progress being lost.**

"What the . . ." Orrin turned in a circle. Styx was gone. He screamed in frustration and threw punches and kicks at nothing until he felt tired.

[Way of the Water]: first gate reset.
Test your progress and unlock the first gate?

Breathing heavily, Orrin sat on the ground and put his head in his hands. "Think, stupid. Attacking him wasn't the answer. He isn't moving to attack me. How do I test my progress without fighting?"

The water around him churned together and coalesced back into the waiting form of Styx. He stood normally for a moment before dropping into Formless again.

"Test my progress . . ." Orrin murmured to himself. How could he be so stupid? [Way of the Water] wasn't about attacking. Honestly, sometimes he felt like it wasn't a fighting style at all. Dodging all attacks couldn't be considered a fighting style, could it?

Orrin stood up and fell into Formless. "Let's see if this works, then."

He moved into a different stance, taking Ocean. Styx copied his movement. He swung his foot up into one of the first attacks Styx had taught him: Scorpion Fish Strike. Again, the watery teacher mirrored his movements.

Orrin spent hours moving from stance to stance, repeating every attack, move, counter, and dodge that he could remember. He fell into a trance, watching Styx watching him. Moving together until they were one. Orrin couldn't say when their arms connected, dancing through the various elements of [Way of the Water]. His arms pushed while Styx pulled, the attacks speeding up as Styx stopped copying and instead synced with Orrin's waltz. They gracefully combined moves in a way that Orrin had never thought to try, reading the other's tiniest movements. Speeding up as the strikes and kicks moved with frantic energy, chaotically missing each other in a frenzy that ended when Styx pulled away violently.

Orrin was dripping with sweat. Styx bowed his head and disappeared.

[Way of the Water]: first gate unlocked.

Chapter 64

[Way of the Water]: first gate unlocked

"What does that even mean?" Orrin asked the empty air. Instead of an answer, the prompt for his fighting skill popped up.

[Way of the Water]: 25% 5/20 completed.
Continue or save progress?

Orrin groaned at the lack of explanation. He was tempted to continue training at the next stage, but he could feel his body back in the real world starting to get cold. The magic water heater unit had a timer that you had to manually activate. He'd spent more time in the skill training room than ever before. He thought it had to have been ten hours of going through the forms with Styx. In the past, he had needed to reactivate the shower's heat function every ten minutes.

I spend an hour training with Styx for every minute in real time. A one-to-ten ratio is insane. Orrin considered the implications of the magic of this world letting him train in time dilation. There had to be time magic out there.

Orrin grinned as he saved progress and quit. He was going to find a way to unlock time magic for sure. Daniel would be pissed.

After toweling off and getting dressed, Orrin made his way out for more training. He'd been focusing on activating [Side Steps] as much as possible, but with [Way of the Water], it was getting harder for anyone to trigger the skill. If he simply stood still, the skill let him get hit in retaliation. Not that he minded. He was so close to increasing both [Heal Small Wounds] and [Increase Will] that he'd started casting the spells to the exclusion of all others.

By the end of a spar with Madi, Orrin felt his system notify him of something.

"Yes!" Orrin jumped up and down. He'd been casting this spell every time one of them hit the other . . . really just healing Madi.

> **[Heal Small Wounds] Level 3 (10,000)!**
> **Upgrade to [Heal Moderate Wounds]—Upgrade Available. 12 AP**

Orrin whistled. He remembered getting [Heal Small Wounds], level three, from his Heal 200 People of Dey Quest. He'd forgotten that it cost six ability points, but seeing the price double to twelve for [Heal Moderate Wounds] put into perspective how much the spell cost. From what Lyra, the elven elder of healing, had said, he shouldn't buy the upgrade unless he wanted to close off all the other branches of healing.

"[Diagnose] was the main one, right?" Orrin asked himself. He didn't want to spend five ability points on something that sounded like it did what [Analyze] and [Identify] already did, but he trusted the information enough to not buy [Moderate] right away. He put it out of his mind for now. Madi was still holding her spear at the ready position.

"Did you get a notification?" she asked when he finally stopped staring into space.

"My healing spell maxed out."

Madi dropped her guard and came in for a high five. She'd seen Daniel and Orrin do it a few times and was trying to implement their rituals into her own life. Orrin slapped her hand.

"Do you want to continue fighting?"

Orrin shook his head. He'd been putting off visiting Amir since he returned. He'd made a promise to the coffee maker and wanted to let him know what he'd learned from the elves, at least. He was going to try and use Assign Class to make him a [Healer] regardless of what Lyra had told him. Maybe assigning the class would open up [Heal Small Wounds].

"I need to run some errands," Orrin said, tossing his [Ice Sword] into a corner of the training square. It would melt in a bit. "When I get back, do you want to play a few games of Kala?"

Madi smirked. "You're not going to beat me. I've been playing longer than you."

Orrin waved his hand. "Same wager? One silver a game?"

Madi laughed as she reextended her spear and went to stab a dummy. "You're just giving me money at this point."

Orrin washed the sweat from his body with a basin of water and a small towel before leaving. He didn't want to waste all the house's water and had barely worked up a sweat with Madi. The first gate of [Way of the Water] was still a mystery, but the skill itself seemed easier to use. Madi hadn't come close to connecting a single hit on him.

Trudging down the streets, Orrin found Amir pulling in the furniture from outside. He stacked the chairs and folded the tables, leaning them against the wall.

Orrin grabbed a chair and helped.

"Welcome back. How have you been?"

Orrin handed the chair to Amir. "Fine. I had to go back to the elven forest, but I got to talk with the leader of their Hospital. I learned a lot about being a [Healer]."

Amir's hands paused on the chair before he shook his head and took it. "I'm guessing the elves wouldn't take a human in for training."

Orrin wanted to kick himself. He hadn't even thought to ask Lyra if that was an option. He could probably get Arandir to strong-arm her into it but—

"It would probably end the same anyway. I would likely be the only human in their forest. Besides, my father needs help with the shop. I can't leave him by himself."

Orrin grunted as he tried to fold up one of the tables. Amir smirked and showed him the small contraption that released the pin. He took the table and set it inside.

"Would you like a cup?" Amir stuck his head out the door.

Orrin smiled and nodded enthusiastically. Amir waved him inside.

While his back was turned, Orrin pulled up Assign Class.

Choose Target

Orrin selected Amir.

Choose Class:

Orrin selected [Healer].

Replace [Brewer] with [Healer]?
Yes or No?

Orrin paused. He had to double-check.

"Amir, if you could become a [Healer], would you want to?"

His friend had pushed the last chair onto a stack and closed the door to the shop. It was early afternoon, but Orrin knew from experience they closed for a few hours so Amir and his father could take a break and grab a late lunch during the slow hours. He imagined having to pull all those chairs out twice a day, as well as putting them back away in the middle of the day and night.

"It has always been my dream, but I don't see how it could happen at this point. Even if I wanted to move back to Odrana, I'm not sure I could get into the Hospital there. There have been talks of trouble between Dey and Odrana lately. I don't know the particulars, but my da said we should keep out of it. People are likely to target us anyway as he still speaks with a slight accent from the northern country, but . . ."

Orrin mulled over his choice. If the class change worked, Amir could train on his own. Orrin could shuttle him to Lyra for a few pointers, and Amir could continue working with his father. The downside was Amir might talk and let people know how he got the class. All that was even if the change to [Healer] worked or if it gave him access to the core healing spell in the first place. What if he changed Amir to a [Healer] and he still couldn't heal?

"I will not give up, though. If it takes a decade, I will find a way to help others." He finished his rambling as he pushed a cup of steaming-hot coffee across the small counter.

Orrin took a sip. "Coffee cures everything."

Amir laughed. "My da says the same thing."

Orrin set the cup down and stared into it. The worst-case scenario was Amir got his hopes up. Orrin could deal with rumors that he could change a class. He trusted Amir, despite the fact that they had never been in a party together or fought side by side. Amir wanted to help people. He would give up anything to . . .

Realization hit Orrin. Amir wanted to be [Healer]. He was ostracized for being different . . . just like his own mom had been.

She worked a lot as an emergency room doctor now, but Orrin had been born just before her residency. She'd had to scrap and claw for her position, working twice as hard as other doctors. He had overheard her talking to his dad about jackass doctors who assumed she was a nurse or patients who refused to be seen by her because she was a woman. Amir was a kindred spirit. He wanted to help but was being hindered by things that didn't matter at the end of the day.

Orrin made his choice. "There are a few options for you according to the elf I talked to. You could spend a lot of time doing first aid and training. There is a chance you could get [Heal Small Wounds] from doing that. If you did, you could change your class to [Healer]."

Amir sighed. "I've heard that. I've been volunteering at an alchemy store down the street. They don't charge for bandages if you purchase their creams and poultices. I get to help people wrap up their burns and cuts. I don't mind it, but I don't see how I'm helping."

"There might be another way. I'm . . . not sure it will work. Also, if it did work, you could never tell anybody about it. You would have to lie and say you got [Heal Small Wounds] from your work at the alchemy shop."

Amir frowned. "I won't do anything illegal. If you've stolen an amulet, return it."

Orrin put his hands in the air. "Nothing illegal. I didn't steal an amulet."

Amir's frown deepened. "What you are telling me sounds too good to be true. You told me in the past that you received [Heal Small Wounds] from your class. Did you find a way for me to gain the same class? If I had [Heal Small Wounds], I might be able to change to [Healer]. Even if I can't, being able to heal people . . ."

Orrin smiled at his friend's faraway look. "Do you promise to keep this between us? You can't even tell your father. I should also tell you there is a chance it won't work."

Amir stirred a spoon in his own coffee lazily. "I have nothing to lose. I promise to keep whatever mysterious thing you are about to do a secret."

Orrin hit yes.

> **Cost to use Assign Class: one (1) Administrator Point.**
> **Accept?**

Orrin frowned at the increased loss of another administrator point but pulled the trigger anyway.

Orrin waited.

And waited.

Nothing special happened. He checked Amir with [Identify].

> **Amir Fallah**
> **[Healer] Level 1**

"Hey, look at that! It worked," Orrin said, grinning.

"What do you—" Amir paused as he glanced at his status. His eyes widened in shock. Orrin watched as his lips moved, reading the various things in his new class.

"Orrin, I am a [Healer]. How?"

"Do you have [Heal Small Wounds]?"

". . . I do. It is at zero of a thousand points. That will take me half a year to level if I work each day." Amir stopped talking and looked up with tears in his eyes. "Whatever you did to me, thank you. A thousand times, thank you."

Orrin sat back and sipped his coffee. "I told you already, we're friends forever. You gave me coffee. It's the least I could do."

Chapter 65

Orrin gave Amir all the pointers on healing that he had gleaned in the past months and promised to give Amir more help in the future. He even considered bringing Amir along for some leveling, but the boy shot the idea down.

"I need to be careful at first. If the Hospital finds out there is a new [Healer] in town, things could get dangerous."

Orrin tapped his finger on the empty mug in front of him. "If you ever need help, go to Lord Catanzano. Tell him I sent you. He'll help."

Or else . . . Orrin thought darkly.

He totally rejected the three—no, four bags of coffee that Amir handed to him. Yep. It would be a dick move to accept that as a gift . . . right? Orrin took a deep whiff of the beans as he walked back.

"Again!" Sasha shouted, making Daniel attack a log the size of a full tree with a dagger. "Stab harder."

Orrin lounged with Madi. They watched Daniel get put through the wringer and enjoyed every moment of it. Madi even brought out some lemonade.

"How's your training going?" Orrin asked, sipping the refreshing drink.

Daniel's thrust took a chunk out of the wood. He was supposed to be using his skills to put his entire arm through the log but had succeeded in taking only the first few inches off.

"Amazing," Madi answered, turning away from the spectacle. "I reached [Spear Proficiency] level two yesterday."

"You unlocked it?"

"No." Madi's smile widened. "I earned it. I hit my teacher and sent him flying. When he landed, I got the notification."

Orrin was impressed. Fighting classes had to train for years to level up their skills without spending points, and there was no guarantee it would happen. He'd yet to receive a single weapon proficiency, despite all his practice. It was getting to the point that Orrin was considering spending some of his sweet, sweet ability points on [Sword Proficiency].

"That's awesome, Madi," Orrin congratulated her.

They sat in silence, except for Daniel's grunts in the background. Madi opened her mouth but closed it before speaking.

The third time she stopped herself from talking, Orrin rolled his head and blinked in an exaggerated motion. "What?"

"Huh?"

"You want to say something. What is it?"

"I don't—"

"Madi, you didn't even notice that Daniel took his shirt off. What's on your mind?"

"He took his shirt off?" Madi's head snapped back around. "No, he didn't."

"No, he didn't. But you thought he might have."

Madi sighed. "I wanted to know if you thought about changing my class."

Orrin knew she had been talking to Daniel about this. His friend had brought it up multiple times. They'd argued over the pros and cons. He hadn't told Daniel about Amir, but seeing it work gave him a bit more confidence. "Do you know for sure what the class you want does? Like, you aren't going to regret it?"

Madi sat straighter and put her cup down. "Orrin, when I first got [Prism Conjurer], I was so happy. It isn't unheard-of to unlock, but not a lot of people get it anymore. I thought that the superior version was just a story. I'm sure Daniel told you about that. Denna is a [Superior Prism Conjurer], but every story we tell has someone with a made-up class. I wanted to be able to do what she does in the stories. She can use light and fire magic to create different attacks. [Sunbeam], the spell in that book we found at the Guild, do you remember? That's one of her core spells. Most of her story is stuff like 'Denna cast [Sunbeam] through the fourth circuit and green light filled the cavern,' which isn't a real skill or anything. When you said the class actually exists . . . I'd risk it. I want this, Orrin. Please."

Orrin watched Daniel hacking away with his dagger. The cuts were getting deeper. "You'd have to start over at level one."

Madi froze. "You don't know that for sure, right? Maybe my levels would transfer over or—"

"I used the power. It resets the class to one. You might even lose [Sunbeam]. What if Denna used a skill book for that attack and you can never find another?"

Madi paused and then did something Orrin had known she would. Madi was her father's daughter. She had thought through her options and figured out exactly what she wanted, but now that she knew she hadn't had all the facts, she asked for time to think about it. "Those are good points. I hadn't considered . . . Can I have some time?"

Orrin grabbed her hand as she stood up to leave. "Madi, I'm not saying no. If you want this, I'll do it."

She squeezed his fingers. "Thank you, O."

Orrin stood in the shower, letting the water hit his back as he activated [Way of the Water].

"Hey, Styx," Orrin said as the watery man formed.

"WELCOME."

Orrin didn't move for a full two seconds. "What?"

"WELCOME."

"You can talk?"

"YES."

"What the fuck, dude? You've never talked before."

"GATE."

Orrin poked Styx's arm. His finger dipped into the water, depressing the shape a bit. When he removed his hand, Styx formed up normally.

"The gate upgraded you, huh?"

Styx didn't respond but stepped side to side as he had in the past when Orrin asked a question that couldn't be answered clearly.

"This is great," Orrin cheered. "I have so much to ask you. What's up with the statues?"

"LATER."

Orrin considered the answer. Either Styx wanted to train first, then talk or . . .

"I have to get past more gates to learn about that?"

"YES."

"Damn." Orrin scratched his head. It didn't really matter. He had come here to level his skill up. He wanted to fight Daniel and put him on his ass without using a buff or debuff. "Let's train, then."

Styx moved his head in what might have been a nod. Orrin fell into Formless.

Styx sat on the ground.

"What?"

The watery hand patted the floor. "SIT."

Orrin sighed as he knelt and then sat down. "What are we doing, Styx?"

"FOCUS."

Styx held his hands out, inches apart, as if he were about to clap.

Orrin copied him.

"FOCUS."

"I am."

Styx shook his hands.

Orrin watched a few small water particles shake off and land around him. The water didn't stay on the marble tile but disappeared after a moment. *What? Where did it go?*

He looked around where Styx was sitting. The floor should be wet where the man was standing, right? Orrin thought back to the long fights. Even when he'd destroyed Styx in a battle, the man pulled himself back together. The floor should have kept some moisture, though. Orrin couldn't remember ever thinking the floor was slippery.

"FOCUS."

Orrin almost argued that he was, but while he was turning his head up, a little light refracted off something between Styx's hands. Orrin focused not on his teacher but on the space between his palms.

A single water droplet hovered between Styx's outstretched hands. Not touching him but flying in the space between.

"Are you using magic?" Orrin asked excitedly.

"REFLECT."

Orrin was stumped. He asked more questions, but Styx only sat still, repeating the one word over and over.

"REFLECT."

"I don't know what you are talking about," Orrin shouted.

He'd tried attacking Styx, but he just reformed and yelled his single-word response. He'd sat in the same position and held his hands out. He'd tried to scoop some water out of Styx and drip it between his hands, but the water didn't float like it did for Styx. He was missing something.

Or maybe [Way of the Water] is supposed to be used by a [Water Mage] and I've reached a roadblock.

Orrin shivered at the thought. He could buy a spell, but that would suck. He didn't want to spend more ability points on things right now. He was still trying to weigh the different options from [Heal Small Wounds] leveling up.

"REFLECT."

"You reflect," Orrin countered, slapping Styx's arms to dash water across the room.

Orrin's hand slowed as it neared Styx and then was pushed away.

"What the fuck was that?"

"REFLECT."

Orrin sat still and watched the bead of water. He had thought it was part of Styx's body, but the way it rippled was different. It was like a heartbeat of power hit it from both directions, keeping it from moving. Like Styx was holding it there with his will alone. Orrin couldn't sense any mana or magic coming from Styx.

"How are you reflecting, Styx?"

The man of water didn't have distinct facial features, but Orrin swore he could make out a smile.

"AVOID."

Avoid what? Avoid the water falling down? Orrin reached out and took a handful of water from Styx. He let it drip from one hand down to the other.

"Like this? Avoid the water?" Orrin moved his hand back and forth, letting the drops splash to the ground.

Styx didn't respond.

"This is pointless." Orrin let the rest of the water fall out of his hand and made to stand up. "I've wasted too much of my day doing this. I'll come back when I've—"

As Orrin stood, Styx moved a hand to strike his leg. Orrin fell into a dodge. Styx's arm was overextended, and Orrin used Piercing Dive to counterattack. His hand went through Styx's arm, severing the watery appendage. Water splashed to the ground.

Except one drop of water that shot away from his palm to land ten feet away.

It undulated just like the one between Styx's hands.

"Oh."

Four hours later, Orrin got his notification.

> **[Way of the Water] 30% 6/20 completed.**
> **Continue or save progress?**

Orrin bowed to Styx and left the simulation. Turning off the water, he toweled off. He said a silent thank-you to Arandir for the advice about practicing in water for his water skill. The feeling of the shower hitting his body repeatedly helped him understand the movements better. He wasn't sure he would have noticed that first single drop of water if the feeling hadn't been so different from the hundreds of drops hitting his back.

He held his hands slightly apart and pushed. Every time he attacked or dodged using [Way of the Water], Orrin was using his body's energy. The push of his hand created movement, while the drag away from an opponent created friction. With his fighting skill, he could use these forces in a minute way to make a bead of water hover.

Orrin watched the single drop of water shiver between his hands until he lost the train of thought and it dropped.

To be honest, he had no idea why this was part of a fighting skill. He didn't think it was practical to make water hover in the middle of a fight, but it was the first time he hadn't needed to get his ass beaten to level up the skill.

Orrin kept playing with the new skill until Daniel fell into the bed next to him.

"I'm never using a dagger again," Daniel muttered, his face in his pillow.

"Take a shower. You stink."

"Maybe I'll use it one more time." Daniel turned his face and threatened Orrin. "Just a little stabby-stabby on you. Where have you been? Madi came looking for you."

"Taking a shower and leveling [Way of the Water]. Did you break the tree in half?"

Daniel laughed. "It was the size of a tree, wasn't it? I got halfway through it with one strike, but Sasha said that was good enough for now. Did your training go well?"

"I can make a drop of water hover between my hands using the power of my mind."

"..."

"..."

"You could just say no." Daniel grunted as he swung back off the bed and gathered a spare set of clothes. "I hope you didn't use up all the water."

Orrin moved the bead between his hands, ignoring Daniel.

Chapter 66

Orrin continued training with Madi and Daniel over the next few days. He even received permission from Silas to bring Amir along on a few monster hunts.

At first, Lord Catanzano was against another person joining, but when Orrin explained Amir was not affiliated with the Hospital and would be healing Madi's injuries for free, he relented. He uncharacteristically gave Orrin advice to pass along to Amir as well. Mostly the information was about specific areas of town where he could heal without consequence or other [Healers] who had been able to carve their own niches. Orrin made sure to write down the names so Amir could visit them later. However, the most surprising topic that came up wasn't advice at all.

"If your friend is resolute in his path, I would be willing to take him under my house's protection," Silas said, not even looking up from his paperwork. The poor guy was practically swimming in requests, orders, and backlogged grievances. Madi had complained he didn't sleep enough and had taken to bringing him dinner in his study. "He would serve for a time healing my men each week or when needed but would be under my protection. The Hospital would likely want to talk with him, but there are no specific laws that he must join them."

"That's . . . kind of you," Orrin responded, scratching his neck. "I don't know what his plans are, I just know he wants to help people."

"Commendable, but unless he has someone willing to take care of scheduling healing sessions, deter the Hospital from sending investigators after him, or keep him fed when he starts healing every person with a sob story for free, he'll be dead or broke in a few months."

Orrin clenched his fist. "Maybe a lord of Dey or even the new [Hero] could put in a word to the Hospital that the new [Healer] in town is off-limits?"

Silas glanced at Orrin and spread his hands over the papers in front of him. "I have other things to do than get into a pissing contest with the Hospital. My offer remains the same. He would need to work as a [Healer] for my house for a time, but I won't call on him too much. If he escaped the notice of the Hospital, then he's likely too low a level for them to worry about. Let me know what he decides."

Orrin told Amir, who promised to think about it. They met up a few times, but Amir never seemed eager to meet with the lord of Dey. The third day after Silas had made his offer to Amir, Orrin brought him along on a monster extermination.

Normally, local scouts found various high-experience monsters for the trio to hunt. The information would get relayed to Silas, who would send a guard to show them the area. Lately, he hadn't been able to afford a guard, and they'd only been given a general direction. Neither Daniel nor Madi minded having Amir along. He always brought cookies and coffee, making the treks through the woods or fields more of a retreat from the constant training. Working with them, Amir was able to gain six levels in [Healer] in just a few days.

After meeting Madi, Amir asked to meet Silas. Orrin didn't ask if they'd made a deal, mostly because he wasn't sure if it was a good thing or not.

Orrin was sure that Amir was more excited to be spending time with Madi than gaining levels. He had a crush on her that was obvious to everyone . . . except Madi.

Orrin didn't spend all his time leveling. He also continued to practice his [Way of the Water] skills. Madi in particular was fascinated with the magic that was not magic. The water droplet moving between his hands didn't cost any mana to manipulate, and it irked her that she couldn't figure out how to do it.

"It makes no sense," she complained. "I've seen attack skills that throw fire or some other element, but they always use mana in some way. The closest thing to what you're doing was this performer at a festival when I was younger. He could move the wind without mana. My father said it was a scam, but now that I'm seeing this . . ."

Orrin was hesitant to go back into Styx's training. He'd spent so much time in the last session trying to get the single bead of water to stay between his hands. Somehow, he knew the training was only going to get more difficult.

Instead, Orrin focused on his other skills and spells. He worked on [Camouflage] while his friends looked for him in an elaborate game of hide-and-seek. Madi figured out a way to use her spells to see his heat signature, proving that the spell was not foolproof. It only worked when she was close, though, which gave Orrin some hope.

He also hit a major hurdle with his increase-stat skills. Specifically, he maxed out [Increase Will] to its ten-thousand-mana-used marker. He had been watching the counter closely and smiled for a full two seconds as the numbers turned over with his last cast of the spell.

"What the hell?"

> **[Increase Will] (10,000/10,000)**
> **(1/4 Completed)**

"One of four what?" Orrin shouted at his screen even as he realized the obvious answer. He'd been looking forward to the major increase. The first [Increase Will] had given a plus-one bonus. The second had doubled, and the third level had doubled again to plus four. He'd made a bet with Daniel that it would go to plus eight at the next level. Daniel thought it would just be another two added on or plus six total. None of it mattered in the long run, as Orrin could boost his stats to give a total of one hundred points in any stat, but the saved cost in casting time would have been nice.

"What's going on there, buddy?" Daniel slowed down his attacks with a warhammer and rested on the stick part.

"Skill problems. Go back to destroying your boulder," Orrin commanded.

Daniel grunted as he picked up the large hammer and started swinging at the rock brought into the courtyard specially for him.

At the end of the day, he didn't get an upgrade to [Increase Will] and felt disheartened. He stopped spending time on the other three increase spells and sulked for a day before Madi flicked him between the eyes.

"Get over yourself. You can already make us stupid strong. Don't give up."

Orrin rubbed his forehead and flipped her off, but he did restart his daily casts. He wasn't even disappointed when he maxed out [Remetabolize] and it gave no option to upgrade.

Finally, Orrin made some skill purchases from the store.

> **[Diagnose]—ascertain the target's ailments. 5 AP**
> **[Purify]—remove abnormal statuses. 8 AP**
> **Would you like to purchase for 13 AP?**
> **Yes or No?**

[Purify] was the first skill that Orrin had wanted to buy upon seeing the new list of healing spells. If it worked like he thought it would, he could boost anybody to level one hundred in all their stats and not have to worry about the crash after. When he had overboosted his party in the Aqua Chambers dungeon, they'd all gotten statuses of Fatigued, Dizzy, Brain Fog, and Nauseous. He was sure these would qualify as abnormal statuses. If he could cure them, there was no downside to boosting his party before each fight and getting rid of the side effects after.

> **[Purify]—remove abnormal statuses. 20 MP**

It didn't even cost that much mana . . . well, for him, at least.

[Diagnose] was the skill that Lyra had suggested as the base for other healing skills. Orrin tested the skill out and found it to be similar to [Identify] and [Analyze] in a way—while using the skill, he could see a white light around an injury. It didn't use mana to activate, so Orrin played with it for a few minutes, punching his hand against the wall and healing himself with his lowest-level [Heal Small Wounds]. He wasn't sure, but it looked like if he used [Diagnose] first, the healing spell recovered more health.

In the middle of testing out his new skill, Orrin felt unusually tired and sat down hard.

Daniel found him teetering on the edge of his bed.

"What's wrong with you?"

"I feel woozy," Orrin slurred.

Daniel pushed his friend back and tucked him in. "Did you buy a physical skill? You look like shit, dude."

Orrin realized it as soon as Daniel voiced the problem. He didn't have experience in skills that used up a person's stamina and hadn't noticed the signs that [Diagnose] was draining him. He closed his eyes and napped.

When he woke up, the afternoon had passed and Daniel was snoring.

"Damn it."

Orrin tried to go back to sleep, but his energy had returned. He snuck out of the room and made his way down to the kitchen. He was starving and knew where the cooks kept all the good stuff.

He giggled as he imagined Madi's face the next time he pulled out some tasty treat from his [Dimension Hole].

"—sure he's still alive?"

Orrin paused on the top of the stairs and instinctively activated [Camouflage]. Silas's voice was a bare whisper. Whomever he was talking to kept their voice even lower, so Orrin could make out only murmurs.

"I can't do that. If I did, it would look like I sanctioned it and—" Silas either lowered his voice or moved farther into his office.

Orrin crept down the stairs, trying to avoid each creaky step he could remember. He made it down the hall and waited outside Lord Catanzano's office.

"—kill him." The other voice was male but didn't belong to one of the guards Orrin knew. That wasn't too surprising, though, as Silas had taken over a large portion of Wendeln's forces, and even before that he'd had guards outside the manor that Orrin had never met.

"Even if it comes to that, there is nothing I can do. My hands are tied. He tried something rash and it failed. I cannot and will not risk the entire city over one boy gone mad."

Orrin leaned closer to the door. Silas kept his voice lower and he'd barely heard the last bit.

Does that cup thing on the wall work? I've only ever seen it in movies. Do I even have a cup? As Orrin searched his mind for what kind of cups he had in his [Dimension Hole], he put his head too close to Silas's office door.

The door that was slightly ajar.

The door that was now creaking open from the light bonk he'd given it with his head.

"Who's there?" The guard inside was already at the door, pushing it open.

Orrin boosted his dexterity and made it around the corner at the last second. He held his breath.

"Ellis, who is out there?" Silas asked, his voice carrying farther with the door open.

The guard, Ellis, paused before answering. Orrin's heart was beating so loudly he cast [Calm Mind] on himself. "Nobody. It must have been a draft."

"Close the door and get in here. We have to figure out what to do about him. I don't want to have him killed, but he knows too much about—"

The door closed with a thud. Orrin made his way back to bed, forgetting about his hunger. He sat and thought, wondering if he should wake up Daniel. They could probably get out of Dey if they left now. He was sure Daniel would want to bring Madi. They'd have to convince Madi that her dad was trying to kill one of them again.

Orrin put his head in his hands and had to cast [Calm Mind] on himself for the second time in one night.

Chapter 67

As his spell worked its magic, bringing his racing thoughts under control, Orrin replayed Silas's conversation in his mind. There was too much unknown. He needed help.

Orrin was sure that Daniel would want to talk with Silas before doing anything. The recent fight against Lord Sanerris of Odrana had confirmed something Orrin had been worried about for some time: Daniel was falling into the cliché of thinking he was all-powerful.

If this was one of the stories Orrin had read in the past, Daniel would keep getting out of trouble with some deus ex machina bullshit or by using the power of friendship. Instead, the only reason Daniel hadn't been toasted by Sanerris was because Orrin and Madi had come looking for him and had the forethought to grab the most powerful person around first—namely, Arandir.

"I guess Arandir sort of satisfies that trope," Orrin muttered to himself. He shook his head, clearing his thoughts. "Who's the Arandir of Dey?"

Orrin ran through the powerful people of the city. He couldn't go to the other lords of Dey; Orrin barely knew them, and they'd likely side with Silas. Amir wasn't powerful. Hell, he wasn't even level ten.

Orrin considered Guildmaster Pritus for all of five seconds before discarding that idea. He trusted her about as far as he did Silas. He might be able to ask around and find the Dragoon team, but he didn't need someone to fight Silas. He needed information.

Tony.

Orrin threw the blanket off and slid his feet into his shoes. *Why didn't I think of Tony before? He knows the way Silas works. He'll be able to help.*

Slipping back into [Camouflage], Orrin made his way out of the house. He knocked on the front door lightly so the guard outside would open it. While the woman was looking for who had hit the door, he squeezed by her and was off.

Orrin was learning. He didn't [Teleport] to Tony's house. The last time he had tried that had resulted in less-than-pleasant results. Instead, he walked. Few people were on the streets, and the stars twinkled brightly in the sky as he approached Tony's townhome.

"About time." Tony was standing at the door, rubbing his eyes. "You've been screaming your thoughts so loud that you woke me up. Come in. Tea?"

Orrin ran up the stairs and followed Tony into the back kitchen area. He paced in a quick two-step back and forth as Tony put a kettle on.

"Sit down, boy." Tony's voice echoed in Orrin's ears. "You're too worked up."

He guided Orrin into the spare chair and sat across the table. "I'm only catching every other word, but if you are in trouble, let me know now. I can see about getting you out of the city, but—"

Orrin cut Tony off. "I overhead Silas talking about offing someone who knows too much. I'm worried he's going to try and kill me . . . or maybe Daniel . . . but probably not Daniel—that would be stupid, right?"

Tony waited for Orrin to stop talking before he answered. "Killing either of you would be the dumbest thing he could do right now. I've caught wind of the little demon king problem. The upper crust is doing a good job of keeping it contained, but those who know still talk sometimes. The fact that there is a [Hero] in town is the only thing that is keeping half the richer folks from running for the hills. You might be surprised to know that quite of few of the people in the know also think highly of you and the little Catanzano girl. Sof wants to buy you dinner at some point, by the way. I told him I would let you know . . . if you ever stopped in to say hi."

Orrin narrowed his eyes. "Are you seriously inviting me to dinner right now? Silas wants someone dead, and it very well could be me."

Tony sighed in Orrin's mind—something that he still hated. It was weird seeing Tony's passive face with a closed mouth but hearing the full weight of a bored-dad sigh in your head. "What exactly did you overhear?"

Orrin stumbled trying to recall the words. "He said that he might have to kill someone who knows too much. He can't risk the entire city over a rash decision."

Tony sucked his cheek and chewed, the hollow depression on one side making him look even older than he was. "Have you done anything rash lately?"

Orrin rubbed his face with both hands. "When am I not doing something rash? I negotiated . . . well, more like acted like a middleman . . . I helped Dey and the elves figure out a way to fight the Demon Lord together. I might have unlocked a few of my Administrator skills and helped a friend become a [Healer]. I overheard Silas talking while making my way into his pantry to steal all his best food. Take your pick."

Tony leaned back in his chair and let out a laugh. Without his tongue, the bark of laughter sounded more coarse and animalistic, but Orrin warmed at the sound still. Tony laughing meant he was being an idiot about all this, right?

"You just happened to negotiate a deal—that I'm sure Silas is taking credit for, by the way—and you also made someone into a [Healer]? A healing class that the Hospital spends more gold than you can imagine trying to figure out? Do you know about their amulets? Did you use one somehow?"

Orrin waved the question off. "I can change a person's class. That's not the point. I want you to help me figure out if Silas is coming after me."

Tony's smile stayed on his face, but it seemed plastered on instead of real. "Not the point? You can just change a person's class and you think the lord of Dey is coming after you? Boy, the entire world will be after you if that comes out. Who else knows about your power?"

"Daniel, Madi, Amir—the guy who I made into a [Healer]—and Arandir," Orrin counted off. "Arandir is the—"

"I know bloody well who the leader of the elves is, you imbecile." Tony stood up and got his kettle. His hands shook as he poured two cups.

"I don't want any tea, thanks."

"I know, but you'll drink it anyway," Tony replied as he slapped the cup down on the table. "It'll calm you down. Now start again, from the beginning."

Orrin felt bad as he started filling in Tony on the events of the last few weeks. He'd been unconsciously avoiding him. After Orrin had told Tony about being an Administrator, the man had changed. He was still a curmudgeon, but Orrin saw the slight looks of fear when they talked about his powers. It was hard for Tony to reconcile his own knowledge of Administrators with the kid who had puked all over his house multiple times.

As Orrin recounted purchasing [Assign Class] and his reasoning for doing so, Tony laughed again.

"What's so funny?"

"You had no guarantee that your plan would work and went for it anyway," Tony chuckled. "You've either got the biggest balls or the best luck of anyone I've ever met. Maybe both."

Orrin warmed at that. He still felt silly for all the worrying he'd done, but everything had worked out in the end. Amir was happy with his class.

"Everything you've told me makes me think that old Sly-lus isn't after you." Tony took a sip of his tea and grimaced. He added a dollop of honey to the cup and stirred it with his finger. "He's an asshole, but he wouldn't discuss killing you while you were in the same house. That also knocks Daniel out of the equation, unless he was out?"

Orrin shook his head.

"You're missing something," Tony announced. "You didn't hear everything or you're recalling it wrong."

"I was a little worried I might get caught sneaking around," Orrin said, defending himself. "In case you forgot, that house is crawling with guards. I'd like to see you do better."

Tony's smile darkened into something ferocious. "Don't resist."

"What?" Orrin started to say when he felt fingers on the back of his neck. He slapped the back of his own head, but nothing was there. Yet the sensation continued.

"Tony?"

"I'm going to take a look. Just focus on the room you were in."

"I was in the hall." Orrin rubbed the hair on the top of his head. "Tony, this is really uncomfortable."

"I'm being as gentle as I can. Retrieving an exact memory is delicate. Don't think of too many things—I might scramble your brain."

"What?"

"I'm kidding. It's perfectly safe. Just shut up."

Orrin shivered as goose bumps raced down his spine. He tried to concentrate on Silas's office and what he overheard. Intrusive thoughts about what other secrets Tony could overhear kept creeping in.

"I don't care how you cheated on a test in third grade . . . what's a third grade?" Tony paused. "Never mind. I've got it."

Tony was silent and still for a few seconds. As his eyes refocused on Orrin, he shook his head. "You are safe. The words he used . . . *sanctioned . . . one boy gone mad . . .* It's not you."

"We can't be sure, though. Maybe we could go for a walk and you take a peek under the hood?"

Tony's visage froze. "Are you asking me to spy into the mind of the lord of Dey?"

Orrin rushed to pull the words back into his mouth. "I don't mean like that! You get passing thoughts, right? Maybe if I walk in Silas's room when you're outside, you could tell me if you get any murdery feelings or thoughts directed at me."

"I'm having murdery thoughts about you right now." Tony's hands clasped tightly around his mug. "If I have not made it clear in the past, let me do so for you now. I do not mind-rape people's thoughts except in cases of extreme danger or if ordered by the leaders of Dey. Asking me to do so, even in jest, is not something a friend would ever do. I stay in my house, not because I'm a misanthrope, but to minimize my contact with the public. Do you understand?"

Orrin dropped his eyes to the table. "I'm sorry, Tony. I shouldn't have . . . I'm sorry."

The heavy air in the kitchen sat still for a minute before Tony let out an exhausted breath. "My class and position do not allow me to act without consequence, Orrin. What I can do is give advice. You have Silas's daughter's ear. Use it. Don't try and plan the perfect situation or set them up. Tell your friend what you heard and discuss it with her. You overheard something in the middle of the night and overthought it. I'm nearly certain he is not discussing you, although if I were in his shoes, I'd have killed you long ago."

Orrin snapped his head up to see the smirk on Tony's face. "He did try once."

Tony's smirk turned into a sad smile. "No, he did not. He rolls the dice with people's lives, but Silas Catanzano does not kill people without much thought and even more reason. Trust me on that."

Orrin almost asked more but kept his mouth shut. He'd pieced together enough about Tony to know the mind mage and Silas had worked together in the past. He also knew Tony had lost someone named Reed. He hadn't asked anyone about it because he didn't want to overstep. *Did Silas kill this Reed guy? Tony didn't want him to but thinks Silas had his reasons? Who was he?*

"I guess I'll ask Madi," Orrin finally said, looking down at his full cup of tea. "I told you I didn't want any tea."

Tony winked and pulled the cup to himself. "More for me, then."

Orrin crept back into the Catanzano manor in the early-morning hours. The staff was making their way in as well, so he had an easier time slipping into the shadows with them. Daniel was still asleep when Orrin crawled into bed.

"Wake up, sleepyhead," Daniel shouted, pushing the mattress down so Orrin rolled over. "We've got so much to do today."

"Fuck off," Orrin groaned. He couldn't have closed his eyes for more than a few minutes. He peeked at the window and saw the sun was fully out. All right, more than a few minutes.

"I was going to grab Madi and see if she wanted to go to your little coffee shop place," Daniel said, strapping on his clothes and armor. They rarely went out without being fully ready for a fight. No scouts had returned yet, so time frames were iffy, but the [Hero] and his team weren't taking any chances. "I hear they have really good pastries, and I woke up with a sweet tooth."

"I'll go with you," Orrin muttered, trying to rub the sleep out of his eyes. "I have something to talk with the two of you about."

"Oh?"

Orrin threw his pillow at Daniel. [Side Steps] activated, and his friend blurred to the side. "Damn it."

"Sweet! That put me over the edge. I'm at level four now. Thanks!" Daniel was lost in thought staring at his status screen when another pillow hit him in the face. "Come on, dude."

Chapter 68

Orrin filled them both in on the walk to Amir's shop. Madi had to grab Daniel's arm and haul him down the street.

"Let me go, Madi," Daniel said as he struggled. Orrin noted his strength was much higher and he could have gotten away easily if he'd tried for real. "I'm going to ask your dad a few questions. I don't care who he is, he doesn't get to threaten us. I warned him last time what would happen."

"Are you an idiot?" Madi let go abruptly, letting Daniel fall. "I'm stopping you because I'm worried for your safety, not his. Besides, Orrin didn't say my father was threatening one of you. There is a war going on right now, if you haven't noticed. He could be talking about a deserter or a spy. He could be talking about someone who didn't want to pay their taxes because they found some information about someone of rank that could create a little chaos. Let me talk to him and I'll find out."

Daniel dusted off the imaginary dust on the sleeve Madi had grabbed and shook out his coat. "I want to be there when you do. Orrin can tell him what he heard and—"

"Yep. Tell the guy who pays for our food, housing, and equipment that I was sneaking around at night and overheard plans to murder someone. That'll be great for me," Orrin said, smiling. Tony had been right. Sharing the burden with his friends made it seem less scary. Or maybe it was being out in the light of day. The sky was blue. The air was crisp. Orrin was on his way to have coffee. Things were okay.

"What were you doing walking around the house at night, anyway?" Madi poked him in the side.

Orrin blushed and pointed ahead. "We need to hurry or we'll have to wait in the line forever."

He ran.

Daniel and Madi shared a look. "He was raiding the kitchen, right?"

Daniel raised his hands in defense. "Don't look at me. I was asleep."

After grabbing a few pastries and coffee, the trio made their way back to the house. Amir wasn't working, but his father had given Orrin an extra bagel. "On the roof."

Orrin could see the man was beaming with pride. He winked at Orrin so many times that Madi asked if he had something in his eye.

"I guess Amir is out healing," Madi said as they sat down at the kitchen table. "I'm glad someone got the class they want."

Orrin groaned. "Daniel, you have to stop teaching her how to be passive-aggressive. Madi, I promise you that when all this shit"—Orrin waved a finger around in the air above his head, encompassing everything—"stops, I'll do whatever you want. I think a war on two fronts, dealing with my own new powers, and trying to disrupt an assassination attempt might take priority."

Daniel decided to speak up, too. "Don't forget, you'd be level one. You wouldn't be able to do much when the Horde gets here."

"I know, I know. Sorry, Orrin. I'm just impatient. I think calling it an assassination attempt might be a little too much, don't you?"

"What assassination attempt?"

Orrin started at Silas's voice as he wheeled himself into the kitchen.

"Father!" Madi jumped out of her chair and gave the man a hug. He rested one hand on her back. "I'm glad to see you're taking care of yourself and leaving that dark office. We brought some food home. Would you like anything?"

Silas moved toward the table and appraised the various pastries. The three of them had been using camp rules and tearing small pieces off each to share and try. Silas took half a bagel that hadn't been touched yet.

"Thank you. No one is going to answer my question?"

Orrin wanted to activate [Camouflage] and slink out the door. Madi shuffled and opened her mouth, but Daniel used his normal charm and tact to start the conversation.

"We heard you're planning on killing someone, and me and Orrin want to make sure it isn't one of us," his friend said, crossing his hands over his chest.

"Orrin and I," Orrin corrected out of habit.

"What?" Madi asked. "I didn't hear what you said, Orrin."

"It doesn't matter."

"Who am I killing?" Silas glanced around, bemused. "Where is this information coming from?"

Daniel and Madi pointedly looked everywhere but at Orrin.

He closed his eyes in frustration at his stupid friends. "I overheard a conversation about killing someone last night. I didn't mean to eavesdrop, but here we are."

Silas stiffened almost imperceptibly, but Madi knew her father too well.

"It's true, then?" she asked, crossing her arms to mirror Daniel.

Silas put the bagel half back down and turned his chair around to leave.

"Where are you going?" Madi moved in front of him.

"Madeleine Catanzano, move out of the way, right now," Silas demanded, using his lord voice. "I will not discuss secrets of state with my daughter and her friends, even if one of them is the [Hero]. There is nothing here that concerns you."

"Hey, Silas, if it isn't me or Orrin that you want to kill . . . that's all you have to say," Daniel called out from his chair. "We understand you're basically at war right now. It's just . . . given our history . . ."

Silas's shoulders dropped a bit. "There are no plans to remove you or Orrin, no matter how much easier that might make my life at times."

Madi uncrossed her arms and put them on her father's hands. "Thank you. We all appreciate your honesty and all the hard work you are doing for everyone. I love you."

Orrin couldn't see Silas, as the man's chair was turned away from him. Madi's face flashed through several emotions as she watched her father respond. "Please remember that in the future. If you'll excuse me."

He left the way he came, not taking any food with him.

"There we go." Daniel reached across the table and snagged the bagel Silas had abandoned. "No plans to kill us today. That's a good day in my book."

"Someone is going to have a bad day, though," Orrin said as he leaned back and felt the pressure lift. "He didn't deny there's going to be a hit on someone, did he?"

Daniel shrugged. "We've killed people before. I'm sure he's got his reasons."

Madi was staring out the doorway still. "Daniel, I'm taking the day off from training. I'll be back later." She left before either of them could say a word.

"Sweet," Daniel said, putting his feet up on the table. "What should we do today?"

Orrin rolled his eyes. "I'm going to keep practicing. I might try and [Merge] a few skills together later."

"No fun." Daniel threw a small piece of bread his way. Orrin dodged and let it fall to the floor. "Let's go exploring. I want to talk with a few blacksmiths about working some runes into Gertrude's dragon bone parts."

"That's cool. Any specific runes you want?"

"Fireball would be cool."

Orrin stared at his friend. "You didn't read the rune book Madi got you, did you?"

"Of course I read the book. It was very long and had lots of words."

"Fireball is not a rune."

"It should be."

"While I agree it should be, it isn't. The runes on a weapon have to be something to enhance the weapon or the user. You might be able to find someone who could make you catch on fire . . . actually, maybe I should come with you. That might be something I'd pay for."

Daniel frowned. "You can be a dick sometimes."

Three shops and three rejections later, Daniel was angry. "What's the point of having dragon bone if nobody in town will put runes on it for me?"

Orrin watched around them, keeping vigilant. Although Daniel had become a local celebrity, there was always the chance someone could try to attack him. Odrana wasn't his only enemy.

"You were rude as fuck to that last guy," Orrin retorted while keeping his eyes peeled. "He knew a few runes that might be cool to have. You didn't need to insult him."

Daniel grabbed Gertrude off his back and held it high in the air. "Why would I want a rune to make this girl invisible? I want my enemies to see her cleaving through the air before she strikes them."

"You could have used that to sneak your weapon into places without using me as a pack mule," Orrin muttered.

"I heard that."

"I meant for you to hear it."

The fourth rune-carver merchant inspected Gertrude closely. "I can do up to three runes on this much surface area. Do you have anything in particular in mind?"

The old woman was holding Gertrude straight out in one hand while stroking the bone portion of the hilt with the other. It was unnerving to Orrin. He struggled to lift the sword unless he'd boosted his strength. This grandma had to be pushing ninety years old and was handling Daniel's sword like it was a broom.

"We've been to a few other places that said they could do five runes on it," Daniel complained. "What kind of runes do you know?"

"Excuse my friend," Orrin jumped in quickly. "My name is Orrin, and this is Daniel. Is there a reason you would recommend three runes while the others said five would be all right?"

The old woman didn't change her expression, but when she turned to Orrin, it was if Daniel ceased to exist. "So polite. You can call me Ziv. If you want five runes, I can do five runes. Only three will work at a time, and switching the charge between them will degrade the rune and dragon bone. In perhaps a year or two, either the rune will backfire and cease to work or the bone will shatter."

"Ziv, I'm sorry for earlier. No one told me that," Daniel tried to apologize, but Ziv continued to speak only with Orrin.

"He can be an idiot, but he's a friend," Orrin jested.

Ziv smiled. "There is a chart of available runes in the back. Let me fetch it for you."

Daniel leaned over as she shuffled into the back. "I'm considering going back to each of those other scammers and threatening them a little. Total assholes."

"Just be nice," Orrin advised as Ziv came back. She put down a list with marks on the side and pointed out a few.

"The more common weapon runes are Invisibility, Lightweight, Torch, or Expand. Lightweight might be good for this weapon, as it is a little on the heavy side."

Orrin gaped . . . *a little on the heavy side?*

"I have the [Light Weapon] skill," Daniel said. "Would that make a difference, ma'am?"

"Don't call me ma'am. You may call me Ziv. [Light Weapon] and Lightweight serve the same purpose, so you don't need that rune. Hold the weapon and show me how you swing it."

She directed Daniel toward a training dummy in the corner.

Daniel moved back a few steps to get enough room and swung Gertrude around. He let the sword clink against the wooden figure.

"Like an enemy is attacking you," Ziv ordered. "Not like you're out for a walk in town."

Orrin chuckled.

Daniel's fists gripped the hilt of his sword, and he dashed forward. His sword swung over and he cleaved the dummy in two.

"Better. Do you move fast like that often?"

"Faster still."

Ziv pointed to two runes. "I would recommend these two. Crooked will let you redirect the sword to hit at a different angle. With your speed, you can feint better against an enemy. It takes only a little mana, so even a melee fighter like yourself should be able to recharge it daily. This one is Return. It works like the skill. Do you have that as well?"

"No, Ziv, I do not."

"A quick learner." Ziv nodded at Daniel. "Return is costly, as I have to link two different runes and you'll have to purchase more dragon bone. Enough to make a ring will suffice. The rune on the ring can be triggered and the sword will return to your hand. The two runes are twins that want to be reunited when the mana is activated."

Orrin could see why she'd recommended the two. With Crooked, Daniel could cover some of his amateur sword-fighting skills, even with [Sword Proficiency], and fight opponents with more experience. Orrin could see a multitude of ways Return could be handy.

"How would I use that in combat?" Daniel asked.

Ziv smiled at him and patted his arm gently. "He did warn me that you were an idiot."

Chapter 69

As Orrin theorized about all the ways Daniel could use Return and Crooked on his sword, Ziv brought Gertrude into the back room. The two runes and the small ring of dragon bone that he would need to wear in the future set Daniel back stacks of gold.

Ziv finally brought the weapon and ring back to the front of the store. "There is technically enough space for another rune on this weapon, but more is not always better."

Orrin and Daniel made their way back to the Catanzano house, and Daniel went immediately to the training square to practice. The evil glint in his eye made Orrin return to his room instead. He didn't need to be Daniel's training dummy. Silas was paying people to train Daniel . . . They could get beat up a bit today.

Orrin instead pulled up his new favorite pastime: [Merge].

He had bought almost every type of [Ward] he could think of in an attempt to create an [Ultimate Magic Ward], but the system was laughing at his attempts. The closest he'd gotten was putting together a combination of [Earth Ward], [Wind Ward], [Fire Ward], and [Water Ward] called [Elemental Ward]. Surprisingly, when he added [Ice Ward] as well, [Merge] lost the ability to combine the different skills. He'd kept away from going through with the combination for a few reasons.

Merge: [Earth Ward], [Wind Ward], [Fire Ward], and [Water Ward]?
Compatibility: 100%

Chance of original spell loss: 100%
Variations: 1
[Elemental Ward]—creates a ward around yourself and your party within 50 feet that protects against Elemental Magic for MP maximum. 20 MP
Cooldown: 30 days
Accept?

While he thought that Elemental Magic was code for earth, wind, fire, and water, Orrin wasn't completely sure. He would lose the four spells if he went through with the combination. Although the cost for one cast of [Elemental Ward] would be worth it in the long run, he wouldn't be able to use [Merge] for a month. That was something that Orrin just couldn't take right now.

The reason? Orrin had gone on a shopping spree.

[Boost]—(Spell Modifier) Modify a spell to perform additional effect based on MP. 4 AP
[Split Spell]—(Spell Modifier) Modify a spell to split effects across targets. 5 MP. 4 AP
Would you like to buy [Boost] and [Split Spell] for 8 AP?
Yes or No?

Orrin had been eyeing these two spell modifiers for a while and had finally broken down the night before. Now with a little time to himself, he could experiment.

Merge: [Lightstrike], [Boost], and [Split Spell]?
Compatibility: 100%
Chance of original spell loss: 0%
Variations: 2
Cooldown: 2 hours to 4 days
Review Choices

Orrin bit his lip. He had been hoping to just get [Lightstrikes], the spell that the system had hinted at back when he completed the Obtain Level 10 Quest.

> **Variations:**
> **[Lightstrikes]—cast unerring beams of light that hit multiple targets (up to five) for 10 HP damage. 5 MP. Cooldown: 2 hours**
> **[Flash]—cast a burst of light that hits all targets within 20 feet for 100 HP damage. 50 MP. Cooldown: 4 days**

Orrin smirked. He could imagine the shit Daniel would give him if he took a spell called [Flash]. He selected [Lightstrikes] and upgraded his basic attack.

"Finally," Orrin muttered to himself as the spell slipped into his mind. The cooldown timer for [Merge] started counting down as Orrin looked through the rest of his spells. "Two hours to figure out what to get next. I hope Daniel is having fun."

Orrin spent the next hour going through the list he'd created in his head. [Heal Small Wounds] could be combined with [Split Spell] but not [Boost] for some reason. He couldn't even cast [Boost] and [Heal Small Wounds] normally. The spell-modifier options could be mentally added to a spell before he cast it. Technically, he could create the same effect of [Lightstrikes] by casting [Lightstrike] with [Boost] and [Split Spell]. The mana cost would be the original ten MP from the actual spell plus the five MP from [Split Spell] and whatever he put into [Boost]. He'd been sticking with just five MP for [Boost] until he had a better handle on its capabilities. Orrin could cast the same spell for twenty MP or [Merge] the three into [Lightstrikes] and cast it for five MP.

It was weird that he couldn't boost up his healing spell, but [Merge] gave him an interesting option with [Split Spell].

Merge: [Heal Small Wounds] and [Split Spell]?
Compatibility: 100%
Chance of original spell loss: 0%
Variations: 1
[Healing Hands]—heal up to 5 HP per touched target. 5 MP
Cooldown: 5 days
Accept?

Orrin considered the spell as a mental exercise. He didn't need to be able to heal multiple people at once, but could someone with [Healing Hands] let a bunch of people touch them and cure a bunch of people at once? Was it limited to two people, or could you use ten fingers to touch ten different people? The workarounds and cheats Orrin imagined gave him pause.

I don't need this, but I should remember to tell Amir about it.

Orrin did make one mistake while playing with his new spell modifiers. He wanted to test what [Boost] could do. On [Lightstrike] the spell modifier had made the damage stronger for the upgraded spell. Orrin wanted to try out an idea but couldn't pick between two spells to test his theory.

[Boost]'s description said he could perform an additional effect. He'd imagined that meant making the spell stronger. He looked at [Ice Sword] and [Fire Sword], then decided to play it safe and use ice.

The summoned sword was bigger than Gertrude and fell out of his hand. It dented the wood floor.

"Fuck." He'd tried to add a bit of [Toxic Touch] into the mix as an effect.

"Orrin? You alive up there?" Daniel's voice echoed from the bottom of the stairs.

"I'm fine," Orrin yelled back, dismissing the sword and checking the timer. Daniel had lasted an hour and a half.

"Come down here real quick."

Orrin pulled a small rug over the damaged wood floor and hurried down the stairs.

"What's up?"

"Madi sent a messenger. They found some more good monsters for us to kill. You got all your shit?"

Orrin glanced down at his outfit. "I'm not the one who has to get all his toys to kick ass."

Daniel smirked and rolled his eyes. "Let's go."

They made their way down the streets of Dey, pushing through the crowds of people. The general population was moving around more, finally getting over the upheaval. The lords of Dey would protect them and so would the new [Hero]. Who cared if a bunch of demons might show up any day now? People still had to eat, do their laundry, and go to work.

Orrin's stomach growled as they passed a stand. The glistening meat roasted over a low fire, and the merchant carved pieces directly onto a piece of bread that he rolled like a tortilla.

"I'm getting one of those, how about you?" Orrin stepped into line to grab an early dinner.

Daniel glanced toward the outer gate. "We don't have time to wait in line, O. We can grab something when we get back."

"I'll catch up. I can find you both with [Map]."

Daniel hesitated and then pulled a gold coin out of his pouch. "Get three. We can eat as we walk. I'll stall Madi as long as I can. She wants to meet us right outside the front gate."

Orrin watched Daniel walk away. The line moved quicker than he'd hoped, but he still had lost sight of his friend by the time he had the food. He pulled up his [Map] and saw the two marks showing his party members on the other side of the Wall.

"It's getting late." A guard stopped him as he began to head out. "Make sure you're back inside before the sun sets. We won't be letting people in after dark."

Orrin nodded his thanks and kept moving. They'd been warned that new procedures would start soon. Silas didn't want to chance adversarial forces moving in at night.

Not like they could stop me from using [Teleport] anyway.

Orrin spotted his friends and ran up to them. "Hey, guys, I didn't catch what these are called, but I've eaten half of mine and it's pretty good." Orrin held the rolled meat sandwiches out.

Daniel took his food woodenly but didn't respond. Madi hadn't turned toward him.

"Mads, you hungry? How far away are these monsters?"

"There are no monsters, Orrin. Maybe we should head back insi—"

"Would you go if it was Orrin?" Madi interrupted Daniel. The dim light of dusk made it hard to see, but Orrin could spot twin trails of moisture down her cheeks. "If it was him, would you still say it was too dangerous?"

"That's not fair, Madi," Daniel said in a calming voice, talking to her like he would a wounded animal. "You don't even know if he's alive."

Orrin glanced back and forth. "Somebody going to fill me in?"

Madi rubbed her eye and took the food from Orrin. "Odrana has Brandt. They're probably torturing him—or worse—for information about Dey. He's worked with most of the lords at one point or another. He's the person my father is planning on having killed."

Orrin took a peek at Daniel. His face looked aged, harder than he remembered. "We have to go get him, then, right?"

Daniel shook his head. "Tell him where he is, Madi."

Madi swallowed a bite. Orrin noticed she had barely chewed. "The informant my father used believes he's being held in Sanerris's castle. Brandt tried . . . he's been charged . . ."

"Brandt snuck over to Odrana and tried to assassinate their leader," Daniel cut in. "Don't lie to him, Madi. Brandt was angry and did something stupid. It's been months since he left. We don't know how long he's been held prisoner or if he's for sure even alive."

"He's alive," Madi said forcefully. "If he wasn't, my father wouldn't be sending someone to kill him."

Orrin didn't understand. "I'm confused. If he's alive, why wouldn't your dad try to save him . . . or kill Sanerris?"

"Killing Lord Sanerris would be next to impossible," Madi said, crossing her arms. The sandwich was already gone. "He'd have done it already if he could. The people guarding one prisoner wouldn't be as hard to get around. He's defenseless, probably starved and scared . . ."

"Madi, we can't storm into Odrana. I like Brandt. He's a good guy, but what would he say if he was here?" Daniel put his hands on Madi's shoulders as he talked. Orrin could see they were shaking.

"Probably something stupid that we'd ignore anyway, right?" Orrin caught Daniel's eye and tilted his head.

What the hell, man? We have to try, right?

Daniel's lips tightened into a thin line, and he jerked his head toward the Wall behind them. *We have to stay and protect the people here. The Demon Lord and his Horde could show up any day.*

Orrin put his left pointer finger on his right palm and bounced the digit around. *I can [Teleport] us there and back in no time at all.*

"You haven't been to Odrana," Daniel said aloud. "We would have to travel there or pay someone to get us there with [Teleport]."

"Even better," Orrin responded in kind. "Saves me some mana to use on the bad guys. Also, after I heal up Brandt—if he needs healing at all, that is—I'm sure Madi is going to kick his ass for making us save him. I'll need the extra mana."

Madi choked out a laugh and rushed Orrin. He awkwardly hugged her back when she fell into his arms.

"This isn't a good idea," Daniel said again. "I don't want to leave him any more than you do, Madi. You know this isn't smart."

Orrin patted Madi's back. "Yeah, but let's be honest. We never do things the smart way, do we?"

Chapter 70

Daniel stopped arguing after that and helped them plan.

"Madi, how much did you find out?" Daniel asked. He stuck his sword into the ground and leaned against it.

Why does it look so cool when he does stupid shit like that? Orrin sighed internally.

"Only what I've told you. Even my father hasn't been able to find out more information. If he knew for sure exactly where Brandt was being held, he'd have . . . acted by now."

"Orrin, do you think your elf friend might know something?"

"I can ask, but once we make any moves, Silas will know," Orrin responded, pushing down the urge to kick Daniel's leg out from underneath him. He had one foot propped up backward on Gertrude. "If all we need to do is get in and out, I can sneak in with [Camouflage]. I just need to get close enough to—"

"We are not sending you in alone," Madi cut him off. "There are a lot of skills and safety procedures set up for [Camouflage], which is one reason people choose [Invisibility] over it."

Daniel and Orrin tilted their heads in sync.

"What? I can study and read books, too."

"I think we're rubbing off on her a bit," Daniel said, stepping away from his sword to nudge Orrin.

"She's adorable when she tries to be like us." Orrin smirked. "I might have a way to get us all in together."

"We can't [Teleport] directly into his castle. He'll have teleport wards baked directly into the walls."

Orrin smiled and pulled up a spell. He tossed it to both his friends.

Daniel pinched the bridge of his nose and sighed. "How many new spells have you bought?"

Orrin muttered something and tried to change the subject. "We can probably hire someone here to get us nearby. We'd need to pay them a lot or . . . make sure they didn't go straight home."

"First, we are not killing a [Locationist] . . . maybe we can tie them up nicely," Madi said, shaking her head. "Second, how long have you been able to use [Camouflage] on all of us?"

"I didn't say kill them, and how do you tie someone up *nicely?*"

"Orrin . . ." Daniel threatened.

"I bought a bunch of spells when the elves kidnapped you to give to Sanerris, all right?"

"He's hiding something," Madi said as she studied his face.

"I know." Daniel had his hands on his hips.

Orrin threw his hands in the air. "Damn it, guys. I kind of created [Lightstrikes]."

Daniel frowned. "I thought you already had [Lightstrike]."

"With an *S* at the end. I've been playing with [Merge]." Orrin scratched the back of his neck. He'd been warned about using the skill, but he needed the power. He needed to be able to help his friends. If anything happened to Daniel or Madi, he'd be devastated. If the cost of protecting them was a little risk, it was something he was willing to do.

Daniel pointed his finger at Orrin. "We'll talk about this later. It's dangerous to create new spells, isn't it?"

"I made one that already exists. It's not like I went off the deep end and spent hours finding out every combination of . . . Why are you both looking at me like that?"

"You totally spent hours doing just that, didn't you?" Daniel's face was drawn again. "What are we going to do with you?"

"We need more information on Sanerris's castle, and we need to find someone who knows the area and can teleport us there." Orrin ignored Daniel and listed the plan item by item. "Should we go, just the three of us? Amir would help and could heal Brandt if he needs it while I help fight any guards we come across. Tony might be able to just waltz right in and make everyone forget Brandt was ever there."

Madi and Daniel shook their heads together. Madi glanced at Daniel before she started to speak. "Tony reports to the lords of Dey in an unofficial capacity, but he has enough power that Odrana would see it as an act of war."

"Amir is a sweet guy, but you can do anything he can do better," Daniel added. "Hopefully we won't need to fight anyone."

Orrin laughed. "You had to jinx us, didn't you?"

After figuring out a few more details, the trio made their way back into Dey and went about the tasks they'd assigned themselves. Madi visited the Guild. She wanted to find a quest that brought them close enough to the border that it could be used as an excuse for being away. She was also going to put out some quiet questions regarding getting a [Teleport] there, dropping hints that Orrin might not be able to make it with her and the [Hero] on this outing.

Daniel went to Silas to check on the status of the Pass reconnaissance, which wouldn't be out of the norm for him. Orrin smirked thinking about how Silas sighed every time Daniel caught his eye. The [Hero] was a micromanager who needed to feel involved and up to speed on every aspect of the plan to deal with the Demon Lord. This trip would be the same as the three other times this week that he'd annoyed Silas with questions. Only this time, he'd be fishing for a better timeline under the guise of going farther afield to train. That was something Silas would likely jump at, giving him a few days away from Daniel's nagging.

Orrin went to half a dozen shops, buying a random assortment of things. Most of the shopkeepers knew him at this point and waved as he entered their stores. He tried to be discreet as he stocked up on mana potions, health potions, and some food, grabbing vials from different vendors.

When they regrouped in Daniel's and Orrin's room, Madi slapped a piece of paper on the table.

"A small group of bandits has popped up along the road leading into Odrana. The Guild quest is for information only, since it is so close to the border. The Guild doesn't want us attacking a patrol unit from their army if the reports are wrong," she explained.

"It's five days of travel on horseback. That puts it outside your [Teleport] range even if you knew where to go, Orrin. I was able to find a few people with [Teleport], but they can only move ten miles. The only ones who can move more are helping set up the barracks at the far end of the Pass."

"Damn it," Daniel cursed. "Your dad said they don't have any concrete reports on the Demon Lord's Horde. They've sent a few of the stealthiest people they have to check out the surrounding areas, and all have returned unharmed so far. Of course, he could be lying to me, but I don't know."

"Isn't that good news?" Orrin asked, laying out the provisions he'd gotten on Daniel's bed. He was trying to separate things into three piles. It would be best for Madi and Daniel to carry their own packs with some supplies, just in case they got separated. "If the scouts can't find anything, we have more time. Let's say one of them comes back tonight and reports movement. That would still give us a day or two before the Horde reaches the front line. Even longer before they reach Dey, if we can hold them back a bit."

"Madi, if it takes five days to get to the Odranan border, how much more do we have to go to reach Sanerris's place?" Daniel asked and picked up a blue root vegetable up from his bed. "What is this?"

Madi took the long tuber from his hand. "You've eaten this like five times. It's a potato."

"Potatoes are brown."

"No, they are not."

Orrin snatched it away and put it back down on the bed. "Madi, how far into Odrana do we need to go?"

"From Dey to the border is about a hundred and fifty miles," Madi answered. She turned and walked over to a pile of books sitting next to Orrin's bed. "I think I brought . . . Yes, here it is." Returning to the table, she opened the book she'd retrieved. "I gave you this book ages ago, Orrin. It has a pretty good map of . . . here."

Turning a quarter of the way through the book, she spread out a two-page doodle of the world of Asmea.

"Daniel can draw better than that," Orrin complained. "Are the distances accurate?"

"From the border here, we have to travel northeast about another hundred miles to reach Mistlight. That's the Sanerris city stronghold. They have a school for [Mages] there."

"It's a port town, right?" Orrin remembered a sliver of conversation with Tony. "Could we go by boat?"

Madi shook her head. "Even if we could, it wouldn't be safe. The elves travel by longship and oar along the coastlines. Odrana has a few trading vessels that go farther out to sea, but they keep track of every passenger and item on the ships. The water is dangerous."

"Orrin could get the elves to help us," Daniel offered. "If we can't find someone to [Teleport] us the whole way, that would be eight days to get there and eight days to get back. That's too long. How long would it take to go by boat?"

"Two days, maybe three."

"Coming back won't be a problem if we travel on land, but I don't know if I can [Teleport] to the middle of the ocean. I have to have some image in my head of where I want to go. It won't take eight days to come back, either. I can jump us back easy enough."

"If you have the mana left."

"I can always blood cycle."

Daniel glared and then perked up. "I almost forgot. I have [Home Base]. I can get us all back in an instant."

"So, we have multiple options." Orrin finished separating supplies and filled two small bags with some food, a blanket each, and two potions of each type. He moved to his neglected mortar and pestle. He pulled out the penidrops he'd bought and started mashing them. A few regen potions would be helpful for them all to have. "We'll go to the elves and see if we can take a boat or travel by land. The problem is the Guild quest. It gives us an excuse to get away, but if Silas finds out we just jumped to the elven forest, he'll know something is up."

"Do you think Arandir would tell him?" Madi asked, watching over his shoulder as Orrin boiled the smashed mush.

"I don't want to chance it."

They sat in silence for a few minutes as Orrin continued his process. He hadn't made the regen potions recently and still had one left from his first batch but the recipe was easy for him to remember. He'd also made enough solo dinners over the years that his cooking skills weren't terrible. Making the regen potions wasn't any harder than following the directions for a box of macaroni and cheese.

After he began drying the powder residue, leached of the poison, Madi left. She made them promise not to leave in the dead of night.

As she closed the door behind her, Daniel chuckled. "She knows us so well."

"We should hide in the morning just to mess with her," Orrin agreed and kept stirring his powder around the small flame.

"In the cellar or on the roof?" Daniel suggested half jokingly. "You know there is a ladder to the roof in the training yard? There's a nice view of the sunset against the Wall. Silas has a great spot here. You can see for miles in either direction."

". . . that could work," Orrin muttered, forgetting to stir penidrop filtrate for a moment and nearly ruining the entire batch. He quickly stirred once and turned to Daniel. "How high in the air do you think you could throw me?"

Chapter 71

"If you die, I'm going to kill you."

Orrin ignored Daniel, pulling himself up higher on the ladder. "I've never had a problem landing at a different height. Why wouldn't I be able to start in the air?"

It was early morning, and Orrin was climbing to the top of the Catanzano manor's roof. Orrin's theory involved his [Teleport] spell. In the past, he'd always started from a flat surface and used the spell to jump to something he could see or a place he'd been before, as long as it was within the spell's range. Currently, [Teleport] let him move fifty miles in a single jump. He wanted to test an idea he'd had.

Could he [Teleport] during a fall?

Daniel had thrown two mattresses on the ground in the training courtyard. The [Hero] had essentially stolen the yard from Silas at this point, forcing all the other guards in the household to train elsewhere. Daniel wouldn't have cared, but Madi had mentioned spies and keeping his skills hidden. Lord Catanzano had sent his men away.

Orrin planned to jump not from the roof but from a controlled height. Even if he landed wrong, he was reasonably sure he could heal himself. He'd finished the regen potions and handed one off to Daniel, who would force it down Orrin's throat if he needed to.

"I don't see why you can't jump from the top of the stairs," Daniel complained.

Orrin finished climbing and turned around. He hung from the top of the ladder, one hand holding the roof. Daniel was holding the base steady.

"I could, but this is more fun," Orrin said as he teetered on the edge. "Here goes nothing."

He landed and bounced off the mattress stack, rolling to a stop when he hit the wall nearby.

"Orrin! Are you okay?" Daniel ran to his friend's side.

"Damn, I was hoping that would work."

"What in the . . . Why?" Madi rushed into the yard and took in the sight. Orrin brushed dirt off his sleeves, tousled but unharmed. Daniel squatted nearby. Mattresses and a ladder stood by guiltily.

"Orrin wanted to test out [Teleport]. I convinced him to only jump from a ladder. He wanted me to launch him into the sky." Daniel betrayed him immediately.

"Coward."

"Orrin—" Madi elongated his name in the way his mom used to when he was in trouble. "You know the entire manor is warded against [Teleport]."

". . ." Orrin glanced at Daniel, who was holding back a laugh.

"It's not my spell."

Orrin sighed and picked himself up. "Madi, do you know if [Teleport] works when a person is falling from the sky?"

"Why would you be falling from the sky?"

"I need to be able to see into the distance. If I have Daniel throw me or create a balloon, I could see farther away and [Teleport] where I want to go," Orrin explained. "It sounds stupid, but the way the horizon works—"

"I know the theory of the curvature of the world. We've tried to build towers high enough to see the far side of the Pass in the past. It's not safe to go that high up."

"I'm not talking about building a tower. If this world is even roughly the same as our home planet and I did the math right, if I go even a hundred feet up, I can see over ten miles."

Madi paused, began to speak, and shook her head. "You won't distract me. We can talk about that math later. If you go too high, sometimes things attack. I don't know of anyone with [Teleport] who would be foolish enough to do something that dumb when they could just travel for a few hours instead."

"If I can get to five hundred feet, I can probably see thirty miles. Daniel throws me in the air a few times and we make it all the way to Odrana in an hour."

Madi hesitated again and stomped her foot as she turned around. "I'll have the wards turned off around the yard for ten minutes. Don't try anything until I get back."

"Good job." Daniel patted him on the back. He rested his hand and slapped him a few more times, making dust billow. "You took a good tumble there."

"I didn't even think about the wards," Orrin grumbled, moving away from his well-meaning friend.

Daniel whistled as he picked up the top mattress that had bounced halfway off the stack with Orrin's descent.

"... Daniel? Did you know I wasn't going anywhere because of the wards?"

Daniel continued to whistle as Orrin chased him around the yard.

Ten minutes later, Orrin was grinning from ear to ear. [Teleport] would allow him to jump even in midfall. The spell stopped his velocity and set him a few inches above the ground no matter how high he jumped from or how long he fell.

The hitch in his plan was that even boosted to maximum strength and starting from the top of the Catanzano manor, Daniel could only throw him fifty feet. It wasn't straight up, either, but a sort of angle up and away from wherever he was.

As Orrin hurtled through the air, it was hard to make out distant places, too. He was spinning, and Daniel couldn't get a handle on how to throw him better.

"If anybody is watching this, I'm sure my father will ask me all sorts of questions tonight," Madi said, putting her hand over her face. "You two look like imbeciles."

"Madi, do you have hot air balloons or know anyone with the [Fly] skill?" Orrin asked, ignoring her. Despite her complaints, she'd been laughing and had even jumped off the roof once with Orrin. He'd teleported them both safely back to the roof before they hit the ground.

"[Fly] is one of those spells that people guard with their life. You can't unlock it? I thought you could do anything?" Madi's question wasn't sarcastic. Orrin narrowed his eyes at her, but she genuinely seemed to believe he could simply take any spell or skill he wanted.

"My running theory is I have access to most of the base spells and skills, but some things are unlocked once certain spells are leveled or maybe when combined through [Merge]," Orrin explained. "Is there anything else you can think of that might be of use? I don't need much control, just more than Daniel's uncoordinated ass can handle."

"Hey! I'm trying."

"Trying to kill me," Orrin muttered.

Madi sat down on the edge of the roof and dangled her legs over the side. Daniel sat down next to her.

After a minute, she snapped her fingers. "There was this fighter from Veskar a few years ago. He made shields in the air. He could make a few in a row and run up them like steps to attack from above . . ." She trailed off. "I think he broke both his legs when he jumped from too high once. I don't know what happened to him after that."

Orrin searched his store. "There's something called [Quick Step] that lets me kind of double jump, I guess? I'm not sure it's worth it. Nothing else really stands out."

Daniel patted the ledge between himself and Madi. "At least enjoy the view. We don't stop and take this all in enough."

Orrin settled in and watched the city come to life. People filled the streets, going about their business, as the three of them stewed in their own thoughts.

"I'm not sure we have the time to build a hot air balloon," Orrin started, but Daniel popped him on the head.

"You don't know how to build one of those, and even if you did, it would be too suspicious. We can find high points and move as fast as we can. I don't think going to the elves is a good plan. We should head out and do the Guild quest. Today. You can increase our dexterity and we can run for it."

Orrin absent-mindedly rubbed the spot Daniel had hit. "What are we waiting for, then? Let's grab some breakfast and go. I can [Teleport] us pretty far out. I think I can do about thirty miles east if I remember the place right."

Madi shook her head. "Orrin has been using too much mana today already to [Teleport] us too many times. We shouldn't rely too much on Orrin boosting our speed. We can take some horses and move out. We don't need to tip our hand on what we're up to. There are a few villages we can drop the horses off at tomorrow if we feel that we should make a few jumps instead."

"I've got a regen potion, and I still have three full cycles of my mana left. That's before I fully boost myself up."

"She's right, O," Daniel said, eyeing what was left of one of the mattresses on the ground. "We need you at full strength at all times. Getting Brandt back to Dey as fast as possible is our priority. We are not trying to get back at Sanerris."

Orrin raised an eyebrow at that. "You don't want revenge?"

"Madi may have made a good point—that killing the leader of Odrana right before the Demon Lord gets here might be bad timing."

Madi reached over Orrin and rubbed Daniel's head, fluffing his curls. "He's learning to listen. Isn't it adorable?"

Orrin rolled his eyes. "I guess we still have to get down."

"The ladder is right there," Madi pointed, confused about what Orrin was getting at.

Orrin linked his arms around both his friends and laughed. Then, with a quick boost of strength, he threw all three of them off the ledge.

The rest of the day was spent traveling. Madi had taken care of the logistics, and Silas either hadn't been made aware yet or didn't care that they were taking on a Guild quest. Orrin's bet was that Madi had kept it from him somehow.

"I hate horseback riding," Daniel complained as the Walls of Dey faded behind them.

"Is this the same road we first met you on?" Orrin glanced around. Most of the traveling they'd done in the past had been a bit more to the north, and this road was maintained much better than the roads to small villages and farms.

"It is. It's the main route to Odrana, with a town or two along the way. Hopefully, we can avoid those and find a barn to stable the horses until we get back."

Orrin tried to find any sign of that first fight, but the push of people coming and going from Dey moved them along even once out of sight of the city. "Why are there so many people on the road?"

"Word has begun to get out that something dangerous is coming," Madi said with a sigh. "Some people leave for the country when a Horde is coming, and others go into the city, thinking they can get some easy experience or even a bit of thieving."

Orrin watched a mother with three small children push past them. She was wearing rags, and the oldest of her children carried the youngest on his back. Orrin waved her over and handed her a few gold pieces. She cried and thanked him, but then the mass of others began to push in, asking for help.

"Back away." Madi's voice rang over the sudden mob. "In the name of Lord Catanzano, back away."

The people dispersed. Orrin couldn't find the family anymore.

"What are you doing? Do you not understand we are trying to be a little sneaky here?" Madi berated him.

"She had kids." Orrin didn't try to argue anymore and tried to pick up speed with his horse.

Once the sun began to set, people started disappearing off the road to make camp, and they were able to put a few more miles behind them before Daniel pointed.

"That barn is as good a place as any."

The farmer wasn't keen on feeding and looking after three horses until Daniel stacked up three gold pieces. The horses were taken and phase two of the plan began.

"You guys sure? I still haven't tested out [Purify]. It might not work."

Madi pulled her backpack higher up and cinched the straps. "Keep the dexterity just over the limit tonight. We can rest for a few hours tomorrow if it doesn't work for me."

This was the part of the plan that Orrin didn't like. Daniel had told Madi about his initial run through the forest and suggested Orrin use [Increase Dexterity] to let them run. With nobody on the roads at night, they could cover a lot of ground. At full speed and less than thirty dexterity, Daniel had run the length of the forest and to Dey in less than twenty-four hours. How much faster would they run at fifty dexterity?

Orrin had a few bags of coffee ready for them when they got tired, but Madi assured them both that if this didn't work, they could always [Teleport] back and use the horses. What was the worst that could happen?

Chapter 72

The good news was that [Purify] worked and had cleared Madi's Dizzy and Fatigued statuses when they hit her twenty minutes after they started running. Orrin had purposefully not reapplied [Increase Dexterity] or [Increase Strength] to her and let the side effects hit while they were still close to the horses. A quick misstep from Madi and Orrin's [Identify] had shown what he knew to be true—Daniel and Orrin were exempt from the overuse side effects of his increase-stat spells. However, the dexterity wearing off on Madi gave a solid hit to her ability to stay upright.

The bad news was that [Purify] worked. Orrin didn't realize how much that would incentivize both Madi and Daniel.

"I hate running," he complained for the twentieth time. They'd been at it for four hours. Daniel had convinced Orrin to tweak the numbers a bit more and pushed Madi's dexterity to seventy. He had used [Utility Ward] as the base and reapplied [Increase Dexterity] as needed.

Orrin knew Daniel was a good runner. He did the sports and moved the ball. He probably had an amazing sprint time back on Earth, but with the increased stats, it was superhuman. Daniel kept running forward to check the trail. No matter that Orrin was running [Map] nonstop and would see anyone or anything that they would come across well before needing a warning. *He's such a show-off.*

"I'm not fond of it, either," Madi shot right back. When they'd left Dey, her hair had been done up in a traveling bun. The sweat had destroyed the glamour of it all. "How is he quicker than us?"

Orrin did his best to shrug as they ran. He didn't want to have to explain their theory that even with the boosted stats, it only unlocked potential. In a previous life, in gym class, Orrin had had to run a mile in under ten minutes for a passing grade. He'd barely made it. With his dexterity at one hundred points, his legs moved faster and landed steady despite the uneven ground. The increased strength made each push off the ground throw his body into the distance at greater speeds. He was holding back a little to stay with Madi but figured they had to be moving as fast as the horses at a full gallop. Orrin didn't know the exact speed that people could run—or even horses, for that matter—but Madi knew the landmarks leading to the border and assured them both they were moving fast.

"How are you doing?" Madi huffed. "Is your mana pool almost empty?"

Orrin checked again. He'd used [Utility Ward] and kept his will topped off the entire time, but juggling all three of their dexterity and strength stats while also casting a [Heal Small Wounds] every once in a while to relieve their hard breathing was intense.

"I'm at about half but doing fine. Didn't you say just a bit more like an hour ago?"

Madi slowed down to a walk and then stopped completely. She rested her hands on her knees and took deep breaths. "I'm feeling it more and more each time we rest. Sorry, give me a minute."

Daniel timed his entrance perfectly. "Why are you two stopping? There's a village about three miles from here. I saw the lights—"

"Shut up," Madi and Orrin said together. Daniel's boundless energy was a bit much after no sleep all night.

Orrin threw a healing spell on Madi and walked Daniel up the road a bit. "We don't have the same constitution that you do. We can run faster, but it still hurts after a while. I'm not sure Madi or I can do much more tonight. Do you want to go ahead and get a room at an inn?"

"Does that village even have an inn?"

"That village is Stillrock, one of the main trading posts between Odrana and Dey. They have multiple inns, but we can't stay at one tonight." Madi hobbled forward to join the conversation. "We left yesterday with horses. It should take us four more days to arrive. Maybe three days if we pushed the horses. Do you two realize we just ran a hundred and ten miles in just under five hours?"

"Good to know," Orrin muttered, tallying up the math. Madi had slowed them down a bit but not that much. Knowing that he could run somewhere between twenty and twenty-five miles an hour was nothing to laugh at. *Look at me now, Coach Steele.*

"We can make camp for the rest of the night and then do some reconnaissance tomorrow." Madi took the waterskin off her side and took a long sip. "Don't forget, we have to attempt the Guild quest. I'm hoping Orrin's [Map] finds something fast so we can keep moving."

"We should only travel like this at night," Daniel added. "Even with how slow you two are compared to me, it's a weird sight seeing you jump ten yards a step."

Orrin forcefully laughed and pushed Daniel into the tree line. "Go clear a space for a tent. No fire; we can eat when we wake up."

Daniel saluted and walked off, not realizing Orrin had saved his life. Madi lost a little of her princess shine when she was tired, and she hadn't slept for almost twenty-four hours. She'd taken a deliberate step in Daniel's direction at his light gibe.

"Ignore him," Orrin said as he nudged her with his elbow. "I'll make sure to give him less dex tomorrow."

Madi's smile was positively evil. "Sounds good to me."

Stillrock was much bigger than a village, but Orrin could see why Daniel had thought it was smaller. The town was sprawling, with houses set far apart as they approached with their hoods up. As they traveled into Stillrock, the houses became shops before a barricade and gate blocked the more expensive homes and stores.

"Anything outside the wall is not really Stillrock," Madi explained as they entered through the gate. No guards stopped them or even looked their way. "The town sits close to the Odranan border. A small river separates the territories of Dey and Odrana, about ten miles on the other side of the walls. People from both sides come here to trade and live before going back to their homes. Even Veskar has some semipermanent businessmen who live here part-time."

Orrin ignored Madi as she overshared information, something she'd started doing ever since she'd found out both of them were from another planet. Orrin assumed she must have thought she was filling Daniel in on everything at first.

"Madi, Madi, stop," Daniel finally snapped. "We just need to know where these bandits are attacking and have Orrin count how many there are. That should be enough to satisfy Pritus, right? We don't need to be in town or know anything about it right now. Which way is the fastest?"

Madi brought them down busy streets for the next hour, avoiding the worst rush of the morning and keeping as low a profile as she could. Some of the locals might recognize her, and they didn't have the time for the required political dance that would ensue if that happened.

Luckily, they made it through Stillrock without a hiccup. Orrin felt a twinge of loss that they hadn't been able to explore the charming town a bit more. *We can rest here with Brandt. It might be within my [Teleport] range from Mistlight.*

As they exited the gates on the eastern side, more carts and people filled the street, trying to get into the city. Orrin noticed more haggard faces on this side of the gates and pointed out a cart with a few arrows still stuck to the back.

"Might be the work of the bandits we're looking for," he offered.

Madi sighed and nodded. "You're going to have to do it. I'm too well-known, and Daniel . . . well . . ."

"He'll find a way to have a feast thrown in his honor, I know."

"Hey, you two are getting on—"

"Off I go. Take care of Daniel for me," Orrin said over his shoulder as he made a hasty getaway.

He approached the cart and waved at the couple riding up top. Only one horse was connected to the right side of the hitch. The left side was empty, with a dark stain against the wood. The grizzled older man only growled, but his daughter smiled and waved back.

"Did you two find trouble on your way in?" Orrin asked, pointing at the arrows on the side of the wagon. The old man muttered and reached over the edge. He yanked the arrow out and threw it on the burlap bags they were carrying.

"I don't mean to pry," Orrin said, holding up his hands. "I'm heading that way with friends and don't want to run into anything pointy."

The daughter chuckled. She was at least half the old man's age with an easy smile. She slapped her father's arm and whispered something to him. Then she turned back to Orrin.

"There are always bandits on the roads, but some have been a bit more aggressive in the last month or so. They killed one of the horses, too." She pouted prettily. "Are you with the Guild? Is someone finally going to save us?"

Orrin's bullshit meter spiked.

Daniel's rise in popularity had started in middle school. He'd always made time for Orrin, but he was busy and had his own life. Orrin wasn't unpopular at first. He'd been befriended by a new girl at the school. He hadn't known that she was using him to get to Daniel. She wasn't the last to completely blow him off once he'd made the introduction, but she'd been the first. He'd learned to pick up the signs: over-the-top expressions and near flirting, asking for help in subjects they were doing fine with and snooping for information in a seemingly natural way.

"Me? With the Guild?" Orrin forced a laugh and watched her smile turn brittle. "I simply don't want an arrow planted in my behind." He pointed to the back of the wagon by way of explanation. "Thank you for the information."

Orrin turned and walked away before they could respond. He caught up with Madi and Daniel a minute later.

"What did the couple say?" Daniel asked as they regrouped.

"Couple? I thought that was his daughter." Orrin glanced over his shoulder but couldn't see them anymore. "They said it was bandits, but she was acting weird."

Madi perked up. "Weird how?"

Orrin tried to think of the words to explain it but shrugged it off. "She thought I might be with the Guild."

"Damn it," Madi cursed. "We need to get going, then. If the local Guild chapter finds out we're here, they'll want us to report in on the state of the roads between Dey and Stillrock. Let's go."

Daniel's stomach grumbled. "Lunch first?"

"Eat on the way," Orrin said, fishing some raisin bread out of his storage.

They were able to make it five miles before the sun started to dip again. Walking was much slower, and the people passing them kept Orrin from increasing their stats again. He kept an eye on [Map] but saw nothing beyond the people they passed and the occasional deer. Once a bear lumbered into view on his [Map], but it was moving southwest and disappeared within a few minutes.

"We can make it tonight if we run through the night," Daniel said, pulling apart the chicken Orrin had pulled out for dinner.

"I think we should sleep a few hours then run," Orrin suggested. "I don't know about you two, but I'm still tired from last night."

Daniel snapped a bone between his fingers. "We need to hurry."

"We can [Teleport] back to Dey if we need to," Orrin countered. "Brandt can wait another day. He's not going anywhere."

A choked-off sob from his side made Orrin close his eyes at his stupid words. "I mean, he's held on this long. We need to be in the best shape we can be when we rescue his butt."

Daniel tossed his broken chicken pieces into the fire. "I'll take the first watch. Get some sleep, you two."

Orrin and Madi crawled into their respective sleeping bags. Orrin tried to fall asleep, but Daniel was still moving around, trying to find a comfortable spot to sit.

"Madi? Are you awake? I'm sorry for what I said," Orrin whispered. "Brandt will be fine. He's probably going to give us shit for saving him."

Madi turned over and faced him. "Daniel thinks he'll yell at me for rescuing him. I think he'll yell at Daniel for letting me come at all."

Orrin chuckled. "I'm not taking either of those bets."

Silence swallowed the small camp again.

"Madi? Orrin? I think someone is coming toward us," Daniel whispered. He kicked some sand over the small fire they'd built. "Orrin, what do you see?"

Orrin pulled up his [Map]. More than a dozen white dots were moving in their direction.

Chapter 73

"We're leaving, now," Daniel said, throwing the few camp supplies at Orrin. "Orrin, can you use [Teleport] to get us back to the Stillrock?"

"I can, but we—"

"Don't argue."

Orrin caught the sleeping bag and took an extra second to push the length of it into his pocket. [Dimension Hole] was one of his most useful skills. In no time at all, Orrin had the entire camp stored away. His friends reached out and put their hands on his shoulder. Ignoring Daniel's orders, Orrin jumped them a mile down the road back the way they'd come.

"Orrin . . ." Daniel's voice was tense. "I said to the town. Why am I not seeing buildings?"

Orrin continued ignoring Daniel and spoke to Madi. "I brought us about a mile away from where we were sleeping. We can use [Camouflage Ward] and sneak by them. I counted fourteen people heading our way, but I doubt that group was everyone. We can either track them and get an exact count or just boost up and start running."

Madi looked up at the sky, checking the position of the moon. "It's not even midnight. We could get close to Mistlight."

"Excuse me?" Daniel brushed between them. "Why am I being ignored? I'm in charge here."

Orrin laughed. Madi smirked.

"Daniel, you've been outvoted. We are not going back to Stillrock. Do you have an opinion on what we do next?" Orrin cast [Camouflage Ward].

"We are going to talk about this later," Daniel complained. "We don't have time to track them down. If we're going to run, let's make it to Mistlight today. Orrin, bring Madi to the max with us. We need to move."

Orrin acquiesced and cast [Utility Ward] again before increasing Madi and Daniel's strength and dexterity to one hundred.

Despite Daniel's suggestion that they not try, Orrin checked his [Map] as they ran. Strangely, he didn't find the fourteen they'd encountered before. *They must have run back to their hiding place.*

The river border had a bridge and bored guards on either side, but another application of [Camouflage Ward] made the crossing easy. The sun was coming up when Madi slowed them at an intersection. All three were slick with sweat and exhausted. She pointed to some markings on a crude sign. "Mistlight is another ten miles in that direction. We've made it."

"Orrin, find us a spot nearby to rest. We all need some sleep," Daniel ordered, still trying to be the group leader. Madi nodded at Orrin behind him.

"Yes, sir." Orrin saluted sarcastically and marched into the brush. His mana was at about a tenth of his full mana pool and he needed the sleep. Even with [Meditation], the long two-day run had worn him down. He hadn't fully regained his mana pool once, and casting his buffs on everyone every twenty minutes had drained him.

Orrin made sure to cast [Purify] on Madi as the last buffs wore off. He patted Daniel on the shoulder and nodded at the sleeping bag he'd laid out.

"Get some sleep."

Daniel shook his head. "I'll take the first watch."

Orrin sat down and crossed his legs. "D, I have my [Map]. I'll be able to see anyone long before they get here. None of us are in any condition to fight right now, and I'm not sure I could [Teleport] us more than once. You and Madi need sleep. I need you two rested so you can protect my scrawny ass."

Orrin knew playing the protect-me card was low, but it was true. He wasn't as good in a fight. He was useless to them right now besides his ability to stand guard while they slept.

Daniel's arm snaked out and pulled Orrin into a headlock. He rubbed his knuckles on Orrin's head. "You're an idiot. We wouldn't be here if it wasn't for you. Not just here right now, but alive at all. Stop doubting on yourself already, dude. I can barely hit you with your new watery fight style, and you have more options than a Swiss Army knife. Don't even get me started on your Administrator bullshit. I'll go to sleep, but only because I know you can protect us. I will wake up in a few hours and make you get some sleep, though, even if I have to knock you out." He playfully increased the pressure of his chokehold around Orrin's neck for a second before letting him go.

Orrin watched his friend crawl into his bag. When the snoring began, he wiped at some dirt that had gotten in his eye and refocused on his [Map].

After a breakfast of sausages wrapped in pancakes, Orrin brought their strength and dexterity up to a manageable point for Madi so they could jog halfway to Mistlight before seeing anyone. Once the traffic began, they pulled up their hoods and moved slower. It was midafternoon by the time they made it to the gates of Mistlight, and Daniel was grumbling about wasted time.

"We can't [Teleport] into the city," Madi said, kicking him in the back of the leg. "We can't run in like the wind, either. We have to keep a low profile. Once we get inside, we can do some investigating. Odrana has a Guild chapter, but from what I know, it's corrupt and not worth visiting. Lord Sanerris has all but bought every position of power. I have a few acquaintances I could ask questions of, but I doubt that would be helpful, either."

"Brandt is in Sanerris's house, right?" Daniel's voice was loud, and Orrin kicked him. "Will you two stop kicking me?"

"Shut your mouth then," Orrin muttered out of the side of his mouth. "There are guards up ahead."

The gate they were moving toward made the bundles of people traveling to the city funnel into a walkway just wide enough for a single cart. Madi had avoided the main gate, saying it was too conspicuous. This side gate was the entrance for small-time merchants and people traveling for pleasure. The main gate was for dignitaries and large shipments, which meant tighter security.

Orrin was impressed with the height of the wall. Mistlight's protection from monsters wasn't as tall or thick as Dey's Walls, but there was a cold beauty to the dark-blue material it was made out of.

"There is a quarry about twenty miles east," Madi whispered to Orrin, seeing his gaze. "The Sanerris family kept hundreds of orc slaves and forced them to dig the blue limestone. Nobody knows how many orcs and other slaves died excavating. They were only allowed to cut pieces as big as you can see there."

Orrin noticed the line about five feet up. "That's stupid. Why did they need it so big? Small cuts would have worked fine, right? I'm not an architect, but I've seen old-timey castles. That's as big as a horse."

"Sanerris family secret." Madi shrugged. "They had the money and the manpower. They built the wall. The rumor is it doesn't extend into the ground, and they used other stone for protection there and the base of the city throughout. You'll see how much blue there is once we get inside. When the sun hits the roads in the morning, the entire city shines with a cloudy blue haze. That's where the name Mistlight comes from."

"How big is the city?" Daniel asked, watching a guard who poked around in the pack of the young man in front of them. "Can't we find the castle that Sanerris is in and— Ow."

Madi shook her hand out before rubbing her pointer finger. "Why is your skull so hard? I'll show you when we get inside . . . keep your mouths shut."

Madi stepped in front of them and smiled at the guard. "Would one of you point us in the direction of an affordable inn? Preferably by the shopping district? My guard here can tip you if—"

"Move along." One guard waved Madi through and pointed to a woman behind Daniel. "You, random spot check. Come along."

"Davis Jergson, I will report you again," the woman carrying a tray of vials cursed. "You can't keep pulling me aside so your wife gets the best spot in the market. If you try—"

"Hey, Ephraim. I think this one is refusing a search. Maybe we ought to send her around to the front gate today," Davis yelled over Orrin's head as he snuck through as quietly as he could. The other guard spit at the ground and smiled nastily.

"Come on." Madi grabbed Daniel's arm and pulled. "Don't interfere."

Daniel frowned but allowed himself to be dragged away. His face was still contorted when he turned to complain, but amazement settled over him instead as he got his first view of the interior of Mistlight.

"It's magical," Daniel whispered. "Beautiful."

Orrin agreed. The majority of buildings crawling toward the sky were painted in varying shades of blue. The deep blue of the walls and streets reflected the vibrant shades of the buildings, throwing illusions of movement into every corner. The people moved with an air of ease and calm, completely unlike the purpose and strong stride of the people of Dey. Orrin saw families in swimsuits, holding picnic baskets. They moved north, toward the water, and Orrin could only surmise they were having a beach day. Even the vendors setting up stalls in small grooves between buildings put out their wares with a relaxed air about them. Streamers and flags flew from nearly every window and door.

The people were diverse, too. Dwarves, orcs, and humans crowded the streets. Most of the people moving around wore dark shades of green, blue, and even some purple. The few people wearing more muted colors were standing around slack-jawed, taking in the sights.

"We need to get some new clothes," Madi said to herself. "Orrin. Daniel. Stop acting like country boys and come with me."

Orrin snapped out of it and raised an eyebrow at Daniel.

"Yes, my liege. Whatever you demand, my liege," Daniel replied sarcastically but followed her.

Madi smirked imperiously over her shoulder. "I kind of like that. Keep it up."

Three gold and seven silver pieces later, the trio stepped out of a clothier's shop. Daniel kept tugging at his sleeves.

"Are you sure this color is right?"

"You heard her, purple is all the rage right now," Madi said, watching for an opening in the foot traffic. "Ms. Rose said there's a good inn up this way. We can talk more once we're settled."

Orrin glanced at his own green shirt and thanked his luck that Madi had been focused on Daniel.

"Hurry up, you two," Madi yelled over her shoulder.

The Dragonflight Inn was a step down from staying at the Catanzanos' manor, but they took a room for one important reason: it was within throwing distance of the Sanerris castle.

On the western side of the city, the castle was made of the same blue stone as the walls. Orrin thought calling it a castle was a bit of an exaggeration, but he'd grown up watching celebrities showing off their mansions. It had a lawn all the way around it, separating the main part of the residence from the rest of the city and the wall behind it. Eight towers joined together in an octagonal shape with a slightly higher tower in the middle overseeing the rest of the city. The Sanerris castle loomed over Mistlight like a blue beacon.

"We can rest and eat some dinner," Daniel said, yanking on the long sleeves of his shirt again. "Then we find a way to bust in there and free Brandt."

"It's surrounded by a fence and I can count ten guards from here with [Map] . . . I think," Orrin countered. He sat on the bed and bounced, testing it out. "We should set up a distraction on the other side of the city and try to sneak in."

Madi let the curtain fall from where she was spying out the window and turned to them. "Let's make a plan."

Chapter 74

The plan was simple: Daniel was going to create a distraction a few blocks away. Something flashy and big, but not traceable to him. Madi would help him cover his tracks and make their way back to Orrin, who would be waiting by the gate to Sanerris's home. They would use [Map] and [Camouflage] to sneak inside and find Brandt. Orrin had already tried to find Brandt using [Map], but something blocked his view into the castle. He could make out the grounds, but beyond the inner courtyard was a blank slate.

Orrin had [Teleport] and Daniel had [Home Base]. Either one of them could get the entire party out of Mistlight if they needed to, with Daniel's once-a-month skill bringing them all the way back to Dey in a moment. They wanted to save that as their trump card. Sanerris would probably send people after them if they tried to run over land, and when the shit hit the fan, Orrin didn't know how much mana he'd have left. Sleeping all night and most of the day had helped him reset to a full pool of mana, but he was about to attempt a break-in on the leader of Odrana's fortress.

"If you see my butterflies in the sky, abort and meet by the side gate," Madi said as she pulled a strap on Daniel's chest tight. The contraption he used to carry Gertrude rested on his back since he wouldn't have Orrin around to carry his giant sword.

"We know what to do." Daniel reached over his shoulder and connected his weapon to its holster. "I'm more worried about Orrin going alone. We shouldn't split up. Isn't that one of your rules, O?"

Orrin smiled as he double-checked the vials on his hip. "That's for gaming. There isn't a dungeon master waiting for us to fuck up in real life. I'll be watching to see where most of the guards leave from. We want to keep the element of surprise for as long as we can. More importantly, have you figured out what you're going to do to create a distraction big enough to draw out his guards?"

Daniel's grin chilled Orrin's soul. "I was thinking about bringing a building down."

"Don't do anything that hurts people."

"There are a bunch of empty buildings around—haven't you noticed?" Daniel took a peek out the window. "The fronts are painted and the small lawns are maintained, but nobody comes in or out of them."

Madi frowned. "Mistlight is prosperous. There's no reason someone would buy a failed business. Which building are you talking about?"

"After we bought our clothes, do you remember the street with the guy selling lizards on a stick? I noticed five buildings with the doors locked up tight. There was a thick layer of dust up the steps behind the iron gates of each one."

Orrin pulled up his [Map] and sketched out the local streets on a spare piece of paper. "Show me where they are."

Daniel ran his finger along the squares and lines of Orrin's doodle. "Here to here. I don't know which one I'll go for, exactly, but you should be able to see the dust, right?"

"It's weird, but yes, I'll be able to see," Orrin answered, deep in thought. *Why would there be a bunch of empty buildings on a street with so much foot traffic?*

"Should you boost me up, then?" Daniel spread his arms wide. "Hit me with it."

Orrin rolled his eyes. His base will was twenty-eight. He cast [Utility Ward] at level two, which was the equivalent of casting each increase-stat spell five times at level two. The plus two to each stat became plus six instead, adding up to a total of thirty extra points to each stat for all three.

And it only cost me two hundred MP! Orrin thought. *I guess really only a hundred and ninety-eight MP, but who's counting?*

With his intelligence at fifty-eight, the rest of his spells cost almost half as much, and he quickly got Daniel to the maximum strength and dexterity that he liked. He kept Madi in the sixty range.

"What gives?" Madi's eyes were distant, the telltale sign that she was checking her status. "You didn't push me all the way up."

Orrin scratched his neck and tried to not turn away from her angry tone. "I'll bring you up more once we reconnect. I don't like buffing you even this much when we're all separated. If something happens, you're going to go down hard with side effects. You only have twenty minutes before the [Increase Dexterity] and other spells wear off, so hurry."

Madi didn't argue, realizing Orrin's concerns were valid. Instead, she threw a pillow at Daniel in frustration. [Side Steps] activated, and he blurred to the side.

"We can pillow fight later," Daniel said as he bent and tossed the pillow back on the bed. "Time for a rescue."

Orrin had to wait alone for ten painstaking minutes before the clamor began. He had found a spot that sold books on the curb, mostly trashy romance novels like the ones Silas kept as a keepsake. He posted up to avoid suspicion.

True to his promise, Daniel used a combination of his [Gravity Strike] and [Shooting Star] to pinball around the inside of what Orrin hoped was a vacant building. Orrin heard the screams from a few streets over before he saw the plume of dust rise into the air.

No butterflies. That's good, at least.

More yelling nearby alerted Orrin to the gate opening. Half a dozen guards ran out and made their way toward the disturbance. The guards that remained closed the gate but stood nearby, watching the distance.

"Hey."

Orrin jumped and turned around. Madi smiled.

"Where's Daniel?"

Madi rolled her eyes and pointed to the alley. "He got covered in dirt. He doesn't want to be seen. We only got away because all five of those buildings were under construction. They had taken down the walls between them. We just walked out of a different entrance. Luckily, it was close to some small streets. He got a few looks, but almost everyone was covered with dust when that building came down."

Orrin followed Madi. "How'd you avoid getting covered?"

Madi brushed imaginary dirt off her sleeve. "I was raised properly. I know how to avoid a mess."

"Hurry up," Daniel hissed from in front of them. "Did they open the gate?"

"Yes, but they closed it again." Orrin made sure they were still in a party and cast [Camouflage Ward]. He also reapplied the various buffs that had worn off and cast [Ward] on each for good measure. "We might have to fight our way in."

"I've got it," Madi stated. "Stick close."

"We can't look at each other. Shit, I hate this spell. It makes me want to puke," Daniel complained.

"Madi, tap your spear on the ground every few steps," Orrin called out as loudly as he dared. A small click ahead of him helped him find his way forward. Orrin had to agree with Daniel. Being on the other end of [Camouflage] was disorienting. He knew Madi was ahead of him and could catch glimpses of her whenever she moved. As long as she kept her back to something simple, like the walls of the building nearby, Orrin's eyes would gloss over her, barely able to find her. Once she stepped into the street with the Sanerris estate in the background, Madi's figure reappeared like an afterimage. She shook and distorted a bit. It hurt his eyes and turned his stomach.

"I see why you don't like this," Orrin whispered to his side. He kept [Map] running as Madi approached the gate. Two guards still waited inside the entrance to Sanerris's house. "What is she doing?"

Madi raised her hand and shot a [Shimmersight] at the guard farthest from her. As the lights exploded across the man's eyes, she reached in and yanked the first guard against the metal gate . . . hard.

"That was awesome, Madi," Daniel said, pushing the gate open and punching the stunned guard in the face. "Orrin, give me some rope. I'll tie them up."

Orrin sighed and held out two pairs of manacles. Daniel took them gingerly.

"Do I want to know why you have these?"

Orrin sighed. "I came prepared. Cuff their hands together and make them hug that tree. Hurry up."

They approached the front door in a crouch. Standing by the front door made Orrin feel exposed. Even with [Camouflage] running, he felt like there were eyes on him.

"Any guards inside?" Madi whispered in the wrong direction.

"I can't tell." Orrin reached out and tried to grab her arm. He touched her hair instead. "Sorry."

"This is going great," Daniel complained. "I'm going in."

The door creaked a little as they entered the main entrance to the castle. Orrin sighed in relief that no guards waited right inside.

"This is too easy," Madi muttered. "Where is everyone?"

"Responding to the distraction," Daniel said before moving deeper into the house. "Which way, O?"

Orrin checked his [Map]. "Shit. It's not working. Everything is grayed out, and I can't even make out you two anymore."

"Daniel, get over here and stay close. We might need to drop [Camouflage]. If we get split up in here . . ." Madi trailed off.

Orrin didn't try his other spell but knew from Madi's warning that Sanerris would have teleport wards activated. He checked the entrance hall they were in. It was furnished nicely enough, but not too extreme. A few paintings of people Orrin didn't know lined the walls. Chairs and a few tables rested underneath with trinkets and curiosities for people to peruse as they waited for the lord of Odrana to receive them. Other than the front entrance they'd come through, he could see two closed doors at the far left and right sides of the hallway.

"Which way?" Orrin whispered to Madi.

"I don't know."

"We probably should have figured this out beforehand."

"We can't walk into a shop and ask for the layout of the castle, now can we?"

"This way." Daniel's voice moved to the door on the left. "Follow me."

Orrin checked his mana pool. He could take a regen potion now but decided to wait. He could blood cycle a few full mana pools before he needed the quick boost of a potion. His party was at full health, boosted up, and ready to fight. He'd done what he could. It was time to let Daniel be the [Hero].

Daniel kept one hand on Gertrude's hilt, ready to swing her over his shoulder at any moment. He slowly turned a handle and gently opened the door.

After taking a half step inside, he turned back and smiled. "Dining room. Nobody's here."

The three walked into the lavishly appointed room. Sanerris had spent money on the furnishings here. They stood at the end of a long table that glistened with a fresh wax polish. Silverware was laid out, but no food was on the table. Various bottles lined wine racks along the far wall. A set of doors at the other end of the room exited to what Orrin thought must be the kitchen.

"Should we steal all his alcohol?" Daniel walked around the table and lifted a bottle. "Madi, is this stuff any good?"

"Put it back," Madi hissed across the table. "We need to keep moving before—"

Two servants entered the room with steaming bowls of food. One set her bowl down and turned without incident. The second paused with wide eyes fixated on what appeared to be a floating bottle. He blinked twice and moved to run.

"Fuck," Orrin cursed as he cast an inversed-dexterity debuff on the man. His legs landed funny and he fell like a newborn colt. Orrin hit the woman as well. She hadn't even turned from the noise.

Madi helped Orrin pull the woman to the side of the room as Daniel picked up the man. "Which way to Brandt?"

The man's lips quivered, and a dark stain appeared on his pants. His lips moved and sound came out, but with the lowered dexterity, he couldn't form words. Orrin sighed and motioned to Daniel to hold him tight. He cast an [Increase Dexterity] on the man.

"—sh I can't talk. What is happening? We're just the help. Please don't kill us." The man's eyes darted between the three and settled on Orrin. "Please help me."

"Shut it and answer his questions," Orrin demanded, trying to use a commanding voice.

"Anything you need. We have the good silverware in the kitchen. I can fetch it for you if—"

Daniel shook the man once like a rag doll. "Where does Sanerris keep the prisoners?"

"I work in the kitchen. I don't go into the rest of the castle." The man raised his hands at the look on Daniel's face. "Wait! Wait! Meena takes food to other rooms. She'll know! Let me go. She'll tell you what you need to—"

Orrin reduced the servant's dexterity to zero again. Orrin crouched down next to Meena. "I'm going to let you move in a second. You heard his question, so if the first thing you say isn't a direction, I'm going to be very disappointed."

Meena was young, probably not even Orrin's age. She stared up with huge eyes, and her chest heaved as she tried to take deep breaths. Orrin increased her dexterity until she could sit up.

"I've never been to the basement, I swear. A guard takes the food and brings it down," she said in a panic. Her hands gripped Orrin's pant leg. "Please don't kill me."

"Which way?"

Orrin asked more questions before he reduced their dexterity again and pulled the two into a corner. Madi had been searching and came back with an extra tablecloth. They covered the hyperventilating bodies with the fabric before turning to the kitchen door.

"Through the kitchen, a right at the end of the hall, and find the door next to the old Lady Sanerris." Orrin repeated the instructions

Meena had given. A guard was always posted by the door and would take the gruel they brought to anyone kept below the castle.

Daniel cracked his knuckles, and Madi rolled her shoulders. "[Camouflage Ward] has worn off. Orrin, reapply it?"

Orrin held his hands out to either side and summoned a sword in each. One made of ice and one flickering with flames. "No. Let them see us and scream for help."

Chapter 75

Daniel stepped in front of Orrin with his hands on his hips. "That sounded really cool, but we still have the element of surprise. Don't be stupid."

Orrin frowned but let the swords dissipate. He turned on [Mind Bastion] and let a cycle of blood mana course through him. Using [Heal Small Wounds], he recovered the health he'd lost for a fraction of the cost. When his mana pool was filled to the top, he considered his options and sighed as he dropped the skill. "I did sound pretty badass, didn't I?"

Madi patted his shoulder as she walked toward the kitchen door. "Awesome. Let's do this."

Orrin reapplied [Camouflage Ward]. With the kitchen staff neutralized, the trio was able to sneak by the cooks with ease. Orrin felt uneasy leaving potential enemies moving freely, but the chefs and helpers running around and preparing food didn't look up as one door opened or the other door closed.

The long hall on the other side of the kitchen had doors every few feet, but Daniel crept past all of them, focusing on the end of the path. *If Meena lied to us, we are screwed.*

Daniel peeked around the corner and motioned for them to get close. "There is a single guard at the end of the hall. There is a painting near him, but I can't make it out. Let's take him out. I think that's our way in. Orrin? You good?"

"Ready." Orrin made to move past him but Daniel caught his arm. "How long before our stats dip?"

Orrin hit them both with another round of buffs and gave a thumbs-up. "Twenty minutes. Let's hurry."

The guard was at a higher level than the staff. Orrin hit the man with four inversed [Increase Dexterity] before he looked up. A crossbow fired once and missed him. The second bolt hit his [Ward].

Orrin snarled and hit the man with five rapid-strength debuffs as well. The bow fell from his fingers, and the guard slumped to the ground.

"What the hell?" Daniel asked as he ran up behind Orrin. "How did he get two shots off? Are you hit?"

"My [Ward] stopped the bolt." Orrin kicked the metal-tipped piece of wood to the side. "He was stronger than he looked. I should have used [Identify] first."

"It's fine, guys. We don't have time. Someone is going to find out we're here soon enough." Madi grabbed the arm of the guard and pulled him to the side of the wall. "Help me, please?"

Orrin checked the paintings on the wall and found the imperious-looking blonde woman in a deep-green mage's robe. "If Meena wasn't lying to us, this door should lead down to the dungeon."

Daniel stripped a dagger off the guard's body. "Or right into the guards' barracks . . ." He took Gertrude off his back. "Try not to kill anyone if you don't have to, but if we find Brandt and they resist . . ."

Madi nodded. "We do what we have to. Everyone gets out."

Daniel put his hand on the door and pushed it open. A dimly lit staircase led into darkness. "Brandt, you better be down there."

The walls near the staircase were brick for the first few steps but quickly turned to stone. Orrin could hear something in the distance but couldn't put his finger on what the noise was. Before he could figure it out, they were at the bottom.

Three guards were sitting around a table. The one facing the three of them squinted in their direction, but before he could say anything, Orrin took all three down with a combination of dexterity- and strength-sapping spells.

"This doesn't look like a dungeon," Daniel commented as they pulled the three guards under the stairs. Madi took their weapons and passed them to Orrin. He stored them in his [Dimension Hole].

"It's not built, it's natural." Madi ran a hand along the walls. "It's wet."

Orrin's mind clicked as he placed the noises. "That's the ocean. Are there caves around the coast?"

Madi shook her head. "I don't know."

Behind the table, two paths split off into the darkness. Torches were placed farther in, but Orrin couldn't make out anything.

"This way." Daniel pointed Gertrude to the right. "There are bars along the walls down there."

Orrin muttered about Daniel's eyesight as they made their way down the hall. A cough echoed, and they paused for a moment. A second cough sent Madi scrambling forward.

"Brandt?"

"Now she can recognize him from a cough?" Daniel muttered.

Five small jail cells had been carved from the rock with iron gates hammered into the openings. Behind the first one, wrapped in a threadbare sheet, was Brandt. He was pale and had lost at least twenty pounds.

Orrin noticed the marks along his arms and back before he pulled the small blanket around himself.

"Lady Catanzano? What are you doing here?" Brandt coughed and stumbled to the bars. "You have to leave, right now!"

"Brandt, you idiot," Madi cried as she threw butterflies of light around the cells, looking for a key to the door. "We came to get you out. Where are the keys?"

Brandt's cough rattled, and Orrin stepped up and put his hand out. "Brandt, come here."

Orrin took his hand and cast [Diagnose]. Brandt's body lit up like a Christmas tree. Hundreds of lines of white light radiated from his back, chest, and extremities. Around his center mass was a flickering haze. *That's probably pneumonia or something. Are they trying to kill people down here?*

Brandt kept his right hand behind the blanket but was having trouble keeping it closed. Orrin could see tokens of light along the base of his hand. *They cut off his fingers.*

Orrin's rage built up so fast that [Mind Bastion] auto-activated. He left finding a way to open the cell to his friends and started casting [Heal Small Wounds] on his friend. He tried [Purify] as well. It seemed to work partially—the cuts on Brandt's body began to close over. The old bruises cleared while the fresher purple skin faded to a pale yellow. Brandt moaned, and Madi rushed back to his side.

"Are you hurt? Brandt?"

"Orrin's healing me. I forgot how good it felt not to . . ." He trailed off and glanced at Madi. His eyes flickered to Orrin. "Not be tired. Thanks for the refresher."

Daniel kicked the bars. "I'm not sure I can open this without making a lot of noise. Brandt, join our party. Take my hand. I'll try to use [Home Base]."

"I can't join your party," Brandt said, letting the blanket slip down. A collar of metal was around his neck. "I'm cut off from the system."

Orrin studied the band of metal as Daniel and Madi peppered Brandt with questions. The smooth, dark metal was encrusted with jewels arranged into runes. He couldn't recognize any of them but noticed some similarities to the book the carver who'd worked on Gertrude had shown them.

"We don't have a choice," Daniel was saying. "Orrin, get ready to run. We'll figure out a way to take off the collar once we're outside."

"Wait, Daniel. I might be—" Orrin snapped out of his own thoughts but was too late. Daniel had wedged Gertrude into the hinges and was pulling with his increased strength.

Orrin summoned an [Ice Sword] and wedged it in the bottom half. The metal screamed as it reached its bursting point and then bent with a loud groan. The door didn't fall off, but enough of an opening was created that Brandt could crawl out.

Madi hugged him tight while Daniel watched the path back to the stairs. Orrin cast more healing on him, noting the haze around his chest wasn't clearing up.

"You're sick," Orrin whispered when he gave Brandt his own hug. "It's in your chest, and I can't heal it."

Brandt slapped Orrin's back. "I'll be fine."

Orrin reached up and touched the collar. It was almost ornamental—if he'd seen a noble wearing it, he could have passed it off as jewelry. It felt cold. "I'm going to try to melt it."

Brandt nodded and reached out, taking Madi's hand. Orrin saw her notice the missing three fingers and gasp. Orrin slipped his fingers under the metal and pulled gently before activating [Toxic Touch].

Nothing happened.

He used [Remetabolize] once. Brandt grimaced. Orrin cast it twice more in rapid succession, and Brandt let out a breath of pain. Orrin felt the metal under his fingers give a little and smirked. "Just a bit more."

"Finish that later." Daniel ran back in. "I heard shouting."

Orrin checked his mana. He'd used over half his pool again. He held off from cycling or using a potion. Turning to Brandt, he pulled a sword he'd stolen from one of the guards out of his storage. "Can you fight?"

Brandt took the sword and let the blanket fall from his shoulders. Shirtless and bare, he looked worse than Orrin had thought. With the sword in his left hand, he stepped in front of Madi as if to protect her. "Until my last breath."

Orrin was frustrated. He contemplated letting Daniel handle the incoming guards while he finished breaking the collar off Brandt but dismissed the idea. Madi wasn't going to leave Brandt's side, and the footsteps echoing down the hall sounded like too many feet for Daniel to take alone.

"Try to push through," Brandt suggested. "If we get stuck down here, they can work in shifts to wear down our stamina and mana. They'll have reinforcements . . . Do we have reinforcements?"

The sad glimmer of hope in his voice cracked at the last word. Brandt had been alone for months, not knowing if anyone knew or cared if he was alive. The dazed look in his eyes whenever Madi crossed his sight was enough to let Orrin know Brandt was going to have some trauma to work through.

He cast [Calm Mind] on the knight as Madi shook her head. "The three of us came straight here when we found out you'd been captured."

Brandt hung his head but squared his shoulders. "I'll make sure you get out of here."

"We're all getting out of here," Daniel shouted over his shoulder. "I have a plan."

Daniel took off running, and Orrin threw up a hand in a futile gesture. "What plan?"

Brandt rushed past, dragging Madi by one arm.

"Damn it." Orrin ran as well. He buffed Brandt as he ran and checked him using [Identify]. His strength and dexterity went up, which meant the collar stopped him from forming a party or using his skills, but he could still be affected by outside spells. Brandt stumbled a step but found his footing. He laughed as they began to move faster down the tunnel.

Reaching the end, Orrin saw Daniel already fighting two guards at the foot of the stairs. Five more were making their way down. Madi threw flashes of light at them as she entered the room and kept them from coming farther down with her spear, but it was only a matter of time before one of them got by.

Brandt tackled the guard on Daniel's right and viciously punched his face. When the guard stopped moving, Brandt let out a scream of rage and bodily threw the corpse at the other guard. The man was so engaged with blocking Daniel's strikes that he didn't even see what hit him. The two bodies went down in a flail of arms and legs. A swift strike from Brandt ended the movement.

"We've been trying not to kill them, Brandt," Daniel scolded as he stepped away from the dead guards. "They're just hired guards and—"

Brandt kicked the second guard's body. "That one cut off my fingers. The other would spit in my food before dropping it on the floor every day. They're animals, not men."

"A little help?" Madi yelled out, and the two left it to rush to her aid, only to find three guards falling down the stairs.

"Sorry," Orrin said as he hopped from foot to foot, avoiding the falling guards. "I hit the two in the back with some debuffs. I didn't think that through."

Orrin and Daniel knocked the remaining guards out before they got to their feet, with Madi blinding two. Orrin pulled the last of his rope out of his [Dimension Hole] and tied them in a bundle. "I'm not sure how well that'll hold up. Daniel, what's your plan?"

The [Hero] pointed down the other tunnel. "You said you heard the ocean that way. It has to be an emergency exit."

"That's a leap, D," Orrin said as he peered into the darkness. "Give me two more minutes to get that collar off. Then we can just [Teleport] out."

"[Teleport] isn't going to work down here," Brandt interjected. "There are wards everywhere."

"But will they block the [Hero]'s version?" Orrin asked, wiggling his eyes. "Even if we can't jump here, we don't know what's down that way. We should go back upstairs and—"

Shouting and more footsteps from above interrupted him.

"You were saying?" Daniel raised a hand to point at the door.

"Let's go to the beach?"

Chapter 76

After running down the dimly lit cavern tunnel for a few minutes, the group came across the first split in the path.

"Orrin, please tell me [Map] is working." Daniel bounced from side to side, trying to see into the gloomy darkness either way.

Orrin mentally crossed his fingers as he brought the skill up. He let out a sigh. "It's a freaking maze. Give me a second to figure it out."

Madi hugged Brandt and checked him over as Orrin drew lines in the air with his finger. He cursed and moved back.

"Anytime soon would be great," Daniel poked.

"Not sure you'd be doing any better, asshole."

Madi hushed Daniel. A few seconds later, Orrin whooped. "Got it. Left path. I'm going to need somebody to take my arm and keep me from running into a wall. I have to concentrate on this."

Orrin had them turn left twice, then right. They ran into a three-way split and took the middle route, only to turn around and take the left path instead.

"Sorry."

"You're doing great, Orrin. Keep it up." Madi had one hand on Orrin's elbow and her other clasped in Brandt's. Her weapon swung at her hip.

The echoes of feet and yells from behind spurred them on, but no guards had caught up to them yet. Orrin was hoping they were splitting up along each path to check that they didn't double back to the castle.

After thirty minutes of frantic turns, bumping into walls and scraping skin, plus Daniel's grumbling, Orrin took his eyes off his [Map]. "Straight shot from here. D, can you see any light?"

Daniel was quiet as he peered ahead. "I think so. Good job, Orrin. I knew you could do it."

As they moved forward, Orrin went back to trying to remove Brandt's collar. He grimaced as one of Madi's butterfly lights revealed his handiwork on the knight's neck where his fingers had brushed and acid burned the skin in long stripes.

"Sorry about this," he mumbled, but Brandt just smirked.

"I've been through worse. I haven't seen the sun in over a hundred days. I lost count somewhere around ninety-five. I can't wait to get out of here."

They could see the light of the cave's entrance. The sound of water filled the tunnel. Daniel ran ahead and waved them on. Orrin's [Camouflage Ward] had worn off. He'd been focused on his [Map] and only kept the stat buffs going so Madi and Brandt didn't fall over.

"Hurry up."

Orrin felt the collar begin to give, the metal melting. It burned his hand, but he ignored the pain for now. Finally, with a faint crack, it fell off Brandt.

"Daniel, he's out. Invite Brandt . . ."

As Daniel turned, Orrin pointed behind him. A group of robed figures stepped in front of the exit and raised their hands in unison. Fire, ice, lightning, and more extended from the fingers of all the mages present and struck the [Hero] in the back.

Orrin was close enough to see Daniel's face. He'd been smiling in excitement. He always enjoyed a challenge, and even though he'd complained about it, breaking Brandt out was secretly scratching all his heroic itches.

As the spells hit him, a frown of puzzlement flashed across his brow, followed quickly by shock and pain. Orrin's [Ward] had been obliterated. Daniel glanced down at his armor in surprise. A bolt of ice stuck out from the center of his chest. His right knee to ankle was covered in vines that dug into the skin, blood pouring out like a river.

Their eyes connected, and Daniel's mouth popped open in a little "ouch." Then the [Hero] fell forward, hitting the ground. Gertrude slipped from his fingers.

The sound of the waves crashed in Orrin's ears. Distant shouting and screams were a mere annoyance as he took one, then two steps toward his friend's body. He'd get up and smirk any second. He was going to be so pissed that he'd dropped his sword. He might need a heal or two; that ice spike might have done some damage to him.

A small part of Orrin screamed at him to get down. He didn't want to listen to that part of himself. He needed to get to Daniel. His feet were moving so slowly. Had his [Increase Dexterity] worn off? Orrin checked his status by reflex. Nope, still there. Had Daniel's buffs worn off? Was that why he wasn't moving?

Orrin used [Identify] on Daniel.

> **Daniel**
> **Hero**
> **Level 18**
> **HP: 0/400**
> **MP: 360/380**
> **Strength: 24 (100)**
> **Constitution: 20**
> **Dexterity: 15 (100)**
> **Will: 8 (38)**
> **Intelligence: 10 (40)**

Zero health. Orrin read the status but couldn't comprehend it. *Why isn't he moving?*

Orrin noticed motion. The mages were rushing in. They were going to try and take Daniel before he got up.

"No."

Orrin slipped into Formless stance from [Way of the Water]. He heard Madi shouting but didn't need any distractions. Activating [Mind Bastion], he stepped over Daniel. With one last glance over his shoulder, he caught Madi's attention. "Take care of him."

Orrin exploded into movement. He didn't attack but went into Ocean stance to slide between the different assailants. He blood cycled when attacks hit and reapplied [Ward]. The healing from cycling kept him at full health.

He started using [Toxic Touch] indiscriminately, boosted with [Remetabolize]. People screamed, but he kept going. Scorpion Fish Strike to Returning Tide. Rising Wave before falling back to Formless. Two mages tried to attack from separate directions. Orrin moved into Mist and jumped forward, dodging both the spear of light and the ice shard. Coming up from his front roll, he returned to Ocean and darted forward. The [Ice Mage] fell with a hole through his chest. Orrin pulled his hand out and continued.

"Enough!"

Orrin's falling kick missed. The mage still sparkled with radiant lightning flickering across her skin. She moved back and knelt toward the entrance with her remaining comrades. Of the twelve mages who had attacked, only four were still standing. Six were dead and two were unconscious.

Backlit against the ocean and sun behind him, Lord Sanerris, the ruler of Odrana, entered the cave.

"That is quite enough. You dare to come into my house and take my prisoner? You kill my guards and my students?" The blond hair was not as perfected tousled as it had been when they last met. Orrin could tell they'd made Sanerris run to catch them. "You cannot escape. I will make you beg for death."

Orrin cast [Lightstrikes] at the man before he finished speaking.

Sanerris snarled and waved a hand. Orrin's attack faded in front of him.

He tried again. He sent inversed [Increase Dexterity] at Sanerris. He tried his new spell, [Gust], with a hundred mana invested. Sanerris's robes didn't even stir.

Orrin ran at the man. One of the mages stood up, and Orrin's freshly summoned [Fire Sword] decapitated him. The blade continued its burning arc toward the leader of Odrana, who stood still with a bored look on his face.

"That's enough."

Orrin's sword stopped. He tried to move his arm, his leg, or any part of his body, but it was like he was frozen in place.

Sanerris sneered at him. "I thought you were special."

He stepped past Orrin and snapped his fingers. "Collar him. I want to know his class and skills."

One of the mages stood up and pulled a metal circle just like Brandt's out of his inner robes. It snapped shut around Orrin's neck. He kept fighting, trying to do anything. He couldn't even blink, and his eyes started to water.

No. I have to be able to heal Daniel.

"Hey, asshole," a voice from behind him taunted. "Let my friend go."

"Daniel?" Madi's gasp of disbelief broke through the murmuring of the other mages surrounding Orrin. "You're alive!"

"I never want to try that skill again. Ouch, you bastards pack a big hit."

Orrin couldn't see his friend but let the tears flow fast. Of course, he'd forgotten about Daniel's skill [Edge of Death]. He couldn't remember the exact wording but knew it was supposed to bring him back if he took too much damage. A final healing fail-safe. Orrin had threatened to kill him and activate it multiple times, but seeing the mangled body of his friend had thrown that right out the window.

"The [Hero] of Dey," Sanerris scoffed. "Is that little Catanzano back there? I guess the information I let slip about your knight reached you. I was hoping I could lure one of you here, but to see all three of you . . . and you even got so close."

Sanerris laughed. "There are no elves to save you this time, [Hero]. Put down your sword and let's talk."

Orrin was pointed in the wrong direction and couldn't see. He tried every spell and skill he had. Nothing worked. He couldn't tell if it was the collar or whatever Sanerris had cast on him. He couldn't even see the system boxes but felt them right out of reach.

"I'm warning you once. Let Orrin go. We'll leave and that will be the end of things."

Orrin cheered at his friend.

"And if I don't?"

Orrin could hear the smile on Daniel's face. "We have a saying where I'm from. Fuck around and find out. You don't want to find out."

Orrin had a moment's notice. The motion from his earlier swing kept his momentum moving forward, and the pressure holding him still lifted. He almost face-planted but was able to roll into a crouch.

"Collar the [Hero]. You can kill the other two."

Orrin tried to use his spells, but nothing came. Two mages nearby moved to grab him. The last moved toward Daniel, frozen in place just like Orrin had just been.

Time magic? Orrin was just thankful that he'd learned [Way of the Water] the hard way. The collar locked out his spells and his party options, but he could still fight. His stats were still increased for . . . two more minutes.

The two mages went down with barely a sound.

"Daniel, get home with them. I'll find a way out," Orrin shouted, drawing Sanerris's attention. Madi and Brandt moved in front of Daniel's unmoving body.

"Orrin, we're all going together," Madi argued.

"Nobody will be going anywhere." Sanerris flicked his fingers at Madi.

Brandt threw himself in front of her. His body flipped end over end and, already frail, he hit the ground hard. Orrin let out a breath when the knight pushed himself back to his feet. His right arm was broken, bone sticking through. He'd landed on the hand with missing fingers to soften the blow, sacrificing the bad arm so he could still swing his sword.

What a fucking badass. Orrin admired him for a second.

A pain behind his eyes began to fester. The same spell that Sanerris had tried on him in the elven forest bloomed. He'd never taken [Mind Bastion] off, but the proximity and intensity were ramped up this time.

"Sit in the corner and stop killing my students," Sanerris yelled.

"Eat me," Orrin fired back, running at Sanerris. He feinted left and then barreled his entire frame into the man. Orrin wasn't a match for the taller man normally, but he still had the full weight of one hundred points of strength behind him. Sanerris bounced back, unharmed but flying over Daniel and Brandt.

Madi finally landed a [Shimmersight] on the last mage and pierced his neck with her spear. She spun the shaft twice in the narrow hallway and yelled at Orrin as she swung at Sanerris. "Run."

Orrin ran toward the danger.

"No, you idiot. Get Daniel and get out of here." Madi sent bursts of light at Sanerris. Everything failed to hit.

"When he stops me, you convince Daniel to get the three of you out of here," Orrin whispered quickly. He didn't wait for a response and charged Sanerris again.

"You still haven't learned." The man held his hands out to the side as Orrin ran at him. "You can't touch me."

Orrin screamed as he rushed at the man. His pristine clothes were banged up, but they hadn't done any lasting damage. Orrin whispered to the system. "Now's the time to activate some crazy skill. Suck his powers away or something. C'mon!"

The system did nothing. Sanerris froze Orrin with his time freeze spell two feet from contact.

"I'm going to have fun with you." Sanerris pointed his finger at Orrin. He glanced beyond Orrin, and his face twisted. "No! Where did they go?"

Orrin felt a catch in his breath even through the spell. *They escaped.*

Lord Sanerris began to beat Orrin in a rage.

Acknowledgments

For my team at Podium that made this into a reality. Nicole, Julie, Leah, Brian, and copyeditor Sara, this book wouldn't exist without all your hard work. Nick, I'm forever grateful and awed at your ability to bring these characters to life.

For all my friends and family who calmed my anxiety, cheered me on, and read my first mad scribbling. Kevin for writing a song from Orrin's POV (Melissa, hopefully you didn't have to read this book aloud to him). Nick, Jesse, Tyler, Lawrence, Nikolai, and Collin, for throwing dice and forgiving me when I complained the D&D spells weren't as good as mine. Harrison for talking through different class ideas and being there when I needed to complain.

For my readers. The ones from the beginning, the ones who supported me along the way, and the ones new to this journey. Thank you for giving me a chance to bring you on an adventure.

About the Author

SourpatchHero is the author of LitRPG series I'm Not the Hero. When he's not writing new stories, you'll find him spending time with his two sons and his wife, reading, or playing video games.